Clive Cussler
The Sea Wolves

AN ISAAC BELL ADVENTURE®

CLIVE CUSSLER
THE SEA WOLVES

JACK DU BRUL

WHEELER PUBLISHING
A part of Gale, a Cengage Company

Wheeler Publishing, a part of Gale, a Cengage Company.

Wheeler Publishing Large Print Hardcover.
The text of this Large Print edition is unabridged.
Other aspects of the book may vary from the original edition.
Set in 16 pt. Plantin.

**LIBRARY OF CONGRESS CIP DATA ON FILE.
CATALOGUING IN PUBLICATION FOR THIS BOOK
IS AVAILABLE FROM THE LIBRARY OF CONGRESS.**

ISBN-13: 978-1-4328-9958-5 (hardcover alk. paper)

Published in 2022 by arrangement with G. P. Putnam's Sons, an imprint of Penguin Publishing Group, a division of Penguin Random House LLC.

Printed in Mexico
Print Number : 1 Print Year : 2023

CAST OF CHARACTERS

French Guiana

MAX HESSMANN German spy/prisoner

FOSTER "FOSS" GLY Prisoner

HEINZ-JOSEPH VOLKER German commando

New York/New Haven/New Jersey

JOSEPH VAN DORN Founder of the Van Dorn Detective Agency

ISAAC BELL Chief investigator of the Van Dorn Agency

MARION BELL Isaac's wife

ARCHIBALD ABBOTT Van Dorn detective and Bell's best friend

EDDIE EDWARDS Van Dorn detective

HARRY WARREN Van Dorn detective

HELEN MILLS Van Dorn detective

JAMES DASHWOOD Van Dorn detective

EDDIE TOBIN Van Dorn detective

GRADY FORRER Van Dorn researcher

DICK HOPLEY Winchester Arms representative

JOHN KRAMER Winchester Arms employee

WILLIAM "WILLIE K." VANDERBILT Millionaire sportsman

JOHN PORTE Pilot

WERNER DIETRICH Long Island farmer

JOE MARCHETTI U.S. Navy ensign

GEORGE CALDWELL U.S. Navy captain and Joe's boss

WENDEL CARVER Penn Station security chief

RALPH PRYOR Lighthouse keeper

DEVLIN CONNELL Lighthouse inspector

FRANKLIN ROOSEVELT Assistant Secretary of the Navy

KURT MILLER Roosevelt's aide

CECIL SPRING-RICE British Ambassador to the United States

At Sea

LOTHAR REINHART U-boat captain

EDWARD JOYCE Captain of the *Centurion*

JAMES MCCUBBIN Cunard Line chief purser

PETER SMITH Cunard Line master-at-arms

GEORGE PIERPOINT Liverpool detective

Prologue

Îles du Salut
April 13, 1914

The commandos came ashore under the silvery light of a tropical moon. There were only three men who leapt onto the rocky coast. Two sailors remained with the aluminum boat so that it wouldn't be lost in the treacherous currents that lashed the forlorn island some nine miles off the South American mainland. The assault team carried pistols but understood if they needed them the mission was likely a failure. Their main weapons were knives crudely fashioned from scrap steel. The blades were ugly, but honed razor sharp, like the weapons they were designed to emulate — the basic prison shiv.

The South Atlantic breeze kept the shore cool, but as soon as the men moved into the thick, inky jungle it was like stepping into a hothouse. Heat and humidity made sweat run from their pores and soon enough their uniforms were soaked through with moisture. Night insects and the occasional cry of a bird drowned out the distant pounding of waves on stone.

Knowing the general layout of the island, the team soon found the path leading to their target. Palm fronds met overhead and blocked the moon's weak glow. Many months of careful planning and preparation came down to the next few minutes and the elite soldiers were all too aware of what would happen if they were spotted. The French still loved to use their beloved guillotine.

There were three small isles that made up what was known as the Salvation Island chain. It had been so named because the last six hundred survivors of an estimated twelve thousand men and women who'd tried to colonize the nearby territory of French Guiana had fled here from the fever coast to find sanctuary. All efforts to tame the primeval mainland came to naught until the middle of the nineteenth century when Napoleon III decreed that part of the territory would be turned into a penal colony and that prison labor would be used to conquer the land. The Bagne de Cayenne sprawled along the coast in the form of prisons and jungle work camps and utilized thousands of France's worst offenders as virtual slaves.

The coastal islands too became part of the prison system. Royale Island, the largest, housed four hundred prisoners who had been exiled from the mainland for major infractions of the new penal laws. Another island, Devil's Island, though ominously named, was the most benign place in the entire prison colony. It was reserved for a handful of political prisoners, like the recently released Alfred Dreyfus, who'd been falsely accused of being a traitor.

In a twist of irony, upon his return to France and recommissioning into the army, Dreyfus told only one confidant all that he'd seen and done during his time in Guiana. He'd explained how the prison system worked and gave detailed descriptions of the buildings and the guards' routines. This man, a friend, was actually the German spy the French authorities had thought was Dreyfus. The intelligence Dreyfus divulged to his friend had been crucial in planning the commandos' mission.

The third island of the Salvation group, the one the commandos were stealthily traversing, was called St. Joseph's. It was hell on earth. This was where the most recalcitrant prisoners were housed in what the French called *insolement.* Isolation.

The minimum sentence to one of St. Joseph's nine-foot-by-five-foot cells was six months, the maximum usually five years, though many prisoners had paid repeated visits. Time served on St. Joseph's was always added to an inmate's already existing sentence. Insanity wasn't uncommon among the survivors of such deprivation. Death was the more likely outcome.

Silence was strictly enforced, and the tops of the cells were iron bars open to the elements so that the tropical rains and burning sun were additional torments for the men. Guards walked on catwalks above the cells, making sure none of the prisoners spoke. The minuscule food ration was passed through a slot at the bottom of each cell's iron door and another judas door, higher up, could be opened so a prisoner could stick his head out of his cell if the warden or some other official wanted to speak to him. Once on St. Joseph's there was no medical care, no dental care, zero hygiene. The prisoners lived like penned animals, but with the torturous self-awareness a poor animal never knows.

The prisons on French Guiana were supposed to be a social experiment to reform prisoners so they could return to proper society. Instead, they had created a place more barbaric than any medieval dungeon.

The commandos now came to a large clearing at the end of the path. The jungle had been hacked back for a complex of plastered stone buildings. The structures were brutish in style, and even without knowing their function, they seemed shrouded in dark menace. A gate gave access to a broad courtyard. The lock was heavy duty and the one commando tasked with picking it had to use his largest set of tools. He opened it a fraction of an inch at a time to prevent the rust-ravaged hinges from squealing. The lockpicker placed two wooden shims at the base of the heavy door so that it couldn't swing open farther, or slam shut.

The courtyard was plain dirt that had been raked smooth. Ahead was an administration building and housing for the guards. To their left stood the detention block. The team leader pointed out that a metal roof had been built above the catwalks to shield the guards, a detail that differed from their mission briefing. They waited in the shadows for a guard shift change to occur, which it did at precisely the top of the hour. A guard made his way from the dormitory and climbed up onto the parapet above the cells. He and the on-duty guard spoke for just a minute and then the latter made his way off to his soft bed.

The commandos gave it ten minutes for the new guard to fall into routine. He was soon leaning against one of the roof's support columns, the cherry glow of his cigarette moving from his face as he inhaled to down by his waist when he relaxed his arm. There was just enough light to see the outline of a rifle slung over his shoulder.

The iron stairs up to the guard's walkway were bolted to the side of the building. The lead commando unsheathed his knife and moved as slowly as a stalking cat up the stairs, his footfalls feathery light, his concentration total. He paused when only his eyes were above the top step, and he watched the Frenchman finish his cigarette and pitch the butt off the building so that it hit the courtyard in a shower of sparks.

He started ambling down the length of the cell block, his footfalls slow and lazy. It had to be a miserable duty, the team leader thought as he rose from a crouch and padded after the guard. To his right and left were the iron-bar tops of the open cells. No light penetrated their musty gloom.

The guard was so dulled by routine that

he never felt a shadow stalking him and only reacted when a hand clamped over his mouth in a steel-like grip. He had a fraction of a second to stiffen in shock before the shiv was drawn from ear to ear and his throat opened in a violent gush of blood. The soldier slowly lowered the guard to the floor as his body's functions shut down one by one until his eyelids gave one last flutter and his heart stopped.

He slunk back down the stairs and regrouped with his men. They had fifty minutes to spring their target and get clear of the Salvation Islands before the corpse was discovered and an alarm sounded. They rightly assumed that guards on all three islands would be alerted of the murder by a klaxon or bell and that they would pour from their barracks in droves.

Still, they had plenty of time.

They moved to the cell block's main door and eased it open, careful that its hinges didn't squeal. The hallway beyond was plastered brick, patchy with damp spots and showing mildew growth where the wall met the floor. The smell wasn't bad because of the open cell ceilings, but an underlying odor of corruption and filth clung to the space and filled the men's lungs like smoke. Identical doors ran along each wall, thick metal affairs coated with rust. There were no names listed above them. The prisoners were housed in utter anonymity. Like their freedom, their identities had also been stripped away.

The men fanned out and began tapping a code phrase against the doors, pausing to hear the proper response tapped back by their man. This had all been orchestrated even before the man they were to spring had been sentenced to the penal colony all those months ago. He was a German spying on French industry, especially those working on military contracts. They'd all been lucky he hadn't been shot. The French had acceded to diplomatic pressure and eventually direct threats from Germany and the Austro-Hungarian empire to spare the man's life. Everyone knew he'd be sent here.

Tap. Tap-tap. Tap-tap. Tap. Tap.

Nothing but silence from the faceless, nameless men cowering in their cells in the night. The soldiers moved on. There were only a few cells left to check and doubt began to creep into the team leader's mind. What if he wasn't here? What if their scheme to get him sent to solitary had failed? They could have given him over to the guillotine upon his arrival and no one outside of the French Ministry of Justice would know. It was even possible he'd died on the long passage from France. Alfred Dreyfus had said countless dead were hauled from the prison ship's fetid cages each day and dumped into the vessel's wake.

Tap. Tap-tap. Tap-tap. Tap. Tap.

Tap-tap-tap. Tap. Tap-tap.

They found him. Max Hessmann.

The commando commander quickly opened the door. "Welcome back to the world of the living, Herr Hessmann," he whispered.

A living corpse stepped from the cell and into the weak moonlight. He was tall but gaunt to the point of looking cadaverous. His head was bald but he wore a scraggy beard that would be teeming with lice. His wrists below the cuffs of his rough prison shirt were as thin as a child's. The light was poor, but even so his eyes were sunken into depthless craters and his cheeks appeared sucked into his teeth.

"Not exactly," the man croaked in English. "I'm Foss Gly."

"I have little English," the German commando said.

"Française?"

"Oui."

"*Bon. Je m'appelle Foster Gly.* Call me Foss."

The commando answered in French. "I am Lieutenant Heinz-Joseph Volker of the Imperial German Navy. We are here to rescue Max Hessmann."

"I know," Gly said. Despite his appearance, there remained a commanding presence about him. "Max told me everything. We worked together to get exiled here to St. Joseph's. How long before the guard is discovered?"

"Where is Hessmann?"

"Infirmary on Royale Island, if we're lucky. Dead if we're not. He came down with malaria just prior to the escape attempt that guaranteed we'd be sent here. We couldn't put it off while he recovered. When we arrived here to serve our additional sentence, I was sent to a cell, while he's been on a sickbed. What about the guard? How long?"

"Shift change in about forty-five minutes," Lieutenant Volker answered.

"We just might have enough time. But we need to get moving."

The German seemed a little incensed that this foreigner — his accent said British Isles — thought he could give orders as if he had any standing. "I don't believe —"

Gly cut him off and stepped close so that his full height loomed over Volker. With madness glinting in his sunken eyes, he looked like something from a horrific Germanic folktale. "I saved Max's life twice when he first arrived here. Other inmates knew he was a German spy. These men are all degenerates, but they're still Frenchmen, so they thought they'd teach the odd Boche a lesson. I killed three men defending Max and now he owes me, see. Besides, he's so weak he could never escape on his own, but with me involved the warden will believe I escaped my cell and rescued Max. All the guards know we're tight."

Volker let that sink in for a minute. "They will think you got him off these islands and not suspect a raid from a submarine."

Gly nodded and a ghost of a smile reached his lips. He was a career criminal, a murderer, and a thug, and while most times he opened his mouth to speak only lies came out, tonight he was telling the truth. "Max and I talked about it. He was actually mad at himself for not thinking of this while planning his escape with your military intelligence back during his trial in Paris. He realized too late that having someone like me helping from the inside makes for a stronger play."

"Okay," Volker agreed. "Do you have a plan?"

Gly knew from Max that the commandos planning to rescue him had rowed ashore from an experimental long-range submarine. "We need to row over to Isle Royale and then your sailors need to row over to Devil's Island and wait for us there."

"I don't understand. Why?"

"If we're spotted, we'll never be able to row from shore fast enough. The guards here are lazy and corrupt, but they take great sport in shooting prisoners trying to escape. We'd be sitting ducks leaving Royale in a boat."

"But how do we get to Devil's Island?"

"I'll tell you on the way. This is all for naught if the dead guard here is discovered and all hell breaks loose."

One of the commandos handed Gly a bundle of dark clothing before they left the cell block. He changed out of the tattered striped pants, but slipped the black shirt over his prison-issued tunic. They sidled out of the building, keeping watch on the barracks, and kept close to the perimeter wall as they ran crouched toward the main gate. Once clear and the door was pressed closed again, they retraced their steps to the coast and the waiting rowboat.

"How long?" Volker asked when they were deep into the jungle. His voice was still barely a whisper.

Gly said, "What?"

"How long have you been a prisoner here?"

"It's April 1914, yes?"

"It is."

"Three years."

The commando shuddered. Gly looked like he'd been marooned on a desert island for a decade or more, a scarecrow of withered flesh, with the haunted presence of a man who truly understood deprivation and despair. Volker had faced down armed insurrections in two of Germany's African colonies and knew he was a brave soldier, but the idea of this place and how it diminished both body and soul in three short years gave his bowels an oily slide.

They reached the coast. Gly took in measured lungfuls of the salt-tanged air. As much as he wanted to fill his chest to bursting, he knew his lungs were scarred by the damp and the fevers and illnesses that had racked his body since his arrival in Guiana, and too much would send him into paroxysms of hacking coughs. He'd learned that lesson when he'd been moved from the mainland to the islands weeks earlier. Even so, he could taste something else in the sultry night air, something that hadn't been present on the small launch that had whisked him and Max and other hardened inmates out here.

He could taste the first stirrings of freedom.

Lieutenant Volker used a small flashlight to summon the boat hiding out in the waters of the Atlantic while he and his men hunkered down among the rocks. The wind remained gentle and the surf rhythmic and calm. In a moment, the soft slap of oars played like a backbeat over the sound of splashing waves.

Gly grunted in grudging admiration. The Germans had followed Max's plan to the letter. Their little dinghy smelled of fish oil and looked like it had been battered by years of tropical sun, with faded and chipped paint and gunwales that were punky with rot. Exactly the kind of boat an enterprising inmate could bribe a local fisherman into using to abet an escape from the islands. When they abandoned it after the raid, its discovery would further obscure what really transpired this night.

He refused their offers to help him into the boat. He was weak, his limbs a third of their normal size and the ache of hunger was like a hole in his stomach, but he wouldn't acknowledge his own wasted condition. They had starved him and beat him, but they hadn't broken him. That distinction had sustained him since his arrival.

The sailors maneuvered the little craft away from the stony beach, rowing so that the oars barely made a splash. The currents between the islands were notorious and one of the reasons there were no successful escapes from the prison. There was little need for actual walls or cells, though the men on Royale Island were penned forty to a cell and strapped down at night with an iron bar over their ankles to prevent them from moving in their sleep. The islands themselves were prisons as effective as any brick-and-mortar penitentiary. Even the strongest swimmers wouldn't last more than a few minutes battling the rip current and would soon be sucked far out into the Atlantic.

There were also the sharks. When a prisoner died on the Salvation Islands, their corpse was rowed a short distance offshore, a bell was rung, and the poor wretch was dumped into the water. Local sharks had learned to recognize the bell and were ravaging the body moments after it hit the water. The prison boat rowed back to the pier through a widening pool of the man's spilt blood. In its wake, a frenzy of sleek torpedo-shaped predators writhed and fed.

Gly's knowledge of Royale Island came mostly from what he'd learned from other prisoners during his stay in the mainland prison. He himself had sat in a cage on the boat while the transfer prisoners, including the deathly ill Max Hessmann, were marched off. Gly was then brought to St. Joseph's and dumped into isolation.

The first ten days, they'd lowered iron plates over the top of his cell to keep him in total darkness and to let the temperatures soar until he felt like his flesh was melting from his body. He shuddered away the memory, one of a million he wished he could purge from his mind.

Still, he felt confident that he could lead the commandos to the infirmary. It was close to the guards' compound, which made things tricky, but with all the prisoners penned in their cells, he'd been told that random foot patrols were rare. Once the commandos were ashore, the sailors would row over to Devil's Island and beach midway down its south shore and wait out of sight.

"Why not leave the boat on the beach or

stand it offshore like we did just now?" Volker asked.

"Because the Frenchies patrol the coast of Royale like dogs on the lookout for boats just like this. It's the only way to escape and they guard against it. If the rip weren't so treacherous, I'd say we swim in and send the boat straight over to Devil's Island. Truth is, though, we'd never make it."

The distance between St. Joseph's Island and the spot on Royale where Gly wanted to land was just a few hundred yards, but it seemingly took forever. To the sailors working the oars it felt like they lost eleven inches for every foot they gained. It took forty minutes for them to finally approach Royale Island, a low jungle-covered silhouette rising from the waters. "We only need the two of us," Gly whispered to Volker. "We will be moving around some buildings and a larger force is more easily detected."

"What if we run into more guards than you think?"

"Doesn't matter. It only takes one to raise an alarm. Better go in by stealth and not be seen than to have to depend on force if we are."

Volker frowned. He didn't know Gly and judging him by his appearance inspired little confidence. He doubted the man could even lift a hand to defend himself. But Max Hessmann trusted him with his life, and prior to his capture in France, Hessmann had been a legend in Germany's intelligence apparatus, Sektion IIIb.

"And if Hessmann can't walk?"

"It's the infirmary, there's bound to be a stretcher," Gly said. "Consider this too. If the guards see a large force tonight, even if we manage to escape but only two men are missing from morning muster, they will know Hessmann had outside help and there will be a diplomatic incident."

Volker saw the logic in that. While training for this mission, it had been drilled into him again and again that none of his men could be captured alive. Such an occurrence would light a match to the powder keg that was the current diplomatic status between Berlin and Paris. His orders were to turn his pistol on his men and then take his own life. If they failed, the French would likely blame Germany for the three dead men who tried to invade their penal colony, but there would be no proof. The incident would soon blow over with some bluster and saber-rattling, but no real consequences.

"Okay," he said at last, "we'll do it your way." He whispered to his men the change in plans and gave Gly one of the handmade knives.

"I'm good with a pistol," Gly told him.

"You might well be," Volker replied, "but you're not getting one."

The men stayed low behind the gunwales as they drew closer. Like the previous island, there was no beach, just solid rock getting relentlessly slapped by waves. They saw no movement, no indication that the shore was being guarded, so they rowed in the last dozen yards and Gly and Volker crawled out of the boat as its prow touched ground.

"We'll wait for you to get into position, and then rescue Hessmann," Volker told his men, and gave the boat a shove. He and Gly scrambled over the rocks and into the cover of the dense jungle. A light rain began to patter through the foliage.

"This is good," Gly said with his lips practically touching Volker's ear. "Frenchies don't like to get wet. They think it makes them more suspectable to malaria and yellow fever."

"Does it?"

"Hell if I know."

Just as Gly had predicted, they saw no patrols walking the trail that ringed the island. The rain was little more than a drizzle, but it served to keep the guards under shelter in the main compound. Also, the clouds obscured the moon's hoary glow and turned the jungle into a tangled jigsaw of dark shades and shapes. They were relatively protected, so the wait went quickly enough.

Gly pointed out the direction they had to go, but let Volker take point. His strength, such as it was, wouldn't last if he took the role of trailblazer. Volker moved well. A lifetime of stalking game through the mountains and forests of Bavaria had turned him into a skilled hunter. They slowed as a little light slipped through the patchwork of branches and leaves. The island had a generator for electricity, but it had long been turned off. There was light from an oil lamp spilling through the gauzy curtain covering a ground-floor window of the three-story infirmary building. The aura moved across the window. The lamp was being held in someone's hand. A doctor checking his patients, perhaps. Or a guard making certain all the prisoners were accounted for. Moments later the light vanished, as if the person had exited the ward and closed the door.

A stubby lighthouse sat next to the infirmary, but its lamp wasn't lit.

They moved close to the stone structure, feeling it radiating some of the heat it had absorbed during the day. Volker led. At the first corner they approached, he ducked low before peering around the edge so that there would be no movement at eye level if someone was looking. His tradecraft impressed Gly. Max had bragged about the German military and especially its troops trained in irregular warfare. If anything, he'd downplayed their skills.

They were at the rear of the building and all the windows were dark. At the next corner, Lieutenant Volker repeated his trick. He quickly ducked back and hustled Gly a few feet away from the corner.

"Guard standing atop some low steps at the building entrance. He's got a rifle."

"Is he out in the rain?"

"No, there's an awning over him."

Gly thought for a minute, picked up a coconut that had fallen from a palm tree, and slid around the corner before Volker could stop him. The guard was a few dozen paces from him, leaning against a handrail and watching the rain falling from above. Gly pressed himself against the infirmary, his body so thin he was like just one more layer of brick veneer. The Frenchman appeared lost in some daydream. Gly knew some of the guards had brought family with them to the islands, but this one looked too young to have a wife. He was likely thinking of some girl he knew back in France, a *petit copine* from *l'ecole.*

He moved until he was just at the base of the short flight of steps. The guard continued to lean against the rail, unaware of his surroundings. His rifle rested against the rail, close to his hand. Slowly, and just out of the man's peripheral vision, Gly lobbed the coconut out onto the lawn.

Its movement caught the guard's eye and he stiffened even as Gly mounted the steps, the shiv in his right hand, his left snaking around the guard's face to clamp over his mouth. Gly's hand and the blade touched the man at the same time. There was no struggle as Gly opened his carotid artery with an expertly placed slit. He twisted the man so that his blood soaked into his uniform rather than pool on the stone terrace. Dragging the corpse back into the deep shadows behind the infirmary left Gly panting, but it was worth the effort. He now had the rifle, a Lebel Model 1886 that was probably a decade older than the guard who'd wielded it.

Gly's prison uniform had no pockets, so he didn't bother grabbing any more of the

Lebel's tubular magazines the guard carried in a leather pouch attached to his Sam Browne belt. He checked that the rifle had a cartridge chambered. "Having this gives us cover if you need to use your pistol."

Volker kept his admonishment of Gly's solo assault to himself. He was professional enough to recognize the Briton's skill and ruthlessness and rightly assumed any reprimand would be ignored.

The infirmary door was closed, but not locked. Light spilled from beneath it, possibly from a guard's desk lamp or a nurse duty station. Gly had never set foot in the building. He had no idea of its layout or how many men guarded the sick and infirm prisoners. He let Volker take point again. The commando was in his physical prime and Gly was still winded from killing and dragging his victim.

A door opening slowly would seem suspicious to whomever was inside, so the German agent opened it like he owned the place. There was a seconds-long lag for the man seated at a desk to look up and see it wasn't his partner returning from getting some air. Volker used that brief window of opportunity to attack, lunging hard with the shiv, piercing skin and guiding the blade into the man's heart with well-practiced ease. The guard managed a cry that was little more than a wet cough before his heart stopped and his brain starved for oxygen.

A heavy key ring hung from his belt. Volker cut it free.

Volker turned down the wick on the oil lamp and plucked it from the desk. The closest ward was to their right through an open doorway. They could see two rows of bunks, the men asleep under dingy sheets and threadbare blankets.

Gly stopped the German from entering and whispered, "I should go in. I will be recognized as the man who sprang Max out of here. It'll further confound the Frenchies."

Again Volker could not fault Gly's logic. Hessmann had chosen his partner very well. He wondered what crime Gly had committed to be condemned to this hellish place. Considering how expertly he'd killed the guard, he was certainly familiar with murder.

Gly moved into the ward. Some of the men were awakened by the light, but said nothing. Any change in routine at a prison was something to be suspicious of because it usually meant someone's day was about to go from bad to worse. He held the light so he could see the prisoners' faces. He saw a man he recognized from the boat from the mainland.

"Gadot, right?" he whispered.

The prisoner lying on the cot paused for just a moment before he realized the man standing over him wasn't dressed like a guard or one of the doctors. Recognition widened his eyes. "I know you."

"Foss Gly. I came from the main *bagne* with you."

"You went to solitary," Gadot said, recalling more.

"And I got myself sent here tonight. Is the German here, Hessmann?"

"Your mate? Yes. Last bed under the window."

It was all Gly could do not to sag with relief. He turned away to find Max.

"Wait," Gadot said, and grabbed his arm. "They didn't transfer you here. They never do. You're escaping, aren't you? Take me with you. I've been pretending I'm still sick since I got here. I can make it."

"I can't. My plan's only for the two of us. But tell *les flics* it was me, okay?"

Gadot looked disappointed and sheepish. He pulled aside his blanket. His thigh was gashed deeply and had been left open so fluid could drain into a pan on the floor. "I wouldn't have made it anyway, but it was nice thinking about it. Good luck."

Gly moved on, grateful Gadot hadn't pressed his case because he'd have been forced to kill him and he liked leaving a witness behind. Max Hessmann was leaning up on one elbow when Gly got to him. His color was much better than the last time they'd laid eyes on each other. He'd survived the worst of the malarial fevers and agues and looked to be on the mend. He was in his early forties, just a few years older than Gly, with blondish hair and eyes of an indistinct color. He wasn't particularly handsome or muscular, which served him well. Being a spy meant being invisible.

"Thought I heard your voice," he said in American-accented English. "I was beginning to think Sektion IIIb had forgotten about me."

"Perish the thought. There's a whole slew of them and a submarine, or so they tell me." Gly helped his friend to his feet. "You okay?"

"Truth be told, I'm weak as a kitten, but so much better than I was a few days ago."

Gly lost three minutes trying to find the brass key that fit the lock shackling Hessmann to the bed frame. With Hessmann's arm over his shoulders, Gly and the German shuffled out of the ward. All the prisoners were awake now and watched with varying degrees of suspicion and envy. A few of the older hands, men who'd been locked up for decades, had a knowing look. They were witnessing two men about to throw their lives away.

They understood that death was the only real escape from this place.

Out in the entrance hall, Volker saw that Gly was overtaxed by helping his fellow prisoner and draped Hessmann's other arm over his shoulders and took most of the man's weight. Gly gave a begrudging nod that acknowledged he appreciated the help. He snatched up the rifle and opened the door.

The guard just reaching for the door handle on the other side blinked in surprise and was about to make a joke about perfect timing when he saw that the scene in front of him was all wrong.

"Who are you?" he demanded. "What is the meaning of this?"

Gly reversed the Lebel and hit the guard in the forehead hard enough to crack the thick bone and send him reeling back into the night. The incident wouldn't have drawn attention except that Gly hadn't doused the oil lamp when he'd opened the door. The flare of light had caught the eye of a guard on foot patrol rounding a nearby cell block. His reaction was much better than that of the comatose man lying on the grass at Gly's feet. He began blowing a whistle dangling from a lanyard around his neck, the shrill brassy blasts sending startled birds into the dark sky and causing monkeys who inhabited the island to add to their churlish cries.

"Merde," Gly spat. He raised the rifle and fired. The penalty for an escape attempt was time in isolation. For murdering a guard, it was immediate execution. Gly now faced the guillotine.

Volker stopped and lifted Hessmann in a fireman's carry, astonished by how light he was after only a few months in prison. Carrying the spy, he raced with Gly from the infirmary. Volker steadied Hessmann's legs with his left hand while clutching a Luger pistol in his right. Gly led them back into the thicket of vegetation surrounding the sprawling prison camp and headed to the northern side of the island.

Their destination wasn't far, but the jungle made running impossible. More whistles pierced the night and angry men's voices added to the clamor, while more guards woke and came swarming out of their barracks. Overhead, agitated monkeys squawked and ran through the branches in panicked abandon.

The men came out of the jungle just a short distance from their destination. The channel between Royale Island and Devil's was narrow, but so treacherous that a regular ferry was deemed too dangerous. In order to transfer prisoners, guards, and material to the most isolated of the three Salvation Islands, the French authorities had constructed a primitive overhead cable car system that used muscle power to shunt a dangling basket between low towers erected on each island's coast.

Two guards stationed at the Royale tower, alert to an escape attempt in progress, watched the jungle for any sign of movement. One stood on the ground, shielded by one of the tower's legs, and the other ten feet up on the platform next to the open-topped cable car gondola. Gly shot the guard with the high ground first. He didn't care that the man's back was to him as he watched the jungle to the east. The Frenchman toppled from his perch and hit the wet ground with a meaty thump. Gly had his sights on the second guard even before the first smacked into the earth. This man managed to get off a pair of snap shots with his gun at his hip before Gly drilled him with two rounds to his chest that exploded out his back.

Gly had depleted nearly half of his ammunition, so he snatched up the unfired Lebel from the guard he'd shot off the tower and he and Volker mounted the stairs to the loading platform. The German set his countryman into the tight wooden car and climbed over the edge. Gly followed. He had both rifles now and stood facing aft while Volker started pulling on the second of the two wires spanning the channel. The car lurched out over the water on its metal guide wheels. Volker soon had a steady rhythm but hadn't covered much distance when more guards appeared on the shore of Royal Island. The trio came under withering fire. Gly fired back, alternating pulling the trigger on each of his weapons, estimating placement more than aiming his shots. He just needed to keep the French pinned for a few seconds.

Bullets zipped and screamed past their heads. Several hit the gondola but none penetrated its side. Volker suddenly stopped pulling them across and the gondola pitched as it lost momentum. The Luger spat twice and then twice more. Guards on Devil's Island had arrived at the cable car's receiving tower. Unsure what was happening, they had hesitated and not shot at the men suspended over the water. Both died as a result.

Moments later they finished the traverse and were back down on solid ground. They were still being fired upon, so they raced into the jungle, Hessmann willing himself to move far faster than his body wanted.

Volker's two commandos met them as they reached the shoreline. The boat was beached a short way off. They each took one of Hessmann's arms and carried him the last few yards. The sailors had backed the boat to the rocks and were ready to pull on their oars as soon as all five men tumbled over the gunwale.

Gly quickly shook himself free of them and laid aim over the transom. Men appeared on the stone beach and quickly started taking potshots at the fleeing boat. Gly fired back, more to keep them pinned than in any hope of hitting them from the bobbing craft. Like before, he just wanted to trade time for distance. At fifty yards from shore the fire directed at them diminished as the darkness and the continuing rain made them all but invisible.

"There isn't a prison in the world that can hold Foster Gly," he shouted at the distant shore in English and in his deepest Scottish voice. "Sons of Edinburgh never leave one of their own behind."

"What was that for?" Volker asked.

"Just sowing more doubt about who was doing the rescuing and who was the rescuee."

After an hour of rowing, they came upon a nearly three-hundred-foot submarine lying like a basking shark on the surface. They would have gone past it if not for the lamps left lit on her streamlined conning tower.

"Lieutenant Volker," a voice hailed from the top of the tower. "We heard shots from over the horizon and feared the worst."

"Not to worry, Captain Reinhart," Volker shouted back. "The guards there may know how to bully defenseless prisoners. They fared rather poorer against us."

"Did you find success?"

"He did," Max Hessmann answered for him. "And for that, me and my friend here are most grateful."

"You really did it," Foss Gly said to his comrade, a rare smile cleaving his brutish face. "I kept you alive and you got me out."

"You sound like you think our adventure is at an end. I assure you, it has only just begun. I am known as the Kaiser's favorite spy. We stick together and I will soon make you his second favorite."

Gly thought about it for only a couple of seconds. He'd be arrested immediately if he returned to the British Isles, and he couldn't go back to France, where he'd been living when he'd originally been tried for a string of crimes that had stretched from Paris to the docks of Southampton on the morning of the *Titanic*'s sailing. Lord knew his wife and kid would be better off without him. He had no prospects, no loyalty, and no moral compass. Becoming a spy for the Germans made as much sense as anything else.

"You have yourself a partner."

1

New Haven, Connecticut
August 1914

It was a gray area. That's all anyone could agree on, the politicians and the lawyers and the military people. The current situation was a gray area.

The war in Europe hadn't yet broken out when the first shipment of Springfield rifles, twelve thousand of them, in fact, had left the Port of New York bound for England. They were due in Bristol in just a day or two. The second shipment of eleven thousand rifles was loaded onto a ship still moored in New York Harbor on August fourth when England declared war on Germany. A timely phone call from the British consul in Manhattan to the harbormaster saw the freighter's hawse lines pulled from the pier moments before the declaration was announced. She was technically not in port when the war became official, so she wasn't violating America's strict neutrality. She'd steamed down the East River a short time later on her run to England.

The third consignment, six thousand desperately needed rifles, was where things became sticky, legally speaking. They had been purchased by the British government in the month since Archduke Ferdinand's assassination in Serbia, but before England had actually entered the war. Now that war had been declared, the guns were currently sitting in the Winchester Arms factory in New Haven, Connecticut, and subject to a U.S. military oversight. Current exportation laws meant that them leaving U.S. soil was a direct violation of America's vow to stay out of the latest European war.

Joseph Van Dorn himself had devised the work-around. His firm, the Van Dorn Detective Agency, had been hired by the British government to oversee security for the operation, so Joseph was aware of the looming legal problem and had a plan to sidestep the intent of the law if not its letter.

England had purchased the guns from the United States government and they were to have been shipped by rail from the Springfield Armory in western Massachusetts straight to New York. But as the situation in Europe rapidly deteriorated, concern grew that the weapons wouldn't make it out of the country on time and would then languish in some warehouse for the duration of the war.

Van Dorn's eleventh-hour suggestion was that the English reject the rifles in all three batches and that Winchester Arms buy those same surplus guns. The sale needed to take place before the war's declaration. That date was a closely guarded secret, so the deal went through on July twenty-eighth. Winchester Arms, a duly licensed manufacturer and exporter of all manner of weapons, then sold those three batches of Springfield rifles back to the British government. Again that sale took place before the declaration so it wouldn't violate America's promise to favor nor aid either side in the war.

To further the ruse, the rifles went from the Springfield Armory to Winchester's factory, where they were pulled from their Army-issue crates and loaded into wooden chests stamped with the Winchester name and logo. The first two shipments made it out of the country on time. The holdup with the third group came when plain-clothed Canadian Mounties, His Majesty's representatives in North America, along with their armorer, found fault in several dozen five-rifle crates, causing the inspection and selection of guns to take far longer than expected.

Today was August sixth, the war for England was two days old, and their guns remained on American soil.

To make matters worse, because so many people in Washington had been hastily consulted on the legalities, the German Ambassador had learned of the deal and had already lodged a complaint with the War Department. A reply was being drafted explaining to His Excellency that the U.S. government did not involve itself in private sales made during times of peace and viewed the transaction as permissible under current law.

Despite the certainty in that pronouncement, it remained a gray area.

The workers transferring the rifles from the Army crates to the familiar Winchester packing chests did so with the expectation that federal police would burst in on the operation and arrest them all.

The Van Dorn lead investigator had no such concerns.

Isaac Bell wore his traditional summer white linen suit and low-crowned hat, though his jacket was draped limply over the back of an office chair and the hat sat atop a nearby filing cabinet. Outside the bank of windows where he stood, he saw men down in the factory's loading bay work in the wilting heat wearing denim overalls, often unbuttoned with the straps flapping around the backs of their thighs.

The heat wave was in its second week and showed no signs of letting up.

Archibald Abbott sat at a nearby desk, his face inches from a desk fan, so when he spoke it sounded like it was through an airplane's propeller. "This is ridiculous, we were supposed to guard a couple of trains on a milk run from Springfield, not babysit worker bees swapping one box for another in what amounts to an industrial-sized oven."

Archie was another Van Dorn man and Bell's best friend since college. Their wives were close as well. He had once been a stage actor and still had the good looks of a matinee idol. His hair was burnished copper and worn a little long on the sides and back. In contrast, Bell was blond, his hair neatly trimmed. Handsome, but more intense than Archie, with warier eyes. Both men were in their thirties and had the look of comfort in their own skin.

"Don't forget," Bell said in a deep but languid voice that still carried a hint of his native Boston, "we have junior agents currently picking through three days' worth of Ritz-Carlton garbage looking for a diamond necklace that the owner swears she lost in the hotel. You could join them."

"Ah, the glamorous life of a private dick," Archie mooned. "Remember that time in Tampa with the rum distillery owner stepping out on his wife and he got the jump on us?"

Bell shook his head at the memory. "Doused head to toe in molasses. Had to shave our heads and scrub for hours and we still smelled of it for weeks."

Archie leaned back so the fan wasn't directly in his face. "And look at us now, melting like gelatos so politicians can give the old 'wink wink' to our neutrality. Mark my words, the European war will be over by Christmas. Both sides have too much to lose to fight any longer than that."

"Your lips to God's ear. Our economy is in shambles enough as it is. The New York Stock Exchange is closed indefinitely, and if we lose exports long-term, things are going to get a lot worse."

Just then another detective popped his head into the borrowed office. "Isaac, we need you." The agent was Eddie Edwards, one of Van Dorn's top people and a specialist on railroad crime. He'd led the men who'd guarded the trains carrying rifles south from Springfield. "There's something you have to see."

Grateful for the distraction, Bell turned away from the window and strode after the much older Edwards. Archie got to his feet, but didn't make a move for the door. He would take Bell's spot overlooking the work. Any change in routine could be a diversion and Van Dorns never allowed themselves to be distracted.

"What do you have, KC?" Eddie's nickname was Kansas City. They went down a flight of stairs double time, Bell's custom-made boots making his tread as light as a cat's.

"Guns."

"They are the point of this place, you know," Bell deadpanned. They had to raise their voices slightly. While there was no machinery in the big loading bay, the Winchester factory was still a working arms plant, and the throb of nearby machinery was ever-present.

Edwards wasn't known for his sense of humor, but he said, "It ain't what I found that's interesting. Like the real estate people say — it's the location, location, location."

Bell's mustache twitched with interest. "Lead on."

They crossed the busy room, where forty or so workers were using pry bars to open the wooden packing crates the Army used to store the Springfield Model 1903s. Each rifle was packed in grease to prevent rust and wrapped with oil-proof paper. As soon as a crate was opened, the guns were removed and nestled into the Winchester Arms boxes. Carpenters were at the ready to nail them shut and more men were on hand to load the crates into the boxcars idling on the factory's dedicated rail spur. It went as efficiently as Henry Ford's Detroit assembly line.

The two men turned a corner and approached a washroom. A young agent stood just inside the door and made to confront the pair until he recognized his superiors. Eddie had obviously left him to guard the facilities. The room was dimly lit, with dingy white tiles on the floor and walls and eight stalls partitioned by wood walls with louvered doors. A janitor's closet was near the entrance and stood open. Inside there were mops and buckets and shelves of chemicals, as well as a bundled tarp. In the corner were propped five forty-three-inch-long Springfield rifles still shrouded in wax paper.

Bell looked to the right of the closet door and immediately saw what had drawn Edwards's keen interest. There was a small smudge of yellowish grease, no more than a thin sheen really, but it was an anomaly, a tiny detail out of place, and for a detective there was nothing more intriguing than understanding its deeper meaning.

Most times such things are entirely banal, meaningless points of data that don't lead to a larger conspiracy. It could have been a condiment from the janitor's lunch transferred to the wall from his hand that happened to look like the packing grease. Or it could have been the actual grease smeared by a worker waiting for access to one of the stalls.

But it wasn't.

Isaac Bell had no idea then the implications of the innocuous little smudge and what it revealed inside the closet, the international ramifications or the number of lives about to be torn apart because a careless thief had left behind this single clue.

Bell leaned down to inspect the spot. There was no smearing. It was just a little dollop of grease, as if something had been leaned against the wall while the door was opened.

"You see it too, right?" Eddie asked.

"Had this been transferred from a person's hand, there would have been some sign of streaking."

"That's just a little dot. Made no sense, so I tracked down the janitor and he opened the door. A painter's drop cloth had been thrown over the guns."

"Good catch, KC. What do you think it means?"

"Boss, I find the clues," he drawled. "I'll leave it up to you to suss out their meaning."

Bell turned his attention to the lock. It was a cheap thing and easily picked. He usually carried a small flashlight powered by a single D cell battery, but it was upstairs in a jacket pocket. He turned his head this way and that and finally saw bright scratches inside the keyhole. Definitely picked.

He thought about taking the rifles, but decided against it. Whoever had pilfered them from the loading bay was still out there working and Bell didn't want to tip his hand just yet.

"Stay here for a couple more minutes," Bell told the junior man, and he and Edwards stepped out of the washroom. As they turned the corner into the loading area, Bell started laughing as if his companion had just told a joke. Eddie caught on and guffawed a few times. Just two friends without a care in the world. Bell noted that none of the workers looked up or paid them the slightest attention.

Bell returned to the upstairs office, while Eddie Edwards went out to check on his men guarding the train. Archie had his back to him, focused on the work below. "What's up?" he asked without turning around.

"KC found five of the Springfield rifles in a locked janitor's closet."

That got Archie's attention. "Who steals ten-year-old surplus Army rifles when you work at a plant producing some of the finest weapons in the world? That makes no sense."

Bell picked up the candlestick phone sitting on the desk he was using.

"Seriously," Archie said. "This is like someone snatching a paste earring from a jewelry store when they could have grabbed a diamond tiara."

"Hello?" Bell said to the receptionist who answered his wire. "I would like to speak with Mr. Hopley. This is Isaac Bell." Dick Hopley was their liaison with Winchester.

The line's static hiss was faint since this was a limited-range internal call. A moment later came a smooth voice. "Mr. Bell, it's Dick Hopley. What can I do for you?"

"We have a problem. One of my men found five of the Springfield rifles tucked away in a broom closet." Bell paused, but the arms rep didn't say anything, so he continued. "I need you to make sure none of your men have left the work area prematurely and then I'm afraid I have to stop any more of the rifles being transferred out to the train cars."

"I can see the need to make certain none of the men have left," Hopley said at length. "That may be an indication of guilt, but why stop loading the crates?"

"Because I don't think our thief wants the rifles. He wanted the space."

2

The Van Dorn men made their coordinated move ten minutes after Bell hung up the phone. Dick Hopley performed the head count himself. He was a slender man with a salt-and-pepper beard and fingers stained yellow by cigarettes. He'd given a nod up to the overlooking offices so that Bell knew everyone was accounted for. Bell pointed to Eddie Edwards, who stood by the chainfall mechanism that opened and closed the roll-up main door. He worked the chain, and the big metal door came rattling down, slamming shut with an echoing crash. All the workers looked up at this sudden interruption. The young agent who had been posted in the restroom took up a position near some swinging doors that led deeper into the factory. Other agents led the few Winchester workers who'd been stacking crates in the boxcars back inside through a side door.

Bell came down the stairs and commanded everyone's attention. "We're sorry for the interruption," he said loudly enough for all to hear. "My name is Isaac Bell and I'm in charge of the security detail. We've run into a situation that requires your help. Would you all please line up in rows of four?"

When the forty workers were properly aligned, Bell and Archie walked among their ranks. Bell said nothing, though Archie asked each man his name and home address. It took about fifteen minutes.

"Okay, gentlemen, please remain in place for a bit longer," Bell called out when they were done. He waved to the floor foreman and led him to a quiet spot away from the others. He passed over the list Archie had compiled. "You know them all, right?"

"Sure. Some of my boys have been here twenty years on."

"That's good. Did any of them lie to us about their name or address?"

"Not sure I know where they all live, Mr. Bell," the man said as he scanned the page of information. "The names are correct, and I recognize a lot of the addresses, but some of the younger blokes move from place to place, looking for cheaper boardinghouses, or better ones once they've got some coin in their pockets."

"That's good enough," Bell told him, and motioned for the man to step away.

"Which one?" Archie asked, knowing Bell had already pinpointed a suspect.

"The young blond kid," Bell replied. "His eyes were shifting and he had the worst case of flop sweat I've ever seen."

"What about this one — Kraus? He has the scar across the chin. He seemed a bit jumpy to me."

"If you'd gotten a little closer you would have smelled the schnapps on his breath. He was afraid of getting busted for drinking on the job. No, it's John Kramer who interests me."

"For the sake of argument," Archie said, "let's say we have our criminal. What exactly is his crime?"

"Smuggling, would be my guess."

"What exactly?"

"That's to be determined." Bell sought out Dick Hopley. "We need to unload the train cars again."

"To discover what was hidden in the crate where the rifles were removed?" he asked eagerly.

"Yes."

"That's a lot of cases to be reopened and resealed again," the executive pointed out.

"We've been at this for hours. Must be close to five hundred crates."

"We will only be opening one," Bell said confidently. "Can you shunt the rail cars to another large space similar to this one? And have another car brought in so the men can keep working?"

Hopley nodded. "There's an auxiliary loading bay closer to the main gates."

"Good. Have the cars moved and please get me a handful of men to unload the crates, and I will need the services of a skilled carpenter. These men here can carry on working for now."

Bell gave word to his agents that John Kramer was to be watched like a hawk and prevented from leaving if he tried.

It took just under an hour to get the boxcars moved down the track and for the carpenter to construct a large scale using a thick fifteen-foot-long piece of lumber resting on an iron jack for the balance bar, with pallets hung from ropes to act as the pans. A bunch of the wooden crates had already been unloaded and stacked nearby. Bell and Archie each moved ten of them onto the pans, loading them evenly so that the beam barely moved. They waited a moment, and when the beam remained perfectly horizontal, they knew the two sets of crates weighed the exact same.

The Van Dorn detectives removed the crates and loaded another ten onto each pallet, making certain not to jostle the rig too much and waste time waiting for it to find its equilibrium again. Satisfied that the second batch was genuine, they moved on to twenty new crates.

Soon they were sweating in the afternoon heat. The warehouse had a metal roof that seemed to soak up the sun's rays and redirect them down onto the work floor. Both men mopped at their faces with handkerchiefs they could practically wring dry. At first, the Winchester stevedores scoffed at the two dapper men working their odd contraption, but soon grew to respect their diligence and ability to ignore their own discomfort.

By Bell's count they were checking crates three hundred and forty through three hundred and sixty when they hit pay dirt. As soon as all twenty crates were in position and Bell took away his hand, his pan started slowly dipping toward the floor. He and Archie exchanged a look. Bell reached under the pallet and lifted it up so that the balance beam was perfectly horizontal again. He stepped back, and as before the beam fell out of true.

"Well. Look at that. I didn't notice that any of my crates felt heavier or lighter," Archie remarked.

"I didn't suspect we would. Kramer had to keep the weight as close to a real case as possible. That's why we didn't load more than ten at a time. A small discrepancy would be lost if each side of the balance was too overloaded." Bell shouted over to the workers lugging in crates from the boxcars or returning the ones that had already been checked. "Hey, fellas, I think we're close. Why don't you all take twenty and then come back."

When they were alone, Bell said to Archie, "Okay, let's take them off one at a time."

Removing one crate from each side did nothing to correct the scale's imbalance, so they took off the next two and four more after that until the beam remained perfectly level. The suspect crate was one of the last two to be removed.

"It will be the heavier one," Bell said.

"Why would you think that?" Archie countered. "Could just as easily be the lighter one."

Bell was on his knees with a pry bar, his white suit all but destroyed. "Because Kramer would have added weight to match a real case but couldn't remove weight from whatever he's trying to smuggle."

Archie made to say something, but found no fault in his friend's logic.

Bell worked the bar around the crate's perimeter, jimmying the lid a bit at a time, the nails protesting with almost humanlike shrieks. Finally the lid could take no more and popped free from its base. Inside was some coir packing material that he pulled out by the handful to reveal what John Kramer had so painstakingly hidden away.

There were two heavy deep-cycle batteries secured in place with metal strapping. They were wired to a radio transmitter through a circuit that included an alarm clock with its clacker removed. An antenna wire bent into a convoluted shape to fit the crate's space completed the assembly.

"Not what I was expecting," Archie said.

Bell rocked back on his heels, his hand scratching absently at his sweaty chin. His blue eyes narrowed with concentration as he tried to determine the meaning of this apparatus and its purpose. He used the knife he kept sheathed in his boot to cut the leather loops that secured the alarm clock so he could pull it from the case, careful not to break any of the circuitry by damaging the wires.

It wasn't a standard bedside clock like he

had back in his rooms at the Knickerbocker Hotel. There was an extra face set into the larger circle of numbers that ran one through seven. Bell had seen these before. The clock was designed so that its timer could be set up to seven days before the alarm sounded. This one had been set to ring, albeit silently because of the missing bell striker, in three days. That meant in roughly seventy-two hours the alarm would sound and electricity would be fed to the transmitter. The radio would beam out its rays at a particular unknown frequency. Bell knew he would need a more technically inclined pair of eyes to plumb the device's electronic depths. For now, knowing the transmitter would emit waves of radio energy was good enough.

"Range is determined by the amount of power and the antenna length and height," Bell said more to himself than for Archie's benefit. "These types of batteries are designed to discharge at a slow, steady rate and the antenna is pretty limited because of the rifle case. I bet it can't reach more than a few miles."

"What good does that do?"

Bell set the clock back in its niche inside the crate. "Did you know that a properly tuned radio receiver can get a fix on a transmitter and with some patience triangulate its point of origin based on signal strength?"

Archie saw the implications immediately. "It's a tracking beacon."

"I believe so," Bell said. "Timed so it won't interfere with or be detected by any shore-based radio transceivers. Once it's far enough out at sea, the clock hits zero, the circuits complete, and for however long the batteries last it will be sending out a continuous carrier signal. To a German ship or submarine, prepositioned for an intercept, it's like they're sharks following the blood trail in the water, leading them to a tasty meal."

Bell jammed the lid back onto the crate as best he could because of the nails he'd bent when he'd pried it open. He and Archie hefted the crate and left the warehouse. They spotted the work crew loitering a short distance away, some smoking and a few on their knees playing dice.

"Hey, gents, you can reload the car again." Bell added a little lie to cover the unusual activity. "We found the crate with the defective weapons."

He and Archie returned to the main loading dock. The men continued to work like they were cogs in a large machine, moving crates, opening them, removing the rifles, and re-crating them so they could be returned to the railcars. None of the workers paid them the slightest heed until their suspect, John Kramer, saw them carrying in the single crate between them. Archie was walking backward, so he couldn't see, but Bell had an unobstructed view of the twenty-something worker go ashen and start to look for exits the way a cornered rat would.

"I was right," Bell whispered. "He looks like the poster boy for guilty."

A pair of Van Dorn agents saw the interplay between their boss and the suspect and started across the room to intercept the young man. Kramer noted the movement and his frightened demeanor hardened into something else. Bell recognized it and lowered his end of the crate. Archie followed suit a fraction of a second later, but was too late.

"Everybody down," Bell shouted before actually seeing the small revolver Kramer pulled from his coverall's pocket.

Kramer fired a pair of bullets toward the agents who were closer and began running for the exit that led deeper into the arms factory. Bell saw the disaster as it unfolded, and as much as he wanted to stop it, he knew he was powerless. Agents were trained not to return fire if there were civilians in danger. Bell would have finessed the situation, talked Kramer down or at least shot to wound, but the other two Van Dorn men, greener and suddenly overwhelmed by adrenaline, were quick with their guns.

They had their weapons out before the fleeing suspect had taken another step. They fired with abandon, cycling triggers as fast as they could, their training now all but forgotten. The cascade of shots sounded like a full volley of cannon, and it took long seconds for it to stop echoing in the vaulted loading bay. Bell's ears were left ringing.

He had drawn his own weapon, a boxy Browning 9-millimeter automatic with a round already in the chamber. It was a reflex action for approaching an armed suspect, but Bell needn't have bothered. Kramer was down, falling face-first with four visible bullet wounds in his back and one in his left thigh just below the buttock. No blood spewed from the ragged holes. His heart had beat its last.

Bell turned from the body as his men stepped closer. They had the sense not to gloat, or show much of anything really, but Bell could tell they were proud of themselves, proud that they had survived their first gunfight, such as it was. He couldn't be angry at them. They had followed procedure. But he could rage at the situation and did. Their only real chance of finding out what was going on here at the Winchester factory lay dead on the cement with more holes than an Italian *nonna*'s colander. He was livid inside, but projected to his men only an icy exterior and perhaps a subtle flare of his nostrils.

Kramer's pistol had skittered away when his body absorbed the kinetic shock of so many bullets. Bell picked it up from the floor. As he'd suspected when he heard it fire, it was a cheaply made .22 caliber with a loose cylinder. The next time its trigger was pulled there was a fifty-fifty chance of the gun exploding in the shooter's hand.

Archie approached. He could feel his partner's anger, so he asked a dumb question to distract him. "Do you think he thought he could escape, or did he want to die to protect someone?"

"Young guys like him always think they can make a break for it," Bell said absently, then shook off his own sense of pessimism. There were leads to follow, and he snapped himself into the here and now.

Bell said, "I want to believe that Kramer and his backers only had time to slip a radio into this load of weapons, but we need to check on the other ships hauling guns to England. Arch, get on the horn and contact the shippers. They need to reach their captains and determine if one of the crates is broadcasting. They should be able to use their own wireless to hear it."

"Right." Archie Abbott spun on his heel and climbed the stairs to their borrowed offices.

Bell addressed the other two Van Dorn men. "Go to the Yale campus and find an expert on radio and wireless and get him over here so we can determine what frequency this contraption sends on, to make it easier for those sailors out there."

Dick Hopley arrived in a rush. Only a minute had passed since the shooting, so he'd made good time from his office. He gaped at the sight of his employee lying dead on the floor. "What happened here, Bell?"

"This man, John Kramer, tried to hide a radio in one of the crates. It was set on a timer so it wouldn't begin transmitting until it was well out at sea."

"To what end?" Hopley asked, baffled by such an odd package to smuggle. He couldn't tear his eyes away from the dead man. The sweat on his forehead had more to do with the grisly scene than the heat. He dabbed at it with a bandanna.

"The signal can be tracked back to its source by an enemy ship or submarine the way a homing pigeon can zero in on its loft."

The executive lost all color at the implications. "Those men would have been sitting ducks."

"Cooked goose, if we want to keep with the bird analogies. What's worse is two ships have already left New York and could be transmitting their location this very moment."

"We have to do something," Hopley stammered.

"We are. Archie is contacting the shipping companies now. We'll get the crews searching for the radio before the hour is out. I want to investigate John Kramer's lodgings." Bell had the address from the notes that Archie had compiled earlier. "I would like you to get his employee records. I will need to talk to any of his closer associates here at the factory. Get a list of such men from your foreman."

"Yes, of course," Hopley said, pulling himself together. It was clear the whole situation had him rattled, but getting orders and having something to do seemed to settle his nerves. "I will see to it at once."

"Also, call the police while you're at it. Archie can give a statement and the two who actually pulled the trigger should be back shortly."

Bell made to leave the arms plant. Things were in motion. He just hoped they had direction.

3

The address where John, né Johan, Kramer lived was a large detached home about a mile from the plant. Out front was a sign that read MRS. CASTEAUX'S ROOMS FOR RENT. The two-story structure was painted an inviting beige with white shutters and trim and was fronted by a deep porch with a pair of Adirondack-style rocking chairs. The lawn was well tended but browning due to the August heat. A respectable place, Bell guessed, but perhaps not the type of place a young man would want to inhabit, since he suspected there were as many rules as there were rosebushes lining the porch rail.

The front door was open, in case there was a breeze, but the screen door was closed. Bell knocked and called out, "Hello."

"Be right with you," a woman replied from inside.

Bell could see a living room with a large sofa, two overstuffed chairs, and an upright piano finished in cherry veneer jammed into a corner. Through a set of French doors opposite the home's entry, Bell saw the dining room with a large family-style table for Mrs. Casteaux's lodgers. A woman came through from the dining room, wiping her hands on an apron. She was young and pretty, not what Bell had expected, but perhaps explained why Kramer had chosen to live here.

"Are you the owner, Mrs. Casteaux?"

"Good heavens no," she said with a bright smile. "That's my mother. I'm Catherine. I help out with the cooking and cleaning. I'm sorry to say we have no available rooms, Mr. . . ."

"Bell. My name is Isaac Bell, and I'm not here about renting a room. I'm here about one of your current lodgers. May I come in?"

"Pardon me." She unlatched the screen door and pushed it open as an invitation. "Please."

Bell removed his hat and stepped across the threshold. "I am the lead investigator for the Van Dorn Detective Agency," he said, and showed her a billfold with his picture, title, and company affiliation. "Perhaps you've heard of us."

"I have," Catherine Casteaux replied, caution taking the cheerful lilt from her voice, a reaction Bell was used to.

"I'm afraid one of your boarders, John Kramer . . ." At the mere mention of the name, Catherine's face paled and she clutched at the throat of her blouse.

"What happened to John?" she asked in a rush. Her affection for him, and her fear for him too, was evident in how her eyes dilated so they looked pure black. She didn't burst into tears, but her eyes welled up and her lip trembled ever so slightly.

"He was killed today. Shot, I'm afraid, by two of my men in the commission of an act of sabotage." She appeared steady enough, but Bell took her elbow anyway and guided her to the sofa. "I'm sorry to tell you so bluntly, but I believe frankness in these matters is for the best, don't you?"

"Yes," she said absently, as Bell knew she would. His little question at the end was deliberately intended to distract the listener and prevent their thoughts from spiraling out of control.

"I can tell by your reaction you liked Mr. Kramer, so I am especially sorry for his death. It couldn't be helped. He fired at my men and could have wounded or even killed bystanders."

"He had a gun?" she asked, the initial shock wearing off.

"Yes, ma'am. We caught him trying to smuggle a radio into a valuable cargo shipment. When confronted, he chose to fire at us and run. You didn't know he had any firearms?"

"Well, no. I know he worked at Winchester, but he never mentioned owning any guns himself. I never saw him with any."

"Miss Casteaux, the police will be opening an investigation soon, but time is of the essence. It's possible many sailors' lives are at risk because of what John Kramer was up to. I need to see his room and perhaps any common spaces in your home. Is that all right?"

"Shouldn't we wait for the police?"

"It'll be hours before they get around to coming here. I don't have that kind of time if I'm to save those other men." Bell's eyes never left hers so she could feel the seriousness of the situation.

"John was a spy?"

"Yes, an agent and a saboteur, and if my hunch is right, an attempted murderer. Also, I doubt he was working alone. Was he close to any of your other lodgers, or did he have friends visit him here?"

"He was friendly to everyone, but no one in particular. He and Gary Taylor both worked at the plant and would walk together most days, but that was about it. I never saw them together on their days off." She pulled a key ring from her apron pocket. "I will show you John's room. As for common areas, this is about it except for the kitchen."

"What about a basement?"

"We have one and it's not locked or anything, but there's nothing down there but some old junk."

"I'd still like to see it."

She led him up a flight of stairs. The hallway at the top ran left to right with a closed door at each end that Bell suspected were the shared bathrooms. There were four bedrooms, each locked, but accessible with the landlady's set of keys. "These are all for lodgers. My mother and I have a separate apartment off the kitchen."

"Have you been doing this long?"

"A few years now. I have six siblings who are all much older than me. When they grew up and left the house, my mom decided to take in renters rather than sell and move into something smaller."

Bell didn't ask about the father. No matter what had become of him, it would likely be distressing for her.

"Here we go," she said, and opened one of the locked doors.

The bedroom was a tidy rectangle with a

single curtained window, a bed, a small desk with a chair, and a chest of drawers. The walls were unadorned. A central light fixture hung from the ceiling. The house was old enough for the electrical system to be retrofitted.

Catherine waited in the hallway, as if she couldn't bring herself to invade a man's space, even if he was dead. Bell went first to the desk. Sitting on top was a Jules Verne novel. Bell checked and saw it had come from the New Haven Library and would be overdue in a few days' time. There was a single drawer, empty. The chest was filled with clothes, neatly folded, doubtlessly by Catherine. Bell felt through all of the items but found nothing out of the ordinary. He removed the drawers one by one to see if anything had been stashed behind them. There wasn't.

There wasn't anything between the mattress and the box spring, either, and under the bed was an empty suitcase. Its liner was intact and none of the seams looked like they'd been cut open and restitched.

This was as Bell expected. Kramer was young, but schooled enough in the ways of espionage to be able to smuggle the radio in under their noses. He'd also know not to leave anything incriminating in his immediate living space. There was no deniability if some secret stash was discovered.

Bell understood enough spycraft to know that Kramer was disposable to his handler, so he very much wanted to meet whoever trained the man and supplied him with the delayed-time radios.

"Show me the basement," he said to Catherine.

The basement steps ran under the flight leading up to the second floor. There was a bolt that could be thrown to secure the door, but no lock, as he'd been told. He noted when he opened the door that the hinges didn't squeak. He touched one and his fingertip came back covered with a thin sheen of oil. Someone had recently greased the hardware so that a late-night visit could go undetected. This boded well.

He clicked on the lights. The stairs were made of unpainted wood and the floor was packed dirt. The plaster covering the lathing walls had been left rough. Bell descended and looked around once he was at the bottom. The basement appeared to be divided into many smaller rooms and there was shelving covering many of the walls. They were loaded with all sorts of stuff, from empty canning jars to bits of unidentifiable machinery. The space had a claustrophobic gloom and smelled of dampness and moldering paper.

He called up to Catherine, who'd remained at the top of the steps, "No sense in you coming down. It's going to take me a while."

"Thanks. I don't like going down there much. I'll be in the kitchen if you need me."

Bell went from room to room, opening boxes and cartons of a certain size and moving bundles of papers to see if anything had been stashed behind them. As he searched, Bell unwound the mystery of the Casteaux family from the possessions kept in the basement. It was purely a mental exercise to test his observational powers. It appeared Mr. Henry Casteaux tried to repair broken things he'd find in the trash. He fancied himself an amateur electrician and worked to fix all manner of appliances and motors. He read scientific journals and pasted electrical diagrams into scrapbooks. Judging by the scorch marks on a tool-laden desk in the only room with a barred window, high up on the wall, he hadn't properly grounded something and took what had to have been a fatal jolt. Bell imagined that Mrs. Casteaux and her daughter left the cellar as it was in tribute.

It was in the final room that he found

what he knew would be there. This was the furnace room, the only one spared from Mr. Casteaux's hoarding. Wedged between the boiler's circulator pump and a newish oil storage tank was a canvas tarp that looked like it had been in the basement for decades. Under it were four more deep-cycle batteries and two identical radios. The only things missing were the special clocks. Bell guessed Kramer's handler —

He heard the scrape of a match and then a loud whoosh of hot air blasted him at the same moment he registered a billowing wall of light behind him. He whirled to see the space just outside the furnace room consumed in fire. The bundles of papers stacked nearly three feet high burned like torches and the brittle wooden shelving went up like it was soaked in pitch.

Bell felt a primal stab of raw panic as he faced the growing wall of flame, knowing that his only escape lay on the far side of the basement. He smelled the chemical taint of kerosene that had been used as an accelerant. In seconds, flames began to lick at the wooden joists and ceiling overhead. He tried to rush forward, but the heat beat him back before he was even five feet from the roaring blaze. By the depth of the fire, he knew the unseen arsonist had doused the other rooms between him and the stairs.

He was caught on the wrong side of hell.

4

Dense smoke began to fill the boiler room under the Casteaux boardinghouse, a haze that eroded visibility by the second. Isaac Bell tried to keep his breathing shallow, but he couldn't help but inhale some of the acrid smog and he felt it sear his lungs like caustic lye. His eyes watered and tears streaked his cheeks.

He couldn't wait for the flames to die down because they wouldn't. The house was old, the exposed wood as dry as tinder, and the basement full of papers and combustibles. The whole place would soon be consumed, burned down to a cellar hole filled with smoky remains and ash. Bell felt another stab as he guessed at Catherine Casteaux's fate. John Kramer's handler, the spy who doubtlessly set the blaze, couldn't chance her noticing his escape once she heard the fire and smelled the smoke. He would have killed her before descending the cellar stairs and trapping Bell in the basement. Not enough of her remains would survive the fire to show a slit throat or an expertly punctured heart.

Bell couldn't dwell on her now and cruelly thrust her fate aside. He recalled the latch on the cellar door. It had been high up. Even if he survived a run through the flames and launched himself up the stairs at full tilt, he wouldn't be able to smash the door open. He wouldn't have the momentum nor be able to hit the slab of wood at the proper height to break the lock.

He coughed for the first time, trying to suppress it as best he could. If he hadn't, he would soon be racked with uncontrollable fits.

He considered and discarded a slim sheaf of ideas. There was nothing he could do. He was trapped. The floorboards near the wall separating the boiler room from the rest of the basement turned black before his eyes, smoked heavily for a moment, and then burst into flames. Soon the entire ceiling would be a sheet of fire. Another paralyzing punch of fear nearly overwhelmed him, but he fought it down as if instinct could be ignored.

Think. Something had caught his attention when he'd entered the room. A trivial detail. What was it?

The oil tank. It was much newer than the boiler. Bell looked around. Through the thick smoke writhing along the ceiling he spotted the sealed door for an abandoned coal chute. The boiler had once been coal-fired, but had likely been converted to oil after Henry Casteaux's death. He imagined neither widow nor daughter would want to come down to shovel coal all winter in the basement where he died.

Bell dropped to the floor to take a deep breath of the relatively clean air and held it. He used the boiler and its various pipes as stepping-stones to climb atop the oil tank. The smoke reduced his eyes to weeping slits. There was a twist lock at the bottom of the coal door that hadn't been turned in years, so he sucked in the pain as the flesh of his fingers was squashed between the metal latch and his own bones.

He relaxed his grip, shook out the pain, and tried again. The flames consuming the floorboards and joists drew closer and the smoke grew thicker still. Something heavy crashed outside the boiler room, a section of floor collapsing, and the inferno's roar swelled as if it sensed its victory over the house.

He redoubled his torque on the lever,

sweat breaking out of his pores as the heat built. The latch popped and Bell pulled the door open, leaping through the tight opening as additional oxygen was sucked into the blaze, allowing it to mushroom like an explosion. He hit the ground outside and rolled away from the gush of fire that erupted from the coal delivery door. And he kept rolling when he saw his suit pants were on fire a moment before he felt the flame lick his skin.

He swatted at the last of the fire and coughed out some of the smoke fouling his lungs. He looked up to see all the ground-floor windows had been blown out by the heat. From them, flames and smoke coiled into the sky. A crowd had gathered along the street, men and women, and especially big-eyed children. Only minutes had passed, but the whole structure was doomed. Something inside the building exploded and the crowd surged back. Fear overcame their voyeurism for a few seconds and then their rapt expressions returned. In the distance, a fire engine's clanking bell could be heard.

Bell paid attention to none of that. He surveyed the scene, looking for anomalies, the thread he always believed could be reliably tugged to unravel a mystery. He spotted it at once and felt a flush of adrenaline revive his body and sharpen his mind.

Max Hessmann regretted killing Catherine Casteaux. It had been necessary, to be sure, but still regrettable. When she'd come blubbering up to his room to tell him John Kramer was dead and that a detective had gone through his room and was now searching the basement, her fate had been sealed. While several radio beacons remained, this operation was terminated and Hessmann had to eliminate any loose ends.

Catherine only knew him as Gary Taylor, another worker at the Winchester plant, though he had never actually set foot in the place. It was all a ruse for her benefit, but still, she had seen his face and eventually a police sketch artist would assemble a portrait and he couldn't allow that to happen. John apparently had done the right thing and avoided capture, saving Hessmann the need to kill him as well.

Kramer was nothing more than a dupe recruited at a local bar that catered to German expats. It had taken little more than an appeal to his patriotism of an idealized homeland he had left as a child and a wad of cash. It had been luck that his boardinghouse had a spare room, so they didn't have to meet clandestinely. Those types of meetings were reserved for Foss Gly, who kept the German-supplied extended-play clocks. The radios and batteries were easy enough to purchase and could be kept in a less-secure location, but the clocks were so specialized their discovery would doubtlessly invite too many questions. Gly had them at a safe house in New York.

He'd gotten a few things from his room before leaving the house. Smoke had started to roil from open windows, so a crowd had gathered. To flee immediately would have aroused suspicion, so he'd hung in with the growing throng, answering their questions about anyone else being in the building. He told one and all that the other boarders were at work and that the madam and Miss Casteaux were running errands.

He slowly worked his way to the back of the crowd, becoming not a survivor of the catastrophe but just another gawking witness. He turned to make his escape just seconds before Bell rounded the corner to see the mob watching the fire as though it were the afternoon's entertainment.

Bell looked past the crowd and spotted a man walking away. In itself, that wasn't unusual. Watchers were coming and going depending on the urgency of their afternoon plans. But the man at the center of Bell's attention was the only person within a block other than himself who didn't turn to the explosion. The man didn't even flinch. That wasn't human nature. That was someone fighting to hide his connection to the blaze he was fleeing.

Bell made to run after him and nearly fell to the pavement. He hadn't realized it until that moment, but he'd wrenched his ankle. It could barely take his weight. He looked up the road in desperation. The spy didn't appear to be rushing, but his dark form was receding alarmingly fast. Bell had just moments.

He took a hobbling step and then another. The pain was savage, but tolerable. What wasn't was his speed. He covered five feet in the time it took the fiend to escape a further ten.

Bell then spotted what he hoped was a miracle. Joseph Merkel was standing among the first rank of onlookers and leaning against some sort of handle, like that of a shovel.

"Joe," Bell shouted over the roar of the fire and the approaching fire engine.

The man pulled his gaze from the spectacle and recognition lifted the corners of his mustache into a smile. Merkel had been one of the early Milwaukee pioneers of motorcycles along with other notables like Davidson and Harley. Bell had once owned a Flying Merkel, one of the fastest bikes around. Bell knew he'd sold his company a few years ago and had no idea he was in New Haven.

"Isaac. What happened to you?"

Bell jerked a thumb over his shoulder. "I was in the basement. I don't have time to explain, but do you have a motorbike with you? The guy who torched the house is getting away."

The mechanic caught the urgency in Bell's voice and replied quickly, "Just this. I'm helping its inventor fine-tune the design."

That's when Bell realized his friend was standing on an oversized child's scooter and that it had a small motor attached to the front wheel.

"It's called an Autoped," Merkel said, stepping down off the contraption, but holding on to the control handle's throttle grip. "Push this forward to engage the clutch and drive. Center is neutral, and pulling back on the handle brakes it. Throttle links just like any of my bikes."

Isaac took his place, leaving one foot on the ground to steady the little vehicle. The tires were red rubber and about ten inches in diameter. There was no suspension, so Bell knew to keep his knees flexed. He pressed the handle forward and opened the throttle. The 155cc motor purred to life and the machine began to gather speed. "I'll leave it at the Winchester Arms plant with one of my detectives," Bell shouted over his shoulder. "And thanks."

Like any two-wheeler, the Autoped was unstable at low speeds, especially because the rider stood atop it rather than sitting on a seat, so the center of gravity was high, but within ten or fifteen seconds, Bell had the ride smoothed out and he opened the throttle to the max. Hot wind dried the sweat on his face and breezed through his blond hair. His quarry was three-quarters of a block ahead and had no idea he was being hunted.

Keeping his right hand on the throttle, Bell loosened his Browning from its holster under his left arm and stuffed it in his right coat pocket.

The spy stayed on the sidewalk as he rounded the corner ahead. It appeared to be a busier street than the one where the boardinghouse had stood. Bell stayed after his man, gaining more confidence with the Autoped with each passing moment. He estimated his speed at around twelve miles per hour. When he reached the same corner, Bell slowed and cut wide in his lane so he could take in the scene that fraction of a second faster.

Buildings suddenly grew to three- and four-story tenements with blackened-brick facades and concrete stoops. There were more people walking about. The sidewalks were obstacle courses of crates of fruits and vegetables, bolts of cloth on racks, a shoe-shine stand outside a cobbler's place. A streetcar track ran down the middle of the two vehicle lanes. Pedestrian jaywalking seemed to be a New Haven pastime.

Overhead were strung hundreds of power lines and telephone trunk cables that met in unsolvable knots, like rat nests, at each utility pole. Above all that hung "urban pennants," strings of drying laundry run out from windows and fire escapes. Where distances were too great to run a single line, guy-wired structures called laundry ladders had been erected with fifty or more lines radiating out like spokes on a wheel. Like in most industrial cities, anything white hung out to dry was uniformly gray by the time it was hauled in for folding.

There was a general rumble of noise that permeated everywhere, daunting to strangers, unheard by locals.

The spy was half a block ahead and still moving at a brisk, but not hurried, pace. Bell noticed he was now taking a much sharper interest in his surroundings, looking left and right, checking for tails in the reflections of storefront windows. Before, he just wanted to gain distance from the fire and not attract attention, but now he was practicing tradecraft. Bell slowed a little.

He considered his options. Ideally, he would follow the man to learn where his secondary safe house was located and at least recover the clocks as evidence. But a successful tail needed a half dozen or more agents, multiple vehicles, disguises, and a carefully detailed plan. One man on a motorized scooter with unknown range wasn't going to cut it. That left Bell alone to take the man down. The streets were rough, heavily dug up and hastily repaved, so the ride was brutal on Bell's strained ankle, but he felt good enough to give it a go. He had the 9mm Browning and the advantage of surprise.

And then he didn't.

The spy had the instincts of a cat. Somehow he'd made Bell, because he suddenly took off running. Bell opened the throttle and the man quickly looked over his shoulder and his eyes widened. Bell cursed. His run had been a ruse. The spy hadn't known he was being followed, but by sprinting ahead he had tricked Bell into revealing himself. In all his years of being a detective, no perp had ever shown such craftiness.

He found some satisfaction in confirming his suspicion about the guy he was chasing.

The road was less congested than the sidewalk, so the spy jumped off the curb and started running flat out along the edge of the steady string of cars. The Autoped was more than game and Bell began closing the distance. Then the spy juked hard to the right, ran across the sidewalk by shoving through the crowd, and raced down an alley.

The tires were too small for Bell to speed up onto the sidewalk in pursuit. He was forced to stop and lift the front wheel off the road and then goose the rear end to follow.

The alley was tight, claustrophobic, with little light filtering through the steel scaffolding of the overhanging fire escapes. The smell was a combination of animal manure and rancid cooking grease. Trash cans overflowed and a colony of feral cats were still hackled by the spy's passage. The man had flipped some trash cans in his wake and toppled a shipping crate in order to slow the pursuit. Bell was forced to either weave around the obstacles or kick them aside with his foot. He was losing ground and wanted to abandon the scooter and give chase on foot, but each time he put any sort of pressure on his ankle, it sent a spike of pain all the way to the top of his skull.

Bell finally burst from the alley onto another busy street. This one was four-laned and lacked light-rail tracks. He looked right and saw the spy climbing into the back of a taxi. Had Bell looked left first, he would have lost the man. He spun the scooter and adjusted his stance so as to present a slimmer profile to the wind. He had to catch them before they got out of traffic or the Model T daubed in a jarring yellow paint would vanish.

The cab would accelerate away for a few dozen yards and then grind to a halt as traffic thickened. They were approaching a large construction site and a parade of trucks exiting the boarded-off plot snarled the road's usual flow. Bell drew tantalizingly close, only to have traffic begin to move again, slowly at first, and then suddenly the cab was fifty yards away. Bell wove around cars as best he could, trying to exploit the tight area between the vehicles and the gutter. He had to lean to his right to keep his shoulder from slamming into side mirrors. That upset the Autoped's balance and forced him to lay the scooter over so that his body was no longer centered above the deck, but a few feet out over the sidewalk.

"Coming through," he shouted to get people along the curb to get out of his way. "Make space."

Traffic stopped again and the passenger door of one of the big construction trucks suddenly flew open. Bell ducked instinctively, narrowly avoiding running face-first into the slab of metal. A surprised worker jumping from the cab cursed Bell as he raced away. The taxi was only a few cars ahead now. In the inner lane, Bell skirted around the rear of another truck and found himself coming up directly behind the cab. He could see the pale oval shape of the spy's face as he peered out the rear window. Bell could sense him making the calculations and they came to the same conclusion at the same time.

The spy was trapped. Traffic was stalled in their lanes, but zipping by in the opposite direction. The sidewalk was still walled off by the wooden construction fence plastered with colored posters and notices.

The spy launched himself from the taxi and ran up the street. There was so little space between some of the cars, he had to shuffle sideways to make it through. Bell had it easier. He scrunched down on his haunches and reached up to hold the handlebar and sailed under side mirrors and protruding headlamps with ease. A grin creased his handsome face. He had his man.

The spy sensed him coming because he leaped onto the running board of an open-topped sedan and then clambered across the backseats and out the other side to reach the sidewalk. Bell braked hard and manhandled the scooter to keep after his man. Because of the construction zone, the sidewalk was practically deserted. Bell maneuvered up the curb once again and gave the plucky little scooter everything it had. He halved the distance in moments and halved it again even quicker.

He made ready to leap from the Autoped in a flying tackle and was factoring angles and distances when he saw they were coming up on another break in the fence that gave access to the boarded-off construction pit. He was closer to the road and had a better line of sight, but no time to even shout a warning that a Mack truck was charging out of the work zone. Bell braked hard and then dumped the scooter on its side, scraping against the cement sidewalk so that the last of his suit shredded and his skin was rubbed off in what bikers called a road rash.

The trucker didn't have time to hit his horn and barely got his foot off the accelerator as he sped out of the foundation hole with a load of dirt. The left front fender slammed into the spy hard enough to send him airborne and rip his tightly laced shoes from his feet. Bell slid until he was almost under the still-rolling rear wheels, so he didn't see the body land in a bone-shattering collision with the pavement and tumble several times like a rag doll thrown by a petulant child.

Bell tucked his legs to his chest and covered his head, praying there would be no pain as he slid under the truck just ahead of its back axle as the driver slammed it to a halt. It was so close that the heavy tire came to rest against his hunched shoulder.

Screams began to pierce the air as drivers on the street and the few people walking past the construction site realized what they'd just witnessed.

Shakily, Bell pulled himself from under the truck as the driver lowered himself from the cab. "I never saw him," he said to no one and everyone. "Guy came out of nowhere. I swear."

"I saw everything," a man in worker's overalls said. "He was being chased." The man spotted Bell climbing out from beneath the truck's rear bed. "That guy," he said, and pointed accusatorially. "He was chasing the other fellow. What's going on here? Who are you?"

Bell ignored the growing mob and went to the body. The spy was clearly dead. His neck was broken so that his head was twisted completely around. He lay on his chest, but his lifeless blue eyes stared heavenward.

"I asked you who you are, mister," the witness said with increasing anger and suspicion. His big fists were balled at his sides.

Bell got to his feet and let his natural authority rise in his voice. "I'm a detective with Van Dorn. This man is a murderer and arsonist." Bell was certain of the latter and pretty sure of the former. "Please go find a policeman."

The man's antagonism fled in the face of Bell's statement and he nodded mutely.

Bell stooped over the body again, ringed by curious onlookers. He rifled through the spy's clothing. He found a needle-like dagger attached to his wrist and a small amount of cash and loose change. The dagger had been wiped clean, but Bell could still smell the coppery scent of blood on the blade.

There was nothing more to be learned here, he knew. He righted the little Autoped and fired the engine. Before any of the onlookers realized what he was doing, he'd sped away, back toward the Winchester factory, in hopes of salvaging something from this debacle.

5

The deluge of bad news continued for Bell as soon as he entered the upstairs office he and Archie used as an observation post. Archie was at a desk with three phones in front of him, his tie loosened, and his sleeves rolled up. A pitcher of water dewed with condensation and an empty glass sat within reach. Arch handled stress better than most, but Bell could see the strain on his friend's face.

"Stay on the wire," Archie said into one of the phones. "Isaac is back, and he'll likely have additional instructions."

"Who's on the other end?" Bell asked, filling the glass with water. He drank it down in a single throw and refilled it.

"Bull pen back at the office. What happened to you? You look terrible."

"Thanks. Let's see, caught in the basement of a burning house, chased a murderer/arsonist on a motorized scooter, which I almost crashed into the truck that killed said murder/arsonist."

"The murderer/arsonist being . . . ?"

"His landlady knew him as Gary Taylor. Claimed to work here with John Kramer, but that's bunkum. Not sure of his name, but I am certain he was Kramer's handler. I found a stash of batteries and radios in the basement of Kramer's boardinghouse. The special clocks must be kept in a separate location. A train station locker or a secondary safe house."

"Did you get anything from the guy?"

"Nothing. I want you to remain here in New Haven to lean on the police. I want access to those radios and batteries. Also, I don't know if this place uses a coroner or has a proper medical examiner, but I'd like to know if the spymaster has any distinguishing traits that we can use to pinpoint a place of origin."

"You assume he's German?"

"Cui bono," Bell said in Latin. "Who else benefits if three shipments of rifles never reach the hands of English soldiers?"

"Speaking of which, there's some news on that front. Early this morning a ship exploded about two hundred miles off the British coast. Torpedo suspected. Several other vessels saw it and investigated. There were no survivors, but they managed to ID the ship from a damaged life raft that had floated free in an oil slick."

"The *Mildred E. Burroughs*?"

Archie nodded. "The very same ship loaded with the first batch of guns. Crew of twenty-nine all dead and the rifles consigned to Davy Jones's locker."

"It's our fault," Bell said as the weight of guilt came crashing down on his shoulders. "We were in charge of protecting those guns and we utterly failed."

"You can't mean . . ."

"Arch, the spies slipped that transmitter into that crate on our watch. It's our screwup. Those men are dead because we didn't do our job." His voice was raw with wrenching shame at their catastrophic oversight. He was furious with himself. This had just become personal for Bell, and it took him a full minute to rein in his emotions. He finally said, "What about the *Centurion,* the second freighter? Is there anything we can do?"

"She left port this morning. All attempts to contact her have gone unanswered. I did finally get a call about twenty minutes ago from the harbormaster's office. The pilot who took her out said their wireless wasn't working, but the radioman said he could fix it."

Bell cursed.

Archie said, "Looks like the Huns are taking the fight right to the British in their own backyard."

"These shipments have been in the works for a while and one of the worst-kept secrets ever. If I were the German admiralty, I'd plan for a special mission to take them out as soon as possible. They tracked the *Burroughs* the moment she left port and took her out the minute they reached the prescribed embargo zone around the British Isles. The war's so new and our neutrality is untested, so it would make sense to risk a big strike now and deal with whatever political repercussions arose later."

"I suppose," Archie said, long-term strategy never being one of his strong suits. "Any thought on how to get a warning to the *Centurion*?"

"She's likely already out of range of any shore-based transceivers," Bell replied. His brain was working like an electric dynamo. There was no way he was going to lose a second ship.

Archie got a sudden idea. "Maybe we can bounce a warning from ship to ship to ship. Contact a nearby freighter and have them rebroadcast it out until . . . Oh, range isn't the issue. Their radio is dead."

"Unless someone gets close enough for semaphore or Morse on a signal lamp, that idea won't work."

"They're going to die, aren't they?" A dark tone had crept into Archie's normally unflappable voice. "A sub's lurking out there right now listening for the homing beacon, and when they hear it, those sailors are as good as dead and there's nothing we can do about it."

"Not nothing," Bell said with sudden inspiration. He strode to Archie's desk, wincing when his ankle took his weight, but he didn't slow. He brought the telephone to his mouth with his right hand, while his left held the speaker to his ear. "This is Bell. Who's on the line?"

"Hey, boss, it's Helen." Helen Mills was the agency's first female agent and had proven herself time and again in her short stint at Van Dorn.

"Helen, are you up to speed on everything?"

"Mr. Abbott's kept us all in the loop."

"Good. Here's what we're going to do. Glenn Curtiss had to cancel his bid to win the *Daily Mail*'s ten-thousand-pound prize for the first transatlantic flight because of the war. He's gone out to Long Island to spend some time at Willie K.'s estate at Centerport."

"Willie K.?"

"William Vanderbilt. The house is called Eagle's Nest. His majordomo is Niles or Giles. I don't have the number, so work the phones. Anyway, Glenn's there with the pilots and the plane to give Vanderbilt a demonstration in hopes he'll invest in the company. I need him to come pick me up at . . ." Bell racked his brain for a moment. He hadn't sailed into New Haven in years. "Right! Have him pick me up at the Pequonnock Yacht Club. I'll have fuel ready to top the tanks. Tell them we're on a search and rescue and it's a matter of life and death for the crew of a ship carrying vital war supplies to England."

The United States' official position was neutrality, but Bell knew men like Curtiss and Willie Vanderbilt were already pulling for the British and French over the Central Powers.

He continued his list of instructions. "Get someone else to phone the yacht club and explain what's about to happen and that I need fuel cans and a pump waiting on a tender to take me out to the plane once Glenn lands. Archie is going to stay here in

New Haven for a day or two liaising with local officials. Let Lillian know to either come herself or send up a bag. Also, I want you to call the shipping agent for the *Centurion* and find out her typical speed at the beginning of a journey. I'll call you for that info in a couple of hours, but make sure you get an accurate number, otherwise I'll be looking for a needle in the wrong haystack."

"Got it. Where's Mr. Abbott staying?"

Bell shielded the phone's mouthpiece. "Hotel preference?"

"The Taft is next door to the Shubert Theatre. Tell Helen to have Lillian bring some proper clothes and we'll take in a show."

"The Taft Hotel," Bell told his former protégée. "Let Lillian know he's taking her to the Shubert. Also make sure Curtiss brings me some flying togs. That's it for now, so on the jump with you."

Archie stood. "We've got some time. Why don't we head over to the boardinghouse?"

"You go," Bell said. He made a point to show off the dismal condition of his suit. "I need to find a change of clothes. And I'm probably not getting much sleep in the next day or two, so a little shut-eye is in order."

■ ■ ■ ■

The docks at the yacht club were quiet enough for Bell to hear the approaching seaplane before he spotted it. He was in a little outbuilding along the main pier chatting with Roger, the college-age kid who had the job of rowing yachtsmen out to their boats at anchor. Bell had held the same job at his father's club the summer following his freshman year at Yale. It was a rite of passage for the yachting set and a chance for club members to get to know the next generation of sailors and for the youths to make connections with potential employers when school was done.

Curtiss, recipient of the nation's first pilot's license, had come straight across Long Island Sound, an easy flight in a plane designed to leapfrog across the Atlantic from New York to Ireland. The plane wasn't actually Glenn's. He'd designed and built it for Rod Wanamaker, the heir to a department store fortune who'd wanted to claim the *Daily Mail* prize. Bell didn't know if his friend had squared the mission with the owner, but there wasn't time for niceties. Beg for forgiveness rather than ask for permission.

Bell had wanted to take Marion on a motor trip up to Hammondsport, New York, where Glenn and his team had built the plane, but had just been too busy. But he knew the plane was big. The biggest seaplane ever constructed, in fact. He thought back to the little Fowler-Gage flying boat he'd piloted across Panama the year prior and knew it was like comparing a chickadee to an albatross.

The plane, nicknamed *America,* had a seventy-four-foot upper wing and a forty-six-foot lower wing to give her enough lift to carry all the fuel necessary to cross the Atlantic. She was just shy of forty feet long and took her power from a pair of ninety-horsepower OX-5 V-8 motors attached to tractor-style propellers. Two pilots sat side by side in an enclosed cockpit. Behind them were internal compartments to rest during the flight. She was painted a uniform gray.

Bell and the young rower stepped out into the hot sunshine and stood with their eyes shaded as the plane came roaring overhead, trailing faint lines of exhaust. Bell felt the power of those engines in the pit of his stomach and grinned. He loved all things technical and mechanical and was grateful to live in a time of such tremendous innovation. Just this morning he rode on a newly invented mode of transportation and now he was about to fly the world's biggest seaplane. Sure, people shot at him on occasion or tried to burn him to death in a fire. Every job has its downsides. But the opportunities afforded to him by being Joseph Van Dorn's chief investigator made it all worthwhile.

The pilot banked around and settled the plane lower and lower, its curved underhull seeming to float inches from the calm waters of Winter Harbor. With a kiss, the plane touched down, sending a creaming wake past her sides. She slowed dramatically fast in the highly resistant water. The pilot taxied closer to the pier, but there wasn't enough clearance between the anchored yachts to come in all the way. Fifty yards short of the dock the engines sputtered and died and quiet returned once again.

"That's your cue," Bell said to Roger.

The collegian scampered down into the rowboat ferry, untied the painter, and put his back to it in long even strokes. As he'd told Bell, he crewed for the Elis. By the time they reached the floatplane, the pilot had climbed out of the cockpit and straddled the nose. Roger tossed him the rope and it was quickly tied off to a purpose-built metal loop at the plane's prow.

Then it was Roger's turn to earn his fee. The plane weighed nearly five thousand pounds and was merrily bobbing like a top. He pulled and pulled so that the muscles under his polo shirt bulged and soon the garment was showing sweat stains. He finally gained a couple of inches and once he had the flying boat in motion, her momentum built. It took him ten minutes to weave the lumbering aircraft through the maze of yachts and he was blowing like a humpback whale by the time Bell was able to catch the Curtiss-built aircraft before it hit the rubber tire fenders hanging off the side of the dock. Roger threw him his end of the tow rope, which he cinched to a cleat.

"Hello, Isaac," the man straddling the nose said. He spoke unnaturally loud due to the hour of engine noise he'd just endured. "Hell of a trip."

Surprise and delight raised the pitch in Bell's voice. "Willie K., what the hell are you doing here?"

Vanderbilt was a shade older than Bell, with a mustache as dark as Isaac's was blond and an infectious not-a-care-in-the-world look in his eye.

"My pilot here" — he pointed to a second man standing at the cockpit door —

"wouldn't have the foggiest on how to find the old Peq Club," the handsome heir to the Vanderbilt fortune said breezily. "Isaac Bell, this is John Porte, the unlucky sod who saw his chance at aviation glory undone by the Boche."

Porte took off his peaked cap. He had a broad forehead and a strong chin. "You're my passenger?" he asked.

"Irish?" Bell asked him.

"County Cork. You've been?"

"Passed through Eire a couple of times. Wife's begging me to take her on holiday."

"Take her. Prettiest land in the world," Porte said. "Willie says you're a pilot."

"I am." Bell turned his attention back to Vanderbilt.

Though both were from wealthy families — not that the Bells could come close to the riches the Vanderbilts had accrued since the days of Commodore Cornelius — their friendship stemmed from a mutual fascination with all things that went fast. Willie had once held the nation's land speed record and had gone so far as to build a paved toll road through Long Island so he could race on it. He'd been trying to get Bell to enter one of the Vanderbilt Cup races, but the timing had never worked out.

"I'm sure you know that time is of the essence?"

"Your charming Miss Mills explained the broad strokes," Willie replied after stepping onto the dock. He and Isaac shook hands. " 'Those in peril upon the sea.' "

"Exactly. I need to get aboard the *Centurion,* and if I can't find the radio at least get them to turn back." He called across to the Irishman. "I have some fuel here. How do we transfer it?"

"Don't bother, chum," Vanderbilt said. "The plane has an insane amount of range. I have a man standing by with a pump and fuel at the main dock at Sag Harbor. You two take off now and refuel there."

Bell smiled his gratitude. Hand-pumping gasoline into the seaplane's tanks would have cost precious time. "That's terrific. Are you okay stranded here?"

Willie made a charming self-deprecating gesture. "I'm a member, so I shouldn't have too hard a time rustling up a schooner or yacht to take me back to Centerport. You two get going and be heroes."

Bell had thought the plane had an open cockpit, so he was relieved to find he didn't have to wear goggles, a helmet, and a heavy coat. Willie stripped off a light flying jacket and handed it to him. "Bit drafty, so you'll need it."

"Thanks." Bell shrugged into the coat and stepped across into the cockpit. The plane was so big it barely dipped under his weight. He formally shook the pilot's hand.

Bell shouted to the young Yale rower. "Roger, you ready?"

He'd caught his breath and mopped his face with a towel. "Sure thing, Mr. Bell."

"Willie, give the kid a tip when he gets back."

"Lad looks fit enough to row me across the Sound, so I might hire him instead." He turned a little more serious. "Good luck, you two."

"Thanks," Bell replied, hoping the fates were listening.

Fifteen minutes later, with Roger's help firing the engines by spinning the props, the huge seaplane lifted off the sheltered waters and started climbing sedately. They flew southeast toward the tip of Long Island and the old whaling port of Sag Harbor. Visibility was nearly limitless and once they leveled off at about five thousand feet, Bell was grateful for the warm flying jacket.

Porte had an easy hand on the stick. The minute adjustments needed to keep the plane level were barely noticeable and he kept her nose pegged on one spot on the horizon as if she were a train following a set of rails. Bell knew he was in the hands of an accomplished aviator. It was too loud to hold a conversation, so the two men flew in companionable silence.

It took forty minutes to reach the far side of Long Island Sound. They were just west of where the North and South Forks split around Great Peconic Bay. Bell soon spotted Robins Island and pointed out an adjustment to their course to Porte. He also indicated they should start shedding some altitude. Porte eased back on the throttle to reduce airspeed and banked them slightly until the compass had spun about three degrees. Soon after, they passed over the slender peninsula known as Jessup's Neck, and not long after that, Bell pointed out the town of Sag Harbor.

Where great whaling fleets had once gone out to hunt right and sperm whales, Sag Harbor was now a quiet commercial fishing town. At this time of day, the fishermen were on their way back and the main wharf was wide open. Porte circled the area twice and got an idea of the prevailing winds from a flag in a nearby churchyard. He cut the power further, banking in to line up so that he was running parallel to the pier. He reduced the power even more, and it felt like the props were barely turning.

The big plane soared scant feet above the placid waters, caught in what was called ground effect due to the cushion of air trapped under the wing. The underhull kissed the water, lifted free for a second, and then settled heavily, like a hippo entering a watering hole.

Porte added some throttle to maintain headway and turned them back for the dock. When they neared, they saw a crowd had gathered to watch them taxi in. Few had ever seen a seaplane and no one had ever seen anything as grand as the Curtiss-built aircraft.

Porte chopped the power and let the plane coast to within range of a rope tossed by a mechanic in grease-stained coveralls. He stood next to a small electrical pump and a pyramid of three-gallon gas cans.

Bell caught the rope and pulled the plane in until its nose bumped against the tire fenders.

"Take it you're Mr. Vanderbilt's friend?" the mechanic drawled. He had an unlit cigar stuffed into the corner of his mouth. Bell could only guess how Willie K. knew the man. Doubtlessly connected to his love of fast cars.

"Isaac Bell." He tossed a rope back over

to the man to tie off the plane to a cleat. "At your service."

"Fine-looking machine," the man said without offering his name.

"She was specially built to try to fly across the Atlantic," Porte said as he climbed out of the cockpit to get to the main tank's filling caps.

"That so," came the disinterested response. "Let's get you gassed up and on your way."

"Any chance there's a phone nearby?" Bell asked.

"Dockmaster's office. End of the pier on the other side of that warehouse."

"Thanks." Bell jumped down from the plane while a slender hose was passed up to John Porte.

He found the little shack of an office unlocked but empty. The phone was mounted to the wall and looked like it could have been Alexander Graham Bell's first prototype. Bell pulled the mouthpiece from its cradle and gave the handle a few cranks to alert an operator. Fortunately she wasn't the nosy type to ask why a stranger was using the dockmaster's line. After ten frustrating minutes she got him a wire to the city. He went through a couple more exchanges before the phone in the Van Dorn bull pen at the Knickerbocker Hotel began to ring.

"Van Dorn Agency," came the grizzled greeting from Harry Warren, one of Bell's more seasoned agents.

"Harry, it's Isaac." He had to raise his voice over the waves of static pulsing through the phone system.

"Where are you?"

"Sag Harbor. I asked Helen to get me some information about the ship I'm chasing."

"*Centurion,* right?"

"That's the one. Is Helen there?"

"She's out, but she left a note by the phone. Says 'Tell Mr. Bell.' Aw, how sweet, she still respects you."

"Can it, old man," Isaac growled merrily.

" 'Tell Mr. Bell that the *Centurion* can't go more than twelve knots when her bunkers are full of coal and that her captain likes to go about twenty miles past the end of Long Island before turning north-northeast. She dropped her harbor pilot at ten-fifteen this morning.' "

"Thanks, Harry. Tell Helen good job."

"One more thing, Chief. The ship has five cargo cranes, three forward and two aft of the wheelhouse, a single funnel with a green stripe on top. Hull is black, upperworks white."

"Now tell her great job. I forgot all about getting a description. Wish us luck."

"Luck."

Bell settled the handset back on its cradle to cut the connection.

6

The heat was overwhelming. The men worked stripped to their underwear and still they were covered in layers of slick sweat. Nearly all metal surfaces were painful to touch. In such a confined space, with nearly every square inch of the passageways and workspaces covered in conduits, pipes, and countless valves, it was impossible not to have some part of the body being scalded during a watch. And then there was the smell. It was a rank combination of diesel exhaust, a balky sanitation system, old food, and the collective body odor of forty sailors who hadn't bathed in weeks.

But the men took it all with a sense of a workingman's pride and of getting the job done no matter the hardships. They were a team, a family even, from the lowliest to the most important, and as a team they endured the heat and the smells and the burns and the lack of privacy and all the other privations that came with serving on an Imperial German Navy *Unterseeboot.*

Captain Lothar Reinhart leaned into the periscope's eyepiece as he slowly rotated the device three hundred and sixty degrees. He saw nothing but undulating waves and a sky turning orange as the sun ran for the western horizon. It was odd not to spot any ship leaving or heading to New York, America's largest city.

The crew of the UX had been on station for two days now, and every other time he'd raised the scope to look around, there had been at least one, if not several, plumes of smoke from ships' funnels in their immediate vicinity. On one occasion they'd had to emergency dive to avoid the cleaving prow of a giant express liner heading for Europe.

"Down scope," he called, and straightened.

The UX was still an experimental design and yet already on her second deployment, the first being the rescue of Max Hessmann and his Scots companion. The ship and crew were performing better than expected. The engines hadn't so much as misfired since leaving Germany and the batteries actually stored more electricity and discharged at a slower rate than he'd been told were their specifications.

Reinhart had started his career on a cruiser and had risen to executive officer before learning of the commissioning of the U-2, Germany's first real attack submarine. He'd been a hunter all his life and loved stalking game as much as taking the killing shot. He saw the potential for the same type of exhilaration hunting enemy warships and so had transferred to the *Unterseeboot* as a second officer. In just six years, the naval architects and sailors and officers had constantly pushed the boundaries of what was possible, honing the weapons system and tactics to the point where they believed themselves invulnerable.

The UX was twice the length of the old U-2, had twice the crew and four times the lethality. And with open-water replenishment from either a freighter or what were to be called milch cows, specially designed provisioning submarines, the UX could remain at sea for months at a time.

Lothar could not have been more proud of all their accomplishments. The only blemish, and it was nothing really, was the fact that he hadn't been given the honor of sinking the first rifle-laden freighter out of New York. That had gone to politically connected Captain Egewolf von Berckheim on the U-26. But number two would be theirs.

"No contacts," he announced to the crew in the control room immediately below the conning tower. "Surface the boat and let's top up the batteries while we have time. Maybe get some fresh air while we're at it. One of you has eaten far too many beans."

The men appreciated his easy style of command and laughed.

The radio operator popped his head around his curtained-off cubicle. "Nothing on the detection gear, Captain. But it will likely be some hours still before the freighter is in range."

"Keep sharp anyway, Max."

"Aye, Captain."

Moments later the sub rose through frothing water, emerging like a Leviathan from the depths. Water sluiced off her conning tower and decks, and ran and dripped from the 105-millimeter cannon mounted on her forward deck. A seaman popped the topside hatch and took a cooling bath in the water that always pooled along its rim. He backed down and let his captain climb up onto the bridge in dry and dignified fashion. The diesels were already running and feeding electricity from the dynamo to the batteries. The circulator fan had also been switched on to clear the sub of its malodorous haze.

Lothar Reinhart glassed the surrounding

sea with a pair of binoculars and saw they were still alone. In the distance, he could see Long Island as just a hazy wisp. It was too far away to even see the hundred-and-ten-foot-tall Montauk lighthouse.

He felt it in his blood. It was like those mornings in the Prussian forests when he crossed the fresh trail of a wild boar. His pulse quickened even if he knew tracking the animal might take hours. He felt the same now. His quarry was out there, unaware that its fate was already sealed. He brought an imaginary rifle to his shoulder, peered over phantom sights toward the west, and pulled the trigger.

"Bang."

7

John Porte was a trained navigator, so Bell unpinned a chart of Long Island from the wall in the dockmaster's office, found a pencil and calipers in a desk drawer, and rushed back to the seaplane still being fed gasoline through an India rubber hose. The pump was whisper quiet.

"We'll be able to narrow down our search area," Bell told the pilot. He spread the chart on the seaplane's nose. He checked his watch and did a quick calculation. "The *Centurion* left seven hours and forty-five minutes ago. She travels at twelve knots, so that's —"

"Ninety-three nautical miles," the terse mechanic said without a moment's hesitation. The two men looked at him and he just shrugged. " 'Bout the only talent I have."

"Thanks," Bell said with incredulity. He checked the scale of the map and saw it was set for statute miles instead of the longer nautical one. He looked over at the mechanic again. "Any chance you can tell me how many statute miles that is?"

"A hundred and seven plus about a hundred feet." There was no hesitation.

"Thanks again."

Bell held the chart steady while Porte used the calipers to figure out the proper distance from the Port of New York. They were both surprised by the answer. The *Centurion* was steaming just east of East Hampton, which was only five miles from their current location.

"Probably won't need the petrol after all," Porte said. He made a cutting gesture to the mechanic, who switched off the pump.

"I don't know. It's a big ocean out there." Bell rolled up the chart and helped the pilot recover the refueling hose. Porte replaced the filler caps and gave each an extra pat.

Bell handed the chart to the mechanic with a nod of thanks. "What about payment?"

"I put it on Mr. Vanderbilt's tab. He'll never notice."

"I'm sure he won't."

Porte said to the mechanic, "Depending how long we need to search, I may be back through for more fuel."

"I'll stay till an hour past dark."

"Thank you."

"Not to worry, my time's on Mr. Vanderbilt's tab too."

With the Irish pilot in the pilot's seat and Bell positioned to hand-crank the props in order to fire the engines, the mechanic spun the seaplane until her nose pointed out into the bay and gave it a gentle shove. Bell had paid close attention when the Irishman explained the firing procedure to Roger back in New Haven and had both motors purring before they'd drifted far from the dock.

As soon as he had scrambled back into the cockpit and strapped in, Porte said over the engines' roar, "Want to take her?"

Isaac grinned like a little boy. "I was hoping you'd offer."

There were controls in front of him identical to those Porte used. He inched up the power to build some headway and used the foot pedals to adjust the rudder and set a course out into the broad bay. He turned them into the wind when he got them into position and raised the throttles to their stops. The engines at their backs bellowed and the nose started to bob against the waves as she cut through them. Speed built slowly at first, but he could tell the moment the wings started getting lift because the *America* began to accelerate exponentially as she became lighter and lighter in the water.

Bell loved the feeling of power he had at the controls of such an enormous aircraft. The waters here were a little rougher than back in Connecticut, but the ride wasn't too bad. And then all became smooth as the flying boat broke free of one of her natural elements and rose up into her other.

Porte let him keep on the controls until they'd climbed up to a thousand feet and he'd banked them on the proper heading.

Glenn Curtiss had built an incredible machine, thought Bell, and would have doubtlessly succeeded in his transatlantic attempt.

They soon passed over a strip of beach and left Long Island behind. The ocean below was a deep blue and appeared calm at the moment. Only occasionally would waves create jagged white lines on the surface like bolts of lightning that formed and flashed out of existence in seconds.

From this altitude it looked like a steady stream of traffic was converging on New York in nearly every direction, while just as many ships were heading out to carry American-made goods to all four points on the compass. It was easy enough to tell their direction of travel by the widening wakes churning astern of each freighter and passenger ship. The liners, with their snowy white paint and glossy wooden decks, were easy to spot, as they were, by and far, the largest ships in sight.

The binoculars nestled in a leather pouch to Bell's right had Willie Vanderbilt's initials on them, yet another bit of thoughtfulness from the young tycoon. Bell checked the stern of a big four-funneled ocean liner and grunted with satisfaction that he'd guessed right. She was the *Aquitania,* the current Blue Riband holder for the fastest Atlantic transect.

They found a routine and rhythm quickly enough. When they spotted a potential contact, a proper-sized freighter with the right number of loading derricks, Porte maneuvered the flying boat so Bell could check the name on its fantail. The sun was slowly setting, but they had plenty of time remaining. Ten times, they thought they had found the *Centurion* and ten times they'd been wrong and had climbed back to a thousand feet to keep hunting.

They were now flying thirty miles beyond where they'd estimated the ship to be, nearing the tip of Long Island. Once sea traffic was no longer constrained against the land, the vessels would scatter in dozens of headings and be that much harder to spot and identify.

Bell felt the first inklings of failure. And he knew if he failed, innocent men were going to die.

He happened to look far to the south and saw a white smear of a ship's wake many miles from the regular shipping routes. The binoculars allowed him to note that it was an outbound ship rather than one completing her voyage. Ahead, the sea was empty except for a couple of stumpy fishing boats heading out for the Grand Banks.

With no other prospects, Bell tapped the pilot on the shoulder and pointed south. Porte looked for a moment and nodded when he spotted the ship. He banked the big plane and added a little throttle to reach their distant target that much quicker. Bell kept the binoculars pressed to his eyes as they approached, wanting to determine her identity as quickly as possible and return to the regular sea lanes.

She was a freighter all right, he could tell some miles out, and she looked to be about the right length, though without anything to compare her to but the vastness of the ocean, it was difficult to tell. Nearer still he saw she carried five cranes in the proper configuration and smiled when a band of green flashed from her funnel.

Porte dropped to five hundred feet and arced the flying boat around the ship's transom. She had a classic champagne glass fantail and emblazoned in faded white letters was her name, *Centurion*.

"I bet she's this far south because her captain is worried about U-boats too," Bell shouted.

"I'll make like I'm landing a couple of times and hope they launch a boat to meet us."

"Good idea."

Porte buzzed the bridge perched atop the superstructure until several men came out onto the flying bridge to watch the big aircraft. He then swung around and made like he was going to land alongside the freighter. He pulled up and circled the ship once again. No one aboard seemed to get it, so he repeated the act. This time when he neared the open wing off the pilothouse, one of the men waved and said something to the helmsman, still at his post behind the wheel.

With his Marconi wireless out and knowing the importance of his cargo, the captain understood an at-sea rendezvous like this had to be an emergency that could not be ignored.

The volume of smoke belching from her stovepipe funnel suddenly dropped and the water curling off her bow turned into a ripple as she slowed. Seamen appeared on the deck and started removing the cover off one of the lifeboats, while others prepared to swing the wooden craft over the rail on its davits.

John Porte made a quick estimation of where the tramp freighter would come to a stop and landed the seaplane accordingly. He kept the engines turning at idle and made lazy figure eights while they waited for the lifeboat to be unshipped and the men taken to the oars. He spun out of his last turn, goosed the engines to cut the distance, and then dropped them back to idle.

"I don't want to shut them down out here," Porte said, meaning the motors. "If they don't refire, I'm in for a long night and a humiliating tow."

"No problem." Bell thrust out a hand to shake. "Thanks for everything, and I'm sorry your flight got canceled. What will you do now?"

"I'm already booked on this Saturday's sailing on the *Lusitania.* This war is going to be fought on the ground, at sea, and in the air, I suspect, so I need to be home to do my part."

Bell knew not to wish a soldier heading out luck, so he said, "Hope you give 'em hell."

"Righto that."

Bell clambered out of the plane and waited for the lifeboat, standing on the sponson that helped keep the nose from plowing into waves while taking off. His right hand held on to a wing guy wire as the plane was rolling with the gentle waves.

"Hello," he yelled to the approaching men. "Or ahoy, I guess."

"Ahoy," the tillerman called back. "Quite an entrance," he added when he was closer.

Bell used his foot to stop the boat from crashing into the seaplane and nimbly stepped over the gunwale. A lifelong sailor, Bell kept his balance, but knew to take a seat quickly so he didn't upset the craft's center of gravity.

"I'm the first officer," the man at the tiller said. "What's the meaning of this?"

Bell was curious for a moment why they hadn't used the lifeboat's gasoline engine, but then let the thought slip away. "My name is Isaac Bell. I work for the Van Dorn Detective Agency and we've discovered that a tracking beacon was slipped aboard your ship when the cargo was loaded. This beacon will give away your position to a waiting submarine."

"A tracking beacon?"

"Yes, a radio transmitter on a predetermined frequency," Bell explained. "A German spy smuggled one onto the *Mildred E. Burroughs,* the first ship carrying these rifles to England. She was sunk as soon as she reached the quarantine zone around the British Isles."

The officer cursed.

Bell continued. "I believe the U-boat that sank her picked up her trail close to New York and dogged her across the Atlantic."

"We need to tell the captain and turn around."

"That's why I'm here."

Their conversation had to end because the seaplane had pulled far enough from the lifeboat for John Porte to open the throttles and let the twin ninety-horsepower engines have their way. Their roar was tremendous and the acceleration swift. The aircraft was soon straining to get back into the sky and she skipped off the top of one wave, sailed over the trough, and deflected heavenward off the next roller. Porte kept her in the air and gained altitude before banking sharply and buzzing the lifeboat at less than fifty feet.

The men were splattered with seawater still dripping from her hull.

"Sorry about that," Bell said. "Pilots tend to show off."

The rigid first officer said nothing of the incident and instead ordered the four rowers to get them back to the *Centurion* with their best effort.

Fifteen minutes later, Bell was escorted to the freighter's bridge. The ship was likely only a few years old and well maintained. He spotted no rust and the deck wasn't salt-crusted. Passageways were clean, if not Spartan. The ship's captain regarded Bell through a wreath of pipe smoke, but with the vacant expression of a good poker player. He was in his sixties with weathered and wrinkled skin and silver hair with a matching beard. Like the first officer, he was British and had likely earned his rating coming up through the Royal Navy.

"Captain," said the first officer, "this man says there's a German submarine about to chase us across the Atlantic."

"The war's barely a day old. I highly doubt that."

Bell said, "We foiled an attempt to place a radio transmitter on the ship carrying the last load of rifles for the British Army, and the first ship that left, the *Mildred E. Burroughs,* was sunk the minute she entered the exclusionary zone the Germans have around your home islands." He then added, "My name is Isaac Bell and I'm the chief investigator of the Van Dorn Detective Agency. I personally found the radio hidden in a rifle crate and killed one of the operatives involved in the plot. He was German."

As if finding his manners, the captain took a few steps closer with his hand outstretched. "Edward Joyce, master of the *Centurion.*"

"I would have rather just wired the information to you, but we learned from the harbor pilot who took you out that your wireless is busted."

Joyce nodded, as he had already come to that conclusion. "Sparks has been tinkering with it for some time, to no avail. Do you have orders for me from Mooreland Marine Services, the ship's owner?"

"I do not."

"How about my government? Have they said anything on the matter?"

"Again, no. I'm afraid there wasn't the time. I'm really here on my own authority."

Joyce's stony facade cracked. It was clear he hadn't liked what he'd heard. "That doesn't stand much with me, Mr. Bell."

"I understand, Captain," Bell said sincerely. "I would feel the same if our roles were reversed. But I have a proposal nevertheless."

The captain said nothing.

"England is now in a state of war. A lot of people believe it will be over by Christmas. Me, I don't know, but I do know that whoever mobilizes the bulk of their forces first stands a better chance of winning than not. France and England need to get men into the field as fast as possible."

"Not a debatable point, Mr. Bell."

"If you turn back, you're going to delay the shipment the time it takes to return to New York and get to this spot again, as well as the days it'll take to unload all the crates to find the hidden radio."

"I figured that."

"That's best case, Captain Joyce. What I believe is going to happen is the third shipment of rifles still sitting in New Haven is going to be impounded pending an investigation by the War Department's intelligence branch, and if you tie up again to an American dock, your cargo will likely be impounded too. My country demands her neutrality is respected, and on the first day of the war we already had spies and sabotage and most likely the murder of a boarding-house owner."

Joyce refilled his pipe, tamping the big bowl with a tobacco-stained knuckle. He took his time, and it was obviously his way of deliberating a difficult question. "What do you propose?"

"We keep going, and as we cross the Atlantic we go through all those crates one by one until we find the radio. Middle of the night we toss it overboard, change direction somewhat, and leave the submarine skipper out in the middle of nowhere scratching his head about how his plan went awry."

"What if we reach the quarantine zone the German's established around England and Ireland and we haven't found the radio?"

"We toss all the crates we haven't yet checked, change course like I mentioned, and be satisfied that we managed to deliver most of your cargo."

Joyce turned to his first officer. "What do you think, Dan?"

The younger man shot Isaac a glance and said, "He risked his life to get this information to us and appears willing to risk it again helping us. I believe him about the rifles being impounded if we turn back, and Lord knows our boys are going to need them. I say we follow his plan."

"Agreed. Mr. Bell, it looks like you're going to be our guest all the way to Bristol."

"My pleasure, Captain Joyce."

What Bell had neglected to mention was that the attack on the first ship, the *Mildred E. Burroughs,* hadn't followed the protocol of allowing the crew to take to the boats before their ship was sunk. The sub had ambushed them, and if Joyce and the men aboard the *Centurion,* himself included, couldn't avoid the sub chasing in their wake, they'd all suffer the same fate.

8

Lothar Reinhart was asleep in his tiny cabin when he was awakened by a watch stander. "Pardon, Captain, radioman Schmidt says he's picking up a faint signal."

Like any officer aboard a naval vessel, Reinhart could go from blissful slumber to alert wakefulness in the blink of an eye. He swung his legs off his coffin-sized bed and stood. He wasn't a large man, no submariner could be, but even in oft-slept-in pants and a dingy sleeveless singlet, he had an aura of command. The crew agreed it was his eyes. They were a blue so pale they almost looked silver.

He shrugged into a shirt and slipped his foot into custom nonslip shoes that had been a gift from his parents when he'd gotten his first command.

He slept with a red battle lamp aglow in a wire cage near the curtain door so he could check the chromometer. It was just shy of midnight. "Tell the cook I want coffee and toasted bread with lard."

"Yes, Captain." The man turned sharply and hurried to the galley.

Reinhart poured a little water into his private washbasin and used a cloth to clean the sweat from his face and the back of his neck. He thought back to winter patrols in the North Sea when the cold deck would radiate through the thickest boots and freeze one's feet. Now in the sun-warmed waters of the Gulf Stream, his boat was as hot as a Swedish sauna.

He exited his cabin and closed the curtain behind him. He was only a few steps from the control room, and just beyond was the radio shack, also partitioned by a heavy curtain to help dampen sound. There wasn't enough room for him to enter the tiny space, so he drew back the cloth and peered in over Willie Schmidt's shoulder. His radio operator had headphones clamped over his ears and he was turning one of the dials on his wireless transceiver. He was just into his twenties, with a youth's enthusiasm for new technology and ears as sharp as a fox's.

He felt his captain's presence above him and pulled the headset from one ear.

"What have you got for us?" Reinhart asked softly, like the two were conspiring.

"No more than a faint hum, Captain, but it's on the right frequency. Direction is a little more southerly than I expected, however."

"Does the little boar we are hunting think he's going to be prey and is trying to get around us?"

"Sir?"

"Just a thought, Willie. Why else would he be south of us? It wastes time and coal."

"Unknown, Captain. With the war officially declared, it could be all shipping are taking precautions."

Reinhart smiled at that thought. "If that's the case and the Atlantic trade is running scared, then our U-boat forces have already won a great propaganda victory."

"Maybe that's why we were able to charge our batteries earlier today."

"Perhaps." The captain allowed the thought to linger a moment longer and then snapped his attention back to his duty. "Do you have a bearing on the target?"

"Not yet, sir. I just picked up the signal. I'll need some time to triangulate."

"And you need us to move a few kilometers east to give you two data points."

"Five should do it, sir."

"And five you shall have." Lothar Reinhart had the first scent of his prey, and his hunter's heart soared.

Back in the control room, he issued his orders in crisp Teutonic fashion. "Dive control, bring us up to periscope depth. Engines ahead half when I give the signal and we are safely off the bottom."

The waters around Long Island tended to be shallow where the UX had lurked, so rather than drain batteries and risk plowing into the bottom while blundering about, the boat had settled into the sandy seafloor during much of her stay off the American coast. Men got to work spinning some valves open and others closed in a virtuoso performance honed over many hours of practice. High-pressure air was forced into the big ballast tanks, replacing the seawater, whose weight kept them pinned to the sand. In just a few moments they lifted off the seafloor and the boat quivered ever so gently with the current.

"Engine control, make for half ahead," Reinhart said. "Conn bearing nine zero degrees."

"Half ahead, aye," said one sailor.

"Bearing nine zero degrees," said another as he spun the ship's wheel to turn the big submarine around.

The sub came about sharply as the electric motors powered the churning propeller at the rear of the craft. Ballast control had kept them perfectly level as they ascended off the bottom. Reinhart watched his crew with satisfaction. They worked as if they were part of the submarine themselves, as integral as each valve and knob and switch.

He could also sense their anticipation. They had chosen a life under the waves, a life of danger and sacrifice. The reward for that? The reward was this hunt. To stalk unsuspecting prey from an unseen lair and move in for the kill when the time was right. The chance to bring the war to Germany's enemies.

A cloud passed behind Reinhart's eyes just then and his ever-observant executive officer caught it.

"You suddenly look troubled, Captain." He spoke in a low voice that barely rose above the background din of a submarine in motion.

"When Wolf Berckheim" — he refused to use the nobleman's full title — "went after the *Mildred Burroughs,* war had not yet been declared."

"Yes."

"He was able to follow her across the Atlantic as easily as if she were being towed, and then maneuvered around once they were in the quarantine zone and put a torpedo in her belly."

"He had no idea the U-26 was hunting him." The junior officer saw where his commander was heading. "But maybe now our target is suspicious because we are at war, and he will take precautions. He won't so easily lead the wolf to slaughter?"

"Ach, I don't know. I do know that wireless technology is still in its infancy and radio direction finding is newer still. If we lose the freighter's signal halfway to Europe we'll never find her again. I for one don't want to return to Germany and report a failure."

"What are you suggesting, Captain?"

"That the quarantine zone is nothing more than arbitrary lines drawn around the British Isles by politicians who know nothing of the tasks they've set for us."

Reinhart glanced at the ship's master chronometer affixed to a nearby bulkhead. He calculated time and speed to get distance. He held up a finger to his exec to suspend their conversation temporarily and let a minute tick by. "Engine control, all stop."

"All stop, aye."

Big levers were ratcheted in order to disengage the motor from the main shaft, while other sailors drew down the power being fed to the electric drive. The hiss of the hull slicing through the warm waters slowly abated as her momentum bled away. Reinhart knew his ship and how she functioned and was certain within ten meters that they had reached the five-kilometer limit that radioman Schmidt needed to get a proper fix on their target.

Reinhart addressed his number one. "What I'm saying is that I have no intention of dogging that ship all the way to England. I want us to attack when we're far enough out that there are no witnesses and sink her in unrestricted waters."

The XO should have been shocked and angered by his captain ignoring the precepts of war, but instead he licked his lips in anticipation. "I wager two days out and there won't be another ship on the horizon."

"I bet just one." Lothar grinned wolfishly.

9

Isaac Bell vastly underestimated the job he'd asked of the *Centurion*'s crew. Just removing one of the large square hatch covers at sea was so dangerous that it would never be considered during a routine cruise. A storm could rise up at a moment's notice that would send waves crashing over the rails and flood a hold far faster than it could be pumped dry. They would sink under the waves with the ship's belly full of water.

The sky was cloudless, yet Captain Joyce had spent several long moments looking at the sky all around the ship, moving from the port bridge wing to the starboard, looking aft and fore. He was listening to his instincts, weighing risk versus reward. Pulling off a hatch cover at sea went against everything he'd learned and heard during his twenty years in command.

And then he thought of those men getting ready to fight the Germans. He'd been a junior officer on a ship returning soldiers to England from the Boer War. Many wore their wounds on the inside. It was in the vacancy of their eyes. He couldn't deny the troops today every advantage on the battlefield.

He cupped his hands around his mouth and shouted down to the crewman on deck near the center hatch. "All right, let's be quick about this. And that the hatch goes back fifteen minutes before sundown or the minute the wind shifts."

Wires had already been secured to the four corners of the thirty-by-thirty-foot cover, and the clamps that held it to the coaming had been loosened. The tall, stick-like derrick was operated through a gearbox linked to a power takeoff from the main engine and had little difficulty lifting the multiton metal cover. It rose up from the deck with a metallic scrape and was then swung around so it could be lowered onto the forward hatch cover. It was not loosened from the crane in case the sailors needed to fit it back in place quickly.

The ship's hold was open to the elements. Isaac Bell edged closer and peered down at what looked to be an infinite number of wooden crates enmeshed in tough cargo nets. He did the math. Six thousand rifles in five-rifle crates meant one thousand two hundred boxes to be hoisted out of the hold and opened for inspection. Captain Joyce spared just six men to help. If every crate in each individual net could be inspected in four minutes and returned to the hold, Bell estimated it would take two hundred hours of labor. Daylight this time of year was about fifteen hours, so thirteen days. The *Centurion* would be well inside the zone in which the Germans announced enemy ships would be torpedoed.

He wouldn't let himself think about that.

A second crane was activated and its hook swung over so a crewman could guide it and then attach it to the top of the first cargo net. The bundle of crates was pulled from the hold and lowered onto the deck. Two other crewmen wrestled the stiff net so it was flat on the deck and started pulling crates from the nearly five-foot-tall stack. Soon pry bars began working off the wooden lids to determine if they'd found the radio.

Bell kept an eye on his watch as they worked their way through the first pallet of boxes. The netted bundle of crates below the first group was already out of the hold and dangling from the end of the hoist's steel hook, ready to be searched. The already examined crates then went back into storage and the men started in on the next group. The whole process from start to finish took an hour and a half. A few minutes less than Bell's estimate, but not enough to search the entire cargo by the time they sailed into the quarantine zone.

"That's it, Mr. Bell," Captain Joyce shouted from the flying bridge. "Leave that pallet netted on deck and get the hatch back on." With the sun so far down in the west, Joyce was merely a shadowy silhouette.

Twenty-five crates down, Bell thought miserably, one thousand one hundred and seventy-five to go.

And then he considered the recipient British soldiers, who would have rifles and time to train with them when they faced the German Army on some plowed field in northern France. Those men had a fighting chance now, and by tomorrow he'd make sure hundreds more would get the weapons they so desperately needed.

Captain Joyce put Bell in a cabin usually used by paying customers, but with the war approaching, their only fare canceled weeks earlier. Joyce dined alone in his cabin, but Bell was allowed to eat with the officers. Conversation was about the war to the exclusion of all other topics. He begged off as soon as possible and returned to his cabin. It had been an eventful day to say the least and he was tired to the marrow of his bones. The cot was thin, lumpy, and smelled musty, but he was asleep the second his head hit the pillow.

Unterseeboot Captain Lothar Reinhart cursed his luck as soon as he raised the periscope at first light. His target was right where radioman Schmidt had said it would be, and it would have been simple enough to race ahead of the plodding freighter to get into firing position and slam a torpedo into her belly. The problem was, there was a large ship astern of them and it was steaming in the same direction as his prey. It had to be going a little faster than the freighter because it hadn't been on the horizon at dusk. It would take some time and careful measurements to figure out the relative difference in their speeds, but Reinhart knew it would be some time before the ship passed by and vanished over the horizon to the east.

He'd studied enough ships at sea to know the overtaking could be as much as a full day.

He climbed down from the conning tower. His men all looked on with the hunger of predators on the hunt.

"There's another ship aft of us that looks like she's running faster than our little wild boar." The eager smiles facing him faded. "Don't know how long she'll take to steam over the horizon, but we're not taking her this morning."

"Do you want to just keep following them?" his XO asked.

"Let's get a little distance so we can get some air. The radio detector is working flawlessly, and I want full batteries when we submerge and stalk her again when we're alone."

"Very good, Captain," said his second-in-command. "Helm, steer one eight zero degrees. Make your speed eleven knots. Maintain current depth, but prepare to surface the boat."

Bell woke at first light and made his way to the mess for tea — this was a British ship after all and there was no coffee to be had — and a breakfast of eggs, sausages the English called bangers, and toast. He'd found a folded boilersuit outside his cabin, so he'd donned it this morning and thought he looked like one of the engineering crew.

A youngish man in a uniform that looked too big for his frame approached Bell's table as he was finishing up. "Mr. Bell, yes?"

"I am."

"I'm Freddie Wiles. They call me Sparks on account of me being in charge of the radio and all." He had a thick Cockney accent and shied away from eye contact when he spoke.

"I hear you have your hands full trying to fix it."

" 'Tis true." The boyish-faced sailor blushed in embarrassment, but then brightened as he showed off an electrical apparatus of some kind. It looked like something he'd cobbled together with spares from his radio gear. It had exposed wiring and a single lightbulb sticking out of a repurposed balsa-wood cigar box.

Bell looked closer at Sparks and noticed the downy stubble on Wiles's cheeks and the red shot through his eyes. He'd been up all night. "What is that?"

Rather than explain, he flipped a switch and the bulb lit up with a feeble amber glow. "It lights up when it detects radio waves. If I got it right, it gets brighter the closer to the source, on account of the waves being stronger. Only just now did I tune into the proper frequency."

Bell instantly understood what this meant. "How sensitive?"

"I 'ope sensitive enough," the lad said with a grin.

"Let's go see."

Bell greeted his work team by name when he reached the hatch. It had been loosened and was ready to be lifted clear. He and Freddie Wiles stood well back as the heavy metal cover was hoisted into the air and set down again. They examined the bulb to see if it had brightened, but it remained as dim as it had been in the mess. Wiles looked a little unsure of himself.

The men watched Bell expectantly, wondering about the meaning of their radioman's presence and the device in his hands.

Bell said, "Freddie thought he could pinpoint the radio with that thing, but it doesn't appear to work."

"It should, though, Mr. Bell. I've seen it done many times. It can't decode radio waves, but it can detect them. The light's on. It's getting something. Um, I don't understand why it's not getting brighter as we get closer."

"It was a good try," Bell told the dejected young officer. "I think we have to keep going the old-fashioned way." Bell made a whirling motion with his hand, and the men got to work securing the next pallet of crates to be manually inspected.

The air still held the morning chill to it, but the sky was cloudless, and soon the sun would beat on the metal deck like a hammer in an iron forge with Bell and his companions caught in the middle. A little over an hour later they had finished with the first pallet of crates. Bell noted they had shaved nearly twenty minutes off their time. He also knew that as the day wore on and fatigue seeped into their bones, their efficiency and speed would plummet.

He went to the rail to watch the sea for a moment while the next set of crates was pulled from the hold. That's when he saw a big express liner chasing down their wake. She had two tall masts fore and aft of her three funnels, and Bell had a sudden suspicion why Sparks's cobbled-together radio detector hadn't appeared to work.

"Captain Reinhart." A sailor called his name from outside his tiny cabin while he was working on the ship's log.

"Yes, what is it?"

"Schmidt says the target has slowed and appears to have altered course to the north."

The UX was back underwater and had taken up a position ahead of the freighter. Their boat was far faster both surfaced and submerged than the plodding cargo ship.

They had already determined that the second vessel spotted that morning was now well ahead of them on its voyage to Europe or wherever its final destination. They had the seas all to themselves to play out the final act of the hunt. They'd marked the spoor, tracked their quarry, and now had moved into a position in order to take the shot.

The last time they'd gone up to periscope depth so that he could satisfy himself that no other ships had encroached on his hunting grounds, he'd noted the sun was well down on the western horizon, but there was still plenty of daylight to sink the British-flagged merchantman.

"I'd expect she'd speed up as she burned through her coal reserves," Reinhart said, emerging from his nook with his cap at a rakish angle over one eye. "Though it's a bit early in her voyage for even that."

"XO thinks she might have a mechanical problem."

"Reasonable man, our executive officer," the captain remarked with a fond smile as he entered the helm. His second-in-command heard the comment.

"And our captain is never wrong," he shot back.

Reinhart turned serious. "What's the status?"

"She's moving to cross our bows in about fifteen minutes at a range Schmidt thinks will be less than three hundred meters."

"But she slowed?"

"Down to eleven knots, but holding steady. We can't tell yet how much she's turned to the north until more time has passed and Schmidt can calculate signal strength versus distance."

"Okay, I want to close the distance ourselves rather than lie in wait," Reinhart said. "Helm, ahead half. Make your heading two seven zero degrees. Maintain depth. Flood torpedo tubes one and two. Do not open outer doors."

The men took to their tasks, calling out each as they were completed in a staccato, no-nonsense cadence. Reinhart ducked his upper body into the radio shack and tapped Schmidt on the shoulder to get his attention. Like before, he only removed the headset from one ear. "Sir?"

"We're moving closer in case our quarry has grown wary."

"You understand the signal will get stronger the closer we get, but it will become more difficult to determine their exact heading."

"Doesn't matter. You've put us close enough that even a blind man will be able to sink her."

When the ship's chronometer showed she'd been underway using her near-silent electric motors for a minute and thirty seconds, Reinhart called for the ship's bow to be swung northward in the direction the freighter would pass, and ordered the U-boat to periscope depth. "Open the outer doors and be ready for my final bearings. We've got them now."

He snapped down the handles and ducked to the eyepiece even before the top of the optics tube pierced the waves.

He spun in a short arc left and right and then searched further until finally rotating the periscope through a full three hundred and sixty degrees. He reared back as if slapped. "Schmidt, where is the *verdammt* freighter?"

"Captain, she's dead ahead of us. Signal is clear. She can't be more than two hundred meters."

Reinhart looked again, frustration and anxiety building. He saw the sea had grown a little rougher and that the sun would vanish soon, but he saw no ship. "XO, we're close enough to hear her. Quiet the boat."

The ventilation system that kept the air

from growing too stagnant whooshed down to silence as the fan blades stopped and word was passed from compartment to compartment to freeze in place and refrain from talking. There wasn't even the whisper hiss of the hull cutting through water. Into that silence they all heard the buzzing sound at the same time. It was faint, like a distant mosquito, but there was no mistaking the sound. Something was out there, just not a seven-thousand-ton merchantman.

Reinhart had a weight in the pit of his stomach so heavy that it felt like it could sink them all. "Surface the boat."

Horns sounded and the men jumped to their tasks. Reinhart himself climbed the conning tower as soon as the hull broached the surface. He was there to undog the hatch and take a dousing of the briny Atlantic Ocean. He scrambled out of the boat and stood at the upper helm. He didn't need to use the binoculars slung around his neck. The situation was clear enough.

One of the English freighter's lifeboats was chugging merrily along with its gasoline engine making a keening sound not unlike an insect's buzz. Its helm had been tied off with rope, and it was managing to keep on a relatively true course. Sitting atop one of the bench seats was a rifle case, obviously the one containing the homing beacon. A hand-painted sign had been attached to it. Lothar Reinhart needed the binoculars to read it.

British Royal Navy 1
Imperial German Navy 0

He searched the horizon, but the ship was long gone. Who knew how long they'd been tracking the decoy. Hours for sure. Half a day just as likely. His executive officer joined him in the tight space atop the conning tower. He passed Reinhart a lit cigarette and fired up another for himself. The captain handed over the binoculars so his second-in-command could read the sign before the lifeboat puttered out of view.

"The British not only knew their ship had been compromised, but they found the transmitter less than two days from port," Reinhart said tonelessly, as the shock was still with him. "I have no idea how."

"If they knew all along, why didn't they leave it back in New York? To taunt us?"

"I don't know. That entire ship could have been a decoy and the real weapons are aboard some other vessel. The spies back in America could have been caught even before the first case was loaded and poor

Egewolf Berckheim, storied captain of the U-26, is also chasing a wild goose to England."

"I believe we have severely underestimated the British," the XO said, exhaling smoke.

"Heaven help us if we have. We might just be in for a long and bloody war."

As soon as Bell had spotted the liner behind their ship he'd called after Freddie Wiles and pointed at it. "Could the Marconi signals from that ship affect your detector?"

"By God, it could. There must be so much interference from her that my little gadget is overwhelmed. I bet if we wait until that ship's out of range we'll find the homing beacon in no time."

An hour later Freddie tried his detector near the hold once more. This time the light snapped on instantly, far brighter than it had been when the liner was in their wake. He moved closer to the open hatch and the bulb brightened even more, though it could not outshine Freddie Wiles's triumphant grin.

"Well, look at that," one of the crewmen said.

"I think the crates are too close together for me to detect which one has the transmitter," Freddie said.

Bell pointed forward. "Stand up there and we'll swing each pallet of cases your way with the derrick. Would that do it?"

"I think so."

Freddie moved until he was as far from the hold as possible, but still within reach of the crane's boom. They swung the netted stack of twenty-five rifle cases over to where he stood.

Freddie watched his device intently, but quickly shook his head. "Not in these."

The crates were set aside so they could haul out the cache that had been below them. Once again Freddie studied his detector and frowned. Bell privately had reservations. Without the need to open all the crates, they would be able to check all the cargo in a fraction of the time, but if the device wasn't sensitive enough, then all this effort was for naught and they'd be forced to pull the cargo once again to check it all visibly.

After four more bundles of rifle cases were hauled up from the hold and Freddie's detector failed to react, Bell's reservations became outright skepticism and he was about to call a halt to the whole operation when another clutch of twenty-five cases emerged from the dark hold and Freddie shouted, "Bloody hell, will you look at that."

Bell and the rest of his men couldn't see the light, so Freddie turned the device around in his hands. The little bulb burned like the midday sun. So bright in fact that it suddenly popped in a puff of smoke and the tinkle of broken glass.

"The radio is in one of those crates," Freddie said with extreme confidence. "I tell you, we're going to have those Germans beat in no time."

They needed to open only four of the crates before finding the one containing the powerful radio transmitter, the antenna, the pair of deep-cycle batteries, and the alarm clock that had activated the device as the ship sailed along Long Island's southern coast. It was exactly like the one Bell and Archie Abbott had found in New Haven.

"Go tell the captain we found it," Bell said to one of the crewmen assigned to him. He turned his attention to Freddie. "Well done, Mr. Wiles. Well done, indeed. I confess to having had some doubts."

"Not me, Mr. Bell," he said assuredly. "The principles behind the detector are solid and well understood."

"I'll take your word for it."

"Is that it, then?" Captain Joyce said with a sniff as he approached.

"It is, Captain," Freddie replied.

"Any chance we can scavenge it to fix our set?"

"Not a good idea," Bell said quickly. "If that transmitter suddenly stops sending the carrier wave, the U-boat captain tracking us will get suspicious and possibly fire his torpedoes even if we are outside of their prescribed war zone."

"I wouldn't put it past them," Joyce said after giving it a moment's thought. "Suggestions?"

Bell pointed to the wooden lifeboat hanging from its davit along the side of the superstructure. "Red herring."

Twenty minutes later, Bell and the English sea captain stood at the rail and watched their decoy as the *Centurion* altered course a couple of degrees in a more southern tangent and the lifeboat kept more or less true to their original path.

Joyce suddenly offered Bell his hand to shake. "On behalf of myself and the rest of the crew, thank you very much for what you've done. Not many people would risk their life the way you did."

"My wife wishes I weren't such a person, but I've always been the type to help out when there's a need. Why I became an investigator in the first place, I suppose. People come to detectives to solve the problems they can't."

"I can see that," Joyce said. "Looks like you get to relax for the rest of the voyage. Sorry we aren't as luxurious as, say, the *Lusitania,* but we'll get you there, and I will make certain you have a suite on whichever ship takes you back home again."

"Some quiet time sounds like exactly what I need," Bell said. "This was the second time I've discovered German spies operating in the United States. I have no wish to find any others."

"This is our fight now, Mr. Bell. The Germans exploited an opportunity as hostilities commenced, one they shan't get again. They know better than to provoke your country from its stance of neutrality."

10

The Long Island farmhouse was typical of the area. Weathered white clapboard that needed paint, a slate roof showing patches of moss, and windows that let in drafts in the winter. There was a barn a short distance away, a corral for draft horses, and rolling fields of corn that were a little stunted for this time of the year, as it had been a hot, dry summer. The owner lived on the property, though he now leased out his land to others to do the actual farming. He was in his late seventies and none of his six children had wanted the country life, so this was the end of the farm.

Foss Gly had met the old man when he and Max Hessmann first arrived in the United States and was told not to visit again unless there was an emergency. This most certainly counted. He had driven out in a Model T, taking the better part of a day to make certain he hadn't been followed. Not that anyone in America knew who he was or why he was here. It was tradecraft as Max had taught him.

Even thinking about his name made Gly's usually stony heart hurt. They'd actually known each other for such a short time, but under such hellish conditions that time's consistency had grown elastic, and it was like they'd known each other all their lives.

This was good, he thought. Hurt can fuel anger and anger will bring revenge.

Gly stopped the car on the dusty driveway that looped from the rural road. He wore brown trousers and an over-laundered workman's shirt. His hat was also brown, with white stains from the salt of old dried sweat.

He remained painfully gaunt, though he could now carry himself to his full, considerable height. His eyes still kept the heavy melancholy of someone who'd seen the worst the world had to offer and accepted it as normal.

The old man came to the door as soon as Gly swung open the screen door and rapped his knuckles on the jamb. He was far shorter than Gly, but most men were. He had let himself grow thick through the middle, but he still had the ropy arms of a man accustomed to hard work and hair that remained thick despite his years.

"Where is Max?" he asked. His accent was thick and German.

"Dead."

The farmer rocked back as if Gly had punched him in the jaw. He recovered, looked out on the deserted road as if expecting a raid, and whisked Gly inside. He closed and locked the door.

The farmhouse was tidy enough and there were still touches of femininity left from his late wife, throw pillows on the sofa and a yellowed lace doily under a decorative ceramic pitcher, plus framed examples of her cross-stitching on the walls.

The old German's name was Werner Dietrich and he acted as a resource for the burgeoning German spy network that had been operating in and around New York over the past few years. He was well established in the United States, above any sort of reproach, so he could lend cover to newly arrived spies as nephews from the old country, and his barn was a safe, out-of-the-way space to work. It was here that Gly and Max had built and tested the remote homing beacons and then disassembled them so John Kramer could swap out rifles for the radio at the Winchester Arms factory. The clocks had been special made in Germany and mailed to the farm.

Werner Dietrich indicated Gly should sit at the scarred wood table next to the kitchen while he went to get two cool beers from the root cellar. He opened the bottles with gassy pops and handed one over as he sat. "What happened?"

"I don't know details, but the boarding-house where he and John Kramer lived was burned to the ground with the owner's daughter inside. A man matching Max's description was hit by a truck a short time after the fire started and was killed. I've since learned that John Kramer was shot inside the factory. I have to assume the radio going out on yesterday's shipment was discovered and the operation blown. We may only hope that the first two were smuggled without being detected."

Dietrich looked troubled, shaken even.

"This cannot be," he finally said after drinking from his beer. "Max Hessmann is Germany's greatest spy. He can't be killed by some random truck in a backwater city like New Haven, Connecticut. There has to be some mistake."

"There's one other thing I didn't tell you. A group called the Van Dorn Detective Agency was providing security for the weapons transfer. I was able to observe one of their agents spending time with the New Haven police late yesterday at both the burned-out boardinghouse and on the street where Max was killed."

"What if it wasn't him?" Dietrich asked. "What if that was another man?"

"Max would have met me at any one of the three locations we had mapped out in advance if we ever encountered a problem. That's what I was doing all last night and this morning. Checking each place multiple times in hopes that Max showed himself."

"Maybe he was injured and is in a hospital?" Dietrich offered hopefully.

"There are only a couple and I checked them. I'm sorry, I know Max meant a great deal to you." Gly couldn't believe he had to cheer up the old man when he himself was so shredded on the inside. "You have to accept he is dead. And if I'm not mistaken I can guess who was chasing him. It wasn't random, in a sense. He was being hunted by a man named Isaac Bell, the chief investigator for the Van Dorns."

"How can you guess such a thing?"

"Bell is the reason I was sent to Devil's Island in the first place," Gly spat with ill-disguised anger. "I had a run-in with him three years ago in England when I worked security for a French mining company. He bested me every step of the way. He can outfight, and more importantly, outthink anyone I've ever known. I'm sure he's the one who discovered the beacon and deduced it was planted by John Kramer. Bell would have gone to John's residence and interviewed the owner or her daughter. I'm also fairly sure that Max burned it down believing he had Bell trapped inside, only to have the American turn the tables on him."

"What can we do?"

"I've given it some thought, and I believe we should proceed with the next phase of Max's operation. I will likely rely on you more than expected because I will be working alone."

"Ja, natürlich."

"Germany can't afford to waste her precious few U-boats sinking ships carrying worthless cargo while letting war matériel slip past the pickets."

"How will you manage that? What was Max's idea?"

"I am sorry, Werner," Gly said. "The less you know, the safer it is for both of us. I will say that Max's plan is absolutely inspired. And it just so happens that I was going to take the lead since it calls for someone who sounds Irish, which Max could not no matter how he tried."

"You can?"

"Like a native," Gly said, replacing his rolling Scots brogue with an Irish lilt.

"And what about this Bell person?"

"I may not have Max's brilliance at designing an operation, but I have no doubt I will think of a clever way of disposing of Isaac Bell once and for all."

11

Brooklyn, New York
April 1915

The sprawling naval yard across the East River from lower Manhattan was like a city unto itself. It covered hundreds of acres, had its own power plants, railroad, and grid of streets, and a workforce that numbered in the thousands. The enclosed dry docks were the size of warehouses, and dozens of smokestacks rising into the overcast sky pumped out continuous sooty plumes. On Building Way No. 1, the yard's principal construction slip, the massive hull of America's latest super dreadnaught was being completed. Surrounded by tower cranes capable of rolling along specially reinforced tracks and a tangle of scaffolding, it was planned that the USS *Arizona* would slip down the ways and enter the river in just two months' time.

The air was filled with the sounds of riveters pounding away, steam whistles, the shouts of men, and the clanks of machines. America was serious about her neutrality, but that didn't mean she wasn't going to keep pace with the arms buildup that led to the latest European war, especially when it came to battleships like the *Arizona* and her sister, the *Pennsylvania.* The Brooklyn Navy Yard had been the epicenter of American naval development and construction for over a century and showed no sign of ever slowing down. It seemed to confirm that the twentieth century was going to be America's century.

There were, however, quiet corners of the yard. The original Lyceum building, where old salts and learned scholars once taught junior sailors about the ways of the sea and ships, was currently home to analysts digesting the latest naval news coming from the war with an eye to incorporating hard lessons learned on the front lines in the next generation of capital ships. The job went to young, studious ensigns. Many considered being tucked away in a musty brick archive building, poring over foreign communiques, as some form of punishment and longed to be assigned sea duty.

Joe Marchetti, at just twenty-one, was the youngest of the newly graduated Annapolis cadets to be assigned to the job, but it was one at which he excelled. He saw in each piece of information an opportunity to help his country, and the Navy he loved, to achieve more. He agreed with his superiors that it benefited the United States to let the others fight the battles while the Navy gained knowledge.

He had the trademark olive skin and dark hair of a child of Naples-born immigrants and possessed delicate, almost feminine features, especially his large doe-like eyes. And while he had passed height and weight requirements to enter Annapolis, he was the slimmest and shortest of his class. He struggled with sports and some of the physical requirements as a cadet, but he graduated as valedictorian and no one questioned the ferocity of his competitive spirit.

His instructors all saw that he would go far in the rapidly modernizing U.S. Navy. Understanding new sciences like radio cryptography and the ballistics for artillery shells lobbed over ten miles was what gave the new Navy its edge. It was brains they needed now, rather than brawn.

It was after five o'clock on a Friday night and Marchetti was still in the large room filled with desks that he shared with the other analysts. His office mates had all left for the weekend, boasting of plans to meet up with a group of nice-looking seamstresses who worked at the Navy Yard sewing flags and pennants. It wasn't uncommon for Marchetti to work late or spurn the traditional pursuits of a young officer. He was happiest working, figuring out mysteries or discovering some detail others had missed, and on this night he was hot on the trail of something potentially earth-shattering.

He'd been working on this particular report for the best part of a week. It was actually outside his purview, but once he discovered even a hint of an anomaly, he stayed at it until he found his answers. At last, he was ready. He bundled up his findings in a leather dispatch bag and went upstairs to where his commanding officer, Captain George Caldwell, was still at his desk, though his assistant had left for the evening.

Caldwell sat hunched over a sheaf of papers, a pen poised to notate whatever he was reading. His uniform coat and hat were on a wooden stand over his left shoulder, while an American flag on a pole was over his right. The view out his office window was of a blank wall across a narrow alley. Marchetti knocked on the frame of the open door. "Excuse me, Captain Caldwell."

While usually shy and unassuming, when Marchetti felt he had an important point to make, he spoke with absolute confidence.

The fifty-year-old senior officer looked up. "Ensign Marchetti. Working late again, eh? I believe the Navy is going to start charging you for the midnight oil you insist on burning."

"Er, yes, sir," Marchetti replied, as the comment didn't really deserve a response.

"Come on in and tell me what's on your mind," Caldwell finally said.

He waved Marchetti to a seat across from his desk, the light catching the Annapolis ring on his finger. A veteran of the Spanish-American War, Caldwell was one of those officers who accepted that they would never make Admiral and spent the last years of their career simply marking time. That said, he was fair to the people under him and encouraged independent thought.

"Sir, on top of my other duties, I've taken it upon myself to review commercial shipping losses since the beginning of the European war and I've noticed a disturbing pattern."

"Pattern?"

"German U-boats have sunk a disproportional number of ships carrying militarily important cargos that have originated here in New York. I've run the numbers and statistically their success does not add up."

Caldwell said nothing, so Marchetti continued. "To date the Germans have sunk ninety-two ships in the exclusion zone. Of those, forty-seven came from American ports, thirty-one from New York. Those thirty-one freighters are roughly one-third of all losses. But of the cargos sunk, they are seventy percent of the strategic matériel destroyed."

"What do you mean by strategic matériel?"

"Things like chemicals for making explosives, high-grade steel, machine tools needed to make weapons, processed rubber. Some ships carrying such supplies are getting through, obviously, but the Germans appear to be far luckier than they should be at denying the British what they need the most."

"What's your conclusion?" Caldwell asked bluntly.

"I don't believe luck plays a factor at all. I think the Germans know which ships leaving New York are carrying vital cargo and have a way of relaying that information to their submarine fleet."

"Something like that happened in the opening days of the war," Caldwell remarked. "The spy ring was disrupted."

"Yes, sir, I read about that in a briefing from the Office of Naval Intelligence. A detective agency on protective detail over a shipment of rifles discovered the spies and prevented two freighters from being sunk. Two of the spies were killed, but that doesn't necessarily mean the entire spy ring was disrupted."

"You think there are more? Bold assertion without proof, Ensign."

"I understand that, sir, but nothing else about the types and tonnage of ships sunk makes sense. It's as if the U-boats know which ships to hunt and which they need not waste their time or torpedoes. At least the ones leaving New York."

"Let's say for the moment you're correct, how do they get the information to a U-boat at sea in a timely enough manner for the captain to act?"

"I don't know, sir," Marchetti admitted with a bitterness that spoke of how much it bothered him. "Wireless telegraphy was one of my fields of interest at the academy, so I know the technology doesn't yet exist for transmitting reliably at these distances. We can get lucky bouncing signals off the ionosphere, but that's mostly inconsistent and not useful in this situation."

Caldwell leaned far back in his chair and laced his fingers behind his head in what looked like an indifferent pose. "Tell me if I have this right. You have no explanation for a phenomenon that only looks suspicious if it's approached by looking at it through the lens of statistical averages."

"Yes, sir, essentially that is what I'm saying. However, that doesn't mean I'm not correct. Seventy percent of the strategic cargos leaving New York don't reach England, while something like ninety-five percent from other ports of call do."

Caldwell rocked forward and put his palms on the desk blotter as he pondered the numbers again. At length, he said, "That's a more convincing way of putting it, Marchetti. You should have led with that." He pointed to the ensign's attaché case still perched on his lap. "Is that your documentation?"

"Yes, sir. I've got the list of ships lost, copies of their cargo manifest, and the math work I did to find the pattern."

"Good. Meet me here at oh six hundred tomorrow morning in your Class A uniform."

"Sir?"

"We're going to the War Department building in Washington, D.C., and you're going to present your findings to a friend of mine in Intelligence."

Rather than feel nervous, Joe, né Giuseppe, Marchetti felt vindicated.

12

Joe Marchetti arrived at the corner of 42nd Street and Broadway and loitered for a couple of moments to compose himself and review in his head one more time what he wanted to ask. The Knickerbocker Hotel loomed fifteen stories above the street and was the tallest structure in the immediate area except for the nearby *New York Times* tower, the city's second-tallest building.

The cobbled streets of Times Square were a snarl of automobiles, horse-drawn drays and carts, and clanking streetcars. It was early yet for the lunch crowds to descend on the tony restaurants that had sprouted around the fabled Theater District, so the sidewalks were relatively peaceful.

What wasn't so pleasant was the smell coming from a nearby vacant lot. Local stables and dirt carters had taken advantage of the open plot of land and had left behind an illegal mountain of manure that was easily thirty feet high. Crews were at work shoveling it out so a new building could be erected. If the stench wasn't bad enough, the workers had displaced a black, buzzing mass of flies to rival ancient Egypt's fourth plague.

An odd-looking truck was pulled up to the hotel's entrance. Its body appeared to be covered in steel plates, its side windows and windshield were inches-tall slits, and the spokes of its wheels had been braced with more metal plating. Two plain-clothed men stood watch over the vehicle, shotguns held at port arms. Their eyes never stopped scanning and assessing the scene around them. After just a moment, another man dressed in a fine suit, with kid gloves and a somber hat, strode from the Knickerbocker and opened a rear door to step into the back of the armored vehicle. The shotgunners relaxed their stance when the truck's chain drive rattled as the invisible driver put the truck in gear. It pulled away from the curb with the gentle acceleration of a locomotive.

Marchetti estimated there was an extra ton and a half of iron plate bolted to the truck, and the poor engine was straining. He also guessed that it had been sent from a bank with a sizable amount of cash.

He stepped into the hotel and caught

himself from whistling like a rube. The lobby was elegant, bordering on garish, with enough polished brass to almost make him shield his eyes. Women in dresses as colorful as rainbows strode past arm in arm or sat with their husbands and children on the numerous sofas. Lobby boys and porters crisscrossed the space like meteors, hard-focused on whatever errand they'd been dispatched to complete.

Joe was glad he'd decided to wear his best uniform and had polished his shoes until they gleamed like obsidian. The dark jacket was plain, but the braid on his cap and at the tips of the standing collar and cuffs caught the eye of more than a few hotel guests. One girl of maybe fifteen walked into a potted palm, unable to take her eyes off him.

At the top of the main staircase, Marchetti found a floor plan sign showing the location of the various ballrooms, offices, and other hotel amenities. He saw the Van Dorns had taken a corner suite overlooking Broadway and 42nd. The outer door was a huge slab of wood that he suspected was as armored as the delivery van he had seen outside.

A dozen heads turned in unison when he opened the door and stepped into the open space commonly called a bull pen. The ceilings were high and the accents were all rich woods and dark metals. The two outer walls were lined with closed doors for private offices. There were a dozen desks in the open space, but the men — then he noticed one woman — were huddled around but a single one.

The blond gentleman seated behind it with a black Gladstone bag on the blotter said, "I see none of you highly trained and experienced detectives thought to lock the door while we transferred the money."

"Should I go?" Joe asked, unsure of what he'd stepped into the middle of.

"That's all right," the blond man said. "I doubt you're the spearhead of a Navy amphibious landing. Come on in. Eddie, for the love of God, lock the door."

Joe said, "I'm looking for either Isaac Bell or Archibald Abbott."

The detective slouched opposite the blond man raised a hand to point down at his own head without turning. "Abbott." He then flicked a finger across the desk. "Bell."

Joe crossed the bull pen and wedged himself between the others clustered around the desk. This time he couldn't stop a whistle from blowing past his lips. The Gladstone bag was filled with neat stacks of one-hundred-dollar bills still in their currency straps.

"Give us a second, Ensign," Isaac Bell said, and looked around at the assembled employees. "My question still stands. What does this tell us?"

A bulldog-faced detective said, "That the kidnapper either sussed out the math or made a million dollars' worth of fake hundos to determine how big of a bag is needed to transport the money."

"Harry's not wrong, but what else?" Bell prompted.

"That the kidnapper is smart," a younger detective said. "He's methodical and has planned this out well in advance."

"And what does that tell us, Mr. Dashwood?"

"It tells us," Helen Mills said, "to expect the ransom money handoff to be equally as well thought-out."

"That's what I was looking for," Bell said, and threw her a conspiratorial wink. "Kidnapping is a crime as old as time itself. Supposedly, Helen — not you, my dear, but the wife of Spartan king Menelaus — was kidnapped four hundred times before Paris snatched her up and took her to Troy. It's a straightforward operation that doesn't need a large crew and that usually pays pretty well. Low risk, high reward. But now that there are professional police forces and private outfits like us, kidnapping has become more difficult.

"The handoff has always been the weak link, the place of maximum vulnerability for the kidnappers, and a lot more are getting nabbed when they try to exchange the victim for the loot. As law enforcement has evolved, so have the kidnappers' tactics. They're getting more and more clever, and whoever snatched our client's daughter is a very sly fox indeed. We need to be on our toes." He checked a slender watch strapped to his wrist. "It's time for the first team of observers to get over to Grand Central. Everyone knows their rendezvous points for when the second team takes over. Be sharp."

A handful of the detectives, including the pretty woman whose gaze lingered on the handsome naval officer, left the offices, while others returned to their desks. Soon the sound of typewriters and voices shouting down staticky phone lines grew.

Archie Abbott had left with the other Van Dorns, so Bell waved Joe Marchetti into the vacant chair. Joe introduced himself and they shook hands. He pulled his hat from under his arm and set it on the desk before settling in.

"What can I do for you, Ensign?"

"I'm not sure, exactly. I read a briefing paper about how you and Mr. Abbott broke up a German spy ring last August up in New Haven."

"We got lucky," Bell remarked.

"I guess I'm looking for some of that luck, Mr. Bell. I believe that another spy ring is now operating here in New York, and no one knows how to find it."

Bell's face went stony. He gave no indication that the young officer's statement chilled him deeply. He'd been afraid that this would happen. He wasn't being self-deprecating when he said they'd gotten lucky. Had they not found the guns hidden in the janitor's closet, John Kramer and his unknown handler would have succeeded in stopping all three rifle shipments, rather than only one.

"Tell me," he invited tersely.

Marchetti laid out all the facts as he'd first presented them to Captain Caldwell and then to a pair of admirals in the War Department building in Washington, D.C.

"Let me guess," Bell said when Joe finished. "Either you were ignored entirely, or worse, Naval Intelligence sent a pack of greenhorn Annapolis grads to search the docks of New York on a spy hunt."

"The latter," Marchetti admitted.

Bell called over to a veteran detective who was reading the shipping news section of a daily paper. "Eddie Tobin, this is Ensign Marchetti. Eddie is our resident expert on the docks and waterways of all five boroughs. Tell the ensign how many people work the docks of New York on any given day."

"Oh, I'd have to say a hundred thousand pretty easily. That's not including the ships' crews coming and going. I'm just talking longshoremen, colliers, stevedores, drivers, agents, and the like."

"Thanks, Eddie," Bell said, focusing on Joe once again. "How much time and manpower did they waste looking for a spy among a hundred thousand people?"

"Six men and two weeks."

"Uniformed?" Bell asked, fearing the worst.

"Of course."

"What a joke."

"I'm stationed at the Navy Yard over in Brooklyn, so I know the port pretty well. I knew it was a waste of time, but the admirals in Intelligence thought otherwise. Only one of the officers they sent had even been to New York before."

"I assume the brass thought this was a plum assignment, catching a real-live German spy, so they selected officers for their connections versus their abilities as investigators."

"I heard one of them is a congressman's son, so . . ."

"Gotcha. I'll ask again, since I'm in no real position to dole out luck, Ensign Marchetti. What is it I can do for you?"

"Insight, Mr. Bell. You're the Van Dorn's lead investigator, so you must be good, and you've got experience with how the Germans operated the other spy ring. What advice can you give me?"

Just then the stick phone on the corner of the desk rang. Bell held up a finger to pause the conversation and snatched up the handset. "Van Dorn Detective Agency. Isaac Bell speaking."

"Oh, Bell. Thank God. It's Grover Green," the caller said in a breathless rush.

Green was their client. It was his debutante daughter, Amelia, who'd gone out one evening with friends and not returned. The following morning, Grover Green's butler discovered on their brownstone stoop the ransom note in the black Gladstone bag now stuffed with cash.

"Calmly, Mr. Green. We're near the finish line here and there's no need to panic." The kidnappers had given them four days to get the money together. The drop was in an hour's time.

"An envelope was just delivered to my house. Inside was a picture of Amelia with her mouth gagged and instructions that the handoff is to take place at Penn Station, not Grand Central, and a half hour earlier than first directed."

As one part of Bell's mind processed this new information, he asked, "Did anyone see the deliveryman?"

"My butler. He said it was a lad in a dark uniform with piping and a cap. Much like a Western Union boy. He raced off as soon as he handed over the envelope."

Dead end, Bell thought.

"Please tell me you'll be ready in time," Green pleaded.

"Rest assured, the money came from the bank a short while ago," Bell said soothingly. "My people know what to do. I realize your instructions are to get Amelia back no matter the cost, but you hired Van Dorn for this and we will do everything in our power to secure both your daughter and your million dollars."

Green hadn't been so crass as to openly say he didn't want to lose the money either, but it was implied when he approached Van Dorn to oversee the exchange for his daughter. "Er, yes. Thank you."

"Time is pressing, Mr. Green, and if I'm to get her back I need to leave on the jump. Is everything else about the swap the same?"

"Yes. Leave the bag with the coat check agent and set the claim ticket in a folded paper on the nearest bench. Amelia will be released at the main entrance when the kidnapper leaves with the bag."

"Got it. Don't worry, Mr. Green, we'll get her home safely."

"And the money too?"

I guess he could be that crass, Bell thought and said, "On our reputation."

He hung up and looked Joe Marchetti in the eye. "How'd you like to be deputized as a Van Dorn agent?"

13

Ensign Marchetti's eyes went wide. "Wha . . . What?"

"Half my squad is on their way to the wrong train station, and I need all the eyes I can get. You in or out?"

"In, sir," he said without further hesitation.

Bell raised his voice so the remaining staff in the large outer office could hear. "Attention, everyone. The exchange has been switched to Penn Station and we only have a half hour to get over there and get in position. James, hightail it to Grand Central and tell Archie what's happened. Doubt he can get back in time, but do your best. People, let's go!"

He led the charge out of the Van Dorn suite like it was a rugby scrum. "Clever son of a gun, our kidnapper," Bell said to Joe Marchetti as they practically ran down the hallway and hit the broad staircase two at a time. "He figured we'd stake out the drop well in advance, so he switched at the last minute."

"Does he know your client hired you?"

"In cases like this, the mark always hires someone or goes to the police to handle the exchange. Kidnappers prefer it that way, professional to professional, so to speak. An upset father with a gun and an eye toward vengeance is the last thing a criminal wants to see."

"And the money? You're going to walk eight blocks with a million dollars in your hands?"

"I've got six armed agents at my back, and besides, I've carried far more than this a lot farther."

They strode down the streets of New York in a flying wedge, striding with such purpose that people instinctively got out of their path, the way a shoal of fish will part for a cruising shark. They barely paused at the crosswalks, forcing traffic to bend to their will, and used just eight of their thirty minutes to reach the classical colonnade fronting the entrance to the massive five-year-old Pennsylvania Station. Inside was a Beaux Arts waiting room modeled after an opulent Roman bath. The barrel-vaulted ceiling soared a hundred and fifty feet above the tile floor and was fully two blocks long. Hundreds of people could be in the space at any given time, and it never felt crowded or particularly loud.

Bell's people peeled off to go up to a mezzanine level to watch the floor below. Joe Marchetti stayed by Bell's side. He sensed a heightened tension in the detective's demeanor. His jacket was unbuttoned and his right hand never strayed far from his waist so that the automatic pistol in a shoulder rig was inches away. He made certain that no other passengers got too close, zigging and zagging to avoid even a moment of contact.

"You're afraid the kidnappers will jump you before the exchange?"

"It's been done before," Bell said, changing directions so quickly that Joe had to jog a couple of steps to catch up. "A knife to the back and then an escape in the confusion when the courier goes down."

Bell approached a baggage check tucked into one corner of the concourse. There were two clerks, both young women in skirts with their hair tied up so as to not interfere with their duty. This wasn't the main drop-off point for people boarding trains but an ancillary spot for people to leave small cases, valises, and the like for a few hours while they explored the city during layovers. Lining the wall behind the two clerks were oaken cubbyholes like the key slots behind a hotel desk, only these were a foot and a half square. About half were occupied.

He set the Gladstone with the ransom on the counter and waited to catch the eye of one of the women. She gave him a nice smile and pulled a brass tag from a lower niche, handed it to Bell, and tucked the bag into its new home. The exchange was entirely routine and unremarkable, something she'd done a dozen times already this morning and doubtlessly would do dozens more before the end of her shift. Bell thanked her and pocketed the brass fob.

He turned and started strolling away, Joe Marchetti at his side. Bell was a little concerned about Marchetti's uniform standing out, but with the war raging in Europe, soldiers and sailors seemed to be traveling a lot more regularly. The government stance remained one of strict neutrality, but the armed forces were slowly preparing for the time if that were to ever change.

"I don't know if I could do it, Mr. Bell."

"Isaac, please. And do what?"

"Hand over a million dollars like that and just walk away."

Bell chuckled a little mirthlessly. "For one,

it's not my million dollars. But I know what you mean. And at least two of my agents are watching the check claim as we speak." Bell took off his hat and casually gestured to their left, where a Van Dorn agent sipped coffee at a café, and then swept the hat up so it pointed to a mezzanine, where another agent leaned against the rail and appeared to be a bored traveler marking time by watching the crowd.

When they were out of eyeshot of the check claim clerks, Bell sped up and headed for a door marked NO ADMITTANCE. It was unlocked and he let himself through with barely a check in his stride. He went down a long corridor, none of the people they passed giving them any mind. At one door marked TRANSIT POLICE, he knocked and entered without waiting to be invited in.

The man behind the desk was about Bell's age, but life looked to have ground some of the joy out of him. He was fleshy without being fat and his hair was in full retreat across his skull. He wore a decent suit and the watch chain hanging from his jacket pocket was at least eighteen-karat gold and looked heavy.

He glanced up from the papers on his blotter and opened his mouth to protest the interruption, when he recognized the detective. "Isaac, good to see you. How are you doing?" And then the bonhomie faded as his brain made some logical leaps of deduction. "You're working a case in my station. You need my help. It's hush-hush and probably happening right now. Why don't you ever just stop by to say hello and shoot the breeze once in a while?"

"And prove your suspicious mind wrong? It'd break your heart. Joe Marchetti, this is former Van Dorn agent turned railroad dick Wendel Carver. Wendy, Joe's obviously with the Navy and happened to be in my office when I needed an extra pair of eyes."

The head of Penn Station security stood and held out his left hand. He raised the right to show the limb was a prosthetic ending in a wooden hand. He saw Marchetti had the same question everyone he met had. "Wish I could say it was apprehending a criminal mastermind, but I got knocked down by a spooked horse and the cart he took off with ran me over and turned my humerus bone to powder. So, what's happening here, Isaac?"

"Ransom exchange. Money's already in your short-stay baggage check. I've got ten minutes to bundle the tag in newspaper and leave it on the bench next to it. This was supposed to happen at Grand Central, and

I had everything set up with your counterpart there."

"Jim Saunders. Good man."

"Agreed. Problem is, the kidnapper called twenty minutes ago and moved the show to your bailiwick. Just wanted to give you a courtesy call. Not enough time to get any of your men up to speed to help me, but I wouldn't operate here without letting you know."

Carver didn't look pleased, but he knew Isaac Bell and his integrity. He nodded. "I have time to brief a couple of my brighter lads. You know the observation room?"

"Yeah."

"Go plant the tag and meet me there."

Isaac grabbed up the morning's edition of the *Herald* from Carver's desk and tucked it under his arm. "I'm stealing your paper."

"Leave the sports page."

Bell and Marchetti backtracked to the main concourse. The place was busy. Packs of newly arrived passengers streamed up from the track platforms below, while others wended their way to ticket counters or loitered as they awaited loved ones. This close to the designated time for the drop, he suspected he was under observation. With a million-dollar payout, the kidnapper had plenty of money to hire lookouts and other accomplices. He glanced at the big wall clock, slowing his pace just enough to arrive at the bench right on time. He casually dropped the newspaper containing the luggage tag on the seat without breaking stride.

The two clerks at the nearby claim check never gave him a second's thought. The detective and the young ensign glided on past and circled back to a set of marble stairs. They climbed quickly but seemingly unhurriedly to the upper mezzanine and Bell led them to another wood slab of a door not authorized for passenger use. It was ajar.

There were two men in the uniforms of transit cops with Carver and beyond them was a large window that looked out over the entire concourse. The glass was tinted on the other side so no one could see them up here, while they had an unobstructed view of most of the station. Bell looked quickly and saw the newspaper was still where he'd left it.

Wendel Carver said, "I got word to the janitors to leave the benches alone."

"Good call. I am worried that some bored passenger will grab it for a free read."

"Likely the kidnapper will nab it soon, then."

"Agreed."

For the next ten minutes the men watched the bench and the baggage claim and tracked anyone who went near either. They thought they had their kidnapper when a woman in an ivory dress sat on the opposite end of the bench from the stashed tag. She paid it no heed and bent to adjust her shoe. Once it was fixed to her satisfaction, she stood and sauntered away. The watchers let out a collective breath and kept their vigil.

"Wendel, how is that crazy brother-in-law of yours?" Bell asked, and explained to Joe Marchetti, "Wendel's wife's brother is a lighthouse keep down on the Jersey Shore. Spends way too much time by himself, coming up with all kinds of crackpot ideas."

"Don't get me started," Carver said. "He got transferred to the Flat Point Light after the previous keeper tumbled down the stairs and split his head open like a melon. Apparently back in the eighties, two consecutive keepers died at that light, so now he's paranoid he's next. Every couple of days Bernadette gets a letter from him telling her not to grieve when he dies and gives instructions on what to do with his personal property and who can and can't come to his funeral. Real morbid stuff."

"No more conspiracy theories about Freemasons taking girls across state lines for immoral purposes?"

"He gave that one up months ago. He is growing suspicious about airplanes, though. Hasn't said why, but he says he has serious suspicions."

"Isaac," Joe Marchetti said tensely.

"I see him," Bell assured him with cool detachment.

A man dressed in carpenter's overalls and an oversized hat was heading straight for the bench. He seemed isolated from the hustle and bustle around him as if his mind was focused on the task at hand. And just as it appeared he would grab the paper, he moved on.

Then came a heavyset porter in a black uniform and cap who passed by the bench and picked up the paper.

"Damn," Wendel Carver spat. "I didn't tell the porters to stay clear of the benches." He turned to one of his transit cops. "Go grab him and put the paper back on the bench."

"Yes, sir." The cop saluted and bolted for the door.

"Hold on," Bell said.

14

There was something about how the porter paused at that moment. His head was tilted slightly as he considered his next set of actions. It wasn't the stance of a man who'd picked up some litter off a bench, but that of someone standing on a precipice about to take a leap into the unknown. He seemed like an island in the swirl of humanity, standing calmly with the newspaper in his hand. He nodded as if he'd made a decision and casually tilted the paper so the brass token fell into his palm. He made his way to the baggage claim, flipping the token once like it was a coin.

"That's him," Joe practically shouted. "The porter."

The handoff was always the tricky bit, Bell reminded himself. It won't be this easy.

The porter approached the clerks and set the tag down on the counter. The same girl who'd issued it to Bell took the tag, checked the number, and turned to the wall of cubbies. The porter suddenly slapped the counter and stepped back several paces as if to turn and run. Then he moved forward again so he was in position when the clerk returned to the counter with the ransom money in the black Gladstone bag. She handed it across.

"We got him," Carver crowed victoriously.

And suddenly they didn't. The porter smoothly handed the bag off to another porter as two more appeared from around a corner, each carrying identical black Gladstone bags.

"What the . . ?" one of the cops said.

"Shell game," Bell told him, unsurprised. "Using porters in a train station is a nice touch."

"Watch the bag," Wendel instructed.

"I have it," Joe said. "It's with the guy moving directly away from us near the lady with the red hat."

That porter switched bags with another, and then three more porters came into view. Same uniform, and similar build and age as all the others. One had a bag. Two didn't. But soon they swapped out with yet another porter who'd climbed up from the platform level. There had to be at least twelve porters now and eight identical bags. Their movements were well rehearsed and made tracking the Gladstone all but impossible, especially when they were partially shielded by the crowds of passengers drifting through the concourse.

To make matters even worse, there were handfuls of real porters crisscrossing the station, some carrying bags for passengers, others empty-handed. The men kept moving in and out of view, swapping bags with one another, shuffling them like cards on a monte box so that only a keen observer could keep an eye on the right man and bag.

"This is out of control," Wendel said. "I'm sorry, Isaac, but I've got to put an end to it. Come on, fellas," he said to his two officers. "We need to arrest them all."

Bell didn't move from the window. His eyes occasionally darted about, but his attention barely wavered.

"What about it, Isaac?" Joe asked. "Shouldn't we go down there? The guy with the money could slip away pretty easily."

"I want to watch from up here, but if you're interested, by all means head down and observe."

Joe decided to stay, and from their aerie they watched Wendel and his two transit cops stop the suspicious porters and open their bags. Carver reached into a Gladstone and pulled out blank newspaper broadsheets cut to resemble stacks of hundred-dollar bills. The faux porters were herded into one corner of the big concourse as each was searched and found to not have the ransom. More transit officers joined the operation. Passengers and travelers didn't know what to make of the spectacle and whispered among themselves as they crossed the tiled floor.

Porters with Gladstone bags, seeing others being rounded up, tried to sneak away, but still more police arrived and prevented any from escaping. It was a masterful piece of work by Carver's boys and Bell was duly impressed. Carver came back up to the observation room a few minutes later.

"Didn't find the money, did you?" Bell asked in the form of a question, but it sounded like a declarative statement.

"It only takes one to slip through the net," Wendel said. "There were so damn many of them and we didn't have the time. I'm sorry, Isaac. The money's gone."

Bell continued to watch the bustling concourse rather than turn to speak to Carver properly. "What's their story? What are the fake porters telling you?"

"They appear to be actors from a theater up in Harlem who were hired through an agency called Regent Talent. They practiced the moves over the past couple of days and thought it was going to be a vaudeville-type screwball comedy. It was only this morning they were told it was to happen here."

"Dead end most likely," Bell guessed. "Regent Talent was just a rented office as a front, no doubt, and the names used were all phony."

"If your kidnapper is this smart, then I'd say that's a fair assessment," Carver agreed glumly. "I guess all you can hope is they hold true to their word and let the victim go."

"Amelia Green is her name," Bell said absently. He continued to watch the claim check, where the ransom was first stored.

"They were all carrying newspapers except one guy," Wendel added, as if that detail had importance.

"Let me guess," Bell said, turning to face Penn Station's top cop. "It is either a balloon that could be inflated with a small cylinder of compressed air or some sort of spring mechanism."

Carver's jaw hinged open in gaped amazement as he showed Bell a deflated balloon made of leather attached to a brass cylinder the size of a man's thumb. "How could you possibly know?"

Bell's handsome face split into a knowing smile. "It's three-card monte. No matter how elaborately the game is played, it's always a scam. Follow me."

He took off at a fast clip so that he and his companions thundered down the steps like an avalanche and crossed the mezzanine to the baggage claim. Bell saw the fear in the one clerk's face even before they arrived, but there was no place for her to go. He also noted the out-of-place buttons hidden behind a pleat on the front of her dress. She stood at the counter and waited those last seconds. She put on a chirpy smile. "Mr. Carver, may I be of some assistance?"

"I've watched how busy you've been, miss. Love your dress, by the way," Bell said, and bent to retrieve something from his shoe. "Dozens upon dozens of people coming to store bags with you while they went about their business. At times it was almost manic. What is it they say, like a one-armed paper hanger."

She smiled at that, but tilted her head as if to ask his point.

Bell said, "But no matter how many bags came through here today and how busy you two were, you never used one particular cubby." With that he flipped the knife he'd pulled from a sheath at his ankle and hurled it by its blade at the niche where the ransom had been placed.

Rather than clatter in the empty cubby, the blade pierced a sheet of thick poster board that had been cleverly painted to make the storage space appear empty. The weight of the blade toppled the poster board to the floor with the clatter of Sheffield steel on marble. Behind the false front sat the original Gladstone bag stuffed with the million-dollar ransom.

The collective gasp was music to Bell's ears.

An out-of-breath Archie Abbott and the rest of the team sent to Grand Central arrived at that moment. "Hey. What did we miss?"

"Where's Amelia?" Bell asked the clerk before anything else could be explained. "Talking now is going to make it go a lot easier with the police and prosecutors."

"That's true," Wendel Carver said. "Your name's Cathy, right?"

She hung her head. "Kelly, Mr. Carver. Kelly Donahue."

"Tell us," he invited with the somber sincerity of a priest asking for a confession.

"She's back in the apartment I share with my boyfriend, Stan. It was his idea. He was the one who came up with the plan. We've treated her good," she said quickly, her eyes flitting between Carver and Isaac Bell, unsure of who held the real power here. "I'm supposed to take my lunch break at noon. Stan'll meet me at the Thirty-third Street entrance in the delivery van he drives. We'd let her out the back and leave New York forever."

Bell and Wendel exchanged a look, and both stepped back to talk in private.

"What do you think?" Carver asked. "It's eleven-thirty now."

"As much as I hate leaving Amelia in their custody for a second longer than necessary, breaking up their plan carries risks. If we show up at their place and bust down the door, he'd still have the time to put a bullet in her head or slice her throat."

"Agreed. It's best to let him think they have the kidnapping sewn up all nice and tidy."

"This also gives us time to bring in a couple of detectives from the Fourteenth Precinct to make the arrest as airtight as possible for District Attorney Perkins."

"Good idea." Carver called over one of his cops and said, "Go over to the Fourteenth and bring back Hoyle and Dyson. We'll meet them at the Thirty-third Street entrance. Tell them we're about to bust a kidnapper. If they're not around, try Moe Thomson and whoever his new partner is."

"You've got thirty minutes to get back here," Bell warned the man, "so on the jump."

Kelly Donahue was already in cuffs, guarded by two transit cops, one of whom held the painted poster board that had hidden the ransom money. Archie Abbott carried the loaded Gladstone, and his team had fanned out in a loose protective formation around him.

"Not that I don't like repeating myself," he said when Bell approached, "but what did we miss while we were dithering around Grand Central?"

Archie absently shook hands with Wendel Carver, as they were well acquainted.

Carver beamed. "Your man Isaac saw through what had to be one of the cleverest ruses I've ever encountered."

"Which reminds me," Bell said, deflecting the praise, "might as well let the fake porters go. No sense in charging them with anything. They thought it was all just a stunt."

"I want to wait until after we catch the boyfriend," Carver said. "I want him ID'd as the man who hired them."

"Fake porters?" Archie asked.

Bell nodded. "They pulled an elaborate

monte on us using a dozen guys dressed as porters all carrying matching bags. They passed the bags back and forth like a hustler swirling the marble under and around the three cups to some rube from Iowa."

Joe Marchetti said, "It was a twelve-shell shell game."

"Exactly, only the marble was never in play. The clerk put the bag in a cubby when I handed it over. No problem. When the first porter grabbed the luggage tag and gave it to her, three things happened almost simultaneously. The porter slapped the counter to draw attention to himself. At the same time she reached the recesses, she undid hidden buttons on the front of her skirt to grab the flattened Gladstone hanging from her waist. This she inflated with a small cylinder of compressed air rigged with a trigger. The bag puffed out so it looked like it was filled with the ransom money. This was the bag she handed to the porter."

"And the third thing that happened?"

"Oh, sorry. While the porter settled down and we watched Miss Donahue walk back to the counter with a million dollars in hand, the other clerk fitted a poster board cover on the mouth of the cubbyhole that was painted to make it look empty."

The woman who'd worked side by side

with Kelly Donahue had the feral cunning of a subway rat because she seemed to know people were talking about her. She looked around as if for an avenue of escape and then saw Isaac's penetrative blue eyes fixed squarely on her. He shook his head ever so slightly and she knew her role in the kidnapping, however small, was out in the open.

Bell called out to James Dashwood, another former protégé and now a full agent, to take her into custody.

"How did you deduce all that?" Wendel asked.

Bell laughed and made a dismissive gesture with his hands. "Deduce? Who am I, Sherlock Holmes? I knew immediately the porter's antics were a distraction and never took my eyes off Kelly Donahue. I watched the whole thing."

"I missed all of it," Wendel Carver admitted.

"Me too," Joe added. "I took my eyes off her for just a couple of seconds at most."

"That's all it takes. They'd practiced this and had the timing down pat."

Carver then realized something. "That first actor dressed as a porter was in on it more than the others."

"I'd have to say yes, and I'd also have to tell you that he isn't among the others you detained. As soon as he handed off the bag, I watched him head down to the tracks. He's long gone."

"Small fish, I suppose," Carver said to hide his disappointment.

"Then let's get ourselves the big one. Archie, get the bag back to the First Commerce so Mr. Green's banker can stop chugging Milk of Magnesia. And tell Green he can meet his daughter at the Fourteenth Precinct, where she'll be giving her statement."

"Righto."

The arrest of Stanley Provost was anticlimactic compared to the morning's activities. Kelly Donahue had provided a description of the van and the name of the delivery service emblazoned on its side. At noon, it was parked on 33rd Street just like it was supposed to be and the nervous, acne-scarred young driver leaning out the window with a toothpick in his mouth like some street tough was as Kelly depicted. The van's engine was idling.

The two plain-clothed police detectives fetched from the Fourteenth, Hoyle and Dyson, walked along the sidewalk just inside the ranks of iron light posts, talking like two men who were on their way to a meeting. Stanley Provost paid them no attention. His gaze was fixed on the station entrance with the expectancy of someone who was about to become a millionaire.

Abreast of the cab, Hoyle and Dyson whipped out their service revolvers. Hoyle was closer and had the muzzle an inch from the kidnapper's forehead. "My trigger finger is faster than your foot on the accelerator, so don't even think about it."

Dyson holstered his gun and wrenched open the door, tossing the skinny kid onto the sidewalk hard enough to scrape skin off his cheek. The detective pressed a knee to the small of Provost's back while he whipped cuffs around his wrists, securing the prisoner in no time flat.

Bell had been approaching from the opposite direction and had timed his arrival so that as soon as Stanley Provost was in custody he was at the van's rear doors. There was no lock, so he swung them open. Amelia Green sat with her back pressed against the van's side, her hands bound behind her back and a gag tied tightly around her mouth. Her eyes were enormous with fear and red from crying. Her cheeks were tear-streaked.

"Amelia, you're safe," he said. "Your father sent me to take you home. Everything is going to be all right." He climbed inside and used his boot knife to cut away the rope around her wrists. He gently untied the cloth gag, but let her pull it free, knowing it can be painful, depending on how long it had been in place. "Have they hurt you? Do you need to go to the hospital?"

She pulled the gag free, wincing at the pain, and then worked her jaw to relieve the cramping. "No," she said at last. "I'm fine. They didn't hurt me."

He helped her out of the van. Stanley Provost was on his feet now with two of Wendel Carver's men holding his elbows. Amelia eyed him warily.

"Don't worry about him," Bell said. "He can't hurt you now."

She shook off the hand he'd had on her forearm and walked straight to her kidnapper. She was still a little unsteady on her legs, and the dress she'd worn the night she was snatched wasn't exactly designed for ease of movement, but she still managed to ram a knee into Provost's groin hard enough to double him over in agony.

"Nice shot," one of Bell's men said.

Others laughed or gasped at the audacity and single-mindedness of the assault.

"I think she'll be fine," Wendel said to Bell in a stage whisper.

15

With apologies, Bell sent Joe Marchetti packing soon after the arrest. District Attorney Charles Perkins had been informed of the case and wanted to be on hand for the interrogations and Amelia Green's statement. Bell was asked to sit in as well, but Joe Marchetti had no bearing on the case and was barred from the proceedings.

"I'm sorry, Joe. Thanks for your help today and all, but I have to tell you there's not much I can do about your situation. There are too many people working the docks of New York to ever know which of them is supplying intelligence to the Germans. And like I told you earlier, Archie and I stumbled onto those New Haven spies out of pure chance."

The young ensign was clearly disappointed but also understanding. He held out a hand, which Bell shook gladly. "It's all right. Coming to you was a long shot anyway and I can tell how busy you must be. Thanks for letting me see you and your people in action. It was pretty incredible."

Bell grinned. "All in a day's work, I suppose."

"So long."

"Take care."

Later that evening Bell was having dinner in the suite of rooms he shared at the Knickerbocker Hotel with his wife, Marion. Like Bell, she was blond, but her eyes were a vivid green that could beguile like an emerald or be as cold as the Arctic Ocean, depending on her mood. She had a lovely face that he never tired of watching, especially in moments when she was unaware of his gaze. The look she gave when she caught him staring, a combination of curiosity as to why he was watching her and charmed happiness, remained his favorite of all.

Marion was a film director, one of the only women in the business. Her eye for lighting and her innate ability to get the most out of her actors, which equated to box office success, far outweighed the latent misogyny of her studio head.

Their conflicting schedules meant they were often apart for weeks at a time, so it made the days and nights they had together that much more special. Absence, for Isaac and Marion, truly did make the heart grow fonder and both believed it was the key to the strength and love of their marriage.

Little remained of their late dinner but the bones of Bell's duck and the brussels sprouts that the kitchen staff had erroneously served Marion. They were so hated that she'd actually bundled the repugnant vegetables in a napkin rather than look at them. Bell had just poured the last of a bottle of wine into their glasses.

"Right between the legs," Marion parroted his last statement.

"She could have been the starting punter for the Bulldogs," Bell said with a chuckle, mentioning his alma mater's nickname.

"I told you I know her peripherally, but after hearing she's that kind of woman, I think it's time I get to know her better." Marion set her glass down and stared him in the eye. Bell's sense of danger piqued. "I'm not sure I like your take on the other business of the day."

"In what way?" He knew what she was saying, but had learned early on that showing off his deductive prowess to Marion during a serious discussion was a pitfall as deep as a tiger trap.

"You simply have to help Ensign Marchetti, Isaac. I understand there's a war on and the sailors on the ships approaching England know the risk, but this seems unfair. They're specifically being targeted like they're easy marks. That's just not right."

"I agree with you wholeheartedly, but this is a matter for our government, not a private agency."

"Poppycock!" she said hotly.

Bell suppressed a smile that he knew would infuriate her. "Please, Marion, there's nothing I can do. There are a hundred thousand potential suspects who could be turning information over to the Germans, literally miles of docks and piers and dozens of ships leaving for Europe on a daily basis. Even if I wanted to help, I wouldn't know where to start. It's just too big. You have to be reasonable."

Her eyes went cold and her body very still. Her voice turned to frost. "When, in the history of matrimonial conversation, has a man's request for a woman to be reasonable ever worked in his favor?"

A wry smile softened his lips. "I'd have to say never."

"And I would be inclined to agree with that. Would you care to rephrase your last comment?"

"I would. Marion, please look at this from

my perspective."

"So much better," she chirped happily. "I can see it from your perspective, it is a likely impossible task, but I have never once seen you shy away from a case because of its size, complexity, or likelihood to be solved."

He dipped his head at the compliment and sipped at his wine. "It's neither the size, complexity, nor difficulty that I am balking at. I don't have a client. Marchetti told me the Navy is dropping the matter after their own bungled investigation and Van Dorn has a strict policy against pro bono work. My hands are tied."

"Hah," she scoffed. "How much did the firm make by you saving the girl and the ransom?"

"Ten percent."

"You just put a hundred grand in Joseph 'Ebenezer' Van Dorn's tight little fist. The least he can do is let you look into this spy business for a week. Remind him that if you crack the case, the agency's reputation in Washington is going to skyrocket. That means bigger and better contacts. Appeal to his baser instincts rather than his lofty ideals."

Bell laughed aloud at that. Van Dorn was a good boss and friend who ran a tight ship and had as strong a moral sense as any man, but his first and only love was the agency that bore his name. Ideals had no place for an ambitious man. "Okay, I'll give it a week, but don't expect any miracles."

Marion stood from the dining table, letting her silk dressing gown slip just a bit. "I knew you could be reasonable," she purred, throwing his gaffe back in his face. "Care for your reward?"

He came up to press himself against her, his arms around her slim waist, and used her words back at her. "I am inclined to agree to that."

It so happened that Joseph Van Dorn had to leave New York the following day for a meeting in Chicago with a hotelier looking for better security for his properties. The proverbial cat was away, so Bell called together a handful of his best people — veterans like Eddie Tobin and Harry Warren and some younger agents with fresher perspectives, namely Helen Mills and James Dashwood. Of course, Archie Abbott was in on the meeting as well. They took one of the conference rooms so as to not disturb other agents working the bull pen. Coffee was supplied from a large silver urn and there were pastries from a shop across Times Square that usually had a line out the door.

Bell wore his customary white summer suit.

"Here's the thing," he said from the head of the table. "The Navy believes there's a spy ring working the docks and supplying the Germans with intelligence on which specific ships to target with their U-boats currently blockading the British Isles. They're identifying munition ships, freighters carrying machine tools or arms, and oil tankers especially.

"The powers that be in the ONI — that's Office of Naval Intelligence for all of you not up on government acronyms — sent six investigators to New York and let them scour the docks for a couple of weeks. In uniform, by the way. As you can well imagine, they found absolutely nothing."

"Lucky they weren't tossed into the Hudson wearing their soda jerk whites," Eddie Tobin remarked, and got a laugh.

"Checking the docks to see who is fingering strategic ships is a waste of time. Too many ships, too many people, and too much dockage. I thought about this some last night and realized that we'll never be able to stop the spies from picking their target. What we can do, I think, is stop that information from reaching Germany."

"How?" Helen asked, her dark hair looking like black diamonds in the morning light streaming through the windows.

Bell let his eyes drift to all the faces arrayed around the polished rosewood table. "No idea. That's why you're all here. Let's figure it out."

"The most obvious is telegraph via the undersea cables," Archie said while turning in his seat to see who was just then opening the conference room door.

"My first thought as well."

"English cut them," Grady Forrer said as he stepped in. "Sorry I'm late."

Grady headed the small Van Dorn Research Department, a windowless collection of rooms buried deep in a corner of the office suites. He was an absolute font of knowledge on the arcane as well as the germane and a crackerjack researcher. If he didn't have an answer on hand, he'd ferret it out in no time. He sported a banker's green visor and stays on his shirt cuffs. His black trousers were shiny at the knees and seat and were twenty years out of fashion.

"They cut them?" Bell said, unsure if he'd heard correctly.

"First week of the war. Remember nearly all the transatlantic cables depart North America in Newfoundland and emerge from the sea in Ireland before branching off to other countries. The Brits cut all the lines running to Germany as a way to deprive them of rapid communication with the outside world."

"I did not know that," Archie said.

"Few do, Mr. Abbott. It's not something the English advertised, but it did, in fact, occur."

"I guess we check telegraphy off our list," Isaac said, glancing around. "Other ideas?"

Eddie Tobin raised a hand a few inches and said, "A courier can get information back to Germany on a fast express liner, like the *Vaterland* or *Imperator.* Those ships cruise at twenty-four knots, far faster than any freighter or oiler. This would get the information to Germany several days ahead of their target. More than enough time to dispatch a U-boat or radio one that's already part of the blockade."

"Not bad."

Grady said, "We can cross-reference German ocean liner sailing times with those high-priority cargo ships and see if there's any correlation."

"Okay. What else?" Bell invited.

"A slight variation on what Eddie suggested," Archie said from around an unlit cigar. "The spies could radio a fast warship lurking off our coast and they steam to the waters around England and relay the information to the submarines."

"Wouldn't anyone else be able to hear the transmission?" Helen Mills pointed out.

"Who's listening if they broadcast at three in the morning?"

"Anyone with a receiver and insomnia," she shot back.

"It's something we should look into," Bell said to keep everyone on track. "I for one don't know much about radio telegraphy beyond how to pay for a wireless call from the Marconi offices aboard ships."

James Dashwood said, "A courier could be motored out to sea on an innocent-looking boat, a fishing smack, or something that might rendezvous with the superfast transatlantic ship. That way there's no radio beam to be intercepted."

Eddie Tobin spoke next. "It'd be odd for a fast enough ship, like a destroyer or light cruiser, to lurk in the waters around New York awaiting instructions. Our Navy or the new Coast Guard would send them packing right away, and if they refused to leave, they'd shadow them. And either way, our Navy boys could interdict the courier's boat or pick up any transmission sent to the Germans."

There was a knock on the door and one of the junior agents opened it and introduced Ensign Joe Marchetti. Like the day before, the good-looking young sailor was in his dress uniform and Bell noted a new confidence in his stance and to the set of his jaw. Joe liked that his preliminary work was setting wheels in motion and evolving into a legitimate operation. Bell also noticed a flush come to Helen Mills's cheeks when she saw him and his half-second pause on her face as his gaze swept the room.

"Sorry I'm late, Mr. Bell. They closed the Brooklyn Bridge for a suffragist march."

Bell made quick introductions for those who hadn't met the naval officer and brought Joe up to speed on the morning's discussion. "Since we've all accepted we can't stop German agents on the docks from gathering critical intelligence, we've been focusing on how the information reaches the U-boat picket line around Great Britain."

"I can assure you that the Navy hasn't caught any German warships skulking around New York," he said with conviction. "We've upped our patrols since the war began and so have the Coasties."

"Ensign Marchatti," Helen Mills began.

"Marchetti, ma'am."

"Sorry." She blushed. "How about I'm Helen and you're Joe?"

Archie and Isaac shared a quick glance to confirm they were of one mind. Helen knew his name perfectly well. She was gunning for the young officer, and he wasn't going to stand a chance.

"I'd like that," Joe said with a smile.

Her head did a coy little dip. "You've had more time to consider all of this. What are your thoughts?"

"The trick is to get the information out of New York undetected. I'm not sure if you're aware, but the British have severed all the transatlantic cable feeds to Germany." He paused a beat to see if this juicy piece of wartime news would get a reaction. It did not. "Okay, apparently you are aware. Without cables, Germany will need to rely on radios, which have limited range and a fatal flaw."

"What's that?" Bell asked.

"Radio waves radiate out from the transmitting antenna like the ripples in a pond when you toss in a pebble. They can be detected by any receiver within range. Yours and your enemy's. The more power and the taller the antenna, the greater the range, but still all ears listening can hear your transmission. There are ways to diminish this effect with shielding, but it can't be eliminated altogether."

"Hold on," Archie said. "Isaac told us you're a researcher for the Navy, not a radio expert."

"I'm on a temporary assignment. My primary work is with evaluating how current and emergent technology can be integrated into our warships of the future with a focus on communications."

Archie nodded, impressed. "All right, then. Please, continue."

"If our German spy were to try to radio a nearby ship, every receiver in the city would hear them, and trust me there are hundreds of people listening. They call themselves 'band scanners' and their hobby is to listen in to as many transmissions as possible. Some do it for the simple joy, others are looking to steal research from other radio enthusiasts working on new transmission methods. At any time and across a broad spectrum, people around New York are listening at all hours of the day or night."

"Sounds like a dull hobby," Harry Warren said dismissively.

Bell shot him an annoyed look and asked Joe, "Even if the spy's transmission is encrypted, there would be chatter among these 'band scanners' about a new unknown transmitter in the area?"

"Absolutely. I know a number of them and reached out a while back. Nothing unusual was broadcast on the days and nights leading to the sailing of the targeted freighters."

16

Bell looked around the conference table. It appeared his people had put faith in Joe Marchetti to have the answer to this mystery and were equally disappointed when the navy officer had nothing. "Where does that leave us, exactly?"

Joe said, "Out of the city. Someplace rural where they can erect a tower tall enough to signal a ship far enough out to sea that it doesn't look suspicious to the Navy or Coast Guard."

"Montauk?" Helen suggested.

"Possibly." He gave her a warm smile and then quickly looked at the others so as to not seem so interested. "Or anywhere along the southern coast of Long Island. It's deserted for the most part and there are few if any amateur receivers out there. I've asked around the community and so far no one knows of any new transmitters."

"I've heard of experiments done from balloons," James Dashwood said.

Marchetti nodded vigorously. "That was going to be my next point. There may not be an antenna at all. As he said, an aerial in the form of a tether can be launched on a balloon from an open space and hauled down again once the transmission's been sent."

"Hot air or helium?" Bell asked, a pen poised over a notepad.

"Helium for sure. The air in hot-air balloons needs to be reheated periodically during flight."

"There can't be that many retailers of helium gas, so it'll be easy enough to check if any have new customers or unusual orders."

"Better include outfits in Jersey and Philly," Archie Abbott suggested.

"I am," Bell said, jotting a note. "Connecticut too."

He set down his pen and looked each of his people in the eye. "We're not dealing with a criminal. Criminals, as a rule, are dumb. True, we have faced some real masterminds in our time, but most of the crimes we see are straightforward hit jobs — your garden-variety purse snatchers, then there are pickpockets loitering in the hotels we protect, or we get the truly ambitious guys who go into truck hijacking. In the case of murder, nine times out of ten it's the husband, the wife, or a business partner, depending on the victim. Like I said. Dumb."

His people chuckled.

"This is a different situation. We're dealing with spies who were selected by their government for this job because they are smart, likely very well trained, and highly motivated. We got lucky in New Haven. They managed to slip one radio by us and that cost the lives of the ship's crew. That mistake is one hundred percent our fault. The Germans would have taken out the other two if Eddie Edwards hadn't spotted a single grease stain on a bathroom wall.

"That operation was designed to target those specific ships, and once it was over the spies would have begun the next phase of their plan, targeting other freighters identified by dockworkers sympathetic to the German war effort. Now, I bagged one of the leaders in New Haven, but another, and possibly several accomplices, are alive and well and at it again.

"This was planned out in Germany, by people who have a long and storied history of espionage dating back to the Napoleonic Wars. They have what's known as institutional knowledge, knowledge built up over generations. And they will use every shred of it to preserve their nation's sovereignty and win the war. The spy in Connecticut almost killed me in the fire at that boardinghouse. They're that good. That's who we're up against. Not some thug knocking over a jewelry store or a cutpurse at Grand Central, but intelligent people who will do everything imaginable to succeed at their mission and not get caught."

Again, his wintry gaze swept the room, hammering home the seriousness of their case. "Give me ten minutes to write up some notes and I'll post individual assignments in the bull pen."

The investigators shuffled out of the conference room, talking in low voices, leaving Bell, Archie, and Joe Marchetti.

"Arch," said Bell, "Joe and I are headed to Long Island to go antenna hunting."

"We are?" Marchetti asked.

"Indeed, and you're going to give me a tutorial on how a radio works, its strengths and limitations. I feel it's the key to what the Germans are doing, and I need more than my rudimentary grasp of the subject. As an example — how difficult would it be for a small group of spies to erect a sufficiently powerful antenna?"

"It's possible, but it wouldn't be easy and it's not something they would want to dismantle after each transmission, only to have to set it back up for the next time they need it."

"So then I'm right that we could drive out there and find it."

"That's a couple thousand square miles," Archie pointed out.

"Yes, but they would need to stay near a road because the girders and such for their antenna are too heavy to transport by hand." Bell looked to Joe for confirmation and continued when the ensign nodded. "Majority of people on Long Island live close to the city. We really only have to check Suffolk County, and that's mostly farmland except along the coasts. Now we're down to a couple hundred miles of roads. Two days tops."

"You are nothing if not confident, my friend," Archie said. "That puts you back before Van Dorn returns from Chicago."

"Exactly. Joe, how about it?"

"I'll need to telephone my boss and request some leave."

"Call from the bull pen."

The car was simply the finest Isaac Bell had ever owned. Built in New Brunswick, New

Jersey, the Simplex Crane Model 5 with custom Brewster coachwork looked like it was formed using some of the new aerodynamic principles shaping aircraft design. The fenders, painted the mesmerizing blue of a propane flame, blended into the automobile's body with the curving grace of a big predatory cat. The bodywork was a pearlescent gray that shone with the sun, but also helped hide the inevitable manure dust that blew along New York's streets all summer long.

Under the hood was a one-hundred-and-ten-horsepower in-line six-cylinder engine displacing an eye-watering five hundred and sixty-three cubic inches and easily capable of pushing the car past a hundred miles per hour. The motor was so finely crafted that the exhaust was merely a soft murmur and there was no clacking of the valves as they opened and closed, as with so many other cars on the road these days.

This particular Model 5 was a two-door convertible coupe with a rumble seat in back that could be hidden under a black leather tonneau cover. For inclement weather, a soft top could be erected around the cockpit. Bell had commissioned the car for his specifications and hadn't bothered with many of the luxury touches the manufacturer was known for, like wood-trimmed cubbies and fold-down writing trays for the back passengers. He did keep the two spare tires strapped above the rear bumper and added one of the new Delco electric starters. No more hand-cranking an obstinate engine on a snowy winter morning.

Even a man of Bell's means, thanks to his father's bank in Boston, had to cringe at what all the power, style, and luxury cost. The Simplex was as expensive as the average house.

After crossing Blackwell's Island Bridge from Midtown into Queens, Bell drove Joe Marchetti through the busy streets until they reached a tollhouse on Nassau Boulevard. Bell paid the attendant a dollar and fifty cents to gain access to the Long Island Motor Parkway. It had been built seven years earlier by his friend William Vanderbilt as a place to indulge in his passion for racing cars. When not in use as a track, the motorway was open to the public as one of the premier roads in the country.

No sooner had the Simplex's tires hit the smooth macadam than Bell put the hammer down and the car accelerated like a thoroughbred out of the starting gate. Joe Marchetti let out a whoop of pure joy as Bell brought the engine to its redline before upshifting so smoothly there was barely any hesitation. By the time he hit fourth gear, the tollhouse was a little toy in the rearview mirror and the wind blasting the screen hit at a hundred and ten miles per hour.

There were no interchanges, no cross streets, nothing but a handful of tollhouses, where access to the motorway was controlled along its forty-two-mile length. There was also little traffic on a workday since the road was used mostly by weekend enthusiasts. But when Bell did come upon other cars, he shot past them so quickly that the drivers didn't even know he'd been there. A few tried to accelerate after him in sport, but all quickly fell away. There was simply nothing on the road that would catch Isaac Bell in his Model 5.

All too soon they came to the end of the parkway near the village of Brookhaven, just beyond Lake Ronkonkoma. Bell throttled down to a reasonable speed.

"Change of plans," he told Joe as he wheeled the big car into the parking lot of the town's post office.

Inside, an elderly clerk manned the counter. He was hand-sorting envelopes into several different piles. He looked up when a bell attached to the door chimed and regarded the two men from under a green banker's visor. "Can I help you gentlemen?"

"Hope so," Bell said, and showed him his Van Dorn badge and credentials. "To the best of your knowledge has anyone erected a radio antenna mast out this way?"

"Not the question I was expecting, but I'll bite. And the answer is, not to the best of my knowledge."

"If something like that were put up along a country road or behind some farmer's barn, is that something your mail carriers would notice and mention?"

"You're from the city, right?"

"Yes."

"Plenty to do there? Shows and restaurants? Hustle and bustle?"

"Yes," Bell said a little warily.

"We have growing grass and old fishermen repairing nets. So if something does change we all talk about it for days. Just a month or so ago, a farmer over in Yaphank had a Holstein calf with a heart-shaped blaze on its forehead. Some folks walked ten miles to see it. Others rode in on the LIRR. For a cow."

"I think I see your point," Bell said.

"I'm sure that you do."

"Does this apply as far out as Montauk or Greenport?"

"News of a heart-shaped blaze on a cow

would likely make it that far east. A new radio tower? Maybe yes and maybe no. How tall?"

Bell looked to Joe Marchetti for the technical details.

"At least a hundred feet, possibly more."

"Could still go either way. Best you head on out and ask. Hit up the postmaster in Riverhead, just to be safe. His name's Pete Peterson."

"Will do. Thank you for your time."

Back in the parking lot, Joe said to Bell, "That was a good idea."

"Thank you. I'd forgotten that rural post offices are frequently the epicenter of local gossip. Might as well let the natives gather intelligence rather than us wasting shoe leather."

The roads leading out to Long Island's North Fork were mostly gravel tracks carved through farmland and second-growth forests. The majority of the bridges were wooden and designed for lighter horse-drawn carriages, though metal spans were being introduced.

It was hard to believe a city of five million souls was a two-hour drive away. This part of Long Island was as rural as any Midwestern county.

The North Fork was a bust. They explored

countless single-lane tracks that branched off into the woods, but most ended at abandoned logging camps or private cabins. None of the postal employees they interrogated knew anything about new radio masts, and so they ventured back across Long Island until reaching the town of Riverhead, the Suffolk County seat and their best option for finding a decent hotel before it grew dark.

They lodged at the Long Island House on Main Street and could hear the rush of water along the Peconic River. As they were near the courthouse, the other lodgers there that night were attorneys from the city with cases pending out here. Not surprisingly, Bell and a few of the lawyers had plenty of mutual friends.

The following morning, they gassed up the Simplex and took the road to the South Fork, a region better suited for an illicit German radio tower, as it was closer to the open Atlantic. They took their time, trekking down as many county lanes as they could find.

After the tenth dead end in a row, Joe remarked, "As thorough as we're being, it's possible that our spies paid a farmer to put it up on his land far enough from a road that we wouldn't spot it, but still accessible overland by a truck."

"I know and I was thinking about flying over the area in a plane if we don't find anything this way."

"Because of the way you drive, why doesn't it surprise me you're a pilot too?"

Bell grinned. "We live in an age where life comes at you faster and faster. If you don't keep up, it's going to steamroll right over you."

"That's why you drilled me all about radios."

"Exactly. Like, I had no idea they can already transmit voice wirelessly. I thought it was all Morse code."

"First voice sent was in 1900. First radio program just six years later."

"It won't be long before people have radios in their living rooms to listen to news and music," Bell said. "Consider this, just eleven years after the Wrights flew at Kitty Hawk, an airline was launched in Florida to take paying passengers from St. Petersburg to Tampa. It folded after a few months, but aviation is going to change the world, mark my words."

Like the previous day, there were dozens of spurs and lanes off the main road out to Montauk that they needed to investigate. And also like the previous day, they found nothing. The town of Southampton was just opening up to early spring tourists lodged at the many seaside hotels. There was a radio enthusiast in town that Joe had spoken to days earlier to learn if he'd picked up any odd transmissions. The man said he'd ask a few others he knew in the region.

They met the radio aficionado for lunch at a downtown restaurant and all Bell got for the price of a meal was a lot of technical arcana and a negative answer about unusual transmissions.

Bell and Marchetti continued out all the way to Montauk Point. The trip had been a bust. Outwardly Bell remained cool as ever, but inside his frustration ate at him. He parked the car in a small lot next to the one-hundred-and-eleven-foot octagonal light-house. As all lighthouses have different exterior markings to help orient ships at sea during daylight hours, the Montauk tower was painted white with a thick band of brown halfway up.

"I guess we'll have to do an aerial survey," Joe said as the engine pinged and pinked as it cooled.

"Then there's the coast of New Jersey. Up near the city it's populated, but farther south is rural, just like this. The Germans could have erected their tower on some coastal farm and we'd never see it. There's just too much territory to cover."

Bell didn't look at the young naval officer as he spoke. He was watching the lighthouse keeper as he went about his duties. In the background was the sound of waves battering Montauk Point and the occasional screech of a gull.

Bell let his eyes climb the lighthouse to its apex, where a glass enclosure protected the station's massive Fresnel lens. Inspiration hit just then like an adrenaline jolt. He tapped Joe on the chest to get his attention and pointed up at the top of the lighthouse.

"What if the radio tower was already in place?"

"Damn," Marchetti breathed as he immediately got what Bell was hinting at. "They could dangle a cable from the light platform, send their transmission, and reel it back in, in no time."

"Let's go talk to the lighthouse keeper."

The man was just coming out of the tower with two gleaming metal buckets. Lamp oil, Bell guessed, and imagined the man had made innumerable journeys up to the top to fill the oil reservoir that kept the lamp shining all through the night.

His face was heavily lined and the hair that coiled out from under a battered sea captain's cap was as silver and stiff as old pewter wire. His pants were baggy, and his shirt so oft-laundered it looked ready to fall apart. His expression soured when he spotted the two strangers approaching.

"This ain't a place for tourists." His voice sounded like rocks tumbling down a chute.

Bell caught his Cape Cod accent, so he let a little more of his native Boston shine through when he replied, "Good thing then we're not tourists."

The keeper tilted his head ever so slightly. "Boston?"

"Back Bay originally," Bell replied, and sensed he had to explain his expensive car and clothes or the man's working-class sensibilities would prevent him from being of any assistance. "But my father did all right, so Beacon Hill after that."

"Suppose I can't blame a man for his birthright."

"My name is Isaac Bell, this is Navy Ensign Joe Marchetti." Bell paused, but the keeper gave no indication he wished to share his name. "I'm a detective working a case that could potentially lead to a group of German spies. Have you been approached by any strangers in the past few months?"

"Nope."

"How about whoever spells you when you have time off?"

"I take two weeks off a year in the spring. Other than that, I'm always here tending the lamp."

"Tough life," Joe said. "And as a seaman out on these waters pretty frequently, I want to thank you. Your light's guided me home on more than one occasion."

The praise seemed to crack a little of the man's hard facade. "German spies, huh?"

"Yes, sir," Joe answered. "They're getting word of what ships are carrying valuable war matériel to the U-boats blockading England. We've been all over Long Island looking for a radio transmission tower."

"When I saw the lighthouse," Bell added, "I thought it was possible the Germans could hang a wire off the top when you aren't around."

"I'm always around," the keeper said.

"You do sleep," Joe pointed out. "Is it possible they could access the tower during the day when you're asleep?"

The man grudgingly nodded.

"You lock the tower during the day?"

"Aye."

"If you'd let me, I'd like to examine the lock."

"Suit yourself, but you can't go inside."

"Why's that?"

"Ain't allowed for civilians to be inside a working lighthouse. The Bureau of Lighthouses made it a new rule when it was taken over by the Department of Commerce two years back. New inspector's real keen on that now."

Bell had his doubts about that. He knew from his friend at Penn Station whose brother-in-law was a lighthouse keeper that many were eccentrics, for who else would be drawn to such a solitary profession? He grabbed a leather satchel from under the Simplex's rear tonneau cover and followed the grizzled old mariner to the tower door. It was open, as he was still in the middle of his chores.

The lock wasn't particularly expensive — there wasn't anything to steal from a lighthouse other than the expensive Fresnel lens, which weighed over five tons, so good luck with that — but it was rugged enough to withstand the salt air. He pulled a flashlight and magnifying glass from the leather satchel and peered inside the lock to inspect its pins. He saw no telltale scratches that would indicate it had been picked.

That didn't mean a spy hadn't somehow gotten hold of an extra key.

He again felt the enormity of the task he'd

set himself. With Marion's insistence, he thought. Like he'd told his people, spies weren't like regular criminals. They were smart and motivated by more than the desire to get rich off someone else's work. He considered how many isolated lighthouses dotted the tristate area. It would take forever to check them all and vet each and every keeper. If not for the dead-on regional accent, this guy could be a German agent for all Bell knew.

And what if their mission didn't rely on radio transmissions at all? This could be a wild-goose chase of the first order. He'd promised Marion he'd give it a week, but his gut told him he'd need months, and even then there was no guarantee.

With a regular case, you have a victim. That person has family, friends, and rivals — people who are suspects — and eventually you crack the case and expose the criminal. Here he had nothing but hunches and three hundred and fifty miles of coastline spanning New York, New Jersey, and Connecticut, much of it uninhabited.

He took a deep breath to prevent himself from showing frustration, and stood. "Looks fine, so I guess there's no need for us to remain. Joe?"

"No. I can't think of anything either. Sorry

to take up your time, sir."

"No bother."

Bell turned to head back to the car, but stopped himself. "One question. All the lighthouses in the area have keepers, right?"

"They do. There's talk one day of automating them with electricity and all, but it'll be some time yet. Though I do have a telephone now."

"Okay, thanks, and have a fine rest of your day."

The two men returned to the car and Bell fired the engine, pulling out of the lot with an aggressive spin of the rear tires and a roaring burst from the exhaust. A man couldn't be expected to quell all signs of his frustration.

They were quiet for several minutes until Marchetti asked, "Any reason to check that other lighthouse near Southampton?"

"The Shinnecock? It's awfully close to town. It'd be a risk for the spies to transmit near where their signal could be intercepted."

"That's my take on it too. Where does that leave us?"

"With either too many leads or none at all," Bell replied. "We could search for radio towers and question every lighthouse keeper from Groton to Cape May and still not find much by way of results."

"I think you're right. I was going to suggest radio direction finders, but we'd need to be near enough to the transmitter at the exact time they're sending to do any good."

"And they might be using some system other than radio. Maybe a powerful signal lamp sending a code to a waiting ship." Bell fell silent for a moment before saying, "The possibilities to this case are literally endless."

17

After Bell dropped Joe off at the Brooklyn Navy Yard, he motored across the bridge and into the city during the tail end of rush hour. It took thirty frustrating minutes to get to the Knickerbocker Hotel. Automobiles were becoming so commonplace that the city needed to come up with a better system of getting them through intersections. He'd heard about a system of lights deployed in Cleveland and hoped something similar would be adopted in Manhattan. There simply weren't enough cops to run the semaphore signalers currently in use.

Most of the Van Dorn staff was already gone for the day when Bell returned to the office. He checked messages left on his desk and was about to head up to his suite when Archie rolled out of the restroom.

"Hey," he said. "How was Long Island?"

"A bust," Bell told him. "Anything on this end?"

"Nothing. None of the sailings of Germany's express liners matches with the sinking of any of the suspicious ships. Doesn't look like a courier crossing the pond is getting them the intelligence. Also, there are surprisingly few helium wholesalers, and they have just a handful of customers. No new regulars cropped up, so it doesn't look like our spies are lofting their antenna wire with balloons."

"Joe and I were inspired when we got to the Montauk lighthouse and considered a wire could be dangled down the side."

"Not bad."

"The keeper said no one's allowed into the tower and it didn't look like the lock was picked, so no clandestine entry either."

"He could be lying."

"Possible. Or someone has a second key, or the spies are using a different lighthouse, or they're not using lighthouses at all and have some other way of getting their message out and we're looking in the wrong direction."

"What do you want to do?"

Bell ran his hands over his face. His skin was gritty from the long drive. "I want to go upstairs, pour myself a stiff drink, and soak in a hot tub, preferably while Marion rubs my shoulders."

"That's the most sensible thing you've said in days — weeks even, I'd wager."

Bell chuckled wryly. "What a pal."

"You're lucky to have me. See you tomorrow."

"Night."

Marion had left him a note on the dining room table that she was dining with an old college friend who was in town, so Bell had his drink and soak alone. Afterward, he ate meatloaf brought up from the Armenonville restaurant downstairs. Marion came home just before midnight. Bell was awake enough and his wife tipsy enough that their reunion after a night apart was a delight for them both.

At breakfast the following morning, Bell told her about his trip to Montauk with Joe Marchetti, as well as Archie and the others striking out.

"What do you do now?" she asked, a buttered scone almost to her lips.

"I might rent a plane and search for the antenna from the air, but it feels like a long shot. I think driving around out there was a fool's errand, to be honest. There's simply too much territory. I sense that Joe sees it too."

"You're not giving up, are you?"

"No. I just wish I had a clue, a lead.

Anything. We're chasing ghosts and I don't know how to find their haunted house."

Marion watched him intently. "There are too many people working the docks to investigate how they gather information, and you don't know how they get said information to Germany. Right?"

"Trying to kick a man while he's down?"

"Never." She smiled prettily. "There is one more piece to this puzzle and that's to alert the British of the ships you suspect will be targeted and have the Royal Navy escort them once they reach the danger zone."

"Actually, Joe suggested that very thing when he laid out his case with our Navy Intelligence boys. He has no idea if the suggestion was taken, however. He said it was 'under advisement,' which to me sounds like Navy-speak for probably not going to do it."

Bell gulped the last of his coffee and pulled his suit jacket on over the shoulder rig for his Browning 9 millimeter and two spare magazines. He had been toying with the new Colt Model 1911 .45 caliber pistol and deeply admired the semiautomatic for its power and reliability, but on the range he proved to himself over the course of many hundreds of rounds that he was quicker and more accurate with a rapid-fire second shot with the 9 millimeter.

That second shot, which he called a double pull, was something else he'd been toying with. Because the .45's recoil was so heavy, Bell had abandoned the traditional firing stance used since dueling pistols first came into use. That is to present a side-on target to your enemy. Raise the pistol with one hand. Acquire the target through the sights. Pull the trigger and await the results.

Bell had started using a two-handed stance, curling his left hand over his right, which was wrapped around the weapon's grip. With his right elbow locked, a pistol's recoil was transferred up his arm to the big muscles of his shoulders and back. The barrel barely moved. In the traditional stance, the recoil overpowered the weaker muscles of the wrist, which allowed the barrel to rise sharply with every shot. Not a problem if your first bullet took down the bad guy straight away, but if it didn't, the armed thug had critical fractions of a second to return fire.

His new, firmer grip allowed him to fire twice and do so as fast as he could pull the trigger, assured the barrel hadn't risen and the perp was still squarely in his sights. A single full metal jacket round was potentially survivable for the amount of time it took to return fire. With a double pull and two 9-millimeter slugs in the chest, the guy's down and not coming back up.

Bell had recommended this style of shooting to all the other Van Dorns, though he didn't make it a requirement for the simple reason the two-handed stance meant twice as much of your body lay exposed to whomever may be shooting back. He'd leave the decision up to each individual agent.

He checked the drape of the tailored suit jacket and bent to kiss his wife's proffered cheek.

"See you tonight."

"Stay safe."

He threw her his most charming smile. "Don't I always?"

Bell didn't go straight to the office. Instead, he headed into the subway station under the building and hopped the train to Grand Central Station. The barber who'd run the shop inside the Knickerbocker Hotel had been lured away to the echoing station with the promise of a larger staff and bigger facility. It was only a few minutes out of his way, so Bell stayed true and dutifully followed him. Because Bell was a loyal customer, the barber, Gino, would always greet him as if he had just arrived for a scheduled appointment, thus allowing him to cut the line of commuters wanting to kill time in the chair.

"Ah, Mr. Bell. Right on time," Gino said when Isaac walked into the busy shop. "Almost done with this gentleman and you're next."

Bell got a few sour looks from others awaiting a trim, but didn't care.

Three minutes later, he was seated in the chair under a black cape and Gino's shears were working their magic. "What's the latest, Gino?"

"Mr. Saunders and his security people are none too happy of losing out on that kidnapping you foiled over at Penn Station."

"Couldn't be helped. They changed venues at the last minute and left us flat-footed. Good thing their security chief, Wendel Carver . . ." Bell's voice trailed off. "Damn. That's it."

He ducked his head to get out from under the scissors before leaping from the chair. He stripped off the cape and handed Gino a couple of bills from his wallet without looking up. "Sorry. I've got to run."

He rushed to a nearby bank of pay phones and closed the accordion door behind him to shut out the constant din of the busy terminal. He plucked the microphone off the Westinghouse Model 50's cradle and slid a nickel into the left slot atop the cast-iron unit. There was the normal hiss of the wires and then a click and an operator's voice came through.

"Number please?"

"Pennsylvania 6-3927," he said, giving her the number of Wendel Carver's desk, one of at least a hundred numbers he kept in his head.

"Carver," said the Penn Station security chief after two tinny rings.

"Go ahead, sir," the operator intoned, and clicked off the line.

"Wendel, it's Isaac Bell."

"What ho, Isaac. Nabbing more bagmen in my station?"

"No. I need to talk to your brother-in-law about lighthouses. You mentioned he'd been reassigned recently, and I was so distracted by the case that I didn't pay attention to where he is."

"Flat Point Light. It's south of Toms River on an island off Barnegat Peninsula. You'll need a boatman to get you out there."

Bell knew there wouldn't be phone service, so didn't bother asking. "Would I find him there now?"

"Sure. He knows I used to work for you, so it shouldn't be a problem. Just don't get him going on conspiracies."

"Check. Thanks, Wendel, and for your help the other day."

"Any time, boss, er, former boss."

Bell next called the livery stable where he garaged the Simplex and asked that they bring it around to the Knickerbocker and then rode the subway back to the hotel.

He caught Marion in front of her vanity wearing nothing more than a towel as she applied makeup with a light, artful touch. "Meeting the other man?" Bell said, and Marion jumped because she hadn't heard him return.

"For scaring me half to death, now I think I will," she harrumphed with a pout, but couldn't stay mad for more than a few seconds. "Lillian and I have a meeting with Alva Belmont."

"The suffragist?"

"I am impressed."

"I'm a detective. I get paid to know who all the agitators are."

Marion was about to protest, when she saw the grin on her husband's handsome face. He fully supported the right for women to vote, though he wasn't so keen on how much of it was tied to the temperance movement. "You are a rotten, rotten man," she said, and turned back to applying blush to her soft white cheek.

"A fact you've known since the first time we met." He went into their bedroom to pack a light bag, speaking through to the adjoining bath. "I have to go away again. Just overnight, because I have to be back in the city for the Tremont Potter trial, in case they need me as an expert witness."

"Ugh, that little pervert. What is this city coming to?" She came into the bedroom, now clad in a sheer robe. "You do remember we're having Archie and Lillian over Friday for dinner and cards."

Bell cinched his bag and noticed her outfit for the first time.

"Must you leave so soon?" she teased.

The head valet gave Bell a sour look for leaving his car parked at the curb in front of the hotel for nearly an hour. Bell didn't care about that one either.

It took the better part of two hours to make his way through the snarl and tangle of New York and northern New Jersey traffic. He wished there were more roads like Vanderbilt's Long Island Motor Parkway. He'd pay anything not to be stuck behind trucks, buses, cars, horse-drawn wagons, an ox-drawn cart loaded with coffins, and, for a time, a flock of sheep being herded by two boys and a dog. And this was just in Manhattan.

The drive south, once he broke out of the congestion around the city, was still frustrating. As soon as he could make speed, he'd have to slow down for the myriad of small towns clinging to each side of the road. Had he open license, he could have made Toms River in less than an hour. Instead, it took the better part of six.

Bell was old enough to remember a time before automobiles when he'd have needed a couple days on horseback, so he supposed he should feel grateful for the progress. But living on a cusp, as he did, between motorized transport and animal power, meant he had to live with the frustration of sharing the roads with swaybacked nags hauling rickety carts piled with hay and driven by farmers who liked to lumber in the middle of the road and to whom the sound of a blown horn was an invitation to slow the pace even more.

He also recalled the anxiety of trying to find gasoline in rural America, but now it seemed even the sleepiest burgs had at least one station and usually a semi-skilled mechanic. That was progress, in Bell's estimation.

He eventually arrived in the tiny village of Tuckerton, the closest to the Flat Point Light. He parked in a packed-dirt lot near the public pier. There, a small fishing boat's catch was being unloaded with the use of a dipper net suspended from the bow-heavy trawler's single mast. The silvery fish were dumped into the back of a truck, whose bed had been filled with crushed ice. Bell guessed the catch would be on a New York restaurant's table the following evening.

The four fishermen wore tall rubber boots and work shirts and all sported heavy beards, one red, two dark brown, and one silvery white. The dock reeked of fish oil that had permeated the wood and the rot of long-dead mollusks that had once clung to the pier's pilings.

"Afternoon," Bell said, and was met with a wall of suspicion. "I need to get out to the Flat Point Light. Any chance you fellows could help? I'd pay, of course."

"What do you need out there?" the oldest of the men asked. Bell guessed he was the captain/owner and that the two dark-haired fishermen were his sons, by the looks of them.

"I'm a private detective and I think the keeper, Ralph Pryor, might know something about a case I'm working." Bell then quickly added, "He's not a suspect or anything."

The captain thought for a few moments and finally said, "I can take you out at first light tomorrow and pick you back up again when we fill our hold. Twenty dollars cash money."

Bell had no desire to spend a night here nor spend an entire day cooped up in a lighthouse with Wendel Carver's conspiracy-loving oddball of a brother-in-law. "How about we leave as soon as you're finished, I spend about an hour talking to Pryor, and you bring me back. Hundred bucks."

One of the sons slapped the other on the chest and whistled at such a windfall. They most likely needed a month of good catches to make that kind of money. "Take it, Pa," the taller of the two said. "Weather's good and we got hours of daylight."

"A hundred?"

"You know what they say about New Yorkers?" Bell asked and said, "We got more money than sense."

"Now that there's a true statement. We'll need another twenty minutes to unload."

"Any place I can get a quick meal?"

"You passed it on the way here. Maeve's. It's on the right."

"Thanks. I'll be back in a half hour."

18

Once clear of the little harbor, Bell saw the lighthouse tower just a couple of miles south and realized he'd vastly overpaid for the ride, but it was a seller's market, and he really didn't want to spend more time here than necessary.

The tower was circular and made of brick and stood roughly eighty feet, about half the height of the Barnegat Light to the north. It was painted with alternating white and black vertical stripes as a visual day marker. It would have a unique flash period for its light as a night marker. It sat on a stone foundation that had been built on a small spit of an island that had probably once been connected to the rest of the main barrier island. There was a caretaker's cottage and a small pier. When they were close enough, Bell saw a little wooden sailboat with a single mast tied to the jetty. It was how Ralph Pryor went to fetch supplies in town.

The fisherman tied his boat behind the sloop and set about straightening the cabin from the day's labors. Bell leapt from the gunwale to the pier and set off to find Ralph Pryor. He first knocked on the keeper's cabin and called his name several times. No one home. Next, he entered the tower itself. It was a hollow cylinder with a wrought iron staircase coiling up along the outer wall. He saw a figure making its way down, so he leaned against the doorjamb, one ankle crossed over the other, to wait.

Ralph Pryor wore dungaree overalls and work boots, with a derby hat perched on his head. As he reached the bottom step and finally looked up, Bell could see he was a big man, heavy in the shoulders and tall, at least four inches above Bell's six feet. His dark eyes narrowed with feral suspicion.

"Who are you?"

"I'm Isaac Bell. Wendel Carver used to work with me at the Van Dorn Agency."

"You're that detective fellow."

"I am. I'm sorry to just show up like this, but you have no telephone. Would it be all right if I asked you a few questions?"

"Sure, I got some time." He moved over to a wooden panel set into the wall opposite the stair landing. The panel hinged open, and Bell saw that the lighthouse was actually constructed of two walls, an inner and an outer with a void space between them. Two sets of chain loops dangled in the opening and Pryor began to pull on one. The metal rattled as he worked.

"Are you resetting the weights that rotate the light?"

"Yup. Just like a giant grandfather clock. I haul the weights up and when I turn on the light and release them, they drop and an attached chain spins the beacon."

"How many times a night do you have to haul them back up?"

"Every eighteen minutes I do one and then eighteen minutes later do the second."

"All night?"

"All night."

"Good thing I didn't come out here to arm wrestle."

Pryor grunted a chuckle. "What can I do for you?"

"I want to know what happened to the previous keeper. The man you replaced."

"Died."

"I know that. What were the circumstances?"

A wary look crossed Pryor's face. "Was he murdered? Is that what you think this is?"

He started getting twitchy and his eyes lost focus. "I'm next, aren't I? Someone has it out for me. I knew it."

Bell had already decided not to take Ralph Pryor into his confidence, but he had to act quickly before he spun out of control, as Wendel Carver had warned him he would.

"Mr. Pryor, please." The man kept rambling under his breath. "Mr. Pryor. Ralph. Stop it! No one is trying to kill you. This is about an insurance scam, not murder. Someone put in a claim against an old life insurance policy the man had when he was a sailor."

He was winging it, but it was a good bet most lighthouse keepers had been mariners at some point in their lives.

Pryor seemed to settle down a little. "Insurance?"

"Yes. An old policy. I need to verify how he died. That's all. This has nothing to do with you at all."

"You're sure?"

"Not unless you're trying to rip off the Norfolk Assurance and Trust Company."

"Never heard of 'em."

"No reason you would. Please, Ralph, all I want to know is how he died."

"I didn't ask about the details, you know. Two keepers died at this very light nigh on thirty years ago. One had a heart attack and the other hit his head on the pier getting out of his boat, fell in the water and drowned."

"What about now? How did your predecessor die?"

"I'm not sure. I think he might have fallen. I didn't ask the police when I met them after I was assigned the light."

"When was that?"

"Been a month now."

The time frame worked for what Bell had in mind. "Did the police discover the body?"

He shook his head. "No. I hear it was the inspector from the Lighthouse Bureau."

"Who's that?"

"A new fellow named Conner or O'Conner. Haven't met 'im yet."

The hairs at the base of Bell's skull rippled as they came erect. While he and Joe Marchetti had struck out on Long Island, he hadn't given up entirely on the idea of a cell of German spies somehow using lighthouses as a way to communicate with a ship at sea who could then relay information to the German Navy.

How that feat was accomplished remained a mystery. In their conversations as they roamed the wilds of Suffolk County, Joe had admitted he didn't know how a clear enough transmission could reach the submarines or Germany itself. The French had made some headway on long-distance communication, but they had the Eiffel Tower, the tallest structure on Earth, to use as a radio mast.

Bell would let Joe suss out that particular answer while he came at the problem from how the information left the shore in the first place. He understood that spies didn't usually do the work themselves, preferring willing proxies like John Kramer, the kid back at the Winchester factory. Finding a sympathetic inspector was unlikely, though possible. But it was possible one had been bribed or blackmailed into doing the spy's bidding. Pretty clever, actually, he thought, if this was the case. But why draw unnecessary attention by killing a keeper? Unless Ralph Pryor's predecessor had seen something he shouldn't have or saw through the deception.

Doubtful.

He knew he was grasping at straws and still coming up empty-handed. Lighthouses probably didn't have a single thing to do with this. It wasn't even a case. It was really a waste of time and effort.

Bell thanked Pryor and returned to the pier, where the fishing boat captain was napping under the late afternoon sun. He came awake when Bell's boots landed on the deck. "Find out what ya needed to know?"

"In my line of work, the answers you get inevitably lead to more questions. So yes, I did, in a way, but now I need to find out even more."

Bell spent the night at a seaside motel farther up the coast and arrived back in Manhattan around noon the next day. He showered and changed into a fresh suit before descending to the Van Dorn offices.

Archie was sitting at one of the desks in the bull pen with his feet up and tie loosened. He held both parts of a stick phone to his face. "You're in luck," he said to whomever was on the wire. "He just walked in." He pressed the mouthpiece to his chest. "It's the DA's office. They need you in court immediately for that serial flasher you nabbed."

"Tremont Potter."

"His lawyer is trying to pull a fast one and they need you to stop him."

"I'll be there in thirty minutes."

"He'll be there in thirty," Archie repeated to the lawyer in the prosecutor's office and hung up. "Go and keep that little lecher off the streets of our fair city."

"On it, but I need you to interview someone for me. Contact the Bureau of Lighthouses in Washington, D.C. It's under the Commerce Department. Talk to their lighthouse inspector. A man named Conner or possibly O'Conner."

"What for?"

"I've got nowhere else to turn."

Archie laughed. "Whenever I look up 'dogged' in the dictionary, there's your smiling face."

"I have no choice. I told Marion I'd work this thing a week and she keeps giving me pitying glances." Bell grabbed the hat he'd hung moments earlier from the coat tree by the door. "Tell him you're investigating insurance fraud. That's how I handled it with Wendel's brother-in-law. See you later."

Archie watched him go and then picked up the phone again. He waited ten minutes for a long-distance wire to Washington to become free and dialed the Commerce Department building, only to find the newly minted Commerce Department was scattered across the nation's capital in a half dozen separate buildings. Usually a lucky man, Archie didn't manage to call the right location on his first try and had to call another number he was supplied. The wait for the second long-distance line had doubled.

They really needed more telephone wires.

Thirty minutes after being tasked with finding Conner or O'Conner, Archie had the whereabouts of one Devlin Connell, and now his customary luck held. Connell was inspecting the Romer Shoal lighthouse in the Lower Bay just south of the Verrazzano-Narrows.

Archie cabbed down to the Battery, where he hired a water taxi to take him out to the light. It was a beautiful spring day. The breeze off the water was fresh and the scent of the ocean once past the polluted swill that drifted around Manhattan was a delight.

The ride took just over an hour. The taxi was faster than it looked and soon they approached the stumpy little lighthouse sitting on its own rocky island. The tower was no more than sixty feet tall, red on top and white on the bottom. An empty water taxi much like the one Archie had hired was tied to the stone jetty.

As Archie had yet to pay the fare, he had no fear of being stranded, so he leapt onto the dock and made his way to the tower, ignoring the two-story keeper's house.

"Hello," he called once he was inside the tower, his voice booming and echoing in the vaulted space.

"Hello?" a voice called back from the top. "Who's there?"

"Archie Abbott is my name. I'm looking for Devlin Connell."

"Ya found him, but he's busy."

"Won't take but a couple of minutes of your time."

"Ach," he said. His voice had an Irish lilt. "Ya can't come up. New rules. Give me a minute to finish up and I'll come down."

Archie waited outside in the sunshine, a freshly lit cigar smoldering between his fingers.

Devlin Connell's appearance was a startling one. He was tall, but gaunt. So gaunt he looked cadaverous, his cheeks sucked in rather than curving out. His forehead was broad and his hair was sparse, oily and brittle looking. His eyes were sunken into purplish sockets, so he looked like he was sporting a pair of week-old shiners. The bones of his rib cage poked against his shirt and appeared as if they held half the allotment of necessary organs. His wrists were as slender as a maiden's and his shoulders poked through his jacket like the tucked wings of a vulture. His skin was a wan gray, like old bathwater, wrinkled not by time but by some horrible affliction.

Archie managed to keep the revulsion

from showing on his face but not the pity in his eyes. It didn't take a medical degree to know this man was dying, most likely from a cancer.

"Devlin Connell," he said to introduce himself. When they shook hands, it was a bit awkward because the inspector's right arm couldn't fully extend, either through some defect at birth or the result of an accident.

"Pleased to meet you. I'm Archie Abbott and I'm an investigator looking into the death of the lighthouse keeper at the Flat Point Light." He took out a pen and small notepad. These were merely props, as his mind absorbed details like a sponge.

"Bill Sherman."

Archie was too smooth to give away that Isaac hadn't told him the victim's name. "That sounds right. I had to take over this assignment when its lead investigator fell ill. I'm afraid I wasn't properly briefed."

"What can I help you with?"

"As you were the person to find him, I just wanted to get your take on his death. For insurance purposes. There is no payout if it was a suicide."

"Haven't you read the police report?" Connell asked.

"I have," Archie lied, "but we're required

to interview the person who found the body as well. For our underwriters."

"Poor sod didn't off himself, I can say with some certainty. When I found him, he was at the base of the stairs, and when I went up to take a look, I found a lot of spilled kerosene near the top next to two overturned buckets. Looks to me like he tripped on his way to fuel the lamp and took a nasty tumble."

"What did you do after you found the body?"

"I went to fetch the police. I returned to the light with them plus a local doctor who rotates in as the county coroner. He said the injuries he could see — bruising, broken neck, and the like — were consistent with a fall. He also noted Bill's mouth smelled of alcohol."

"That much of a problem among lighthouse keepers?" Archie asked.

"Not if they do their job properly, though most drinkers wouldn't last a week with the responsibility of manning a post."

"What happened then?"

"They took the body away. I asked them to telephone the Lighthouse Bureau in Washington to tell them what had happened and that the light needed a replacement tender. I saw to the lamp that night and for two more until the new man arrived."

Connell must have been used to doubters of his abilities because of his arm, so he added, "Most keepers carry two buckets at a time. I can only manage one, so I just double the number of trips. Not efficient, but it keeps my legs strong."

"As far as you know, had anyone visited the lighthouse recently? Do keepers have a logbook or something like that?"

"Nay. I don't know anything about visitors, but from experience I know it's not likely. Especially for lights out on islands like this one or down at Flat Point. What's the point of rowing out, right?"

"I have to agree. Judging by the size of the caretaker cottage over there and the lacy curtains in the windows, it would appear some keepers have family with them. Did he?"

"Bachelor."

"Did you know him well?"

"Never met him, actually. Inspections like what I'm doing now are a new thing. All part of the reorganization."

"I see. Were you a keeper yourself?"

"Aye, back in Ireland and then in the Pacific Northwest. I got the job of East Coast inspector when I came to New Jersey so my wife could be closer to her ma, who's turned frail in her old age."

Archie tucked the notepad in an outside pocket and the fountain pen into an inside breast pocket, thinking the man's wife was soon to be performing the same duties for her husband. "I think that's all I need, Mr. Connell. Thank you for your time. Just curious, how long does it take to inspect a lighthouse?"

"I'll be here through to the morning. Can't inspect a light when it isn't lit."

"Makes sense. Good day."

"Good day."

19

Eddie Tobin would never be considered a handsome man. His eyes were small, his face a little crooked somehow, and he had such bad teeth and so many missing that his mouth looked like it was caving in on itself. His breath usually kept people at an arm's length too. But as he stood outside Bell's office and knocked on the jamb, there was such light in his eyes that he looked less fishlike and more human than usual.

"I might have something for you, Isaac."

Bell was back from the Tremont Potter trial and wanted to get back on track with what he'd missed while wasting a day in a courtroom with the weaselly little lecher and his equally oily attorney. At least he didn't have to go back the following day. Potter was spending the next eight years at Sing Sing.

The sun had sunk behind the New Jersey Palisades an hour earlier, so he worked by the light of just a single lamp on his desk. His jacket hung over the back of his chair and his shirtsleeves were rolled up past his forearms. A crystal tumbler of something amber and peaty was within easy reach.

"Come on in. Drink?"

"Never said no yet." Tobin took a seat opposite his boss while Bell splashed a couple of fingers of Scotch into a glass.

"Please tell me you're not teasing me. I've had a lousy day."

"It might be something. It might be nothing. But at least it's something we can check out."

"What have you got?" Bell's chair creaked as he pressed back into it.

"There's a group down on the docks who call themselves the Bavarian Brotherhood. Mostly it's a thing for German dockworkers. Not quite a union, but more than a social club. They help each other out during rough times, widows' funds, teaching new immigrants the ropes. Like that."

"Doesn't sound too ominous."

"They're not. Secret, sure, but on the up-and-up as far as I can tell. Here's the thing, though. One of their young members is seeing a girl whose brother is one of my informers. He tends bar at a saloon near the docks on the East River. Doesn't matter. The German boy tells his love that some of the guys in the Brotherhood are working with an outsider on something big."

"What is it?"

Eddie shook his head. "Kid wouldn't tell her what it is, no matter how much she pouted, but he says it's important and he's honored to be part of it and that there's a meeting tonight at ten in their club."

Bell said nothing as he mulled this over.

Eddie ticked off his fingers as he made his case. "A, it's a German group. B, they're acting out of character. C, they're working with an outsider. And D, they're trying to keep it secret. Like I said, maybe nothing, but also maybe something."

Isaac leaned forward, a ghost of a smile cocking the side of his mustache. "Eddie, I'd say this may be the closest thing to a lead we've had since Ensign Marchetti first walked through our door. Where's their clubhouse?"

"Lower East Side, not far from Tompkins Square Park."

"Not many Germans left in that area since the *Slocum* disaster."

Eddie just shrugged.

Bell checked his watch. He had an hour to get over there and scope it out before the mysterious meeting. "I wish Archie was back. He speaks some German. Might come in handy."

"There's a kid in the office, would have been John Schmidt had his father not changed it to Smith at Ellis Island. He's just a page, but ya gotta work with what ya got."

"Is he here?"

"He works nights taking messages."

Eddie followed Bell out into the bull pen. Van Dorn's New York office never closed, but it was usually pretty quiet at night. Much of the work was typing up notes and preparing briefings on ongoing cases. The phone still rang, and on-duty agents still went out on calls, but mostly it was sedate compared to the frenetic day shift.

Eddie pointed to a lanky blond boy of no more than eighteen. He hadn't yet filled out, so he looked like a caricature of Ichabod Crane, all arms and legs and with nearly obtuse-angled joints. Bell had a hard enough time including the youthful Marchetti on something so banal as driving the backroads of Suffolk County. There was no way he was going to take an untested errand boy on a potentially dangerous stakeout.

"Forget it," he muttered to Tobin. "I don't need a translator that bad. That kid hasn't shaved more than twice in his life."

"We all started out that young," Eddie said.

"But our first cases weren't professional spies and saboteurs. I cut my teeth fetching food for the guys who were actually on a stakeout of a cheating wife."

"Want me to come?"

"Yeah, but just to sit in a car a block or so away. If I get into any trouble, I'll need you to alert the boys at the Fifteenth Precinct."

"321 East Fifth."

"That's the place."

Bell changed into dark clothing and pulled a black wool watch cap over his bright blond hair. He also brought thin black leather gloves. He left his shoulder holster and Browning pistol, but kept the little derringer he usually secreted somewhere on his person along with a boot knife sheathed on the outside of his right ankle. His reasoning was that if he was caught, he'd have an easier time talking his way out of it without a large-caliber pistol hanging under his left arm.

He was almost out of his office when his mind tricked him into smelling the smoke and feeling the heat of the fire in the basement of John Kramer's boardinghouse and how close the German spy had come to burning him alive. He turned back and transferred the Browning automatic from its shoulder holster to one he clipped to his belt at the small of his back. "To hell with talking my way out."

Twenty minutes later, Eddie Tobin was in an agency car parked a block and a half from the storefront the Bavarian Brotherhood used as their social club. His view was only occasionally obstructed by traffic, even at this late hour. He'd driven past the four-story brick building situated mid-block of nearly identical structures moments earlier, paying it not the least attention. Crouched in the Ford's backseat so only his eyes were visible, Bell had studied the facades intensely. Retail or offices occupied the ground floors, while there were either apartments or additional office space on the higher levels. Most of the upper floors were dark, while a restaurant on the corner was still open, with two couples still at sidewalk tables with a bored waiter loitering at the door.

The Bavarian Brotherhood was open for business as well. There were two windows flanking its door, one with the shades drawn but the other showing a bar-like room inside with a hazy atmosphere of heavy smoking. Two men leaned outside the establishment, heavy men, thick through the middle with simian arms and complementary apelike faces. They were a show of muscle to deter the curious from getting too close.

Bell had exited the Model T when Eddie found the perfect vantage and jogged back toward his target, ducking down the cross street before reaching his destination. As he suspected, halfway down the street a narrow alley bisected the block of buildings where the Germans had their club. It smelled awful and he had to step over a gray-bearded sot passed out with a bottle at his elbow. Overhead, a few lights still showed like coronas around drawn bedroom curtains. The angry strains of a spousal argument tumbled down and the sound of a woman sobbing quietly in the night was just perceptible.

He was not surprised that the buildings hadn't yet been fitted with iron fire escapes. The Triangle Shirtwaist Factory fire had occurred only four years earlier and despite all the new regulations, most landlords remained unwilling to install expensive safety equipment.

Bell stepped around garbage cans and loose refuse and ignored the scampering of rats. He counted the number of back doors and when he came to the Bavarian Brotherhood's, he saw they had upgraded the typical cheap lock for something a little more substantial. He knelt and pulled a leather case containing his set of lockpicks from his back pocket. He looked around. The drunk had moved on apparently.

Substantial as it was, Bell finessed the lock open in just a few seconds. The sweat on his brow had nothing to do with nerves. The night air remained sticky hot. He opened the door a fraction of an inch. The hinges were quiet, and he saw no light spilling over the threshold. He eased the door open just enough to slip inside and closed it behind him.

He found himself on a staircase landing. To his right, darkened steps descended into the basement, while ahead of him, up two wooden treads, was another door. Light seeped from underneath it. Bell carefully padded down the cellar stairs. The smell of tobacco was overwhelming, like he'd just entered the biggest cigar store he'd ever been to. He had his single-battery D cell flashlight and he flicked it on. The basement was packed with wooden crates of cigars imported from Cuba.

It wasn't a great leap of logic to think none of them had U.S. government revenue stickers. It looked like the Bavarian Brotherhood was branching out into import fraud.

Bell was pretty certain this had nothing to do with his case, but he never left a job half finished, so he remounted the stairs. He knew the building was pretty deep and didn't think the door up the two steps opened onto the club proper. He listened with his ear down at floor level. He heard nothing. The door handle turned smoothly in his gloved hand and again the hinges were silent.

The door opened to a hallway with a heavy beaded curtain at the far end. There were two open doors that led to restrooms and a narrower door he guessed was a janitor's closet. There was one dim sconce on the wall, but most of the light came from beyond the curtain.

Bell kept himself pressed tight to the wall opposite the sconce, his senses straining. He could hear murmurs now and an occasional bark of laughter. He reached the curtain. From out in the bar area, he'd be a black shadow in an otherwise dark hallway. The curtain's beads were made of cheap crystal that would chime merrily at the slightest disturbance.

Using just one finger, he parted two strands so slowly the beads touched without making a sound. He opened a slot no bigger than a keyhole, filled his lungs so he wouldn't need to breathe for a few moments, and pressed his eye closer to the opening. Ten or so men were sitting or standing around a large table covered in green felt cloth normally used for card games. A long empty bar ran along one wall. One of the cigar crates from the basement sat on the floor nearby, opened, and two garishly decorated cigar boxes sat atop the baize.

The men were collectively putting out as much smoke as a Pittsburgh steel mill.

Bell didn't know any of the Germans whose faces he could see. A couple had their backs to him. One of the men seated away from Bell had a slump to his shoulders, a gesture that wasn't uncommon, but it stuck with Bell anyway. The scene was what he'd expected when he discovered the cigars. They were wooing buyers for their cache of stogies they'd smuggled off a freighter newly arrived from Havana.

He was satisfied that Eddie's tip wasn't their case, though he'd gladly drop a nickel to the boys at the Fifteenth Precinct.

The club's main door opened, and everyone turned in unison. The newcomer was on the older side but moved with the vigor of a man on a mission. He shouted something in German and pointed straight at Bell lurking in the hallway. Recognition hit like a tire iron. It was the tramp from the alley. They must supply him with booze to watch the back.

Bell felt a hot burst of adrenaline hit his bloodstream. He whirled, the curtain ringing like a child's Christmas bell concert as he fled. In the front room, chairs were thrown back, and men began rushing for the hallway at the club's rear exit.

He crashed through the first door and threw himself at the second, reaching the alley in record time. He turned left, continuing down the narrow track rather than doubling back the way he'd come. With the pursuers so close, he'd never reach Eddie in time for them to escape in the car. The Tin Lizzie was a good automobile, rugged and reliable, but not exactly quick out of the blocks.

Seconds after Bell reached the alley, the club's rear door banged open again and again as men poured out in hot pursuit. Some were yelling challenges, while others grunted at the effort of keeping up. Bell's shoes pounded the hard cement and flew over obstructions barely perceived in the alley's near-total darkness. He heard one pursuer smack into something and go down in a tangle of limbs and shouted German oaths.

Bell emerged from the alley, nearly colliding with a pair of men walking arm in arm and swaying drunkenly.

"Watch it, buddy," one slurred.

There was enough light from streetlamps and the moon for Bell to see, and he poured on the speed. Like a pack of wolves with the scent of prey in the air, the Germans exploded from the narrow alley, bowling over the late-night revelers. Several more went down in the scrum, but most avoided the accident and kept coming. There were a couple of pursuers younger and faster than Bell who would soon be on his heels.

Bell knew his gun could end the chase in short order, but if things went bad, he was the one without a legal defense. He'd broken into their establishment and they had every right to pursue him. He rounded the corner back onto Avenue B, where the entrance to the Bavarian Brotherhood's club was located.

He barely ducked under the haymaker thrown at him by one of the Germans who'd left their joint via the front door in anticipation of him coming that way. Bell's momentum sent him to the pavement, but he tumbled with the fall like an acrobat and came up running just as hard as before. The bruiser with the fast fists needed a second to untorque himself before he joined the two twentysomethings who were closing fast from behind.

Bell angled himself off the sidewalk as a double-decker bus made its way down the street. He let it pass inches from his shoulder before he hooked an arm around a rear railing and let the autobus yank him off his feet. His body was parallel to the ground for a moment and it felt like his shoulder joint would separate at the strain, but his quick action made his pursuers overshoot.

Bell hauled himself around the back of the bus so he could get to the bottom landing of the open-air staircase that swept up to the second deck. The Germans turned as quickly as they could and started running after the bus, but it was no use. The bus was going too fast and they'd lost too much ground. Bell started up the stairs and threw them an ironic little wave as they began to slow loose-leggedly, knowing their quarry had gotten away.

Then a brass bell dinged, and the bus driver eased off the accelerator and gently started applying the brake. They'd reached a passenger's stop and he was pulling over.

Like a starter's pistol at the beginning of a

foot race, the chime launched the pursuers as if they'd been given a second lease on life. Bell was too close to the top of the stairs to backtrack, so he rushed all the way up as the quickest runner reached the rear of the bus and began to pull himself upward, his chest blowing like a bellows.

The bus stopped for just a moment before accelerating from the curb.

To Bell's surprise, more than half the benches on the upper deck were occupied, but he realized he should have known. On a warm night such as this, catching the breeze from a moving bus was a popular pastime for young couples. He moved halfway down the aisle and turned just as the first of the Bavarian Brotherhood foot soldiers reached the second level.

With so many people around, Bell didn't dare pull out his gun. This would have to happen the old-fashioned way. The German rushed at Bell with his arms spread wide. Bell let him come, and when he was a second away from a devastating tackle, he used the back of the benches on either side of him to kick his coiled legs up in the air and then unspring them with everything he had. The attacker had plenty of momentum, but Bell was anchored by his tight grip. His boots compressed the man's rib cage, cracking a few, and blowing every molecule of air from his lungs. The German was propelled backward like he'd been yanked by a rope and he fell to the deck, wheezing and gaping like a fish.

Bell backpedaled as the crowd reacted in shock to the sudden violence. Two more of the Brotherhood reached the top deck. One leapt over his fallen comrade, while the other briefly knelt to check on his friend. The man rushing Bell carried a wooden stick similar to a patrol cop's billy club. A properly placed blow could break an arm or partially crush the skull.

Rather than wait to be struck, Bell rushed the man, throwing off his timing. Bell had gone low, wrapping his arms around the German's upper thighs so that when Bell stood, he heaved the man up and over his shoulders. The guy hit the floor in a heap. Bell managed to kick the nightstick under a bench just as the third German threw himself at him.

He backed up again, nearing the front of the bus, so when the young gangster leapt at him, Bell managed to hook an arm around the man's shoulders and bodily throw him off the upper deck. The German hit the bus's hood with a shuddering bang, and to the driver's credit he didn't slam on the brakes when the body suddenly appeared in front of him. That move would have rolled the German off the hood and under the front tires of the six-ton vehicle.

Instead, the driver accelerated hard enough so the thug rolled up against the windshield. He was glassy-eyed and dazed, but understood how close to death he'd just come.

Bell whirled and started running for the rear stairs, hoping to catch a break. It wasn't meant to be. Two more Brotherhood members raced up the curving staircase. They were slower than their comrades because they were so much bigger. Muscle hung off them in thick slabs. Their arms were as big as Bell's thighs. Neither had a neck.

One sported a pair of brass knuckles the size of a dime store paperback.

Bell sprang left onto an empty bench and ran for the edge of the bus. He leapt over the side, but kept a strong grip on the safety railing as his body pivoted over the void. His feet hit the lower deck and he scrabbled to find purchase on the bus's smooth side. He hauled himself hand over hand across the length of the bus, trying to keep away from the lumbering goons as they chased after him.

Bell's scrabbling feet finally found an open

window. His boot brushed against someone sitting in the seat next to it.

"Coming through," he yelled, and pushed himself away from the bus so that when he swung back again, he could jackknife his legs and slide through the window.

Bell landed on the cushioned seat and quickly got to his feet, repeating that he was sorry as more passengers either screamed or gasped at his dramatic entrance. He looked outside and saw Eddie Tobin had witnessed the whole thing and was in pursuit. The avenue was four-laned, allowing him to keep an easy pace with the bus. He saw Bell eyeing him and waved. Bell gestured that Eddie should approach the rear platform.

Tobin nodded and slowed while Bell raced down the aisle to the consternation of more riders. The men up top would be heading for the stairs that led to the bus's rear platform. It was going to be close.

"Stop that, you," the driver shouted when he looked up into his mirror and saw Bell running.

Bell reached the empty platform. Eddie had the Model T tucked right up against the bus with just an inches-wide gap separating the two vehicles. Isaac didn't break stride. He stepped out onto the sedan's running board and gripped the passenger-side window frame. Eddie began veering away while Bell looked back over his shoulder. The German brute without the brass knuckles sprang with an unexpected grace from near the bottom of the staircase and landed on the running board next to Bell, one meaty hand clutching at the metal roof. The other he pistoned toward Bell's head. To avoid the telegraphed blow, Bell leaned back as far as he could, nearly banging his head on the side of the bus.

Eddie saw Bell had gone out too far, so he cranked the wheel and Bell fell back in toward the car. The German was flung against the Ford's roof. Bell tried to use momentum to slam the guy's face into the metal, but the man tensed the muscles of his back and core and there was no overcoming his vast strength.

Bell then rammed his boot heel into the inside of the monster's knee. The joint buckled and the German grunted at the pain, but still had fight left in him. He fired another punch at Bell's face. He avoided the worst of it by turning his head, but even the glancing blow blurred his vision and made his ears ring. Bell threw a punch of his own, but the German ducked his head behind one massive shoulder. Bell felt like he'd punched a truck tire.

They traded several more awkward blows, but with Eddie constantly adjusting the wheel, both combatants focused most of their concentration on not falling off the speeding car.

Bell saw a tiny opening and kicked out at the German's knee again, and this time the thug couldn't keep weight on it and his eyes showed the first sign of fear. Eddie kept pace with the traffic, not sure what he could do to help his friend.

Bell knew he had the upper hand, but only for as long as it took the German to work through the pain. "Hard left," he shouted. "Now."

Just as Tobin wheeled the Ford around an intersection and toward a cross street, Bell kicked out and caught the inside of the German's other knee. The combination of centrifugal force and the tearing of ligaments in his good knee tumbled the man off the running board and onto the street. He rolled with his limbs tucked tight. The car behind the Model T had smartly backed off during the fight, so its driver had plenty of room to swerve and avoid hitting the fallen thug.

Bell saw the German sit up and clutch his ruined knee before Eddie took another turn and Avenue B was lost from his sight. No sooner had Bell felt he could relax than a car behind them whipped around the corner and accelerated hard in their direction. A man was leaning out the passenger window with a big silvery revolver in his hand.

The Brotherhood hadn't given up.

"Eddie, punch it."

Tobin had heard the screech of tires as the pursuing car cranked around the corner and already had his foot to the floor. Bell clung to the window frame with his right hand while he groped for his automatic with his left. It was awkward and made even more difficult with Eddie slaloming through traffic.

The German fired and the blast sounded like he'd attached pistol grips to a railway gun. The bullet tore through the Model T's trunk, blew a tuft of horsehair ticking out of the rear seat, did the same to the front passenger seat, and still had the power to drill through the dashboard.

The recoil sent the shooter's arm high into the air. Bell had seconds at best. He finally unsnapped his Browning and pulled it from the holster with his off hand. He cocked the gun and aimed. He fired and the bullet punctured the grille, producing a billowing cloud of steam. The German resighted his pistol and pulled the trigger at the moment the scalding spray from the radiator shot past his head and arm and parboiled his exposed skin. The round missed so badly, it gouged a furrow in the pavement just ahead of his own car.

Bell recentered his aim and fired again. And once more, until the three holes were venting the radiator. The engine quickly overheated and seized in a mechanical howl of grinding steel. The driver was quick enough to engage the clutch to prevent the car from coming to a catastrophic stop, but there was nothing he could do as the vehicle lost power and the Model T vanished into the night.

"You mind stopping so I can ride inside like a normal person?" Bell said through the open window when they were finally clear.

"You got it." Eddie pulled over to the curb.

Bell got into the car, still a little shaken from the night's escapade. He reholstered his Browning.

"Well?" Eddie said after a few seconds of silence. "Was it worth it at least?"

"Ever been hunted by a pack of Germans?" Bell didn't wait for the answer. "Even if the spy was there, trussed up like a Thanksgiving turkey, it wouldn't have been worth it. But insult to injury, they have nothing to do with our case. The Bavarian Brotherhood has branched out into selling hijacked Cuban cigars."

"Damn." A moment later he asked, "Do you at least wanna tell the cops?"

"Not this time," Bell said, massaging the side of his head where he'd taken the punch. "The Brotherhood doesn't know who stirred up their little hornet's nest and it's best they never find out. Let's just call tonight a waste of a perfectly good evening and never mention it again."

20

Bell met Archie for drinks at the Yale Club near Grand Central. Archie always joked about being in the lion's den, seeing that he was a Princeton man, but admitted the food was good and the service excellent. As always, the atmosphere was one of muted elegance.

They ordered martinis as soon as they got to the bar.

"How'd it go?" Bell asked while the barman made their drinks.

"I think it's a total bust," Archie said. "That guy looks like he has one foot in the grave already."

"What do you mean?"

"I think he has cancer and he's not long for this world. He's a tall Irish fellow, but so thin it doesn't look like he'd eaten for a month. He had that look — you know the look — that says he knows his number is about up."

"What about the dead guy at Flat Point?"

"Thank you for not telling me his name, by the way. Connell said it was Bill Sherman, and I said I wasn't sure because I had taken over the investigation and hadn't been properly briefed."

"Did he buy it?"

"You insult me, sir," Archie said with mock outrage as he set down his glass. "I am a consummate liar, Olympic contender quality, in point of fact. Of course he believed me. Seriously, I can't picture Connell overpowering a toddler, much less a grown man who hauls forty pounds of kerosene up a hundred steps ten times a night. Guy also has a bum wing."

Bell thought back to Ralph Pryor's size and strength. He doubted the lighthouse service was home to many weak men. The job was just too physically taxing.

"He could still be our guy if the spy's running him. You said he's Irish. There are factions in Ireland that want to see an end to British rule. I've heard some are pretty radical. Could be a motive for helping the Germans," Bell said. "Maybe the spy killed Sherman."

"I don't know," Archie said, unconvinced.

"To further muddy the waters of this case," Bell went on, "Joe left word for me at the office that he still doesn't know how the Germans manage sending a message reliably across the Atlantic. He mentioned something about newly invented vacuum tubes."

"Like a Eureka vacuum cleaner?"

"The message said tubes, not cleaners, and I don't see how a domestic cleaning machine could transmit radio signals."

"I wouldn't be surprised," Archie said impishly. "They're getting pretty fancy. My staff has one with a light on it to better clean dark corners."

Bell chuckled tonelessly and took another sip of his drink. "It could be time to admit that Joe Marchetti might be wrong about this whole thing and that the Germans aren't marking specific ships, but are just getting lucky with the vessels they sink. By now just about every ship leaving New York bound for Britain is carrying war matériel of some form or another. They're all targets."

"You seemed pretty convinced the kid was right not that long ago."

"I know, and now I have to consider my judgment was clouded because I'd convinced myself the spymaster who died in New Haven wasn't acting alone."

"A theory for which you had no proof,

correct?"

Before Bell answered, another patron in a stylish suit sat at the bar, ordered a Scotch, and opened an evening-edition paper in a ruffled flurry.

"But a theory I have a lifetime of experience tells me is possible," he finally said.

"You remember the last piece of advice Van Dorn gives recruits on their first day?"

"Same thing he told us."

In unison the two friends said in their best impression of the old man, "Listen to your gut. But not when you're hungry. Ho ho ho."

The guy reading the paper suddenly cursed. "Damn those German butchers."

"What happened?" Archie asked, as he was closer to the businessman. Bell leaned forward to hear.

The Yale alum pointed at the bottom left headline. "Says here they torpedoed a civilian ship carrying a delegation of American Navy officers headed to England with a group from the Royal Navy who'd been visiting Washington and the Brooklyn Navy Yard."

"Was the ship out of New York?" Bell asked.

"Ah, hold on." The man opened the paper to an interior page, where the headline story continued, and kept scanning. "Yep. Left the city six days ago. The U-boat got her someplace off the Irish coast. It happened at night. All that was found the next morning was some scraps of wood, an oil slick, and a single overturned lifeboat."

"How many Americans?"

Ever since the death of Leon Thrasher, a mining engineer from Massachusetts aboard the steamship *Falaba* when it was torpedoed back in March, the nation's populace grew angrier with each additional American death reported. Some in Congress were already calling for a declaration of war, though for the time being President Wilson seemed content to write strongly worded letters of condemnation. Bell wondered if this latest provocation would change the famous pacifist's mind.

The man said, "Six Brits, six of our boys. The ship itself was from Sweden. All told, more than a hundred people died."

Bell and Archie exchanged a look. Archie said, "Having a suspicion isn't the same as having proof."

Bell added bleakly, "And without any clues, leads, or even reasonable assumptions, proof is a long way off."

Prospects for a break in the case were snuffed out completely the following morning when two strangers entered the Van Dorn offices. In truth, one was a stranger, a stooped young man Bell had never seen before. The other was an old acquaintance of Bell's who he hadn't seen since they were teenagers. He easily recognized the man who that boy had become. He was tall, thin, and with undeniable magnetism. His nose was sharp and his forehead broad and intelligent. He had the look of a man with both ambition and confidence.

"I'm looking for Isaac Bell," the man said in the cultured mid-Atlantic voice that was common among the privileged elite of the Eastern Seaboard.

"You found him, Frankie," Bell said from the doorway of an office he'd been using for privacy.

The two looked at each other for a charged moment, Bell with an easy smile and the other man with a more critical look to the blue eyes behind wire-framed spectacles. Then the man's face softened, though he did not return the smile. He said, "Frank will do just fine."

"Who's this?" Archie asked from behind his desk, sensing an undercurrent even if he couldn't explain it.

"This is Frank Roosevelt, current Assistant Secretary of the Navy," said Bell.

"Frank, this is my number two, Archie Abbott."

Roosevelt was taken aback for a second as he sought a memory that came quickly. "I believe I've seen you onstage, Mr. Abbott."

Archie stood to shake Roosevelt's hand. "You have a good memory, sir. I haven't acted in years."

"I forget the play, but I remembered you well," Roosevelt said, becoming more charming after his initial touch of frost at seeing Bell.

"You two know each other?" Archie asked.

"Not since we were kids," Bell said in such a way as to close that line of inquiry.

Roosevelt introduced his aide. "This is Kurt Miller, my assistant."

Miller was younger than Roosevelt, who himself was the youngest Assistant Secretary in Navy history. He had a dark complexion and soft features and gave Bell the impression that he wasn't the star of his own life, but seemed happy being a bit player in someone else's — someone like the meteoric Franklin Delano Roosevelt. His briefcase was big enough so that his boss wouldn't have to carry one of his own.

Archie said, "Let me guess, Secretary of the Navy . . . You fellows lost a battleship and hope the Van Dorn Agency can find it?"

Roosevelt was too serious of a man to even smile at Archie's attempt at humor. "No. Nothing like that. Have you gentlemen heard what happened to the *Duchess of Värmland*?"

"Sunk with all hands including six American sailors," Bell said gravely.

"Six officers including one Admiral," Roosevelt corrected. "We know from Captain Caldwell, Joe Marchetti's commanding officer, that Marchetti approached you in regard to your experience with some German spies you identified last year."

"He did," Bell admitted.

"What did you tell him?"

"Just that we got lucky. We found those spies because one of my agents discovered some rifles hidden in a closet that led us to discover a radio homing device in the crate a spy had emptied."

Roosevelt then asked, "And what did you think of his theory of another spy operating out of New York? A group getting word to the German Navy about high-value shipping targets?"

"I was intrigued at first, but my ardor has cooled. What's this all about?"

"Following yesterday's sinking, I've decided that the Office of Naval Intelligence should look into Marchetti's suspicion anew and I wanted to know if you have any insights into the case."

Bell took a moment and said, "I had a couple of ideas, but . . . I have to be honest. There are simply too many parameters, too many people, and far too much territory. If it wasn't for a promise to my wife, I wouldn't have spent five seconds on it. However, given the Navy's resources, perhaps you'll have better luck."

"I should think we will," Roosevelt sniffed. "I happened to be in town and wanted to drop by personally. Thank you for whatever assistance you gave Ensign Marchetti, but he is no longer involved in this case and neither are you. Do you have a problem with that?"

"Not a bit," Bell replied a little indolently. "Like I said, we're swinging at the wind on this thing."

"Very good," Roosevelt said, adjusting the angle of his hat. "I bid you gentlemen good day. Come on, Kurt."

After the door closed, Archie asked, "So what's the beef between you two?"

"Petty schoolboy stuff," Bell replied absently.

"Not good enough. Spill."

Bell let out an exaggerated sigh. "Fine. I spent the summer before my senior year with a friend's family in Connecticut. They belonged to this exclusive beach club, which meant we spent most of our time sailing or playing tennis. It really was a great summer. Anyway, Frank Roosevelt was also in town summering with friends. I knew who he was because Teddy and my dad are old buddies, but we hadn't met. Anyway, there was this girl."

"I knew it!" Archie crowed.

"Frank was a couple of years younger than us, but he had it bad for her."

"And she had it bad for you?"

Bell chuckled at the memories. "Let's just say she didn't make me a man, but she sure did make me a better one. Toward the end of the summer, Frank got up the courage to tell her how he felt, and to her credit she let him down gently. Still, it had to have been humiliating and he shot daggers at me until I went back to Boston in September. Haven't seen him since, but I can guess a man wanting to follow his cousin into the Oval Office doesn't like for anyone to see his defeats."

"Why do you think he came himself, rather than just send his lackey?"

"Archie, I never try to understand the mind of a politician."

21

Located to the left of the White House, the State, War, and Navy Building was considered to be among the ugliest in the nation's capital. Constructed in the French Second Empire style, it had copper mansard roofs and hundreds of stumpy columns flanking ridiculously small windows. On three sides, massive porticoes jutted out toward the sidewalks to allow access to each of the cabinet departments. Many said they looked like the entrances to some ancient Egyptian funereal temple. One critic added that the structure managed to look busy without actually accomplishing any work.

In a second-floor conference room that overlooked one of the building's two internal courtyards, the air was filled with cigar and cigarette smoke and a healthy dose of tension. Seated at the heavy oak table were the Secretaries of State and Navy and their closest aides. For Navy Secretary Josephus

Daniels, that would be Franklin D. Roosevelt, newly arrived from New York. Across from them sat Cecil Spring-Rice, the English Ambassador to the United States, and a couple of his assistants, including a retired Admiral who was a Navy attaché.

Spring-Rice was a thin man, balding, with a gray Vandyke beard and rimless spectacles. His suit was of the finest Savile Row tailoring, though it was a bit heavy for the warm weather that cloaked Washington. A lifelong civil servant and diplomat, his current post was the pinnacle of his career. He was a longtime friend of Franklin's cousin Theodore, and had even been best man at his second wedding. And while the two Roosevelt cousins got along well, they were deeply divided by politics. Rice's friendship with Teddy brought him no special concessions from Franklin, a staunch Democrat.

"Surely President Wilson must respond to this latest German provocation," Spring-Rice said.

Newly appointed Secretary of State Robert Lansing, a Watertown, New York, native and international law expert, said evenly, "The President will doubtlessly respond, Mr. Ambassador, but how your government receives this response is the fundamental question."

"You're saying we might not like it," Spring-Rice said.

Lansing brushed a finger along his walrus mustache. "No more than you like our protests of your Navy harassing our shipping or the denial of trade your country is engaged in by blockading the North Sea."

"We decry the loss of life," said Roosevelt's boss, Secretary Daniels, in a North Carolina drawl. "However, both sides of this conflict, you and the Germans, have expanded your land war into what should be free and navigable waters in what some see as open violation of the rights of neutral nations."

"How can you remain neutral when U-boats are killing American sailors and civilians?"

"These are tragedies, outrages even, but they don't meet the burden of a war declaration," Lansing chided.

Spring-Rice had tried to use sentiment to move the Americans, but saw that they remained unconvinced that the sinking of the *Duchess of Värmland* warranted an armed response by the American government.

"This will eventually create a negative impact on the American economy," Spring-Rice said. "I read several shipping lines are no longer crossing the Atlantic and that orders for goods from factories that typically sell to European countries are already in decline."

"Then sign an armistice with the Germans and be done with it," Lansing snapped. "The French lost eighty thousand men last year in the battle for the Marne and we know that British forces are bleeding casualties in Gallipoli, of all places."

Spring-Rice waved away the idea. "I very much doubt the Germans are interested in ceding the territory they've taken from our French allies. Your own Civil War certainly taught you that sometimes ideas and ideals are worth fighting for. This is a war of German and Austrian aggression and that must be kept in check if the nations of Europe are to remain sovereign. That being said, I have been authorized to be more candid with you than normal."

His change in tact and tone and the unexpected admission grabbed everyone's attention.

"Our situation is more dire than we generally admit to. Stocks of ammunition and weapons are dangerously low. Our people are on reduced diets. We can no longer maintain troop levels overseas and if not for my nation's abundance of coal, our Navy would simply remain in port. We are not yet at a level of desperation, but without a steady lifeline from America, our situation will only grow more grim."

"What is it you are asking of us?" Franklin Roosevelt asked, lighting a fresh cigarette.

"Escorts," the English diplomat said. "Not all the ships crossing over, but the ones carrying the most critically important cargos. I believe a U-boat captain will think twice about firing a torpedo so close to an American destroyer or light cruiser."

"Sounds like a recipe for disaster," Roosevelt chuckled, but then sensed a darker implication. "Or perhaps an invitation for one."

"I don't believe being drawn into your war would be in our country's best interest," Navy Secretary Daniels said.

"I have to agree," Lansing from State added. "I can just imagine some moonless night and a U-boat fires on a cargo ship and clips one of our battlewagons instead. That would get you your declaration of war, Mr. Ambassador, at a cost of the lives of our sailors and whatever soldiers we'd eventually send to your front lines. No, thank you."

Spring-Rice stood and buttoned his suit jacket. "I believe, then, I have taken as much of your time as I dare. Thank you all for seeing us and hearing our concerns."

"One moment, Mr. Ambassador," Roosevelt said, and held a quick whispered conversation with his boss.

"I can't see the harm," Daniels said at length. "Go ahead and tell him."

"Mr. Ambassador," Roosevelt said, "there is a young naval officer in New York who deduced something quite interesting. He ran the probabilities and statistics of which ships the German U-boats manage to sink and discovered an alarming anomaly."

The British delegation retook their seats, clearly interested.

"He deduced," Roosevelt continued, "that the Germans were sinking a far greater share of high-value targets than possible by random chance alone. You are aware of the incident last summer of a radio beacon smuggled aboard a freighter to help a submarine home in on it and sink it?"

"Is that happening again?" Spring-Rice asked.

"Not possible. All ships' radio officers have been warned of this tactic and regularly use their equipment to detect unwanted signals being transmitted from their vessel."

"What the devil is going on, then?"

"Another German spy ring is at work in the Port of New York who can somehow get word to the U-boat blockade around your islands of which ships are carrying the choicest freight."

"Is this true?"

Navy Secretary Daniels answered, "We put some of our brightest men from the Office of Naval Intelligence on it for two weeks. They turned up no evidence of any German agents operating on the docks or in the shipping offices."

"That said," Roosevelt took up the tale once again, "the ensign who first ran the numbers later approached the investigator who cracked the first spy ring in hopes of gaining insight into how the German agents were found out. I was just in New York to meet with the fellow. Isaac Bell is his name. I informed him that ONI is back on the case in light of the sinking of the *Duchess of Värmland* and the loss of some of our senior officers. I told him that his investigative services are no longer required."

"Let me see if I follow, Mr. Roosevelt. ONI looked into the matter, found nothing, and so your man hired a private investigator?"

"Not quite, Mr. Ambassador. Bell was working pro bono. Something about a promise to his wife."

"And what did this man, Bell, find?"

Roosevelt hid his discomfort at the question, but answered honestly. "It occurred to me on the train back to Washington that he never actually told me. Bell said that he had some ideas and then let his voice fade before telling me how much better-equipped the Navy would be at hunting spies. I fear it was a bit of flattery to distract me from his nonanswer."

"Why would he do that, I wonder?" asked Spring-Rice's naval attaché.

"I knew Isaac Bell a bit when we were youths," Roosevelt said. "I don't know what type of man he became, but the boy he was was used to getting his own way. I think perhaps he has insights after all and plans on finding the spies on his own, despite my warning him off."

"And why tell us all of this?" Spring-Rice asked.

"Just because we aren't Isaac Bell's client doesn't mean the British government can't hire him."

"Do you think he has a better chance of learning the spies' identities than your own investigation?"

"I do not. However, as dire as you say your nation's situation to be, if I were in your shoes, I'd want every resource brought to bear to end this latest German scourge."

"This is certainly food for thought, Mr. Roosevelt. Thank you for bringing it to my attention." Spring-Rice stood once again.

There were handshakes all around, an ersatz bonhomie. Under the surface, Spring-Rice was bitterly disappointed, and the Americans were annoyed that the British continued to try to chip away at their nation's neutrality. Roosevelt's olive branch helped, but rancor between the former colonists and their former masters persisted.

22

"We've been had," Bell said to Archie Abbott as he burst through the Van Dorn office's main door.

He removed a pair of supple leather driving gloves and tossed them on a desk. He went to the Haws Sanitary Fountain installed next to the restroom and took several long gulps of water before soaking a handkerchief he pulled from a pocket. He wiped the road grime off his face with a satisfied sigh.

"Care to elaborate?"

"I thought of something last night and didn't want to wait until morning to contact the Lighthouse Bureau, so I hopped into the Simplex and just drove down and back to the Flat Point Light to talk to its keeper."

"Wendel's goofball brother-in-law?"

"The same. I asked him who preceded him. The guy who died."

"Bill Sherman, I believe."

"Try Gregor Theodoracopulos."

The color drained from Archie's face. "Holy hell."

"No way anyone could confuse those two names. Devlin Connell said Bill Sherman to test you and you failed."

The full implications of Bell's discovery hit Abbott like a right cross from a heavy-weight champ. He'd been played the second he'd stepped ashore at the Romer Shoal lighthouse. Nobody does that to Archibald Angell Abbott IV. He was genuinely rattled. "Who is this guy?"

"These guys," Bell corrected. "Remember, the spy I chased down and saw run over in New Haven was one disused coal chute away from doing in Mrs. Bell's favorite boy and walking away scot-free. I think Connell is the legit lighthouse inspector, but he's helping the Germans on the side."

A probationary agent barely into his twenties was answering the switchboard in a corner of the office and called out to Bell that he had a long-distance wire from Washington, D.C.

"Route it to this desk."

The slim phone on the desk in front of Bell rang a second later and he snatched it up. "Isaac Bell here."

"Isaac, it's Franklin Roosevelt."

"Mr. Assistant Secretary, this is a surprise," Bell said, and made a shrugging gesture to Archie. "I thought our dealings were at an end."

"Ours are, but maybe not yours."

"I don't think I follow."

"I was in a meeting late yesterday afternoon with the British Ambassador, a man named Cecil Spring-Rice. I can't go into specifics, but I mentioned that you had been involved in the hunt for the German spies and may be of some use to his government. I wanted to let you know in advance if they do reach out to you."

"I appreciate that," Bell said.

"I assumed you aren't going to let this matter go and thought you might as well get paid for your efforts. I knew you were a detective from stories TR told me, but I asked around last night to some people here in Washington and learned you have quite a reputation. They say a Van Dorn man always gets his man."

"It's our motto and I must confess that this case has stuck in my craw, as they say."

"Do you have any leads?"

Bell played things close to the vest, so the lie came easily. "Nothing concrete. The thing is, this investigation is in two parts. One is the spy or spies and whatever assets they're running. Solving that is a matter of expending more shoe leather canvassing the docks, asking around rooming houses, that sort of thing. The other side of the equation is how the information is sent to the U-boats. That's what interests me. I have no problem letting the Navy tackle the spy. I want the transmitter."

"How do you plan on finding it?"

"I would like to have Joe Marchetti back. This is about new technology and he's one sharp kid. He knows what scientists are working on, what's feasible now or in the near future. He can make intuitive leaps that I don't understand. He mentioned vacuum technology. He tried to explain it to me, but it went right over my head."

Out of the corner of his eye, Bell saw Helen Mills look up from her desk at the mention of Joe's name. If ever a woman's eyes actually shone, hers did.

"I'll tell you what. That summer back in Connecticut I was a lovelorn teenager who blamed you for the choice another person made. I've always been disappointed in myself for that. What say we put all that behind us and I'll see that Marchetti gets assigned to you on temporary duty."

He had to hand it to Roosevelt. The man was a consummate politician, always looking for an edge in any deal and usually getting it. He would go far, Bell predicted. Not because of his famous last name, but because his ambition was matched by his intelligence. Bell wanted Marchetti, and Roosevelt wanted to contain the story of a failed boyhood crush.

"That works for me just fine. Thank you."

"Don't mention it. I'll ring the Brooklyn Yard and have Marchetti over by lunch."

"Thanks again."

Bell hung up the phone and set it back on the desk.

"What was that all about?" Archie asked.

"Roosevelt said the Brits might hire us to help root out the spy and he wanted to make sure I didn't cause a scandal in the future."

"That yacht club thing you told me about. Who would care about that?"

"No one, but he's a careful man with lofty ambitions. But we get Joe Marchetti and I managed to plant the seeds for the Navy to take its investigation far from where we're operating."

"I caught that," Archie said, delighting in Bell's verbal sleight of hand. "Last report I read from Eddie Tobin is that not a single one of his contacts among all the dockworkers, tug captains, fishermen, pirates, and other outlaws he knows has seen or heard anything suspicious."

"I'm not surprised," Bell replied. "We were just talking about how good these clowns are. Their eyes on the docks will be just as circumspect. And it only takes one or two people with German sympathies in the right offices to supply them everything they need."

"Back to what you found out about our possibly compromised lighthouse inspector, Devlin Connell."

"Right. So, he pulled a fast one on you with the name of the victim he supposedly discovered. What else could have been a ruse? You said he looked to be in bad shape. Was he faking that?"

"He could have lied about having a bad arm, I suppose, but, Isaac, you gotta see this guy. He's practically a walking skeleton."

"I wonder why he's helping the Germans?"

"It's always one of the holy trinity." Archie ticked each off with a finger. "Money, sex, or politics. I'd go with the first or the third. Lighthouse inspectors can't make much dough and he's Irish. Well, his name and accent are, but now that I think about it, he could have faked that too. Anyway, if he is really Irish, it's like you said back at your club, he could be sympathetic to the Republican cause and want a free Ireland without English rule."

"Whatever the reason, I want his address so we can set a tail on him. He'll lead us to the spy sooner or later."

The probationary agent called out, "Mr. Bell, Mr. Van Dorn is on the wire."

"How does he know I need to talk to him about this case?" Bell asked rhetorically as he grabbed up the phone. He covered the microphone to add to Archie, "We're going to rack up a lot of overtime hours on this and we can't keep sneaking behind his back. Hey, boss, how's Chicago?"

"I'm in our Washington office." The agency maintained a suite at the Willard Hotel, near the White House and in the center of all the most powerful people in the city. "Just got a visit by a guy called Cecil Spring-Rice."

"Britain's Ambassador to the United States."

"Glad you're not playing dumb. He tells me that my agency had been looking into a German spy ring operating in New York on behalf of the Navy, and now that we're off the case, the Brits want us to keep on it. Outwardly I'm playing along, but inside I'm wondering what my chief detective and his trusty sidekick are playing at. Care to enlighten me before you find yourself without a job?"

"It's exactly as he said. A Navy officer named Joe Marchetti figured out the Germans were getting too lucky with the ships they were sinking. The Navy sent a bunch of Boy Scouts to check out the docks for a couple of weeks. Came up empty, of course. Joe then reached out to me because we'd found those spies in New Haven. We batted around some ideas, ended up going out to Montauk looking for a German transmission tower, and realized lighthouses might be the way the Germans sent radio signals. Went down to the Flat Point Light to talk to a contact, which led to an Irish lighthouse inspector named Devlin Connell, who may lead us to the German and/or Germans."

"You've solved it, then?" Van Dorn asked.

"I don't know who the spies working the port are, but I do think they get the information to Connell, and he passes it along somehow. He's my suspect, but it's going to take some time to verify. We need to catch him in the act."

"How long? I need to know in order to charge the Brits."

"Tough to say. Few weeks. It all depends

on when the next juicy freighter leaves New York."

"Sounds good. Looks like the agency is going to have a banner month. First our share of the ransom money you recovered and now we get to dip into His Majesty's piggy bank. What happens now?"

Bell said, "I find out where Connell lives, and we start tailing him."

"Off you go, then."

"On the jump, boss. On the jump."

23

The boat had been rented through one of Eddie Tobin's smuggler contacts. It was forty feet long, wooden hulled, and had a cramped crew cabin under the bow with a small galley and a head that drained straight into the ocean. It looked like a down-on-its-heels charter fishing boat that hadn't seen much maintenance in years. The paintwork was patchy, the brass all tarnished and pitted, and salt had so stained the open aft deck that the teak looked white.

But she had it where it counted. Under the transom were a pair of hundred-horse gasoline engines that could move the revenue runner upward of twenty knots. She was big enough to ride all but the worst Atlantic gales and fast enough to keep pace with Devlin Connell as he roamed the northeastern seaboard seemingly at random, inspecting the countless lighthouses, buoys, and beacons.

Archie had smooth-talked the Irishman's address out of a female secretary with the Lighthouse Bureau and was overseeing the detail meant to keep tabs on the man.

"God bless Henry Ford" was a common refrain around the Van Dorn Agency. By 1915, Ford's assembly lines churned out fully half of all the cars sold in the United States. This meant that of the three million cars on American roads, about one point five million were identical black Model Ts. They were everywhere, so uniform in their blandness that the mind no longer registered them, or if it did, saw only a vague black shape identical to all the other black shapes.

It took just two teams of agents to trail Connell, who drove a blue Chevrolet Model H tourer. Each agency Model T carried three people. As they wove in and out of sight of the car ahead of them, the three would change positions, one might hide in the backseat. They sometimes stopped for a moment to change hats and jackets, all in an attempt to maintain the utter anonymity of their vehicles. Van Dorn agents were well versed at this maneuver and rarely ever lost a mark.

Most of the roads along the coast were congested enough that they didn't become conspicuous. If the traffic thinned too much, they would use a map and guess which lighthouse Connell was planning on inspecting and rush ahead to a crossroads or gas station, where they could tuck in behind him again. Once they were certain where he was heading, they broke off the chase and phoned the New York office. They in turn phoned a friend of Joe Marchetti, who had access to one of the most powerful transmitters in New York, and he broadcast a coded message at prescribed times.

At sea, Bell and Joe, who'd been told in the morning whether they were heading north or south, listened for the broadcast and adjusted their course accordingly. The system wasn't perfect, and a couple of times they couldn't get into position until long after Connell was at work, but for the most part they had him on a tight leash and were in sight of the target lighthouse before the lamp was first lit.

They had been at it for a week, in which time Connell had visited three lighthouses, one in Connecticut and two on the Jersey Shore.

Tonight was the fourth lighthouse, the Barnegat Light, just north of the Flat Point tower that Bell had already visited twice for this case.

"You know it doesn't have to be due east,"

Joe remarked as they idled roughly fifteen miles east of the Barnegat Light. It was almost dark enough for Connell to fire up the kerosene-burning lamp.

"It doesn't have to be, but it makes sense," Bell replied. They were standing side by side in the enclosed pilothouse. Bell was at the controls, while Joe stood by with a pair of powerful marine binoculars. "If we're right, there are so many variables in play with this system of communication that the Germans would want to simplify things where they can. Keeping a ship due east of the light is easier than maintaining a forty-seven-degree angle or at one hundred and twenty-two degrees."

Behind them the sky was a deep purple as the last of the day's light faded over the western horizon.

"How often does the light flash?" Bell asked.

Joe's teeth shone white in the gloom as he smiled wickedly. "Correction. The question should be, what is the light's characteristic?"

"Characteristic, huh?"

"Yes. It's called a characteristic."

"So much for me beginning to like you," Bell deadpanned. "Okay, smart guy, what is the light's characteristic?"

"White light every ten seconds. I'll make

a sailor of you yet, Mr. Bell."

"I was racing twenty-twos while you were still in diapers."

"There," Joe said louder than he'd meant, his finger pointing west as the Fresnel lens atop the Barnegat Light flared like a mirror catching the sun and went dark. He waited a moment, counting silently, and then said, "Eight one thousand. Nine one thousand. Ten."

On cue, the light flashed again as the multi-ton lens rotated atop the nearly one-hundred-and-seventy-foot tower, casting out a beam of light that swept each point of the compass in ten-second intervals.

Bell unscrewed the lid of a Thermos-brand vacuum bottle filled with strong black coffee. "Time to settle in for another night of watching Devlin Connell's handiwork as he keeps the lamp lit and the chains under tension. Get some sleep and I'll wake you just before midnight."

On their first stakeout together, they'd decided the likeliest time for Connell to send a signal was between midnight and two a.m. That deep into the night, there were fewer small craft out on the water to spot and report something anomalous. Bell took the hours from sunset until midnight, when they would both stand watch for an hour.

After that, Bell would sleep while Joe watched for anything out of the ordinary until dawn.

Isaac Bell had many tricks to keep his mind occupied while on a stakeout. It was the only way to ensure boredom didn't dull his senses and make him miss some vital activity or observation. Usually, he would think about his current case, coming at it from different angles, studying the individual pieces that made up the puzzle in order to see if there were other ways they could fit together.

On this case there were no such musings. Either he was right about Devlin Connell acting as a German agent or he was wrong. If it was the latter, he was at an impasse because he had no other ideas for how the spies were getting information back to Germany. He'd already looked at every angle, every idea no matter how strange — could a homing pigeon cross the Atlantic? It took a few calls to track down a pigeon racer in Weehawken, New Jersey, and the answer is no. If Devlin wasn't part of the equation, the Germans had a piece of technology far in advance of anything Joe Marchetti had even dreamed of, some sort of unidirectional radio with tremendous range.

And if Devlin was part of the loop, and he got word out to a ship that was far enough from the coast that it could then resend the information transatlantic, nothing was heard on land that could be interpreted as a viable signal. Joe said that such a setup was much more plausible than a Jules Verne–inspired unidirectional transmitter.

From time to time, Bell had to run up the engines to get back into position because of the tides, current, and wind.

His only choices came if Devlin was involved. It would be easy enough to have him arrested and lean on him to nab the master spy and his network of lookouts on the docks, but wouldn't using him be better? The British were in a bad way. The noose of the U-boat blockade was tightening. What if he could deliver the means with which the subs were communicating with each other? From that, couldn't the British devise countermeasures, render the deadly U-boats deaf and dumb?

The very audacity of such a plan sent a jolt of adrenaline through Bell's body far more stimulating than any mug of coffee. He wanted to wake Joe and discuss it with him, but there were still hours to go on his shift. He passed them easily, his mind working at a lightning pace concocting, altering, rejecting, and honing various ideas and schemes to make a plan that was feasible.

At five minutes before midnight, Bell nudged Joe Marchetti awake. He'd curled up on the deck of the little bridge in a light sleeping bag. The air was plenty warm, but there was an underlying damp chill that rose from the ocean's depths and seeped into a man's bones during a long, lonely night.

"Almost time," Bell said. He hadn't turned away from the metronomic flash of the Barnegat lighthouse for hours.

As a trained sailor, Joe Marchetti snapped awake quickly. He was on his feet in seconds and had helped himself to the Thermos for a blast of caffeine. "I suppose if anything had happened you would have woken me earlier."

"Correct. I might have seen the navigation lights of a couple of ships, but they were too far out to be sure. And old Mr. Fresnel's lens has been merrily flashing away every ten seconds like, well, clockwork."

Bell was about to share his idea with Joe and get his opinion when the light suddenly stopped flashing. It took him an instant to register the change, since he'd been so used to the beam sweeping by so quickly. The light now held steady, pointing straight at them, due east on the compass. Next it blinked in rapid fire, not rotating, but flashing in a random pattern that was beamed to a precise location out to sea. It lasted just a few seconds, less than thirty for sure, and then the light swung away only to return ten seconds later as if nothing had interrupted its monotonous labors.

Joe had a small notebook ready for just such an event and quickly wrote down a string of fifteen letters.

JHVTOLRCKGEFHWQ

He showed it to Bell.

"Code for sure," he said.

"You were right," Marchetti told him with a hearty slap on the back.

"Now let's see if I'm lucky too." Bell fired up the twin engines and engaged the drive, swinging the boat nearly on its axis so its nose pointed due east.

Keeping the lighthouse at their backs, Bell ran the boat hard. The seas were mild and there was ample moonlight to see if any big rogue waves were heading their way. Joe had already told him that the light from the Barnegat tower could be seen as far as twenty-two miles out and so he'd positioned their craft inside that radius, but not too far, in hopes of catching a glimpse of the spy ship.

Twenty-plus-knots speed. Seven miles. Twenty minutes, give or take.

Bell felt the thrill of the chase, the electric tingle throughout his body that heightened his senses and made him feel all the more alive. He glanced at Joe and saw the same hunter's gleam in his eye. He did not regret his decision to try to woo Marchetti away from the Navy. He would be a real asset to the agency if he could get him to join. Joe had a knack for investigative work and a handle on all the latest technology. Bell decided it was time to let Helen Mills into his scheme and laughed aloud at how underhanded it was.

"We'll get 'em," Joe yelled, misinterpreting Bell's outburst.

As they got farther out, the sweep of the lighthouse's beam sank lower and lower on the horizon at the same time it dimmed. The waves began to grow heavier. Both men were seasoned sailors and knew to absorb the shock of the boat pounding into the waves on flexed knees. Bell held the wheel. Joe clutched a teak rail bolted onto the dash for that exact purpose. Occasionally he used one hand to bring the big binoculars up to sweep the sea ahead of them, but so far they hadn't spotted any other vessels.

Bell kept looking back over his shoulder to help maintain his bearings. The light was as faint as a firefly and its precise timing was lost, as waves occasionally blocked its revolving beam.

"We've got to be close," he said over the engines' snarl. It was more a prayer than an observation.

The seas remained empty. They were now well past the reach of the Barnegat Light and still there was nothing but waves and lines of sea-foam and the indifferent stars.

Fog started to rise from the ocean's surface as they passed into a patch of cold air, thin wisps and streamers at first, but it quickly built into a dense cloud that enveloped their boat and made their exhaust echo back into the cockpit. Bell had to slow. Visibility went from nearly unlimited to practically zero.

Guided by the compass and adjusting for the current as best he could estimate, he kept going another mile, then two. Nothing. The Germans were gone. Bell shut down the engines to let them cool.

Waves slapped at the hull as they bobbed impotently. A brass clip on a lanyard pinged like a flat bell against a metal rail. The fog was as thick as it had ever been, like the steam room back at the Yale Club. Straining, Bell thought he heard another engine out in the mist, something much larger than their own in-line sixes. He turned a full circle, hands cupped to his ears, trying to isolate the noise, but it was impossible. Sound echoed and rebounded through the fog with no discernable pattern.

"Do you hear anything?" he asked Joe in little more than a whisper. His eyes watered trying to make out anything in the fog. Was that a shape? No. It was nothing.

"Maybe," Marchetti said, unsure. "I thought I did, but it sounded like it's coming from all around us."

"Yeah. It's the fog."

They waited, heads cocked like hunting dogs, but whatever they had heard or seen was gone.

"They must have run as soon as they received the signal," Joe said in his normal voice. There was no need to pretend anyone was out there with them. "Which way, north or south?"

Suddenly, the prow of a ship burst through the fog no more than twenty feet from the borrowed boat, towering over them like a sharpened cliff made of steel. Bell had killed the engines, so there was nothing they could do as the large ship slammed into their craft at a shallow angle. Wood splintered as the gunwale took the brunt of the collision.

Bell and Joe were both thrown off their feet and tumbled against the cockpit wall. Something down in the cabin crashed violently against the deck. The boat bobbed heavily in the turbulent water the larger vessel churned up. The boat was fortunately pushed away by the ship's passage so that when the fantail slid by they were far enough from the churning props to keep from being diced up like so much chum.

No sooner had the ship appeared than it was gone, swallowed by the fog so completely that there wasn't a sound to be heard, not her great boilers and steam gear nor any foghorn or even the hiss of her hull cleaving the waters.

Bell and Joe got to their feet, asking in unison, "Are you all right?"

"I'm okay," Joe said, massaging the shoulder that had taken the brunt of his body slamming into the wall.

Bell went to start the engines while Joe stepped back to look down at the main deck below. "Don't start them yet," he warned. "It's pretty bad."

Bell moved from the controls to survey the damage. Their boat appeared to be six inches narrower, thanks to the impact. No doubt the hull had been compromised and they were probably taking on water. Bell raced down the short ladder and swung into the cabin below the pilothouse. He saw right away that the radio they'd set up had been destroyed when it fell from the dining booth table.

There was an access hatch built into the floor behind the tiny galley to get to the engines and bilge. He opened it while Joe unclipped a powerful flashlight from near the door.

The beam flashed off the surface of the water that was accumulating in the bilge. It wasn't climbing fast enough to mark visually in the few moments they stared, but both knew more was shipping aboard every second.

"Eddie's smuggler buddy said the bilge pump has some battery backup but primarily runs off the engines."

"Let's get out of here and hope we can make it to shore," Joe said. It wasn't fear in his voice, but healthy concern. "I'll rustle up some life jackets."

"Good idea." Bell turned to climb back up to the bridge.

"Think that was them?" Joe asked before Bell vanished up the ladder.

Bell paused. With the taste of defeat on

his lips, he said, "Who else is lurking out in a fog bank in the middle of the night?"

24

Roosevelt's face was red with rage as his normally cool veneer melted. "I demand that you tell me who it is."

"I can't do that," Bell said levelly. "My client has a right to confidentiality."

"To hell with that," Roosevelt thundered. "This man has the blood of six American officers on his hands, plus the Brits and the others aboard the *Duchess of Värmland.* Not to mention all those other ships he identified for the U-boats to sink like lambs to the slaughter."

Bell tried to cross his legs, but his body protested every movement.

Two nights previous, Bell and Marchetti had limped westward at barely three knots to protect the hull from more damage, while the bilge pumps strained to keep ahead of the flooding. After the first hour, it became clear that the men would have to bail out the boat, and they took turns filling two three-gallon galvanized pails and laboriously dumping them over the side. Even with some cloth wrapped around the wire handles as padding, their hands soon throbbed in agony. It didn't look like their effort made much difference at first, but toward the end of each half-hour shift, they noted the water level had dropped some.

At dawn they shared the roast beef sandwich Bell had kept wrapped in butcher paper in a bag with the now-empty Thermos bottle. They didn't reach land until nearly eight in the morning. They beached the boat near the sleepy town of Lavallette, having drifted miles north with the current. Both men were exhausted from the physical and psychological marathon they'd just endured. Their hands were misshapen into claws from carrying the buckets through the night and their backs ached like they'd been gored by a bull.

Luckily there was a phone in town and after a few hours of sleep on the beach they were driven back to New York by James Dashwood, who'd drawn the short straw in the office and made the arduous roundtrip drive.

After a good night's sleep, Bell had briefed the other agents on his team about their adventures and made certain a constant watch was maintained on Devlin Connell. He added a third car to the detail to make it that much more difficult to spot. He also outlined his idea for the next phase of the operation. A few phone calls confirmed that Roosevelt and Ambassador Spring-Rice were available for a meeting. Bell chose the Van Dorn offices at the Willard Hotel in Washington and hopped the express at Penn Station for the hours-long trip with Joe Marchetti.

Spring-Rice said, "Steady on, Mr. Secretary. No need for that."

Roosevelt turned his ire on Joe, who'd traveled in his dress uniform. He looked like he wanted to be anywhere but sitting so close to the second most powerful man in the Navy. "You took an oath to obey your superiors. Tell me who you identified or so help me God you'll spend the rest of your career on the oldest ship in the fleet shoveling coal with a spoon."

"Frank, lay off the kid," Bell said in a tone that got Roosevelt's attention. He glared at the detective, but Bell plowed on, unfazed. "There are other developments that supersede your need for justice, some things I discussed with Ambassador Spring-Rice prior to this meeting."

Roosevelt fumbled for his cigarette case

and used the few seconds it took to light one to calm himself. "What developments?"

"We saw the boat the Germans are using to rebroadcast their messages once they get them from their contact on the shore. It's big. We estimate a hundred and fifty feet."

"Why is that important?"

"They have some new technology on board. Something that requires a big ship with a lot of available electrical power. You tell him, Joe."

On familiar ground, Marchetti got over his intimidation before the Assistant Navy Secretary. "We ran into them, literally ran into them, several miles beyond where they should have been. I believe this is because the ship has a tall radio mast that doubles as a crow's nest for a lookout that extended their operation range but allowed them to remain in sight of the shore-based signal."

Bell had coached Joe on the ride down to be cautious around Roosevelt. A man with his intellect could infer the Germans were using lighthouses if they gave away too much information. If Roosevelt got wise, he'd have arrest warrants for every keeper from Fort Lee to Fort Lauderdale.

"Go on," Roosevelt said when Joe had paused.

"They have some new technology aboard

that ship. I believe they have perfected a way to eliminate one of the side bands to the main carrier wave in a radio transmission and I believe they do it with a very special type of vacuum tube."

"I don't think I follow that, Ensign."

"I won't bore you with the technical specifications. What I think the Germans have is a powerful transmitter that can signal to a special type of receiver over great distances. The vacuum tubes reduce background static to the point a message is coherent from here all the way to Germany. They have a powerful radio facility at a place called Borkum Island that could receive these transmissions."

Ambassador Spring-Rice added, "Our intelligence wallahs believe they also have a special radio ship called the *Ancona* they use to communicate with their U-boat fleet."

"So, the spies pass their information on to this ship and they, in turn, transmit it back to Germany," Roosevelt said. "From there it's radioed back out to the U-boat fleet?"

"Yes, sir." Marchetti nodded eagerly. "They pass the intelligence on to the blockading U-boats. They have the name of the ship, its destination port, and a likely description, plus its approximate arrival time at the picket lines."

"The designated target wouldn't stand a chance," Bell said in summary.

"What is it you're after, exactly?" Roosevelt asked.

Joe and Bell exchanged a quick glance. Bell finally said, "We want to steal a couple of those vacuum tubes."

"What on earth for?"

Marchetti took the lead again. "First, it's an engineering breakthrough worth studying, but more importantly, if we get our hands on one, it's likely we can jam up their transmissions with artificial static. They wouldn't be able to get the names of the ships to Europe, and our spy ring is out of a job."

"There's another factor," Bell interjected. "It's something I thought of on the train ride down. As I understand it, submarines work pretty independently. They are given assigned patrol zones and left to fend for themselves. They hunt alone, picking at any ship that enters their area."

"That's how we figure it," Roosevelt agreed.

"A single hunter by himself isn't nearly as effective as a coordinated effort of many working together. It's believed that's why our ancestors created language, to better hunt for game. What if this new technology allows the German submarine fleet to act in unison? They could coordinate attacks and become far more effective. A lone wolf will surely die, but hunting together, a wolf pack is about as deadly a killing machine as there is.

"Even if we somehow keep ourselves out of the war," Bell continued, "the Atlantic will become such a bloody killing ground that our international commerce will grind to a halt. Our economy will stagnate. We just clawed our way out of a two-year recession that saw business activity cut by a quarter. What would happen if suddenly we were no longer exporting goods to our strongest trade partners? Factories shuttered. Forges gone cold. Whole industries bankrupt. Mass homelessness, breadlines at every soup kitchen. Hungry children who can't understand why their mother won't feed them. Think depression, Franklin, rather than recession."

Roosevelt nodded. His was a political family tied to the successes of the country. He could see that the grim reality of what Bell described was true. He looked to Joe Marchetti. "Do you think you can counter such a communications network?"

"Not without studying one of the tubes,

that's for sure."

"We'd like a crack at them too," Spring-Rice said. "You chaps aren't in this fight, so it's even more important to us. And we are paying the tab."

"Of course, Mr. Ambassador," Roosevelt said smoothly. "Tell me what you need, Bell."

"For one, I need for Joe to be cashiered out of the Navy."

"What?" Joe cried. This was the first he'd heard of it.

Bell turned to him. "I need you with me on this. I don't even know what a vacuum tube looks like and you're a commissioned officer in the United States Navy. If, God forbid, something goes wrong, your presence on a German warship would constitute an act of war. The diplomatic repercussions would be disastrous."

"That's a fine point," Roosevelt said.

"If you're a Van Dorn agent, we can plausibly say we are being paid to act as industrial spies looking for proprietary equipment. We're still in Dutch, but it keeps Uncle Sam out of it. If we encounter no problems, I'm sure Mr. Roosevelt can reinstate you once the mission is complete."

Bell looked to the Assistant Secretary, who nodded his head. "Is that all?"

"Not even remotely," Bell said. "We need a lure, a target so juicy the dockyard spies will fall all over themselves to get a report back to Germany. This will give us an idea of where the ship will be lurking."

"How, exactly?"

"I'd rather not say," Bell said quickly. "Again, that information belongs to our client."

"How about it, Mr. Ambassador," Roosevelt cajoled. "Care to share?"

"On the advice of Mr. Bell," Spring-Rice said stiffly, "I would rather not at this time."

Roosevelt nodded in acceptance of being outmaneuvered. "What else?"

"I'm not certain just yet," Bell admitted. "My plan is evolving as we pick apart the details, but I'll let you know."

25

Bell and Joe shared a cabin on the night train back to New York and parted company at Penn Station. Joe had to return to the Brooklyn Navy Yard to clear out his clothing and personal effects. The agency was putting him up at a hotel near enough to the Knickerbocker to be convenient, but at a far cheaper room rate. Joseph Van Dorn was still reeling from the cost of repairing the boat Bell had nearly ruined. Just towing it to a qualified shipyard in New Jersey had cost a pretty penny.

Bell hoofed it to the office and locked himself in the boardroom with all the reports his agents had written about tailing Devlin Connell. He had been looking at the case with such a broad view that he'd neglected many of the details. He found it was usually something minor that gets overlooked during an investigation that comes back around to derail the whole thing. There were reams of notes and dozens of photographs he hadn't yet perused.

He now had concrete proof that Devlin Connell was the conduit from the actual spies on the docks in Manhattan to the Germans out at sea. He had to give them credit. Had the German ship stayed in one spot, lurking as Eddie Tobin said, they would have drawn the attention of the Navy or Coast Guard. But because Connell had access to all the lighthouses in the area and inspected them in a schedule he'd shared with the skipper, the ship could cruise up and down the coast without raising any red flags.

Someone knocked on the door just minutes after he sat down. "Come on in."

"I think I cracked it," Helen Mills said, sticking her perfectly coifed head into the boardroom.

"Cracked what?"

"When you and Joe got back to the city from your little misadventure, he gave me the code phrase he'd jotted down. I think I figured out which ship they're targeting next. We might be able to get word to them."

Bell now faced the quandary that so tore at the souls of men in positions of command. He knew sailors were going into harm's way and he had the potential to warn them, but at the cost of revealing key information to the enemy.

"I don't recognize that particular expression on your face," Helen said in a motherly tone. "I think it's your look of indecision."

"You're not wrong," he said. "Do we save those men and possibly tip our hand, or do we do nothing and let them die to protect our secret?"

"I don't think this should be your call."

"How could it not. I'm lead investigator, after all."

Helen's expression went a little stern and protective. "Our client is the British government. Let them decide. Cable their ambassador and lay out his options."

He studied her for a moment. She had a good head on her shoulders, a keen mind, and great instincts, but she was still young and relatively unscarred by life's trials. If he was honest with himself, he begrudged a little of her naivete and of not yet seeing how dark so much of the world can be. He didn't like being the one to erode even a tiny bit of her youthful optimism.

But he must. "He'll sacrifice those sailors without a second's pause and never give them another thought."

"Oh."

"Right, 'Oh.' In the end, it's my call. I

decide their fate. If I tell Spring-Rice, they die. If I don't and I save them, I risk the entire operation." He invited her to sit at the table with him. To give himself more time to consider his options, he asked, "How did you break the code? As I recall, it was just a string of fifteen letters."

"I didn't. I looked up the sailing schedule in the shipping news to see how many ships leaving New York that day had a fifteen-letter name. There was only one, called the *Gayle Peterhouse.* Half her cargo is sacks of ammonium nitrate, which is used to make explosives."

Bell felt a strong sense of relief. He said, "I don't think it's that simple. Let me see the code."

She carried a clipboard and showed him the piece of paper.

JHVTOLRCKGEFHWQ

Bell needed only a second to spot her mistake. "Look here. If this was a simple substitution code, we'd see a pattern. There's four non-sequential letter *e*'s in the name *Gayle Peterhouse.* We don't see that repetition in the code. There are codes that change a letter's meaning every time it's used, but that's pretty complex stuff and likely not workable in this situation."

She looked crestfallen. "And there I was thinking I was being ever so clever."

"Joe and I have talked about this. We think they send the name of the ship as well as a basic description. Size, color, number of funnels. That sort of thing. So maybe the first five letters are the name, then the next denotes size. The *WQ* at the end could mean she's got five masts or two funnels or whatever they'd worked out in advance. I'm afraid without their key it's really unknowable."

"Call me a silly goose."

"Not at all. It was a good idea and when the ship you thought it was happened to be carrying the right type of cargo, it couldn't have felt like a coincidence."

"No. When I saw the cargo manifest, my heart practically jumped out of my chest."

"That's the thing investigators have to always be wary of, getting so enamored of our own theories we begin to see what we want to see."

"Thanks. I guess there's still a lot to learn."

"You're doing fine. Now scram so I can get back to these reports."

After she left, Bell couldn't concentrate on the dry, heavily detailed but ultimately boring reports. Did it really matter if he knew where Connell stopped for breakfast each morning he set out on an inspection?

He closed the file he was currently skimming and set it atop the stack of the ones he hadn't gotten to yet. It had only been a couple of weeks, but there had to be a whole file box of notes and pictures. He ambled out into the bull pen. Archie wasn't around. Joe had returned from checking into his hotel and was talking with Helen Mills. Judging by her laughter and how she kept touching her hair, she was enjoying the attention. He decided to take a drive. Rather than read about Connell's habits, he thought he'd check out where the man lived. Get a feel for him.

He walked to the nearby stable where he kept the Simplex, rather than have it brought around, and was soon on a ferry across the Hudson. Once across the river it took only twenty minutes to reach Connell's neighborhood.

The house was on a typical suburban street in Hoboken. White clapboard, two curtained windows flanking the front door, which was painted a bright yellow. The yard was ornate but looked neglected. The driveway was empty, meaning Connell was out, perhaps on another inspection or just running errands. Either way, Bell simply rolled on past the house as if it held no special interest. There was a one-car garage or large shed in back.

He wondered about the case. Had he committed the same error as Helen? Was he seeing patterns because he wanted to? He'd been right about Connell being in on the spy ring. But was that like Helen discovering the ship was carrying chemicals used to make explosives? To her that had seemed to be an important clue, but ultimately wasn't. Devlin Connell was working with the Germans, but was he important? Was he just one of a dozen ways the Germans were sneaking information out of the United States?

The stakes were rising every day the great European powers blasted each other with artillery and sent men charging into machine-gun fire from their trenches. Soldiers were dying at an unprecedented scale and it seemed that man's collective humanity was being sacrificed as the industrial age matured.

Bell vowed to not lose his.

On his way back to the Knickerbocker, he detoured down close to the Battery where the White Star Line had its headquarters in a neoclassical building at 9 Broadway. Their docks were up near 18th Street, but would be overwhelmed with passengers and crew getting ready for the *Olympic*'s afternoon sailing. Coming here meant he was bound to find someone he knew.

While Bell generally preferred to travel on Cunard Line ships, he had plenty of contacts at White Star, including operations people here in New York. He knew his way around the building and climbed unescorted to the third floor. The place was a buzzing hive of activity, with workers moving around at almost a sprinter's pace. Playing in the background was a shrill symphony of telephones ringing, accompanied by brass messenger cylinders clanking through the pneumatic tube system. An army of typists carried the beat.

He'd failed the sailors aboard the *Mildred E. Burroughs* and saved the men of the *Centurion.* To many that meant the ledger books were balanced. But not for a man like Isaac Bell. The ledger would never balance and that was something he had to live with for the rest of his life. Burdened with the feeling that he could have, and should have, done more kept Bell constantly motivated.

He found the vice president of operations, George Allenby, at his desk with a view of the street below. "Isaac, what a surprise," he said affably. "What brings you down to the tip of Manhattan?"

"Afternoon, my friend. How are you doing?"

"Sailing day, you know. Always a madhouse around here."

"That's why I came. Don't ask how, but I have word on good authority the Germans are really gunning for shipping this week."

"Bloody savages," the Englishman said with a sneer.

"A point I won't argue. I just want to warn you and ask that as the *Olympic* sails that she broadcast warnings to all other ships she encounters to be even more vigilant than normal."

"We usually do, mate. But thanks for the warning. Is this part of a case you're working?"

"Call it tangentially," Bell deflected. "Could you cable London and have your other ships issue the same warning?"

"Sure," Allenby said, a hint of concern tightening his voice. "Do you have anything specific?"

"I'm afraid not. Sorry, I've got to run now."

His next stop was at the Cunard Line's office to deliver the same message. He felt a sense of satisfaction. Though Helen was likely wrong as to the name of the ship Devlin Connell had ratted out to his German masters, there remained a vessel crossing the Atlantic that the U-boats especially wanted to sink. Hopefully, they'd hear the warning and find some way to complete a safe crossing.

He considered this a small plus in that lopsided ledger he carried in his heart.

26

The crates were massive wooden boxes stenciled with numerous arcane numbers and codes. The only plain text anyone seeing them could read was the name of where they had originated — Bethlehem Steel, Naval Armaments Division. Judging by the size and weight, each box likely contained a barrel for the main gun on a giant warship. There were nine crates in total, which jibed with the number of cannons on the latest dreadnaught-class ships.

They had arrived in New Jersey on a special train and had then been barged up the Hudson River to Pier 92, which had a crane powerful enough to lift each of the hundred-ton crates. The site was also chosen because it was far enough north on Manhattan Island that most anyone working the Hudson docks would have taken note of the unusual cargo as it was barged past.

Representatives from Bethlehem Steel

were on hand, as well as Ambassador Spring-Rice's naval attaché.

The ship berthed at Pier 92 was nearly three hundred feet in length. Her pilothouse was located at her very aft so that her deck was a large open space punctured with a series of hatch covers over her compartmentalized interior holds. Her holds had already been filled and the hatches secured. Except for the last of her cargo, which would be lashed to the deck, she was ready to set sail for Bristol.

Dockworkers and riggers set up for the first of the lifts, slinging multiple steel cables under the first crate and latching them to the crane's heavy forged-steel lifting hook. The men were masters of their craft. When the big steam engine atop the crane began to heave on the load, the crate remained within a degree of perfectly level. The container came up off the barge in one smooth maneuver. More steam and smoke belched from the crane's stack and vents as the cab rotated ever so gently until the piece of naval artillery was over the cargo ship's deck.

Stevedores awaiting the payload stayed well back until the crate was lowered to just a foot or so above the metal plating. Then they set to work directing the crane operator to position the heavy load to its exact resting place, and then finally had it lowered with a metallic clang. Chains were threaded through pre-welded pad eyes and the crate was secured to the decking so snugly that no matter what weather the ship endured, the enormous box wouldn't move.

Eight more times these steps were repeated. The extra nine hundred tons of cargo settled the ship, called the *San Gabrielle,* a few inches deeper into the inky river. When the last cannon barrel was aboard, the representative from Bethlehem Steel shook the British attaché's hand and left the port. A retired Admiral spoke a few words with the *San Gabrielle*'s captain before he too took his leave. The ship was scheduled to steam downriver at the turning of the tide the following morning.

From a sixth-floor roof a block inland from the pier, Isaac Bell had watched the five-hour process through a pair of binoculars. He'd regularly swept the other nearby anchorages to see if anyone was giving the loading any special attention. It didn't appear so, but the harbor was always so busy it was difficult to tell. At times he estimated there were five hundred workers within sight of the *San Gabrielle* and the river traffic was so thick it looked like he could walk across the Hudson and never get his feet wet.

"That about does it," Joe Marchetti said. He'd stood the long vigil at Bell's side.

"If they don't jump at this one, I need to a find new career."

The crates had arrived from Bethlehem Steel as advertised, but there were no precision-bored naval cannon barrels inside. Each was loaded with a hundred tons of scrap iron and slag, the waste product of making steel that Bethlehem was more than happy to get rid of. The *San Gabrielle*'s sailing schedule had been posted three days earlier for all to see and now their sham parade of gun barrels was complete.

"With bait like this we'll get them hook, line, and sinker," the young officer predicted.

It had taken a week to organize all the moving parts for the final chapter of this case and to his credit Franklin Roosevelt had pulled out all the stops. Had Bell not known any better, he would have been convinced that nine fourteen-inch cannon barrels had just been loaded onto the ship and that they were soon bound for England.

The *San Gabrielle* really would depart on time and cruise out past the Verrazzano-Narrows and turn eastward as if to cross the Atlantic. However, once clear of traffic, the ship would turn south for Baltimore, where her real cargo of Portland cement sacks would be off-loaded. The big crates would be dismantled and their contents quietly dumped in a landfill.

"It's up to Archie and his team tomorrow morning," Bell said.

Abbott would lead the three-car flying squad tasked with tailing Devlin Connell and reporting back to Joe and Isaac. Once they knew which lighthouse he was heading for, the two of them would fly into pre-position and wait for Connell to send his signal to the waiting German spy ship.

Bell and Marchetti were free to time their operation as they saw fit. However, Archie and his team needed to wait until dawn to move in on Connell because none of them knew how to tend a lighthouse and the lamp could not be allowed to go out.

"Tomorrow is going to be another marathon day," Bell warned. "Get plenty of rest tonight."

Joe looked a little sheepish at Bell's suggestion. It didn't take the eyes and instincts of a trained investigator to see what was happening.

"Let me guess," he said. "You've made plans with Miss Mills."

"She has tickets to a comedy at the Cohan Theatre called *Cousin Lucy.* As soon as it's over I'll escort her home and then it's back to my hotel. Promise."

"It's fine," Bell said, offering some empathy. He recalled any number of nights he went without sleep early in his relationship with Marion. They'd talk the night away and he'd dash off at dawn to put in a full day at Van Dorn's San Francisco office.

He added, "Just be at the Knickerbocker no later than seven. Weather should be cooperative tomorrow."

"And if it isn't?"

"Either we're in for a bumpy ride or the powers that be don't get a sample of Germany's new vacuum tube technology. Regardless of what happens during our little caper, Archie will arrest Connell and the spy ring will be shut down."

27

With the majority of the attendees in uniform, the event playing out in a large meadow on Long Island certainly had a martial air, but it was also infused with the mischievous eagerness of a bunch of little boys at play on a perfect spring afternoon.

William Vanderbilt, Bell's friend Willie K., had provided the land near his Centerport estate for the event's use and so was naturally an honored guest. He'd had a tent erected in the middle of the action complete with an elaborate field kitchen and a pair of trucks converted into mobile ice chests for keeping all the champagne, wine, and beer chilled. Lunch had been chateaubriand drizzled in a red wine and wild mushroom sauce as well as asparagus slathered in hollandaise. And Willie's chef and staff continued to serve up all manner of delicacies for any and all who joined him.

Officers below the rank of colonel had the

good sense to know the millionaire's largesse was meant for senior staff and could only eye the bemedaled chests of the men enjoying the fine spread from afar. There were other pavilions on the vast field for them to socialize with the civilian representatives, but nothing as grand as the Vanderbilt marquee.

The event was the first annual North Atlantic Military Exposition, a showcase for military men and the armorers who supplied them to mingle and eye the latest wares. The American companies that had shown up wanted to sell weapons to the Allied powers, while the handful of non-German European arms firms hoped that they could license their designs to American manufacturers.

The occasional boom from a piece of artillery firing or the rattle of a machine gun being tested served to punctuate the military hymns and marches being played over a tin-horned gramophone. The only enlisted man allowed in the tent was the lowly private whose job it was to replace records and crank the grammy's spring handle. He would no doubt be called an organ-grinder's monkey for the rest of his enlistment.

Bell was on hand too and so was Joe Marchetti. They lolled in leather camp chairs alongside Vanderbilt and a pair of French pilots. A coterie of officers and civilians approached, small talk was exchanged, and then they moved on. Willie K. had a cut crystal flute of champagne on an overturned ammunition crate that served as their coffee table, while Bell, Joe, and the pilots either drank sarsaparilla or something else nonalcoholic.

Also on the makeshift table was a field telephone with a line that had been spliced into the main cable and run out to the tent sitting in the middle of the vast open pasture.

Bell received irregular but steady reports from Archie and his team following Devlin Connell. They'd caught a break. When Connell had left his Hoboken home, he'd turned north and caught a ferry to Manhattan and then crossed over to Long Island. He was either going to the Shinnecock Light near Southampton or the one all the way at the tip of the island at Montauk Point. Either one was far closer than they'd expected, which meant they could spend the day enjoying the festivities rather than flying south to some lighthouse in Jersey or north to Connecticut. At the speed the French could fly, they wouldn't need to leave until it was nearly dark.

The sound of an airplane approaching soon drowned out the gramophone and the sociable conversation. Bell didn't see the plane until after it had landed and taxied to where two other planes sat. He didn't recognize the make or model, but knew it would garner little attention from the French and British officers. Its fuselage was a narrow, almost toylike affair and its wings looked as delicate and vulnerable as a butterfly's. The builder had tried to make the biplane look more capable by mounting a Lewis gun on the upper wing and forging an awkward trigger extension so the pilot needn't lift himself from the seat to fire it over the prop. Also, the little four-cylinder engine appeared woefully underpowered.

In contrast, Bell had been shown pictures of what French designers at Nieuport were building. Their model 11 was a purpose-built air-to-air fighter plane with a nine-cylinder rotary engine and a better than one-hundred-mile-per-hour top speed.

No, he thought, the little canvas moth sitting out in the field would not stir any interest for its builders.

It was only when the plane's unmuffled engine sputtered to silence that Bell heard the field telephone ringing right in front of him. He snatched it up and put the speaker to his ear.

"Bell."

The line was full of static. He could hear a voice amid the distortion, but the sound was too vague to understand.

Bell set the microphone on the table and stooped over it awkwardly so he could jam a finger into his other ear to deaden the ambient noises. "Repeat your message," he said a little louder. Several men eyed him for being rude.

"Isaac." Bell recognized his name but only knew it was Archie because no one else would call. His voice sounded like he was shouting from the bottom of a well protected by an iron roof during a hailstorm. "He just drove past Shinnecock. He is going to Montauk."

"Our target is Montauk," he said to verify.

"Yes. Montauk."

"Great job. Keep an eye on him and grab him in the morning."

"Will do. Good hunting."

Bell cut the line. The two French pilots, Didion and Bonneville, and Joe Marchetti had been listening in.

"A little farther for us," Jacques Bonneville, the lead pilot, said in passable but accented English. "But should be *pas de problème*. Uh . . . no problem. You still wish to arrive at eleven?"

"I'd prefer sunset actually," Bell said. "Just to be certain we catch them. But the last time, he made contact with the ship at midnight. An hour cushion is the best we're going to get."

"Our craft has tremendous endurance, Monsieur Bell, but we cannot stay aloft forever."

"Jacques, I'm just grateful you're here and that Willie K. told me all about your marvelous flying machine months ago when your participation at this expo was first announced."

He smiled. *"Oui, elle est tout à fait remarquable, notre petit amour."*

Just then, the light filtering into the tent faded measurably, like a partial eclipse, because the bulk of Bonneville's *petit amour* swiveled over the festive pavilion as it rotated with the wind around its mooring mast. The breeze kept blowing for a few more seconds and the massive shadow moved on.

They passed the rest of the afternoon amicably. Bell won ten dollars off a general who thought his aide-de-camp was a superior marksman with a pistol. The young lieutenant matched Bell shot for shot over the first twenty rounds, but then failed to get the center ring on their twenty-third bullet fired. For the last shots of the best of twenty-five, they were dead even again. Bell said if the lieutenant ever left the Army, Van Dorn was always hiring.

As the sun finally began to set, burnishing the sky in golds and pinks, and the day's events and demonstrations came to an end, the pilots started prepping for the mission.

Their aircraft was built by the newly renamed Zodiac company, a prominent fabrics and rubber manufacturer outside of Paris that had grown from its founder's love of ballooning. This was their prototype dirigible, or in French *dirigeable,* essentially a hydrogen-filled rubberized cloth envelope, tapered to give it some aerodynamics with what resembled a sleek wingless aircraft slung under its enormous belly.

The long, rakish gondola had enough room for four seated men as well as a highly tuned one-hundred-and-twenty-horsepower engine to spin its "pusher"-style propeller. Flight control was achieved through a cruciform combination of vertical and horizontal stabilizers at the rear, in addition to being able to lower or raise the nose by shifting weights along a rail built between the gondola and the envelope.

The nearly two-hundred-foot airship was

a dark green color due to the proprietary doping compound used to make it impervious to gas seepage. With typical French flourish, the sharklike crew accommodation was painted a festive yellow with green accents on its corners and around the windows and half-sized side door.

Her name was stenciled on the rear portion of the crew module. *L'Avocat.* The Avocado.

While Emile Didion checked over the engine and made certain they had supplies of spares, especially lubricating oil, Jacques Bonneville checked the tension in all the control wires that transferred motion of the wheels and levers in the cockpit up to the fins, as well as the counterweight trolly. Bell and Marchetti double-checked the small vulcanized-rubber boat they would deploy from the airship once they'd located their target. It had also been supplied by Zodiac. The boat would be slung under the dirigible during the flight, and they wanted to ensure the oars and other supplies were secured aboard. They also rustled up Thermoses of coffee, some for the pilots and some for themselves, for the long trip to shore.

The airship shifted and swung as the wind grew from out of the east. In the few days it had been on display, the little wheel under the fuselage to support the back half of the lighter-than-air craft had worn down a fifty-degree arc of grass in the field. Tonight, for the first time, it had rotated beyond that range. Bell and Bonneville exchanged a silent worried look. If the weather held, they'd be bucking a headwind the entire way.

"Can you fly her alone?" Bell asked.

"Technically yes, but another set of eyes and hands makes it much safer. Why do you ask?"

"Exchanging your copilot with an equal weight of gas cans."

Bonneville frowned. "I think not. We will just have to leave sooner and spend less time loitering over the ocean."

"I don't know how big of a window I need. That's the problem."

"I understand, but I need Emile. We are flying over the ocean at night. This is something we have never done. I am sorry, Monsieur Bell, but my decision is final."

"And probably for the best," Bell admitted. "I tend to throw caution to the wind too often."

The Frenchman grinned. "Well, tonight you throw our green avocado to the wind. How about that?"

Bell groaned at the bad joke, delighting

Bonneville even more.

At last, the men and machine were ready. The pilots buckled themselves into adjoining seats with matching controls in front of them. They were separated by an open bulkhead from two more seats — one for a radio operator and observer, though the radio had been stripped for this flight, and the other for a flight engineer, a role that Bell would fulfill as needed. Zodiac had provided a ground crew to help launch and recover the dirigible. One of those men was now nearly to the top of the mooring mast, ready to release the mechanical clamp that held the nose to the wooden pole. Other men held ropes attached to the gondola so they could back the airship safely from its mount before letting go and allowing *L'Avocat* to claw its way into the sky.

The scene was lit with electric floodlights powered by a sputtering generator. Lights also glowed above the heads of the men watching the spectacle from Vanderbilt's sumptuous tent.

"Ready on the mast?" Bonneville shouted out the cockpit's open side window.

"Oui," the man called back.

"Ready on the lines?"

"Nous sommes prêts."

"Release."

The technician on the mooring mast ratcheted open the clamp and freed the airship from the tower. The men holding the mooring ropes pulled back ever so gently as the big blimp floated a few feet above the ground. Unlike an airplane that has brakes to prevent it from moving until the pilot is ready, the dirigible's engine couldn't be fired until the craft was in position to leave the field. The men maneuvered their charge a short distance from the mast with her nose still pointed into the wind.

"Démarrez le moteur," Bonneville shouted to the crew when he had the throttle and choke settings aligned.

One of the men walked the wooden prop through one revolution to fill the cylinders with fuel and air and then gave the blade a hearty shove. With a puff of blue smoke and a few pop-like misfires, the engine quickly settled into a powerful roar. The men had to redouble their efforts to prevent the airship from creeping forward as the prop bit into the sultry night air.

A chorus of cheers and raised glasses came from the men in the pavilion, now all a little buzzed from an afternoon of drinking.

Bonneville fed in more throttle and pulled a release that dropped dozens of ballast weights. This was the ground crew's cue to let go of the ropes. *L'Avocat* rose quickly without the ballast and Bonneville adjusted the trim so the ship climbed nose up, using the motor as well as the hydrogen's natural buoyancy to gain altitude.

"My first time flying lighter than air," Joe had to shout over the engine, but there was no mistaking the glee in his voice.

Bell didn't bother responding. He'd had two near-death experiences, once on a runaway balloon and another when the zeppelin-like airship he'd been on had come apart in midair. Third's the charm, he thought wryly, and settled in for the two-hour flight.

28

The headwinds were far worse than Bonneville or Bell thought they would be. It took nearly three hours and half their fuel reserves to fly the length of Long Island and circle out about twenty nautical miles, roughly two miles past the reach of the Montauk Light. Bell hadn't forgotten that they'd encountered the German spy ship a few miles past the Barnegat Light on the night they'd caught Connell sending his coded message. To make matters worse, they only reached the designated search area at eleven-thirty.

A three-quarter moon had risen as they'd bucked the winds eastward and it seemed to shine twice as brightly because of its reflection off the glass-smooth water. With their fuel load so depleted, Bonneville had little trouble flying up to around six thousand feet. The air was much cooler at that altitude, so each man had worn an insulated flight suit for the duration of the trek. Below, it was easy to see the wakes of the few ships transiting into and out of New York Harbor. The white lines were for the most part perfectly straight.

Bell studied the sea with big marine binoculars. He could see the sweep of the Montauk Light as its beam brushed the ocean. Were they already too late? He had no way of knowing. And would Connell signal in the same direction, due east, as he'd done before? Judging by the handful of ships still traveling at this late hour, due east or due south were both viable options. North was out because the residents of Fishers Island would certainly notice that something odd was occurring at the ever-dependable lighthouse.

Because of the consistent wind, Bonneville was forced to ramp up the engine from idle to power them back to the search area. Their fuel reserves continued to dwindle, though Bell took some satisfaction in seeing that shipping was diminishing in the area he suspected the German ship would receive Connell's signal.

And still the night wore on. Nothing out of the ordinary happened. Ships continued around the tip of Long Island, while the Montauk Light maintained its mesmerizing five-second sweep. Bell felt the pressure mounting and doubt creep into his thinking. Had this been a fool's errand from the outset? Had he misjudged the entire situation or had Connell sensed a trap?

It was nearing one-thirty in the morning. There was a single ship down below, its wake like a chalk line on a classroom blackboard. Bell's doubts were turning to dread.

The pilot waved Bell forward. He knew Bonneville wanted another check of their remaining fuel. He'd performed the routine task periodically as the night wore on. After getting the request, he made his way aft in the low-ceilinged space to where the motor was humming along. He swung open a soundproof hatch to gain access to the engine, the noise now more of a throaty growl. He pulled up the gauge stick that plumbed to the bottom of the fuel tank. He wiped it clean on a rag and reinserted it before pulling it out a second time. While the gasoline wasn't as viscous as the fluid that clung to an oil dipstick, he could read the gradations. They were below a quarter tank. Not good.

Bonneville seemed a decent enough sort, but cautious. The low reserves meant he'd want to return and land the dirigible at Willie Vanderbilt's country estate, probably immediately. And Bell wouldn't blame him, but he had just this one shot at recovering one of the Germans' advanced vacuum tubes. Sure, Archie would arrest Connell in the morning and put an end to his spy ring, but Bell wanted the coup, Connell, and their critical piece of radio equipment. He hated losing, but this was Bonneville's airship and the Frenchman had the final say.

Bell crawled forward, slowly, pausing to gaze out the window for a moment before making his way to the cockpit.

"How is it?" Bonneville asked over his shoulder.

The view from the cockpit was much better than from Bell's little window aft. The moonlight made the dark sky appear purple and vast, with the few clouds appearing like distant wraiths twisting through the night. Bell spotted a shooting star streak past impossibly fast and then vanish as it burned up in the atmosphere.

"A quarter tank. Maybe a little less."

"That's it. I'm sorry, Monsieur Bell. We must turn back. We should have when we had a third of a tank, but I wanted to give you all the time I could."

He reached to the throttle to increase airspeed to make his turn. Bell stopped him with his own hand. "We have to stay. I need to get aboard that spy ship."

"My hands are tied." He tried to shake his hand free from Bell's. Bell held on.

"Jacques, listen to me, please. I need to get on that ship. It's vital to your war effort."

"So you've said."

Like any military operation, the British Admiralty had told their French counterparts all about the necessity of using their airship, but that didn't mean the French told their pilots what was at stake. In war, secrecy is paramount.

"Right." Bell made the call to trust the pilot and the hell with secrecy. "The Germans have developed a new type of radio, one that can broadcast the whole way from here to Berlin. They are using it to order their U-boats to target ships carrying all the gear and equipment you and the British are buying from American factories, items vital to your holding off the Huns from marching into Paris.

"Every time they broadcast a new target's specifics, that ship is hunted until it's sunk. That's less weapons getting into the hands of your troops, less cloth to make uniforms, leather to make boots, less oil and coal to fuel your Navy as well as your factories."

Bell could tell he was getting through, so

he pressed on. "We can make a real difference, the four of us. We can save the lives of your soldiers and those poor wretched civilians who usually pay the greatest price in war. We have to stay, Jacques. The wind is out of the east, has been all night. Once we're away, climb back to altitude and cut the engine. Drift like a balloon and use the engine only as needed. You can do this. You have to do this."

Duty and caution was the conflict furrowing the pilot's brow. And as Bell had hoped, duty always took precedent to those dedicated enough to their principles.

"*D'accord.* Okay. We stay until there is one-eighth of a tank remaining. Any less it would be suicide."

Bell bought himself a half hour at best, probably less because the wind appeared to be picking up. It felt like a great victory, nevertheless. He gave Bonneville's shoulder a squeeze and returned to his mid-gondola vigil.

"We've got twenty minutes," he said to Joe, "half hour, tops."

They continued to scan the ocean, watching the few ships in the area to see if any acted suspiciously. It took Bell a couple of minutes to realize that the chalky white line of a ship's wake he'd tracked earlier looked like it was slowing. He called Joe over and pointed out the anomaly. "What do you think?"

"He's slowing down. I put him at about twenty miles from the light. And almost exactly due east. That's them, Isaac. It's the Germans. They took the bait."

Bell rushed for the cockpit again. "Jacques, we have them. They're slowing off our starboard side."

He stood behind the pilot as the man worked the rudder while keeping the engine at idle, ensuring it couldn't be heard from below. The dirigible was a solid two miles farther east than the ship. When he was aligned with the Germans he nodded to Didion to work the ballast controls. By opening a pair of valves, hydrogen vented from the dark green envelope and the airship began to drop from the sky. They had no way to judge their altitude or the rate at which they were falling, so it came down to the experience of the two aviators. They'd practiced this maneuver over the countless months since Zodiac had delivered the airship for trials.

Bell returned to the crew compartment and opened the main door. The ocean was noticeably closer than before. And their rate of descent seemed to be slowing. Didion was balancing the release of hydrogen knowing that additional ballast in the form of iron pellets stored under the gondola would allow them to ascend again later. Bell could no longer hear gas hissing out of the envelope as it was released. They were down from six thousand feet to just a few hundred as smoothly as if they'd ridden an elevator. Momentum kept the craft sinking lower and lower. The two pilots really knew their business.

With fifty or so feet to go, Bell used his boot knife to cut a loop of rope that kept the two-man raft snug against the gondola's belly. Once he'd severed the line, the rubber raft dropped twenty feet to the end of a second tether and stopped. It twisted in the airship's slipstream. Its impact with the water was his and Joe's cue to jump. Once the airship drifted so it was no longer overhead, Didion would release the remaining ballast and Bonneville would guide them home.

Joe crouched at Bell's shoulder, waiting for the swinging boat to splash down. When Bell turned to look, the young officer gave him an excited smile, like this was all fun and games. Bell was less upbeat about the next part of their operation. Sneaking aboard the German ship undetected wasn't going to be easy.

The Zodiac boat hit the water with a splash of white foam. Bell severed the rope tethering it to the airship. Joe jumped as he was putting the knife back in its scabbard, and then it was Bell's turn. The rush of air past his ears grew louder as he accelerated downward and there was that instinctual squeeze to his heart as if his body knew it shouldn't ever fall this fast.

He hit feet-first and went deep, his body in a swirl of agitated bubbles. The water was icy cold. He opened his eyes against the sting of salt and began swimming up after his bubbles. He reached the surface and sucked in a few lungfuls of air before looking around. Not ten feet away, Joe Marchetti was throwing a leg over the raft's elastic gunwale. Bell began to swim after him. Neither wore shoes, so the going was easy enough.

Joe helped him into the raft and the two men lay still for a few seconds to catch their breath. The French dirigible was already a half mile north and slowly powering its way into the night sky. The only way it was at all visible was when its bulk blotted out the smear of bright stars as it passed between them and the earth.

"Okay," Bell finally said while he opened

the equipment bag tied off on the raft's floor. "That was the easy part."

Bell handed out towels, dry clothes, and canvas shoes, so he and Joe wouldn't lose more body heat. He strapped on his 9 millimeter, took a bearing on a compass, and gave Joe one of the two oars. They had a small gasoline motor that could be secured to the transom, but that was for the long ride to shore once they'd completed the mission.

It was close enough to two a.m. for Bell to assume that's when Connell would send his coded signal. There was no way he and Joe could paddle to their rendezvous in time. Bell risked firing the outboard motor for the first mile. They were still beyond where they could see the Montauk Light directly, but its flash was noticeable as a reflection against the sky. They were steering due west, heading straight for the light, and hopefully the darkened German ship in between. After ten minutes, he cut the motor, pulled it from the transom, and he and Joe started rowing, throwing everything they had into each stroke.

The wind at their back was a godsend. They rowed shoulder to shoulder on their knees. Bell sliced apart the equipment bag and draped it over them like a wide cape so it acted as a primitive sail.

The more he thought about his speech to the French pilot, the more he recognized that he and Joe could not fail. Lives, maybe tens of thousands of them, depended on the next few hours. Without exchanging a word, he and Joe picked up their pace.

29

Bell knew the moment it was two o'clock exactly because the Montauk Light no longer strobed against the night sky. It had stopped rotating and its lamp shone steadily eastward. Just as the Barnegat Light had the night they encountered the spy ship, the Montauk Light blinked rapidly for several moments and then returned to its five-second characteristic flash.

The two men redoubled their effort, straining arms and shoulders until their muscles screamed in protest. They ignored the pain and dug even harder.

A metallic clang shattered the otherwise quiet night. It came from dead ahead. They slowed, panting, tired but not yet spent.

"We were right," Joe whispered.

"It only made sense," Bell replied.

The German ship emerged from the darkness. She showed no light at all, not even the mandatory red and green navigation lamps near her bridge, but the moon's glow was enough for them to see details. It appeared a little larger than it had the night it had rammed them — at least two hundred feet. She had two cargo derricks on her main deck and one aft of the superstructure and was virtually indistinguishable from any other all-metal coastal freighter plying the waters of the Eastern Seaboard.

What Bell and Marchetti had deduced from their first run-in with the ship and mentioned to Roosevelt was that the Germans erected an observation tower whenever they received a signal from shore. Most shipping passing close enough to a lighthouse will sail within the light's reach. It simplified navigation. The temporary tower allowed for a trained watcher to see farther over the horizon and thus let the ship stay far enough from the coast to remain undetected.

The sound they'd just heard was the clang of one of the metal struts hitting something as sailors dismantled the ungainly scaffolding that grew atop the boxy pilothouse just behind the funnel. The tower was also the reason the ship loitered after retrieving the signal. They didn't want to leave the delicate-looking assembly in place while they were underway.

Bell estimated they would need at least twenty more minutes.

They silently rowed closer to the ship, crouching behind the gunwale as best they could. The sailors seemed intent on their job, so they were able to tuck under the ship's fantail without being spotted. They could hear the engine idling through the hull plates. They used their hands to walk the raft forward to where the anchor chain plunged into the sea. The depth off Long Island was rarely greater than sixty feet.

They tied the raft to one of the rusty links and Bell led them up the chain. The tide's sweep meant there was enough tension on the chain for them to climb almost silently. Bell paused at the top, daring to take a quick peek before ducking down. He'd spotted nothing out of the ordinary. The bridge was pitch-black. It was likely, however, that someone was inside on watch, which made this the most dangerous part of the operation.

There wasn't enough room to crawl through the hawse hole, the opening where the anchor chain was fed from the chain locker under the decking. Bell had to go over the fairing. He moved slowly, almost oozing his way over the top of the railing. He couldn't afford to draw any attention.

He put out an arm as he lowered himself to the deck, moving as deliberately as a stalking cat.

He used his hands and toes to crawl behind the raised hatch covering of the first cargo hold and waited while Joe Marchetti repeated his performance.

Bell gave consideration to what would happen if they were caught. He assumed shot, if the Germans had firearms aboard. If not, they'd likely weigh the two of them down with chains and toss them over the side. Bell recalled a jail cell conversation he'd once had with an underworld enforcer. He'd explained reasonably that when weighing down a victim, you have to wrap the chains around the torso and not the legs. Why? Bell had asked, and the man replied that when a body is eaten, sometimes the feet get gnawed from the ankles and the corpse can float back to the surface.

If it came to that, Bell would request ankle chains and hope the Germans weren't savvy to the latest body-dumping protocols.

He and Joe slow-crawled to the superstructure using every scrap of cover and shadow they could find. They could hear the crew continuing to dismantle the observation tower, which Bell realized was also likely their transmitting antenna, making both men acutely aware of their limited time.

The steel door leading to the interior of the superstructure had been left open to increase ventilation. They assumed the radio room would be located one deck up and close to the bridge. Bell drew his pistol. He intentionally hadn't chambered a round and gripped the weapon by its barrel. He needed a club right now, not a gun, and he knew the amount of strength it took to render a man unconscious versus how much of a blow would be fatal.

The ship's interior was much darker. The floor was just inky blackness and the white walls felt indistinct in the gloom. They could make out several closed doors, and to their right, heading toward the bow, was an alcove. Moving slowly, Bell and Marchetti stepped toward the alcove, the fingers of their left hands brushing the wall so that they wouldn't become disoriented as they moved farther from the pale moon-glow that seeped through the open doorway.

The staircase was in the alcove, as Bell had thought. The steps were steep and narrow. A choke point, if ever there was one. If someone started down while Bell and Marchetti were climbing it, the mission was over and they'd count themselves lucky if they managed to escape.

Bell swallowed before taking the first step.

The treads were worn wood and silent as he climbed, not that he had to be too concerned. There was a great deal of background noise with the engine running and waves slapping against the hull. From above, he heard the sound of a chair scraping back against a metal deck. Seconds later there was a flash of dim light, as if someone had pushed aside a curtain. Bell pressed himself as flat as possible, ready to spring.

A metal door opened and closed on the upper deck.

Reaching behind him, he tapped Joe Marchetti's head to make sure he had the younger man's attention and powered up the last couple of steps. The curtained doorway was to the left. At the end of the hall were open double doors that led to the darkened bridge. Again Bell felt certain there would be at least one man standing watch. The only other door had a stencil at eye level — wc. He'd been right. WC was the acronym for water closet. The radio operator was taking a bathroom break. Bell swept aside the curtain and stepped through with Joe moving right behind him.

The room was small and windowless and warmer than even the stuffy companionways because of the radios and some other electrical equipment Bell didn't recognize. Light came from a lit oil lamp. The stench of body odor, cabbage, and cheap cigars hung like a fog in the tiny space. Bell immediately pushed Joe against the wall on one side of the curtain, while he installed himself on the other. Marchetti couldn't tear his eyes off the radio gear. One radio looked familiar to Bell. It was like Freddie Wiles's set back aboard the *Centurion.* The other was sleek and black, with multiple sets of dials and silver toggle switches of unknown purpose. It exuded tremendous power without even being in use.

Bell heard the door to the head creak open and then clank closed, the gush of a toilet cistern refilling sounding oddly loud. The radioman's hand slid aside the curtain a moment later. Bell let him get two steps into the room before bringing the butt of his Browning down hard against the side of the man's skull. Joe was there to catch the slumping figure and ease him to the deck. He then went straight for the radios sitting on a narrow bench table.

Cabinets flanked the pair of radios, multidrawer affairs for all manner of spare parts, tools, and whatever else the operator needed to keep the vital equipment in working order. There was another filing cabinet too, likely for record keeping and logs of all communiqués the ship received and sent. Bell spotted a small safe and bet the codebooks were kept inside. There was no need for him to crack it open and recover the cypher keys, since they were about to shut down the entire operation.

There was an unmade cot jammed in one corner of the room. Bell dragged the unconscious operator next to it and used his thumb to wipe the small amount of blood from his pistol. He smeared it on the bed's footpost. Maybe the ruse would work, maybe not, but it was worth the try.

He turned back to Joe, who was methodically going through the drawers, his eyes wide with interest at what he was seeing. Bell moved close and spoke in a whisper. "Well?"

"They're years ahead of anything I've seen or read about."

"What about the vacuum tubes?"

"Give me another minute."

Bell felt time slipping away. The sailors would have the mast down soon and the ship would come back to life. They would immediately head farther out to sea and probably reassemble the tower under cover of darkness the following night in order to transmit their message to Germany, where the information was relayed to the wolf packs. No doubt the captain or watch officer would check in on the radio shack even before they got underway.

The knot in Bell's stomach tightened.

"We have a problem," Joe said.

And tightened again. "What?"

"They're going to know we stole some tubes." Joe showed him a drawer with delicate glass bulbs nestled in slots that had been lined with soft cloth to protect them from the ship's movement. There were only eight tubes in total. They were a little bigger than a man's thumb, with one end rounded and the other blunt and showing two metal studs that could be slotted into the circuit board inside the radio.

Joe added, "I figured the technology is so new and manufacturing these things so tricky that they would need dozens and dozens to make sure they had enough for a mission of this length. It looks like only two have been blown so far. The others are in perfect order. What do we do?"

When it came to theft, there were two principal ways to go about it. Slyly, like a cat burglar, leaving no trace. Or treat the robbery like a smash and grab, sowing as much chaos and confusion as possible. Bell had hoped to keep this quiet, but that wasn't an option now.

There were a couple of liter-sized metal tins on the floor under the desk. Bell bent and opened one. It had no odor, so he opened another. He sniffed and recoiled at the burning chemical stench of acetone or some other similar chemical solvent. He guessed it was used to clean the delicate electrical equipment of corrosive salt. He pulled his boot knife and carefully sawed off the top of the thin metal can, accidently sloshing some of the acrid fluid onto his hands.

"Grab two of the tubes and leave the drawer open, then open the lamp's glass and give me a hand dragging the operator out of here."

Marchetti placed two tubes in lined metal sleeves he'd brought and slid one in each front pocket. He then swung open the kerosene lamp's glass panel so the flame was exposed, and together he and Bell hauled the unconscious seaman to the doorway. He would be safe enough on the floor because the fireball would mushroom up to the ceiling.

Bell poked his head out into the corridor. He saw no movement on the bridge and heard no one coming up the stairs. He nodded to Joe. Marchetti rushed out of the radio room and hunkered down on the steps. Bell used an underhand motion to fling the full contents of the square tin can at the open oil lamp and turned to run as the volatile liquid arced across the room and splashed all over the radios and cabinets.

A few drops found their way into the lamp and the partially aerosolized cloud of liquid ignited with a deep crump and a blast of overpressure that tossed Bell across the hallway even as he'd tried to get out of the blast radius. The flash of light, after so much darkness, was blindingly bright, and Bell felt wholly disoriented. The detonation had consumed all of the oxygen in the room and hallway, so as soon as the explosion dissipated, air whooshed up from below to fill the void, limiting what actually caught on fire to the bedding and some loose papers.

Joe scampered up to help guide Bell back down to the main deck. There was no point skulking back to the bow, so both men vaulted the rail and fell the ten or so feet to the water. They came up as slowly as possible, pressing themselves to the rust-scaled hull. Men could be heard shouting above on deck, and several raced past close enough for them to hear their shoes slapping on the metal plating. Bell and Marchetti started swimming for the bow. A bell began to sound to roust the off-duty sailors so they could help contain the disaster.

It took just a few moments to reach the bow and their little inflatable boat. Joe made to roll himself inside, but Bell stopped him. "We'll be less visible if we tow it away."

He untied the painter, and keeping their heads low in the water and the raft between them and the German ship, they slowly swam out into the night. The moon was still up, but patches of cloud darkened it for several minutes at a time. The alarm bell fell silent after a few minutes, and looking back they could see no telltale aura of a burning flame. After fifteen minutes, Bell estimated that they were close to half a mile from the spy ship and deemed it safe enough to man the oars.

While he and Joe got situated and took up the paddles, deck and navigation lights flickered on aboard the distant vessel.

"Fire's out, observation tower is down, and it's time to go," Joe guessed.

"Looks like it. Also means we can ditch the oars and fire up the outboard."

"Now, that's music to my ears."

30

It was nearing dawn by the time they were close enough to the Montauk Light to see the keeper's house and other buildings atop its windswept bluff. The little motor might have made for a less tiring night, but it was no quicker than if they had rowed the twenty miles themselves.

The lamp had gone out a moment earlier, a fact that had surprised Bell, as he believed it was still dark enough for mariners to need its guidance. It was a detail out of place, an inconsistency, something to raise his level of concern.

"Something's not right," he said before they made their run through the gentle breakers. "The light should still be on."

"I think so too," Joe admitted. "What does it mean?"

"I'm not sure." Bell pulled his automatic. He'd wiped it down during the night to dry the mechanisms but hadn't been able to re-oil it. He wasn't concerned, though. John Moses Browning designed robust, dependable guns.

He was more concerned with his own abilities at the moment. He and Joe had managed only an hour or so of fitful sleep during the journey to shore. They were both still wet, cold, and exhausted. Thirst and hunger were also a problem.

Bell pulled the tiller hard over and steered the boat a little southward before running it onto the pebbly beach. They were still in the line of sight of the tower, but a hill hid them from the lower outbuildings. They jumped from the Zodiac-built boat and each grabbed a handhold at the bow in order to drag the lightweight craft above the tide line.

Bell made sure Joe stayed behind him as he climbed the bluff to get a protected look at the lighthouse complex. They crawled through patches of grass to get the best view. Bell saw no movement and heard nothing but the wind and the waves. It all looked too quiet.

No, Bell thought, it felt abandoned.

He gestured for Joe to remain hidden in the seagrass and approached the building where the lamp oil was stored. The door was ajar and swung like a slow metronome with the breeze. He pushed it fully open with his left hand, his pistol gripped in his right. The room smelled of kerosene and the floors had a sheen to them from decades of whale oil spillage. He smelled something else, something foul and altogether horrific.

There was a tarp laying on the floor, covering something that was the size and shape of a body. He turned, scanning the outside surroundings for any movement. He looked to where Joe hid and could barely see the paleness of his face screened by some tall grass. Everything appeared as it had been. Bell went to the tarp, knelt, and slowly rolled it back.

Wes Nevins was his name. An agent for a couple of years who usually worked anti-gang cases with Harry Warren. Not married, but seeing a widow with two young kids. Judging by the amount of blood, his slit throat was what had killed him. Bell pulled the tarp down farther. It resisted as if it had been glued to Nevins's corpse. It finally peeled away. His killer, Devlin Connell most certainly, had also gutted Nevins, opening his belly like he was performing some macabre cesarean section.

There was enough blood around the gruesome wound to tell Bell that his coworker and friend had been alive when the Irishman had so brutally slashed his abdomen and maybe lived for ten or twenty seconds with the agony of being eviscerated.

He gently rolled the body to check Nevins's holster. He carried a .38 revolver and it was missing.

Bell went back outside, purging his lungs with some deep breaths. That's when he realized there were no cars in the driveway. It made sense that Archie and his team would have parked a good distance off and hiked in, but there was no sign of Connell's Chevrolet. Bell felt an icy chill crawl up his spine.

He shouted for Joe to come out and Marchetti jogged over to where he stood.

"Connell's car is gone. One of my men is dead in the oil shed."

"What happened?"

"Don't know."

Bell then bellowed out Archie's name, cupping his hands around his mouth and shouting in the four cardinal directions. He strained to hear a reply, but got nothing.

"We need to search the complex," Bell said, and gave Marchetti the safest assignment on the off chance Connell had hidden his car and stuck around. "Start in the tower, go all the way to the top, open any door you come across. I'm going to take the keeper's house."

"Gotcha."

"On the jump, Joe. Even if Archie sent back one of the cars, there's still three other men currently unaccounted for."

Bell went through the keeper's house like a cyclone, moving fast and caring little for the wake of destruction he left behind. Nevins was dead. Archie and the others missing. He felt time slipping through his fingers. The building was large, but logically laid out. He saw no sign of any struggle, no traces of blood, nothing at all to indicate the fate of his friends.

He was out of the house long before Joe had climbed up and down the tower's two hundred and sixty-nine spiraling steps. As soon as Marchetti strode from the tower, shaking his head, Bell started jogging down the long driveway. Joe soon fell in next to him.

Bell couldn't get the image of Archie lying dead out of his head. They'd been rivals and then friends since college. He'd been Archie's best man and Archie had been his. They were closer than brothers and it tortured him to think he might be gone.

At least twice a minute, he would stop and shout out Archie's name and listen for a response. Five minutes after descending the bluff and entering the forest that flanked the access road, he and Joe shared a startled look when he got a faint reply.

"Isaac. I'm here." Archie's voice sounded distant and strained by pain, but it was unmistakably him.

"We hear you," Bell said in a relieved rush. "Where are you?"

"South side of the road. In a gully."

Joe and Bell charged into the woods to their left. The forest was tightly packed with second-growth trees that blocked nearly all the rays of the newly risen sun. Ten yards in, the ground fell away sharply in a narrow cut likely gouged out during the last ice age. Archie lay at the bottom, filthy and disheveled, with a large bloodstain on his shirt.

Bell climbed down as quickly as caution would allow him. The going was steep, and the rocks covered in slick moss. "You've been shot. How bad?"

"I'm still alive, but it hurts like hell. I tried to crawl out of here once I knew Connell was gone, but by then I didn't have the strength. He killed Wes."

"I know," Bell said as he bent over his friend to examine the wound.

"I got cocky, and Connell got the drop on us. I thought he was in the tower, but he was hiding out."

"Stop talking." Bell sliced open Archie's

shirt and used his blade to cut off part of the tail to wipe away some of the dried blood. Archie winced at his ministrations. "No air bubbles in the blood. Good sign."

Panting, Archie said, "I wouldn't have lasted the night with a lung shot." He paused and then took a deep breath. "Considering the pain, I'd say the bullet hit me between two ribs and traveled around my side like a train riding the rails."

Bell rolled Archie over to see if he could spot the bullet, making the man wince and then whimper.

"Sorry," Bell said. "The latissimus muscle is bruised almost black. I think you're spot-on with your self-diagnosis, and we'll add a couple of broken ribs for good measure."

"He's an animal, Isaac."

"I saw what he did to Wes. Where are the others?"

"It was just the two of us."

"You had three cars. Six guys." Bell's tone was more accusatory than he'd intended.

"One car broke down first thing this morning and the other just missed the ferry across the Hudson." Pain began to clip his words into terse syllables. "We had no choice. Wes and I had to keep tailing Connell."

"It's okay," Bell said reassuringly. "We need to worry about getting you out of here."

Bell supposed Archie could have sent Wes to find a phone once they knew the Irishman was coming to Montauk and that's when he got hit. A potential mistake, but he didn't like to second-guess his people. He nodded to Joe, who was crouched on the other side of Archie Abbott, and together they lifted his shoulders and torso to get him sitting upright. In the uncertain light of the dawn filtering through the forest canopy, Archie's skin looked pale and waxen.

Through clenched teeth he said, "You can't lift me up on the left side. Too much. Lift under my right shoulder and left hip, maybe."

"Sure thing. Joe, switch sides with me." While Marchetti was certainly strong, he was much smaller than Bell, so it made sense for Isaac to do the heavy lifting.

Bell and Joe exchanged nods. Bell got his shoulder under Archie's good arm and lifted while Joe pulled up with his hands under Abbott's backside. Archie suppressed the scream they all knew he wanted to bellow, and they got him to his feet. He stood shakily, with his body twisting around and hunched as if to protect his injured side.

Joe went a little ahead of Archie and Bell so he could pull back branches to ease their slow shuffle out of the forest and back to the gravel lane. They laid him on a bed of moss that would be out of the direct sun once it climbed higher into the sky. Archie didn't say anything, but he panted through the pain for a very long minute.

"Our car is hidden a mile ahead, left side of the road opposite a tree that was split by lightning." The detail was delivered with great agony and Archie passed out as the last word left his lips.

Bell told Joe to get the car as fast as he could. "I'm going back to the main house to see if there are any supplies that'll help."

While Marchetti took off like an Olympic runner, Bell jogged the short distance back to the weathered keeper's house. A lifetime of examining how others lived meant Bell knew where to look. He rifled through the kitchen cabinets first and found a couple of bottles of patent medicine. Even though nearly all such potions were nothing but snake oil, one of them boasted it had double the morphine of its nearest competitor. Bell swiped it and a blanket and clean towels from a linen cabinet and ran back to Archie's side.

Arch writhed in his sleep and his eyes

behind their closed lids danced and jittered like a toy top just before it collapses. He began to mutter about someone not answering a phone and then said mournfully, "Oh. Wes. No."

Bell guessed this was a repeat of what he'd said when he discovered their dead comrade.

He was worried. Archie was always larger than life, a center of attention, and seemingly charmed by the fates. He didn't recall a time when Archie ever got more than a black eye during any of the stupid jams they'd gotten themselves into. Seeing him like this, bloodied and in real danger of losing his life, Bell felt a cold fear in the pit of his stomach, something he'd never experienced before.

His eyes burned.

A few minutes later, the sound of an approaching automobile encroached on his silent agonizing. He looked up. Joe was behind the wheel of one of the agency's Model Ts and pushing the car to its very limits. He slowed in time so that when he braked to a stop, he didn't kick a choking cloud of dust over Bell and the supine Archie Abbott.

He turned the car around before hopping out, the motor at idle.

Archie remained unconscious as they carried him to the car and laid him in the backseat. Bell stayed in the rear compartment with him, cradling Archie's head and holding a fresh towel to the wound, which had reopened when they hoisted him from the ground.

"Keep it nice and steady."

"Yes, sir."

An hour later, they found a doctor's office outside of Southampton, recognizable by the caduceus emblem of two intertwined snakes on the sign in front of the two-story clapboard home. Archie hovered between consciousness and oblivion for the entire ride, muttering and occasionally crying out, but never opening his eyes or giving any indication he knew where he was.

Joe parked behind what he presumed to be the doctor's car in the driveway and dashed into the building without need of instructions. He returned a moment later with a man who was too young to be a doctor, so most likely an orderly. He carried a rolled-up canvas stretcher. The two men unfurled it on the ground.

"Gunshot is under the left arm," Bell told the orderly.

"Got it."

Joe and the attendant gently slid Archie

from Bell's lap and lowered him onto the stretcher. The towel he'd placed under Archie was soaked in blood.

Bell crawled out and lifted the front of the stretcher, as Archie was too much weight for Joe to handle. He stayed at their side as they carried Abbott around to the front porch and up the handful of steps. The doctor was waiting just inside. He was either a youthful fifty or a haggard forty, with brushed-back silvering hair, dark brooding eyes, and long precise fingers.

"Take him down the hall, room on the right," he said, even as he pulled back Archie's shirt to take a look at the wound.

Bell and the orderly brought Arch to an exam room/surgical suite with anatomical posters on the walls and a steel-framed bed that could be raised or lowered via a worm gear system. Glass-fronted cabinets were filled with countless jars and bottles of medicines, packs of bandages, and boxes of other medical supplies. It was as clean and up-to-date as any hospital theater Bell had ever seen. The doctor and Joe rolled Archie off the stretcher and onto the bed, which the doctor immediately cranked up so he could examine his patient without having to stoop.

He poured alcohol into a ceramic basin

and swirled his hands through the solution to sterilize them before turning to his patient. "I'm John Ridgeway," he said without looking up. "Tell me what happened."

"Gunshot sometime last night," Bell replied. "Unknown caliber. He spent the night outdoors with no protection."

"Infection's going to be bad, most likely. The bullet has to come out now."

"Not to be disrespectful, but are you a qualified surgeon?"

If he was offended by the question, it didn't distract Dr. Ridgeway from examining the wound track. "I'm head of surgery at Southampton Hospital and I spent the summer of 'ninety-eight in Cuba with the Third Army doing about twenty of these types of operations a day. Lost some, saved most."

Bell paused, absorbing the information before saying, "Good enough for me. What can we do?"

"Nothing. Vincent here is my assistant until he heads back to Columbia in the fall and my nurse will be along in a moment. Once . . ."

"Archie Abbott," Bell said.

"Once Mr. Abbott is under the influence of chloroform, I will remove the bullet and any bone fragments along its trajectory. I will clean the wound as best I can and stitch him back up. Straightforward. But as I said, infection is my real worry."

"I will phone his wife," Bell said. "She'll likely want to bring their family physician."

"The more hands on deck the better. Now leave us."

"Thank you, Doctor."

Bell and Joe backed out of the operating room as a nurse bustled past saying, "I have the anesthesia."

Bell strode straight outside and went to fire up the Model T. He wished he had his Simplex right now.

He issued orders as if Joe were already a Van Dorn agent. "Call the office. Tell them what happened. Make sure they reach out to Lillian Abbott and my wife, Marion. She'll want to come out with her. Book the best rooms you can find here in town. Three at least.

"If whoever is on stakeout at Devlin Connell's house checks in, warn him the man is armed and dangerous and knows he's a suspect. Also, I want four additional agents to meet me at his house in . . ." Bell made the rough calculation. "Four hours."

He could have sent his men in on a raid two hours sooner — the time it would take him just to get across to Manhattan — but there was no way he was going to miss out if Connell had been foolish enough to stick around his little New Jersey bungalow.

The engine fired on the first crank. "Make sure you give everyone this office's phone number and Ridgeway's name. And, Joe, would you please stay with him until everyone else arrives?"

Marchetti saw the pain deep in Bell's eyes. "Never dreamed of leaving his side."

Bell managed to croak "Thanks" before quickly reversing the Ford out of the driveway and turning it west.

31

Isaac Bell had been awake for twenty-two of the past twenty-four hours, but was driven by such anger that he felt fresh and ready for anything. He'd had to buy gas from a garage in Southampton, and while the mechanic was filling the tank, he'd ducked into the diner next door and left with two fried egg and ham sandwiches wrapped in butcher paper.

He ate one-handed as he drove the Ford across the length of Long Island. As he got closer to the city, traffic thickened, but he barely slowed his pace, using aggressive moves to exploit even the slightest advantage to maintain his speed.

There was no ferry service from Long Island across the Hudson to New Jersey, so he roared across the Brooklyn Bridge and into Manhattan. Thankfully, rush hour was over and traffic was manageable. The ferry docks were at the base of Liberty and Cortlandt Streets, a few blocks farther south but on the other side of the city. He'd arrived in New York twenty minutes early by his estimation, but lost all of that advantage crossing over to the West Side.

The two ferry terminals were owned by the railways and usually just carried passengers, but as more and more New Yorkers bought automobiles, car ferries were growing more common. Bell lost another fifteen minutes waiting for the ferry to arrive from the Hoboken terminal, but he was the first to board, which meant he'd be the first off on the other side.

He forced himself to relax. There was nothing he could do during the fifteen-minute crossing but tighten the grip on his emotions. He needed to be cool and dispassionate when he arrived in New Jersey. There was nothing he could do for Archie either. It was best he put his friend's condition out of his head. The surgery was routine, Ridgeway had said. Infection was the concern, but Archie was still young and as vital as a bull. He'd fight any infection the way he used to KO opponents in the boxing ring.

The ferry approached the New Jersey terminal with its engine belching black smoke and white clouds of venting steam.

The captain had to have been a veteran because there was no noticeable bump when they reached the end of their slip. While workers tied off the lines, Bell refired the Model T's motor and retook his seat in preparation for the ramp being dropped.

It came down slowly, like the medieval drawbridge in one of Marion's recent two-reelers. Bell hit the gas as soon as the ramp hit the concrete. Connell's house was on the far side of the "Mile Square City." He was close and anticipation fizzed in his veins like champagne bubbles.

If anything, the waterfront and streets of Hoboken were even more chaotic than Manhattan's. Nearly eighty thousand people were shoehorned among the countless small factories and warehouses. The air was heavy with smoke and the smell of a stockyard hidden someplace in the maze of lanes and alleys. Bell ignored the chaos and maintained his focus.

He remembered the route from his previous reconnaissance and turned onto Connell's street a few minutes later. Everything appeared normal. A couple of kids were playing stickball, while two mothers with push prams had stopped walking their babies to chat under the shade of an elm tree. Connell's house was mid-block. There was no car in the driveway and none of the automobiles he could see matched the description of the Irishman's Chevrolet.

Bell didn't turn down Connell's block, but circled out one more street and cut across several other blocks until turning once again. This way he could come up behind whoever had stakeout duty. Bell found a spot to tuck the Ford and stepped from the vehicle. His clothes were soiled and smelly, but he could easily pass for a factory worker home early for lunch. He tucked the Browning into his waistband and covered it with his shirttail and started down the street.

He wasn't sure which of the cars lining the block was the current stakeout vehicle, so he walked slowly, casually, looking into each as inconspicuously as possible. The kids were still playing ball a block ahead. Things seemed okay. Another half block and he finally spotted the silhouette of a man sitting in a parked car. But something wasn't right. The guy looked like he was asleep and no Van Dorn would ever dare sleep on duty. Bell hurried across the street and approached the black sedan. His right hand found his pistol at the back of his waist, but he didn't yet draw it.

A uniformed mailman making his rounds

stepped onto the block, a heavy leather bag over his shoulder. A dog was barking from inside a nearby cottage. The ballplayers whooped when one of them sent one deep. It was all so normal, but Bell felt cold dread as he reached to open the car door.

The hot copper scent of blood hit him first, followed by the swarm of flies that had already found the corpse. They called him Very Gary. Gary Lawler was his name. Former beat cop who'd had enough time on his feet and wanted a cushier gig. He'd packed on pounds as he reached and then passed fifty, hence the "Very" of his nickname. He usually did stakeouts and hotel security. Good solid agent, married with three adult kids. Loved opera, especially Enrico Caruso because the Italian tenor stayed at the Knickerbocker and had once given him an autograph.

His throat had been opened from ear to ear. Connell had been smart enough to hold Lawler's head down so that the blood leaked from the wound rather than fountained against the windshield. He'd also covered much of the gore by draping Gary's khaki mackintosh over his body.

Even as Bell processed the gruesome scene, he couldn't help but wonder how Connell got the drop on his men, first in

Montauk and now here. Archie was a crack agent, and Gary was as jumpy as a cat normally. The wound was made from behind. He checked the Ford's rear door. Unlocked. An operational oversight when on a stakeout alone, but that didn't explain the scene. Connell would have had to have approached the vehicle unseen, opened the door, slid in, and secured Lawler's head so smoothly and quickly that Gary had been slain like a spring lamb — completely unaware.

Not likely.

These thoughts and their implications went through Bell's head in a single second, possibly two.

By the third he was in motion.

His additional men weren't due for another quarter hour, but he wasn't going to wait. Archie and Wes, and now Gary, hadn't known they were being hunted by an expert and so had been stalked and taken down. Bell knew exactly who and what he was facing and he was going to meet it head-on if he could.

He raced down the street with every ounce of speed his body could muster. The kids stopped playing ball when the stranger ran at them with a pistol in his hand.

"Clear the streets," Bell shouted as he

blew through the ballplayers.

They scattered.

The new mothers with their prams had already moved on.

He doubted Devlin Connell was within twenty miles of his home, but he had no choice but to act like the man was barricaded inside his bungalow with an arsenal of weapons and a death wish. He slowed his approach and used the overgrown hedges as cover to sidle up to the clapboard home. He ducked under a side window and then raised himself to peer inside. The flowery curtains were pulled closed. He shifted slightly to look through the gap where the two panels almost met.

He saw a living room — wallpapered walls, an upright piano with an empty vase on top, antimacassar over the back of the sofa.

Bell immediately saw his mistake and it was like a punch to the gut. How could he have been so blind?

It was the bright yellow door and the poor state of the grounds. The door looked so fresh because it had been repainted in the spring by someone who took pride in their home. However, the ornate landscaping had been ignored for at least a month or two. The two things didn't add up. Inconsistencies are always clues and Bell had missed this one.

He hadn't read all the reports. He'd skimmed them at best because he was confident they already knew they had their man. They never accounted for the woman. She had tended this garden, and she had insisted her husband paint the door, and she had picked the feminine wallpaper and made certain the back of the couch was protected. And there would be fresh flowers from the yard in the vase atop the piano arranged just so by her hand.

There was no record of Devlin Connell's wife ever coming or going because she and her husband, the real Devlin Connell, were dead.

Bell went around to the front door. It was unlocked. He opened it but kept his body clear. Nothing happened. He chanced a quick look. The living room was empty, sunlight streaming through the gap in the curtains, catching a billion motes of dust. The place hadn't been cleaned in a while. It smelled musty, with a hint of something chemical. Bell kept his pistol at the ready as he glided from room to room. In the master, the bed was unmade and whoever had been sleeping in it hadn't bothered with laundry. The sheets were gray and stained, and the pillowcase downright grimy.

Bell checked the bedroom closet. Mostly women's dresses, but a few vaguely naval-looking uniforms appropriate for a lighthouse inspector, he supposed.

He finished his search in the kitchen. There were no signs of violence, but that would have been cleaned up long ago. There was a door that led down to a dirt-floor cellar. A tiny window allowed only a little natural light in the subterranean space, but there was a switch for a single bulb at the bottom of the steps. The air was damp, musty, and the chemical smell first hinted at when he entered the home grew stronger.

On one wall of the basement were shelves for preserved food in mason jars, another had a coal furnace and an empty coal bin. A few odd crates and a couple of old bed frames that might have been children's bunk beds occupied the rest of the basement. On the topmost bed lay all the pictures that had been removed from the walls of the house, formal family portraits of Devlin and his wife and two towheaded boys, who grew taller and older in each successive image. The photos of Devlin did not match the description Archie had provided. Not even close.

Bell moved the bed frames aside. The dirt

under them had been recently disturbed. The soil was brown, where everywhere else in the cellar it was hard-packed black. The area had been dug up in the not-too-distant past. He dropped to his knees and sniffed the dirt. Lime. That was what he'd smelled when entering the house. Chemical lime. He sniffed again. Just below the strong acrid smell lingered another scent, the sickly odor of decay. Murderers often used lime to mask the stench of a victim's decomposition.

It all came crashing down. They hadn't been following Devlin Connell. The Van Dorns had been following a spy who'd taken over Connell's life in order to access lighthouses. The Germans hadn't turned Connell, they'd outright murdered him so their man could carry out his mission.

It was a risk on the spy's part, Bell thought, but if he couldn't gain leverage over the real Devlin Connell, he had no other option. It wouldn't have been difficult. If neighbors asked what had happened to the couple, the spy could claim he was a relative watching over their house while the Connells dealt with an emergency medical condition at an out-of-state sanatorium.

Bell got to his feet. He had to be certain and guessed there would be gardening tools in the shed/garage behind the house. He climbed the stairs, vastly more tired than when he'd gone down them just moments earlier.

He let himself out through the back door and made his way to the garage, his mind whirling. He'd seen the big picture early on in the investigation and so he'd not paid as close attention to the details. While he was driving up and down the coasts of New Jersey and Long Island, he should have spent equal time with all the reports and memos his men had written up. He had warned early on that spies were smart, but he hadn't seen this one coming.

And then he realized it hadn't made a bit of difference to his investigation. Connell and his wife had been dead long before Joe Marchetti had come to him for help. What did it matter if there was no additional layer to the spy operation, no puppet master pulling the lighthouse inspector's strings? It didn't, not in any real sense. He'd thought once they arrested Connell that they could get him to identify who he was working for. Now that point was moot. No harm done after all.

Bell was so lost in his thoughts that he didn't hear the car's motor until he was right in front of the garage doors, and he was far too late to react. The dark blue

Chevrolet H slammed into the double doors under hard acceleration. Bell took the impact all the way from his shoulder to his hip. He was tossed aside as if by a raging bull and hit the ground yards away, rolling as limply as a rag doll. He hadn't been knocked unconscious by the collision, but the right side of his body was a raging sea of pain.

He had just a second at most to look up and see the driver before he raced down the street. The man was as Archie had described him, cadaverous and grim. The spy also took an instant to inspect the man who'd come to arrest him. He twisted his head around as he went past to keep Bell in sight for as long as possible. Bell felt it odd.

The car hit the street, turned sharply to the right, and then was gone.

Bell had tried to get to his feet, but his leg collapsed at the first step, and he fell back to the ground, which was ostensibly a lawn but hadn't been mowed in so long it was like falling into cushions. The spy had kept up at least a pretense of yard maintenance in the front of the bungalow, but had fully neglected the rear.

Bell finally noticed the smell of woodsmoke and heaved himself to his feet. He hobbled, wincing with each step, to the garage's entrance. Garden tools hung from pegs on one wall, another had shelves laden with fishing poles, tackle boxes, and other nautical gear. The floor was dirt, rutted where the Chevrolet's wheels had gouged out narrow tracks over the years. There was a workbench at the far end of the garage and next to it was a little potbellied stove. The grate was open, and flame licked the interior.

The implications were easy to infer. After nearly being captured out at Montauk, the spy had returned home knowing a target was painted on his back. He'd scoped the streets and discovered Gary Lawler casing his house. He'd killed Lawler and then went about erasing any and all evidence that he'd ever been here, burning everything in the stove. Bell imagined there had been codebooks, names of agents and sympathizers, the locations of safe houses, a real treasure trove.

The spy had to have been keeping an eye on the house as he worked and when he saw someone stroll out the back door, he'd figured the jig was up and it was time to flee.

Bell tried to use a wrought iron poker to pull anything useful from the fire, but the tool was too awkward to properly wield with his left arm. His right was still numb.

He considered fetching water from the kitchen sink, but there was no point. He was too hobbled to move quickly enough. By the time he went and came back, everything in the stove would be ash.

He pulled a short-handled spade from its wall pegs and used it as a makeshift cane to recross the lawn. He let himself back in the house. He opened the sink tap and let water run for a moment before filling and refilling a glass he'd found on a drying rack. He only stopped drinking when he could hear water sloshing in his belly. He found a bottle of single malt Scotch, half filled his tumbler with it, and went to sit on the front steps. The stickball kids hadn't yet returned to the streets and another woman was out walking with her toddler in a stroller.

His guys would be here soon enough.

32

Harry Warren and James Dashwood arrived in the first car and pulled right up. They had seen their boss sitting on the steps of the perpetrator's house and so they assumed their man was long gone. Harry killed the engine and levered himself out of the Ford. Young Dashwood was already out and around the car by the time Harry's size elevens hit the street. Both men were sober-faced. Especially Harry because Wes Nevins had been a protégé.

"He got Gary Lawler," Bell said by way of a greeting. "He's still in his car. Throat slit."

Neither man responded, but the tightening of their eyes and the tension in the muscles of their arms and hands were reaction enough.

Bell continued. "I believe there are two bodies buried in the cellar. James, this house doesn't have a phone and this neighborhood isn't all that posh, but someone nearby must have a private line. Check houses and ask at the one with more than just an electrical wire running to it. Call this in to the police. Harry, my right side is messed up. Give me a hand down to the basement."

Harry Warren worked the blunt blade of the shovel like an archaeologist worked his trowel, peeling off layers of dirt so thin that he wouldn't damage anything lying below. Both his and Bell's eyes began to burn when Warren's work got to the layer of caustic lime. The odor of putrefaction grew. They uncovered Devlin Connell first. He'd been buried facedown. They discovered his wife, also facedown, lying at his side. Bell was satisfied just to know his hunch was correct about them. He felt no compunction to disinter them himself. That was up to the police and coroner.

Two police cars were arriving just as they stepped out of the house. James was sitting on the Ford's running board. He stood and went to Bell and Harry Warren. "I sent the other car back to the office. No sense in more of us hanging out here with Hoboken's finest."

"Good call." Normally Bell would have ducked out before the police arrived and had Harry take point with the cops. He didn't this time because of the off chance the spy got arrested instead of taking a pair of bullets from his Browning. He didn't want some mouthpiece lawyer getting his client off on some stupid evidentiary mistake. He'd stay until every *i* was dotted and *t* crossed.

Three of the cops wore dark uniforms with brass buttons and looked like they were dying in the heat. The fourth was older, fifty most likely, and wore a light gray suit, well-shined black shoes, and sported a straw panama much like the one Bell wore during the summer months. By fashion's dictate he was days too early wearing the hat, but through sheer pragmatism, he was savvy as could be. It had been a hot spring.

Bell approached with an outstretched hand. "Detective, my name is Isaac Bell. I'm the lead investigator for the Van Dorn Agency and this is my case."

"Mitchell Shaw," he replied. His grip was firm without turning into a test of strength. "What do we have?"

"German spy murdered the owners of this house, a man named Devlin Connell and his wife, at least six weeks ago, possibly longer. We have had him under surveillance for a couple of weeks, not knowing about the murders. Last night he killed one of my men out at Montauk Point, gravely wounded another, and then today slit the throat of a third agent who was on stakeout. I observed him leave this property in a blue Chevrolet Model H. I do not know his real name, but I can give you his physical description, plus I can have surveillance photographs and notes sent to your department."

"You knew he was a spy?"

"No, I believed the man we were watching was really Devlin Connell, who we thought was working with a spy."

"Where are the bodies of Connell and his wife?"

"Buried in the basement. We removed some soil and lime powder to positively identify the grave."

"And your guy?"

"Sitting behind the wheel of his car down the block."

"Best get to him first," Shaw said. "No sense housewives and kids seeing that sorta thing." He motioned to one of his men. "Find a call box. Tell the station we need the coroner and a van to transport three bodies. Damn but it's going to be a long day."

It was.

Bell finally rolled into the Knickerbocker Hotel at ten p.m. He was dead on his feet, but so filled with coffee that his entire nervous system quaked like a drunk with DTs. The office was dimly lit and quiet. Bell looked around and didn't see any of the senior people until he spotted Grady Forrer rise from a desk and rush up to him. The head of the Research Department looked like he'd been waiting sphinxlike for Bell's return.

"Grady, any word?"

"Archie made it out of surgery just fine. Last report was about two hours ago. He does have a minor fever, which the doctor said can be a result of anesthesia. He said it's early times yet to see if serious infection sets in."

Bell practically sagged with relief. It was the first piece of positive news he'd had all day.

Grady went on. "Mrs. Abbott and your wife are out there now, along with the Abbotts' family physician. Ensign Marchetti has also remained in Southampton in case he is needed to run errands for the physicians. In no uncertain terms, Mrs. Bell said for you to stay here tonight, as there is nothing you can do out on Long Island, but that you are to join them in the morning. She will call your apartment at eight with a list of items she was too hasty to pack this morning but nonetheless needs."

Bell chuckled. "I'm sure it'll be a hell of a list. Grady, before I forget, I need someone to courier out some surveillance pics of Devlin Connell to the Hoboken police and a time sheet of his comings and goings. You have heard what happened, right?"

"Sadly, yes. Jimmy Dashwood came straight here after the police let him leave the crime scene. That was ages ago."

"Our notes and such might help the local cops when they canvass the neighborhood tomorrow."

"I'll organize everything tonight and drive it over myself in the morning."

"Grady, this place would fall apart without you. Anything from the old man?"

"Oh, I forgot to tell you, he's in Southampton too."

Bell wasn't surprised Van Dorn had bolted from Washington as soon as he'd heard. He ran the agency with his eye always on the prize of ever-increasing profits, but he also knew it was his people that made it possible. For as hard as they worked for him, he loved them all like family.

The apartment was in complete darkness, and it was late enough that no traffic noise drifted up from Times Square. Bell came awake like a deep diver finally breaching the surface of some black foreboding lake. He shot upright, violently shaking off his bedding like it was sheets of water and gasping in order to expel the depleted air in his lungs and fill them again with clean oxygen.

He slid back so he could lean his shoulders against the big bed's headboard. His chest heaved as he fought to get control of his breathing. He rarely suffered nightmares, so the sense of dread the dream left behind was especially disturbing. No matter how he tried to recall them, the details of the dream were already gone.

He levered himself out of bed and made his way to the bathroom, where he filled a tooth cup with tap water and drank it down. His eyes in the vanity mirror above the sink looked haggard. He knew he needed a few more hours of sleep.

Back in bed, he had the sudden feeling that he'd let a detail of the day escape his full attention. This wasn't an uncommon occurrence and so he cleared his mind and let the previous day play out as he saw it. He felt certain it wasn't something at the lighthouse, though he mentally walked through the keeper's house once more because the spy had been the last person there.

Nothing there seemed out of place, so that wasn't . . . Damn, he'd been recognized.

That's why the spy had spun in his seat as he'd driven away from the Connell residence. He knew Bell, or at least wanted a longer look to be sure. For his part, Bell had never seen the man in his life, of that he was certain. A man as physically distinctive as that wasn't someone who could be easily forgotten. Bell didn't know him, but the spy's reaction was that of a man who knew Bell.

It made no sense. None of it did, now that he thought it through.

The spy looked so sickly. Archie had believed the man might be dying of some form of cancer. Bell would have thought the same from their brief encounter. But that begged the question, why would the German High Command entrust such an important mission to a man living out his final months?

"They wouldn't," Bell said, and got back out of bed.

He hastily threw on some clothes and went down to the Van Dorn offices.

"Is there anything the matter, Mr. Bell?" asked one of the night clerks.

"No, everything's fine. Grady was going to put together a packet of information for the Hoboken police."

"Mr. Forrer put it in the safe before he left."

"Thanks."

The combination was known by only a handful of top staff. Bell spun the dial through the correct series of numbers and then yanked down on the handle when the tumblers released. A slim leather soft-sided case was on top of other material deemed too sensitive to be left lying around. Bell grabbed it and headed for an office.

He flicked on the desk lamp and pulled the dossiers from the case. The written reports, he ignored. It was the photographs he wanted to see. He set the first one on his blotter and stared for a solid minute. It was taken with a state-of-the-art German-made telephoto lens and showed the spy walking down a sidewalk in what Bell assumed was downtown Hoboken. His hat was pulled a little low, but his features were clear enough.

As he'd seen the day before, the man was gaunt, drawn, with eyes so deep-set they appeared as two bruises. He was thin, his shoulders naturally hunched, and his back stooped. His left arm was down by his side, but he kept his right bent at the elbow and held tight to his body. It could have been a mere quirk of motion at the exact moment the shutter snapped the picture, but Archie had interviewed him and said he had a "bum wing."

Bell retrieved a magnifying glass from a desk drawer. He held the lens in the sweet spot between magnifying the spy's face and getting lost in the photograph's grain. Bell set the picture aside and looked at another. And then another, and all the rest. He spent twenty minutes doing nothing but looking at the man's face and body. He studied how he sat at a table in a restaurant or held his head as he drove by in profile. He got a feel from the snapshots for how the man walked, how he carried himself.

And from all that Bell did not recognize a single feature, not a hint or a spark of anything. He was quite certain he'd never seen this man before in his life.

But the guy had looked as though he recognized me, Bell thought. Was he wrong about that? He replayed that seconds-long encounter. The spy's expression hadn't changed exactly, but he'd shown an oddly intense interest. What if just after the encounter the spy finally recalled where he'd seen Bell and his face lit up with whatever emotion the recognition elicited? Bell wouldn't have seen the epiphany, but that didn't matter. It had happened, he was certain.

Bell kept a catalogue in his head of all the faces he'd ever encountered and could picture them and recall the salient details of his meeting with each of them with ease. Not so with the man in the photograph. That the spy recognized him but he didn't recognize the spy was an unusual feeling.

How could someone who looked so sickly be healthy enough to run a spy ring? What afflicted him? Archie said he had the stamina to carry buckets of fuel up to the tops of the lighthouses he used as cover for his espionage activities. Whatever ailed him didn't affect his strength or endurance. If he'd been ill prior to the mission and was recovering from it, he would have put on weight in the months he'd been operating in and around New York, so that wasn't it either.

He went through the pictures again. What did it matter what afflicted him? Bell tried to see the man as he might have been when he was healthier and heavier. He was so stripped of flesh and fat it was hard to see him any other way. All Bell could imagine of the man's face was some grotesque mask that gets inflated with air and balloons out.

Someone knocked at his door.

"It's open."

Grady Forrer stepped into the office. "They told me you were in here with the dossier I put together."

"Getting an early start, eh?"

"It's eight o'clock."

Bell was shocked. The office he'd grabbed at random was windowless and he hadn't bothered strapping on his watch when he'd come down in the middle of the night. He had no idea this much time had passed. He neatened the stack of papers and pictures and slid them back into the case. "I need to get out to Southampton."

"Of course," Grady said. "If Archie's awake, please give him my regards."

"Will do." Bell paused. "Let me ask you something. You've seen the pictures. What do you think would cause a man to be so sickly looking, but leave him with full strength?"

"Hard to say. I'm not qualified as a physician."

"Don't be modest. I'm sure if you sat for your medical license this afternoon you'd pass with flying colors. I'm just looking for an opinion, not a lifesaving diagnosis."

"Thyroid problems would be one guess, but I noted on some of the logs that he went out to eat a great deal and tended to eat enormous meals. A great many soldiers returning from the Philippine campaigns had a similar pattern, hearty appetite but gradual weight loss."

"And?"

"They were eating for two, so to speak."

"Huh?"

"Parasitic worm infestation. Easy to get in the tropics and devilishly hard to get rid of."

The bolt-out-of-the-blue hit Bell and almost knocked him off his feet. He grabbed the leather case from Grady's startled hands and pulled out the pictures once again. Could it be? He spread several on the desk, glancing from image to image. Was it possible? The height was right. He'd been tall, but he'd also been an ox of a man, thick-shouldered and broad chested.

That was three years ago, Bell thought. Three years doing hard time in hell.

He still didn't see it, but it technically could be him.

Bell needed to be certain.

"Grady, put yourself down for a bonus," Bell said over his shoulder as he ran out into the bull pen. At the communications desk he filled out a telegram request and thrust it into the operator's hands. "Top priority and get word to us in Southampton as soon as you get a reply."

"Yes, Mr. Bell," the junior agent said with awe in his voice. He had never sent a telegram to Paris before.

Bell wrote out a name on another ticket and caught up with Grady before he left the building. "Give all that stuff to someone else in the outfit. I have a research job for you." He handed the telegram request to Forrer. "I need to see a picture of this guy. You'll likely find him in French newspapers from early last year."

"Is he French?"

"German."

33

There were no official records for the shortest drive time between Manhattan and the town of Southampton. Had there been such a record, it would have been shattered that morning. The Simplex and Bell had become a symbiont of man and machine during the reckless drive, each seemingly pushing the other so that the pair flew down Vanderbilt's expressway and then on through twisting country lanes at unheard-of speeds. Bell was operating on too little sleep and too much adrenaline, but knew himself well enough to know his reflexes had not yet been affected.

He drove straight to the doctor's home and braked in a cloud of dust. The driveway was crowded with cars. He recognized Lillian's Rolls-Royce and suspected the pearlescent Pierce-Arrow tourer belonged to the family doctor. Bell believed the Model T parked among the more luxurious marques came from the company motor pool and had likely been driven by Joseph Van Dorn himself.

An agent stood on either side of the clinic's front door. One of them, Bell was surprised to see, was Helen Mills.

"Morning, boss," she said, smiling sweetly.

"Let me guess, the old man has you on guard duty?"

"He's on guard duty," she said, referring to the other agent, "along with two others walking the property. With the spy still on the loose, Mr. Van Dorn is taking no chances. He tasked me with sticking to Mrs. Abbott and by extension Mrs. Bell. Not guarding exactly. More like babysitting. We got out here first thing this morning."

"A good idea," Bell conceded.

He slipped past the two and entered the home/office. It smelled of antiseptic.

"May I help you?" asked a nurse in a crisp white uniform behind a counter.

"Yes. I'm here about Archie Abbott."

"Are you Mr. Bell?"

"I am."

"The doctor is in consultation with Mrs. Abbott, Mr. Van Dorn, and Dr. Rosenstein. It's best not to interrupt them."

"That's fine. May I at least see Archie?"

"The patient is asleep."

"Please, I am the one who found him. I won't wake him, but I just need to see him. Please." Bell gave her such a doleful look that he knew she'd relent.

She glanced about for a second and then got to her feet. "I will just open the door a crack. Please no talking and don't tell Dr. Ridgeway."

"On my honor," Bell said.

She led him down a short hallway. They could hear muffled voices coming from behind the closed door of Ridgeway's office. Opposite was another closed door. The nurse opened it about a foot and stepped back so Bell could see.

Curtains were drawn over the room's sole window, so the light was uneven and murky. Archie lay on his back on a tilted bed, the left side of his chest swathed in clean white bandages. His color was good and he seemed to be resting peacefully. It was still too early to say he was in the clear, but he didn't yet show signs of infection.

The nurse closed the door and shepherded him back to the waiting area. He took a seat on a sofa, but rose a minute later when the doctor's door opened and people filled the hallway. Marion had an arm around Lillian's shoulders. They both already looked tired and it hadn't yet been twenty-four hours. Van Dorn's face was as unreadable as ever. The other man had to be Dr. Rosenstein, the Abbott family physician. He looked to be nearing retirement age and so had the calm demeanor of a man who knows his business.

"How is he?" Bell asked as Marion slid in for a small hug and a kiss on the cheek.

"He's good," Lillian said. "Weak, of course, but he managed to say a few words to me this morning. He's on a great deal of pain medication, so . . ."

"Infection?"

"Not yet," Joseph Van Dorn replied.

"It's still early," Rosenstein cautioned.

"The surgery went as expected," Ridgeway added. "The ribs weren't badly broken and the bullet remained intact. I was in and out in thirty minutes."

"That's good." The less time a person's left open on a surgical table, the better chances of a full recovery.

"It's time for all of you to leave my offices, and you're not to return until at least four this afternoon," Ridgeway warned. "Lillian, if you can't fall asleep in short order, drink two tablespoons of the laudanum tincture I gave you. Same goes for you, Marion. Archie is going to be here for a week if things go well and much longer if they don't. You need to rest if you're to be of any use to him. Understood?"

"Yes," they said in unison like admonished schoolgirls.

"Now go."

"Let's talk back at the hotel," Van Dorn said to Bell out of the corner of his mouth as they left the office. He paused to talk to the guards.

Bell drove Lillian's Rolls with her and Marion sitting close together on the back bench. Helen sat in the passenger seat next to Bell. Lillian just stared at the passing scenery without really seeing it. Marion held her hand and gave occasional directions to reach their hotel. The place was right on the beach, long and painted in brilliant white with red trim like California's famous Hotel del Coronado, though this place wasn't quite so grand or ornate. There were valets waiting under the porte cochere, so Bell eased the stately car to a stop and stepped out as a doorman opened the rear doors for the ladies.

The season wasn't yet in full swing, which meant they had little trouble renting a top-floor two-bedroom suite and other smaller rooms just down the hall for the security detail as well as Dr. Rosenstein. The suite was bright, with tall windows overlooking the Atlantic and plenty of fresh air.

Joe Marchetti sprang up from the couch as soon as he heard the keys rattling in the lock and had his hair smoothed down by the time the others entered the suite. "No calls, Mr. Van Dorn."

"Joe, what are you still doing out here?" Bell asked, surprised but glad that the Navy man had stuck around.

"Mr. Van Dorn asked me to cover the phones while he was at the doctor's office."

"He isn't an employee," Bell scolded his boss.

"Close enough for the time being," Van Dorn grunted. "Lillian, would you and Marion please excuse us? We need to talk shop."

"Of course," Marion said. "I think I'm going to dose Lillian with the laudanum and let her get some decent sleep."

The two women retreated to the bedroom they shared. Joseph Van Dorn had taken the other, which had left poor Joe sleeping on the couch. Not that he seemed to mind now that Helen Mills had turned up here in Southampton.

Van Dorn took one of the two chairs in his spacious room and immediately lit a cigar. He never smoked cheap, so the addition of the cigar to the salty air blowing in from outside perfumed the suite. Bell motioned for Helen to take the chair opposite Van Dorn, but she indicated she'd rather stand next to Joe. Not one to pass up an opportunity, Bell plopped down with an exhausted sigh.

"What's the latest on the investigation?" Van Dorn asked around his cigar.

"I believe I've identified the spy."

The silence that followed was an indication of just how shocking that revelation was.

"Who? How?"

"I am awaiting confirmation from our mutual friend in Paris, Henri Favreau."

"Best fixer in the world, in my opinion," Van Dorn interrupted.

"Agreed. Anyway, I believe the spy is the Scotsman who nearly stymied my run to smuggle that Byzantium ore across England, Foster Gly."

Van Dorn couldn't contain his shock. "How is that even possible? He was turned over to the French and convicted three years ago. They shipped him off to their penal colony in South America."

"He was. And about a year ago, a German spy named Max Hessmann was also sentenced to the Bagne de Cayenne, as it's known. I remember it because it was a big scandal, as the French wanted to shoot the fellow. A lot of saber rattling by the Germans got him sent to Guiana for life instead. I have a theory that the German High Command had a plan in place to rescue him that somehow involved Foster Gly or he made himself a part of it."

"I saw some of the surveillance pictures our guys took," Van Dorn said. "He looks nothing like how you described Gly. Are you sure it's him?"

"Boss, I looked at those pictures for hours last night and I didn't recognize him at all. It was only because he seemed to recognize me that I went back and studied them so intently. Otherwise, I would have trusted my gut and remained convinced I'd never seen the man before in my life. It was when I asked Grady about what could make someone so emaciated and he suggested tropical parasites that the possibility hit me.

"I have Grady looking for a picture of Hessmann, which I'll bet a year's wages will be the guy I ran down in New Haven following our discovery of the radio beacon. The French authorities would never admit that Hessmann and another prisoner escaped their inescapable penal colony, but Henri Favreau has the right kind of contacts to get at the truth. I am convinced that

Hessmann and Gly escaped the *bagne* together. I have no idea what kind of bond they formed, but Hessmann's next spy mission brought him to America and Gly came along for the ride."

"The timing seems to fit," Van Dorn said, still sounding unsure, but not outrightly dismissive.

"If it is Gly, I have to go after him," Bell said.

"You will do no such thing," the old man fired back.

"What?"

"You heard me. Gly is long gone. He would have driven straight to the German consul's office, and they would have escorted him onto the first German-flagged ship leaving New York."

"And if he didn't?"

"He did. But if he didn't, he has the advantage. He knows who you are from your run-in with him in England. He knows where you work and has a great many sympathizers to the German cause who you are not aware of. He will be hunting you, not the other way around."

Bell thought back to his night tangling with the Bavarian Brotherhood. He'd gotten away, but it had been a close thing. The old man had a solid point.

Van Dorn went on. "I have something more important for you, anyway."

"What's that?"

"The Germans are bound to connect the fire on their ship to their fake lighthouse inspector being unmasked. They might suspect a few of their tubes were stolen and will do anything to get them back in order to protect their technological edge. Joe, are the vacuum tubes still in the hotel safe?"

"Yes, Mr. Van Dorn."

The old man turned back to Bell. "After young Mr. Marchetti got word to me that you and he had been successful snatching the tubes, I reached out to Roosevelt and Ambassador Spring-Rice. They both want their prize as soon as possible. Roosevelt is sending his assistant . . ."

"Kurt Miller," Bell offered.

"That's the one. He's coming to New York with a couple of guards to take one of the tubes down to the radio laboratory at the Washington Navy Yard. Spring-Rice requested that you escort their sample to England. Joe, care to see this thing through to the end?"

His grin could have lit up a cavern. "I wouldn't miss it for the world."

"I thought as much. The Brits are eager to pick your brain and show off some of their communications breakthroughs as an extension of the North Atlantic Military Exposition that Vanderbilt put together."

"Aren't you forgetting Archie?" Bell asked.

"I haven't. But ask yourself this — do you have any skills that will help him in any way, shape, or form? Hmm. Didn't think so. Lillian, Marion, and I will take care of Archie. We know you. You'd just be in the way."

Van Dorn wasn't wrong on that either. Bell hated hospitals and the countless hours of empty waiting that took place in them. He generally paced like a caged lion, to the annoyance of others.

"We can give you regular updates through the Marconi wireless."

"Thought of everything, haven't you?" Bell said, a little amused.

"Don't I always? You're all set for the *Lucy* tomorrow and Roosevelt's man will meet you in the office at seven sharp."

The phone in the main part of the suite rang just then. Helen Mills went to answer it. She listened for a moment and thanked the caller. She returned to the bedroom. "That was the office. Isaac, a cable came in for you from France. All it said was 'Confirmed.' "

"Henri Favreau?" Van Dorn asked.

"Yes," Bell said. "Looks like my theory is

panning out. Hessmann and Gly escaped from Guiana. All I need now is for Grady to track down a snapshot of Hessmann and we'll have our proof." He looked over at Joe Marchetti. "We should get a move on right after lunch. I'll have some food brought up."

"Okay. Um, Helen and I were going to go down to the restaurant, if that's all right by you."

Bell couldn't help but smile. "Not at all. Enjoy. Be out front at one-thirty."

Van Dorn begged off lunch and Lillian was sound asleep, so Bell and Marion ate cold chicken salad and grapes on the suite's balcony overlooking the beach and the waters of the Atlantic. They each had a single glass of wine. Bell told her about Gly and warned her that the Germans might be looking for him.

"It's best you make yourself scarce until I get back from England."

"We're safe enough out here for the time being," she said, and he agreed. "Once we know Archie is on the mend, I am sure I can find some directing work down at Edison's studios."

"I thought you didn't like the head guy down there."

"I heard Plimpton's going to resign, so it'll be okay. I am going to miss you."

"There and back in no time. Afterward, let's go someplace."

"Like where?"

"We haven't been back to San Francisco in years."

Marion clapped her hands like an excited little girl. "Ooh, yes. A suite at the Palace Hotel?"

"If that's what you want."

"I do."

"Done."

Bell met Joe out front at the appointed time. Joe was holding Helen's hand and she looked like she was enjoying it. Bell gave them a little distance to say their goodbyes, chuckling silently when he realized Helen was the taller of the two.

"I wish I was coming with you," Helen said to him.

"That would be nice," Joe said and added, "You know, Isaac and Marion were married on an Atlantic crossing."

Helen's face showed mock shock and she said teasingly, "Giuseppe Marchetti, that almost sounds like a marriage proposal."

He replied in a serious, portentous tone. "Almost? Helen Anne Mills, when I ask a girl to marry me there won't be any doubt because it's going to leave her eyes glassy, her knees weak, her heart racing, and her heart mine."

"Oh," Helen managed to whisper.

Joe saw all of that in Helen just then, and the corners of his mouth lifted in a boyish smile.

"Kiss her already," Bell called from the front seat of the agency's Model T. "We've got to go, but first we need to get my car from the doctor's office."

Helen's blush deepened. Joe gave her a chaste kiss on the cheek and whispered in her ear, "We will continue this conversation in a couple of weeks."

"Oh, yes we will."

34

The unseasonably hot weather broke the following morning. It was raining and bitter cold and Roosevelt's man, Kurt Miller, was twenty minutes late arriving at the Van Dorn offices on the second floor of the Knickerbocker Hotel. Bell and Joe still had enough time to get down to Chelsea Piers, but Bell still found it inconsiderate. When he finally arrived, the slope-shouldered aide had two big Navy enlisted men in their summer white uniforms at his side. One had a case handcuffed to his wrist.

"Do you have the tube?" Miller asked, shaking out his umbrella.

"Sure do."

"Any problems?" The question was asked with little regard to the answer.

"Nothing we couldn't handle," Bell assured him, just as disinterested.

They had earlier retrieved one of the cylinders from the office safe, where it had spent the night. Marchetti handed Bell one of the padded tubes. He unscrewed the precision-milled cap and carefully slid the glass bulb into his palm. Its interior was an intricate web of soldered wires and miniature components.

"It works?" Miller asked.

Joe took that question. "There were two compartments in the drawer where they kept them. One for unused tubes and one for tubes that had broken down. Those showed signs of heat scoring and carbon smoke. As you can see, that one there is crystal clear and operable."

"And the other one?"

"We leave for England at ten," Bell told him.

"That was quick work," Miller said. He pulled the key for the attaché case from his pocket.

"The Van Dorn Agency prides itself on its efficiency and discretion," Bell said as he slid the vacuum tube back into the protective cylinder and retightened the lid.

Inside the handcuffed case were wads of newspapers. Miller pulled out some to make a nest for the container and Bell settled it into its new home. Miller closed the lid and repocketed the key. "I believe that concludes our business."

"It does. Good day, Mr. Miller," Bell said as brightly as he could. He did not like Roosevelt's man.

"Good day." Miller left, looking like a piece of lunch meat sandwiched between the towering sailors.

"That guy's one cold fish," Joe observed when Miller was gone.

"Couldn't agree more." Bell moved over to an office with a window overlooking Times Square. He waited longer than expected for Miller and his minders to hit the street. They went straight to a car that had been idling at the curb. He and the sailor carrying the attaché case took the backseat, while the second sailor sat next to the driver. The car immediately pulled away, doubtlessly heading to Penn Station and the next express to Washington.

Bell scanned the streets. Traffic was the normal mix of streetcars, autobuses, cars, and horse-drawn wagons. As it was early on a cold and drizzly Saturday morning, there were few pedestrians about. He ignored the ones walking steadily by and concentrated on anyone who seemed to be loitering, but even among those few, no one was watching the Knickerbocker. One guy who might have been a lookout waved when another man joined him, and together they stepped into a restaurant. Just a couple of buddies meeting for breakfast.

"That wasn't an inconspicuous departure if the Germans are watching, but it would look as if Miller's in the clear. At least he has some muscle with him. They have no idea who you are, so just take a cab to Pier 54. I need you to take my trunk, though."

"What about you?"

"Subway surprise."

"Huh?"

"I'm taking the subway and will use it to lose anyone tailing me."

Joe looked a little nervous and finally said, "I've never been on a luxury liner. I don't know what to do when I get to the dock."

Bell had been going back and forth to Europe from the time he was a boy. It was all second nature to him and Joe's admission made him like the ensign all the more. "Tell the taxi driver you're sailing first class. Wait, you did remember your dress uniform?"

Joe nodded. "But I'm really not supposed to wear it. I'm still temporarily a civilian, remember?"

"No time to get you a tux, so you'll just have to bend that rule. Besides, it's a British-flagged ship. What do they care if you're wearing an American Navy uniform?"

"Okay."

"Once you're at the first-class boarding area inside the terminal building, there are dozens of officers and pursers to help get you and the luggage onto the ship and squared away. I'll be an hour or so behind you. Stay in the cabin until I arrive."

Van Dorn had sent an agent out to the Cunard office the day before to buy the tickets and they'd been in the safe when Bell had secured the two state-of-the-art vacuum tubes. Bell handed one ticket to Marchetti and put the other inside his jacket. He also gave Joe the second vacuum tube.

They went downstairs to the bell captain's station. When traveling with Marion, there was a minimum of three large steamer trunks plus a couple of hatboxes and various other pieces of luggage. Bell had just a single small trunk and Joe had a big leather suitcase with a monogram that didn't match his name.

"My uncle's gift when I went off to college," he explained when Bell noticed that anomaly.

Bell chuckled. "Have them hail you a taxi and I'll see you in about an hour. There's going to be two agents following you on a loose tail to see if anyone is following. Nothing to worry about. Just being cautious."

Bell left the lobby and went downstairs and through to the subway platform. The lobby had been clean, but he wasn't sure about the station. Again, it was early on a Saturday morning and there were only a handful of people waiting for the train. None paid him any attention or averted their gaze if he happened to meet their eye. No one looked like a German agent on a stakeout.

When the train came through, no one got off the car in front of Bell. He stepped in with three other people — two college-age guys wearing matching school ties and knickerbocker pants talking baseball, and an older gentleman with a furled umbrella in an out-of-fashion suit. The car was nearly empty. Bell lurched as the train got underway and grabbed for one of the overhead straps, using his right hand so he didn't flash the shoulder holster under his left arm.

A few people boarded at the next stop.

Bell continued to monitor the older gentleman and the two collegians. Nothing seemed out of place. Surely Gly would have had the German agents in the city watching the Knickerbocker Hotel with a description of their lead detective. He was out here acting as bait so Joe would reach the ship without incident, and yet no one had appeared interested.

They came to the next stop. Bell didn't move as the doors swooshed open. But then he fled the subway car at a near-sprint. The two young men sprang at that instant, rushing for the exit closest to them. Bell then backpedaled into the car as the door chime rang. He ran to the door the boys had used just as they tried to jump back aboard. One nearly made it had Bell not been there to push him back enough for the doors to fully close.

His sneer of contempt turned to a look of horror when he realized Bell had his tie clutched tightly in his fist and the train was beginning to move. He tried pulling back, but Bell's grip was too tight and soon he needed to concentrate on sidestepping in pace with the accelerating subway train. He pounded on the glass. Bell yanked hard, slamming the guy's face against the car. Real panic and desperation overtook the agent as the train gained ever more speed and the brick wall that delineated station from tunnel was fast approaching.

He heard murmurs and gasps from the passengers behind him.

Bell let go so the kid could pull free, but kept it close enough that his momentum carried him into the station wall hard enough to empty his lungs and crack a couple of ribs.

Bell turned to see the reaction of the other passengers just in time to sidestep a short-bladed rapier stabbing at him. It was held in the steady hand of the old gentleman who'd been at the hotel station. The weapon's odd handle made it obvious it had been secreted in his umbrella. He would have run Bell through except he hadn't expected his target to let the kid go at the last second.

The man recovered remarkably quickly and thrust again. Bell spun around one of the numerous floor-to-ceiling poles to keep the blade at bay. The elder man stepped back to give himself more fighting room, since he had the advantage of a two-foot-long needle-thin blade. Bell pressed his attack by grabbing the pole in both hands and whipping his body around it in a lightning move. The soles of his shoes slammed into the swordman's extended arm.

The man crashed into the subway car's wall and the sword clattered to the floor as his breath exploded out in a pained whoosh. Bell let go of the pole and used the inertia of his move to deliver a haymaker punch that corkscrewed the guy to the ground. He'd be out for hours.

Bell flipped open his badge and showed it to the small group of uncertain passengers. "Ladies and gentlemen, I'm a detective with the Van Dorn Agency. This man is part of a German spy ring we've been tracking." Bell replaced the rapier in its umbrella scabbard. The train was already slowing for the next station. "I have to go back for the other two that already got off the train. Please find a transit cop and have them coordinate with our offices at the Knickerbocker Hotel."

He didn't know if the people believed him and would act on his request, nor did he really care. These were low-level operatives, possibly from a group like the Bavarian Brotherhood. Small fish with no useful information.

As soon as the doors opened at the next station, Bell dashed off the train and climbed the steps to the street. He hopped into the first taxi in the line and told the driver to take him to the Astoria Hotel over on Fifth Avenue. He watched the station recede behind them as the cab merged with the traffic. No one came rushing out and no other vehicles pulled away from the curb.

He overtipped the driver as he rushed from the cab and into the lavish hotel. The lobby was busy with well-dressed guests heading for breakfast. He moved through the dallying people like a shark through a shoal of mackerel. It would be unseemly to run down "Peacock Alley," the nearly thousand-foot corridor that connected this part of the hotel to the Waldorf tower, but Bell certainly rushed past any and all he encountered. As he strode on the plush carpeting, he removed his tan overcoat and flipped it inside out to turn it into a black overcoat. He did the same with his hat, which went from brown to gray. The shape was hard to get just right, but it looked good enough.

Five and a half minutes after entering the Astoria, he strode from the Waldorf totally unrecognizable at any moderate distance. He nodded to the bell captain, who whistled up a taxi loitering on 33rd Street. "Chelsea Piers."

35

The ship dwarfed everything around her. From the waterline to the top of her four funnels was the same height as a nine-story building. Her hull was a riveted wall of steel more than sixty feet high and almost eight hundred long. So long in fact she stretched almost a quarter of the way to New Jersey. She was no longer the biggest ship in the world — that honor went to Hamburg America Line's *Vaterland* — but she was an impressive sight nonetheless.

As equally amazing was the chaos on Pier 54 as her ten a.m. sailing time drew nearer. The streets outside the long customhouse that ran the length of the pier were a sea of passengers and porters, taxis, trucks, and wagons. Uniformed officers worked to direct the flow of people, luggage, and goods aboard as orderly as possible. The ship's chief purser, a friend of Bell's named James McCubbin, likened it to herding cats.

Bell left the cab while it was still snarled in traffic and slid through the clamoring passengers and equally overwhelmed crew. The smell of coal hung heavy in the air, as the barges had just recently departed after filling the great ship's bunkers. An ocean liner made no money in port, so the furor to get her turned around and back out into the North Atlantic was unrelenting. The terminal hall was filled with rows of tagged luggage. Cunard allowed for twenty cubic feet of luggage per passenger, and it appeared to Bell's qualified eye that most people had gone well over. He too was familiar with having to pay the overages when traveling with Marion.

As he wended his way through the crowd, he became aware of hearing the words "submarine" and "U-boat" with disturbing frequency. The Germans had recently posted in many leading newspapers a warning that to sail to England was to sail into an active war zone. He got a sense by listening to his fellow passengers that most dismissed the warning, while others appeared to take it to heart.

He made it to the first-class boarding area and presented his ticket to the agent.

"Your luggage, sir. Has it already been tagged?"

"My friend came through with it earlier. I'm all set."

"Very good, sir. Enjoy the crossing."

"I always do."

Bell paused at the top of the steep gangway and looked over the railing. The Hudson was a shadowy dark green and a long way down. Just inside the ship, he met the chief purser, James McCubbin, who was greeting passengers and directing porters like the master he was.

"Mr. Bell, I was delighted to see your name on yesterday's amended manifest," cried McCubbin.

The purser was sixty-two but looked younger. A native of Liverpool, the vessel's home port, he had been with the line for most of his career and was the reason his passengers invariably remarked that a crossing under his care was always their favorite.

"Last-minute business in London," Bell replied. "I know this is inopportune, but may I have a few minutes?"

It was poor form of Bell to ask, and such was McCubbin's professionalism that he showed no irritation at the request, for he knew it had to be important. "Of course." Bell stepped aside and McCubbin conferred with two subalterns, who were talking to reporters about which celebrities and other

VIPs they could interview. McCubbin joined him a second later out of earshot of everyone else.

"What is it?"

"I am acting as a courier for your government, and I want the item locked away, but not in the main safe."

"I can put it in my private safe. It's under the desk in my cabin. Key never leaves my person."

"Perfect. I'll meet you at the purser's station and we can go down together. Also, I'd like to know if there are any last-minute passengers, people who booked this morning, specifically."

"None. Last ticket sold was yours and before that at least a week ago. Now let me share a couple of things with you. Number one is Cunard is forcing me out to pasture."

"You're retiring?"

" 'Fraid so, my friend."

Bell shook his hand. "Congratulations or condolences, depending on how you feel."

"Oh, condolences, most certainly. I have maintained a successful marriage by being gone eleven months out of the year. I fear dear Annie will turn me out after the first couple of months."

"She'll be delighted to finally have you home. And later we must get together and celebrate," Bell said. "Now, you mentioned two reasons."

McCubbin pulled Bell closer and lowered his voice to a conspiratorial whisper. "Captain Turner requested that Cunard have a detective aboard from now on. He's an inspector from Liverpool named Pierpoint, George Pierpoint. He is going to search the ship once we're underway, looking for stowaways. The captain is afraid of German saboteurs. I don't believe our Inspector Pierpoint would mind another trained man with him as he performs his sweep. I'd consider it a personal favor, Isaac."

Bell nodded immediately. "Just this morning I had to shake a trio of German agents. It's less a favor and more of a necessity." He opened his suit jacket to show the purser that he was armed. "I applaud Captain Turner for his foresight."

Noting the gun, McCubbin said, "And I yours."

Bell found Joe Marchetti in the first-class cabin they were to share. It had two bedrooms, a parlor, and a private dining area. They would have to use the communal bathrooms just down the hall. The walls were sheathed in intricate parquetry using exotic woods. The ceiling was coffered, and only the fact that the single window was a porthole leant any hint that this wasn't a suite at a premier hotel. Their view of the deck was partly obstructed by one of the lifeboats.

As Bell had almost been a passenger on the *Titanic,* he didn't mind that the ship carried an expanded number of boats.

"I tell you, this is the life," Joe gushed as he continued unpacking his case.

Bell's trunk had already been delivered to the room and so he unlocked it and swung open the lid. "Little different than sailing on a destroyer or cruiser, eh?"

"I don't think the captain's cabin on a battleship is half as nice as this."

"Probably not. And wait until you taste the cuisine. Cunard hires only the best chefs and serves only the freshest food."

A few minutes later, as they finished unpacking and seeing which items of clothing needed to be pressed by their cabin steward, someone knocked on the door. Not expecting anyone, Bell pulled his Browning, but left it down by his thigh. He backed away from the door in case the visitor tried to rush into the room, and nodded to Joe.

Marchetti opened the door and stepped back smartly so Bell would have a clear shot.

Their precautions were unnecessary. It was the purser, McCubbin.

"Cubby," said Bell. "What can I do for you?"

"Refrain from ever calling me that again. Also, I have a little free time."

"How? It's almost ten. We're about to sail. You have to schmooze with the passengers as we set off."

"We received word earlier that the government commandeered a ship called the *Cameronia.* She belongs to a line we're partnered with. She was about to set out for Glasgow but is now heading for Halifax as part of the war effort. Troop transport, if I were to guess. Anyway, her forty-odd passengers and their luggage plus her three female crew members are sailing with us. A delay of at least an hour, possibly two. I can take you down to my cabin to lock up whatever it is you need made safe."

"Perfect. But let's hurry. I want a look at the newcomers as they board." Bell holstered his pistol. Joe had hidden the heavy metal cylinder on the far side of his mattress. He retrieved it and the three men left the cabin.

McCubbin had thought far enough ahead to have two stewards, perhaps the biggest on his considerable staff, for they were both taller than Bell, escort them down to the chief purser's cabin. There were a few ladies already lounging in the salon reading room, where tea and sandwiches were being served. The room was tall-ceilinged and well illuminated by a large arching skylight. They passed through fast enough that no one approached McCubbin with any last-minute requests, which was what he spent most of his day filling.

Next came the skylit lobby for the main staircase, which wound around the ship's two principal elevators. The intricacy of the plasterwork covering the walls and ceiling was truly remarkable. The floor was real marble. They descended two decks in short order, passengers instinctively moving aside as they passed.

McCubbin's cabin was just off the lobby on C Deck, tucked into a corner next to the much smaller assistant purser's cabin. The rest of the staff was berthed in communal dormitories deeper in the guts of the ship. The purser ignored the main ring of keys he carried and took a smaller ring from his trouser pocket. He unlocked the cabin door and told the two stewards to wait until they were finished inside.

The cabin was simple but cozy because of the dark wood paneling. There was a bed, desk, and dresser, and tartan curtains over the promenade-facing porthole. In the desk's footwell was a squat black safe that looked to be bolted directly to the deck.

"Pardon the familiarity," the purser said after taking off his uniform jacket and beginning to unbutton his crisp white shirt. He reached in to grasp a sturdy necklace he wore around his neck below his undershirt. He unclasped it and slid a brass key into his palm. His joints popped as he got down on his knees and opened the safe. Joe handed him the cylinder, which McCubbin managed to make fit around whatever else the man kept under lock and key.

"I think those knees won't mind retirement, James," Bell quipped when he stood and began to secret the key once more. He was relieved the vacuum tube was safe.

"Mind your manners, Mr. Bell," McCubbin said with a twinkle. "Your time will come soon enough."

"Too true," Bell agreed. "We've got things worked out with the Admiralty. They are sending men aboard as soon as we reach Liverpool. They will escort us off before the rest of the passengers."

McCubbin buttoned his jacket and turned to a small mirror hanging from a wall to straighten his tie. "If you need to get at your mystery item during the crossing, you generally know where to find me day or night."

"Of course." Bell swatted Joe Marchetti's chest with the back of his hand. "Ready to enjoy ourselves for a week?"

"Oh yeah."

"Oh," Bell said, recalling a detail. "What about teaming up with your Inspector Pierpoint?"

"You can meet him at the purser's bureau at two o'clock."

"Okay."

An hour later a string of taxis arrived at Pier 54 and the passengers of the Anchor Line ship *Cameronia* arrived with their luggage. Stevedores swung into action to get the bags and trunks aboard, while stewards formed the people into two groups. Watching from the height of the main deck, Bell saw that one group was headed for second class, while the other, with finer clothing and more luggage, was destined for first.

He hustled back up to C Deck and was casually leaning against the rail at the gangway when the first of the passengers climbed the ramp up from the dock. He studied the newcomers as they gaped and gawked at their new accommodations. None looked particularly German or suspicious. Bell hadn't really been worried.

If Gly and his people didn't book some spies onto this ship, what were the odds of them booking another that was then commandeered at the last minute only to get transferred to the very liner on which Bell was a passenger? A million to one? More like a billion to one.

He joined Joe for lunch and then both went up to the rail with throngs of other passengers to wish New York a raucous goodbye. Women waved handkerchiefs and men their hats. Some cars down below blasted their horns. Just past noon, two hours later than expected, the great ship started easing out of her berth, ready to turn downriver with the help of waiting tugs.

It was Saturday, May 1, 1915, and the RMS *Lusitania* began her journey to infamy.

36

The purser's office was located on B Deck in front of the grand stairway. Its all-white walls and multiple panels of beveled glass made it look like an ice cream parlor, in Bell's estimation. Two men stood near its entrance, one in a Cunard uniform, the other in a suit. They were both in their fifties, graying and a little paunchy perhaps, but each had a capable air. Bell assumed one was George Pierpoint and the other one the ship's master-at-arms, Peter Smith.

They seemed to recognize one of their own as he approached. Their conversation dried up as he took the last few steps down the stairs and drew near.

"Bell?" the ship's policeman said.

"That's right. Master-at-arms?"

"Peter Smith. This is Inspector Pierpoint."

"Call me George," the man said.

"I'm Isaac."

There were handshakes all around.

"I familiarized myself with the ship on the crossing over," Pierpoint explained. "But I thought it best to have a real expert with us."

"A good idea," Bell agreed.

They headed for the stairs and started down. Joe had asked Bell if he could join them on the sweep, but Isaac had said no. It was professional courtesy, with a word from McCubbin, that got Bell on the search party. He didn't want to press his luck and bring along someone who wasn't part of law enforcement.

On D Deck, one above the main, the master-at-arms led them through the opulent first-class dining room and into the kitchen that served both first class and second. An army of chefs in white were hard at work preparing their first service at sea. Orders were shouted back and forth while the kitchen crew worked like it was a ballet. The sound of chopping never ceased. Aromatic steam bubbled from countless pots, while the smell of roasts in the multiple ovens made Bell's mouth fill with saliva.

They exited the double doors into the second-class dining room. While nothing like the premier class — diners here ate at long communal tables — the room was well appointed, and there were countless decorative touches. A rotunda in the middle of the room opened up to the deck above.

Just beyond was another set of stairs. They descended to the main deck, where the majority of the second-class cabins were located. They began to search, checking in lavatories and bathing rooms, peering into any cabin whose occupants had left the door open. Peter Smith carried a passenger manifest, so they grabbed one of the stewards and had him use his passkeys to check that the unoccupied cabins weren't secretly being used. They asked the man if he'd seen anything suspicious and were assured he had not. No one had. They had him open supply closets and storage lockers until they were satisfied nothing untoward was occurring. They climbed another flight and again found nothing.

One deck higher was the shelter deck. There were more nooks and crannies to be checked, countless restrooms and storage areas. Above them were the second-class public spaces, the smoking room for gentlemen, and a parlor for the ladies. The rooms were abuzz with conversations. The three men paused at the entrance to both lofty rooms and surveilled the passengers in a rather overt fashion to see if anyone reacted in a way that set off their instincts. All seemed to be in order.

Another mixed-gender lounge and additional promenades were located on A Deck. Satisfied that nothing was out of place in the second-class area of the ship, located at the *Lusitania*'s stern, they performed a sweep of the austere third-class accommodations located at the bow. The spaces were full of noise — children's riotous games or their wails for attention, arguments in a number of languages, music played on folk instruments — and since there was little soundproofing built into the walls, there was the sound of the ship cutting through the water and the thrum of her massive engines.

As before, they found nothing.

Next came the no-passenger areas of the ship, like the crew's accommodations, additional storage for everything needed on a transatlantic voyage, baggage and mail rooms, and then all the ship's cargo holds. Bell's seasoned eye noted there were a great many ammunition crates among the more mundane cargo being hauled to England.

The ship was divided into six principal zones, the three separate passenger sections, the crew accommodations, the cargo holds, and finally engineering. Because Master-at-Arms Smith had no experience in the working parts of the ship, Captain Turner had ordered his second and third engineers to perform a thorough search of the engine rooms, coal bunkers, and machinery and ancillary spaces.

All that was left for the trio was the first-class accommodations, the least likely place for stowaways, which in Bell's calculating mind made it the most likely of all.

As before, they started low and as far rearward as they could. That meant the maze of cabins on the main deck. They again used the services of a steward to double-check that the empty cabins were indeed empty. As these were the smallest cabins in the first-class area, there were many that were going unused this trip. It was nearing five o'clock. The kitchen would be a madhouse, as the first seating for dinner wasn't far off. But it still had to be searched, no matter the inconvenience.

The dining room was being set for supper by an army of servers under the supervision of an eagle-eyed headwaiter in a smart tuxedo. The three law enforcers slipped through the doors and back into the kitchen. It was noticeably hotter and busier. The din of knives chopping and pots and pans being rattled atop the metal stoves was ear-shattering.

The men passed through the main cooking area and started at the rear of the kitchen, where there was a warren of storage rooms, separate bake shops, pantries, and liquor and spirit lockers big enough to hide an army.

It had become routine for them, so when Inspector Pierpoint opened the door to the portside pantry he actually had his head turned to make a comment to Peter Smith. Three men exploded out of the pantry like Ivy League linebackers. Smith was knocked back and fell to the kitchen floor, while Pierpoint was brushed aside like he wasn't even there.

Bell had been a few feet away and hadn't been hit by the stampede. The sheer number of people working in the kitchen slowed the stowaways' rush for freedom. One of the chefs tried to block two of the intruders and was pushed back against a stove. They held him in place long enough for his jacket to catch fire from the multiple blue-flamed burners. He started screaming and dancing wildly, and his hat tumbled from his head, allowing his hair to burn away like a noxious firework.

Chaos reached a fever pitch in an instant. Screams and shouts from the kitchen caught the attention of the waiters out in the dining salon and soon several of them entered to see what was happening. The burning chef knocked over an oil-filled pan that hit the floor just as it burst into flames.

The stowaways were temporarily trapped by the fire. Cooler, more experienced staff began to react. The burning man was knocked to the ground and staffers started beating at the flames with dishrags, aprons, and even their bare hands. The executive sous-chef managed to knife one of the intruders in the shoulder.

Master-at-Arms Smith got back to his feet and he and Pierpoint entered the fray, and what had been pure bedlam seconds earlier began to shift as the crew got the upper hand. The grease fire on the floor was burning itself out with the help of a five-pound tin of salt being dumped onto it, and the chef who'd been set afire lay on the floor smoldering and miraculously only mildly singed.

It had been a masterful performance that even fooled Bell for a couple of seconds, but he looked back in time to see a fourth man slink from the pantry and head aft to escape the kitchen through the second-class dining room. The man had just reached the swinging doors when Bell realized what was happening. He took off after him at a sprint, pulling his pistol with practiced ease.

He was running at full speed when he reached the door and put out his left hand to brush it aside so he could keep after the fugitive. The escapee was smart. As soon as he'd exited the kitchen, he'd gotten low and braced his back against the door, planning on remaining there for a few seconds to ensure his flight hadn't been noticed.

Bell hit the door with the expectation that it would swing freely, but instead it held as if it had been nailed shut. He broke no bones, but cracked his head hard enough to drop him to the floor like he'd been hit with a Louisville Slugger and his left wrist was definitely sprained. On the other side of the door, the stowaway gave a wry smile as he got to his feet. Perfect. He started running. A few of the second-class wait staff looked like they wanted to intercede, but ultimately did nothing as he crossed the room.

Bell lost five or so seconds on the floor and another two swaying when he regained his feet. He pushed through the door and saw his man slightly hunched over as he dashed out the far door. He started his chase anew.

Beyond the dining room were some cabins and the stairs up to C Deck. Bell understood humans in flight instinctively head for high ground. The man wouldn't be lurking in the shadows down some second-class passageways. He mounted the stairs two at a time and was just reaching the next landing when a brass ash can the size of an umbrella stand was chucked at his head. He had to fall flat on the steps to avoid the projectile, but was unable to duck the stinging cloud of sand and ash and stubbed-out cigarette butts that hit his face and ground into his right eye.

Again, he was slow getting up, his eye burning and tearing heavily. With his left hand currently useless, he had to holster his pistol in order to mop at the injury with a handkerchief using his right. He loped up the last few steps. Judging by the expressions and positions of the handful of passengers in the entrance lobby, his quarry had run out onto the port side of the shelter deck promenade.

Still pressing the cloth to his eye to ease the pain, Bell went after him. Though the covered deck was partially protected, wind whipped along the promenade at a steady beat. The ship was far beyond the Verrazzano-Narrows and had turned to run parallel to Long Island. The sea reflected the brassy light of the sun as it settled closer to the distant horizon. The promenade ran almost the entire length of the ocean liner, but lockable gates prevented second-class passengers from going forward, so Bell turned and rushed aft.

There were a few huddled couples and single men at the fantail watching the ship's four massive screws create a wake that churned and roiled like a horizontal waterfall.

"A man just ran through here," Bell shouted over the wind.

Several passengers pointed to the open metal stairs that gave access to the B Deck promenade. Up there was more open deck space, the ladies' salon, and the smoking lounge, plus the interior stairs. Bell had to hurry. His man was expanding his options with every turn. He pounded up the stairs and confronted his first dilemma. The fugitive could have gone left down the port rail or right down the starboard.

Bell went right, moving quickly but cautiously. The pain in his right eye was a major distraction. It left him a little disoriented. There were more passengers here, mostly couples enjoying the late afternoon air prior to dinner. None of them had the confused look of someone who'd just encountered a stranger rushing past. The stowaway had to have gone left. Bell cursed. Ahead were the open doors to the interior spaces. He was just about there when Foster Gly rushed through, his right arm held awkwardly at his side.

Bell tried to step back from the unexpected encounter to give him fighting space, but Gly moved like lightning. His left fist shot out and caught Bell on the back of the hand pressing the handkerchief to his eye. It had been a fast, instinctual punch that hadn't been properly aimed, so Bell managed to shrug it off.

He knew he was okay. His left arm wasn't up for a fight, but his right felt good and Gly appeared to have lost use of his own right arm in the years since they'd last met. Bell threw his left in a lazy feint that Gly had to defend against, which left open his other side to a swinging right that hit the vulnerable floating ribs. There was so little flesh on the man that it felt to Bell like his hand actually touched bone.

Gly grunted and had to step back. As much as Bell wanted to press the attack, his vision was blurred with fresh tears. The grit was working its way out of his eye, but it cost him half his ability to see.

"Never thought I'd see the likes of you again," Gly said in an Irish lilt.

"Feeling's mutual," Bell snarled, and this

time he came at Gly with abandon.

It was too late when he realized the subterfuge and its implications. Gly wasn't Irish. He was from Scotland. He'd been sent to America as a spy and had learned tradecraft from their very best agent. From the moment he killed the real Devlin Connell he'd been playing a specific role, that of an Irish lighthouse keeper with a damaged right arm. It was an act. He'd convinced everyone of it because he never once broke character. Archie had been convinced, the agents following him had been convinced. Even Bell, when Gly had just now left himself intentionally open for a punch hard enough to crack one or two ribs, was convinced.

Bell came at him in an open lunge, moving within striking distance with his guard down because he'd dismissed the damaged arm entirely. This allowed Gly to stop pretending he had an injury and react, thrusting his right hand inside Bell's jacket to retrieve the Browning.

He should have fired when the gun was still under the coat, but he drew it out, and Bell countered by using his sprained left hand to accelerate Gly's movement and bash the back of his right against the door frame with enough speed to deaden his nerves. The gun flew out of Gly's grasp and spun down the deck even as Bell's left hand went numb.

Gly stomped Bell's foot with his boot and turned to run for the doors to the starboard promenade across the lobby. Bell allowed himself just three seconds to scan for the dropped pistol before giving up and racing after the spy, his hatred of the man as clouding as the tears streaming from his eye.

Gly raced across the ship and out the starboard doors. Bell was a little hobbled by the boot stomp and so lost some ground. Turning forward, Gly ran just a short distance until he realized there was a sizable gap, plus handrails, between this deck and the promenade reserved for first-class passengers. Bell exploded out onto the deck, the wind hitting him in the face. He saw Gly, who turned, mounted a railing, and leapt. He hit the far rail with his chest and let out a sharp grunt, but he was a seasoned street fighter, a man who could brawl through any pain.

He began pulling himself up and over the rail to gain access to the central part of the ship.

Bell sprinted down the deck and went over the rail like a spring. He hit just a couple of feet from where Gly was struggling to get onto the deck. It was a race. Whoever won had a huge advantage and could end the fight right there. Bell with an arrest, Gly with another murder to his credit.

With his left arm now numb from elbow to fingertips, Bell was forced to use the underside of his chin to hold himself steady as he reached higher on the rail to pull himself over. Both men struggled awkwardly, grunting and scrabbling until, miraculously, Bell and Gly hit the promenade at the same time. They both got to their feet. Gly had the advantage of speed, and so he took off running again. He ducked and weaved through passengers out strolling the deck. Bell considered shouting for help, but knew it would just get civilians hurt.

He loped after the murderous Scot as best he could. Gly reached an exterior set of stairs that took him up to the boat deck. Here there was no protection from the wind. It was a cool evening, and the twenty-plus knots of the ship's forward speed made the deck feel icy.

Gly now had an even greater advantage. His ribs hurt, but he could deal with it. He had two functioning arms, while Bell was reduced to just his right and vision from only his left eye. There were still a lot of people around, and doubtlessly one or two would try to break up a fight they thought was between gentlemen.

Another set of stairs rose up to the top of the ship. A little chain was drawn across them with a dangling sign that read CREW ONLY. Gly waited for Bell to appear and spot him before stepping over the chain and climbing to the *Lusitania*'s roof, some seventy-five feet above the waves.

Bell reached the top of the ship just a few seconds after Gly, but he didn't spot his quarry. Though the area wasn't meant for passengers, it was ringed by a safety railing. Most of the space was taken up by the ship's four oval funnels, as well as dozens of air scoops that looked like the throats of giant tubas. To Bell, it all looked like a forest of oddly shaped five-foot-tall mushrooms. Then there were the iron and glass domes and pyramid skylights over various public spaces, like the lobby and the Verandah Café. Gly could be hiding anywhere.

He had his boot knife in hand. The shadows were lengthening, but there was still plenty of light. Bell kept his head in constant motion as he stalked Gly across the industrial landscape. It was too windy and noisy to trust his hearing, so Bell constantly spun to check that Gly wasn't sneaking up behind him.

A couple of the skylight fixtures were the size of greenhouses.

Bell tried to keep as far away from potential hiding places as best he could, but it was nearly impossible. He brushed past one of the air intakes near where the guy wires supporting the second funnel were secured to the decking, when Gly threw an elbow into his groin from his hiding spot tucked under the scoop's fluted mouth.

Eighty percent of the strike hit Bell's inner thigh, but the other twenty was dead on and sucked the air from his lungs and nearly sent him to the deck. Gly rose from his bolthole and Bell scrambled back to give himself a few seconds to recover. Gly rushed him. Bell didn't yet have the coordination to use the knife effectively, so he turned to run.

He got a half dozen steps away when Gly hit him from behind. He slammed Isaac into one of the dome-shaped skylights, by far the most delicate looking of them all. Their combined weight warped the metal frame and shattered a half dozen panes. Glass shards as sharp as knives rained down into the ladies' parlor and sliced through chairs and divans and glittered in piles on the floor. Fortunately, the room was empty, as the ladies were either at dinner or making themselves up in their cabins for the second seating.

Gly slammed an elbow into the back of Bell's head. The motion bent more of the lattice-like iron frame and more glass broke free. There was a real danger of the whole structure giving way, and a drop from this height was likely fatal.

Gly pulled himself back, leaving Bell lying alone on the faltering dome. He stomped on the metalwork in an attempt to damage it past the point of no return. Bell tried to crawl back, but Gly was there to block him and prevent him from getting on solid ground. The Scotsman slammed his big foot down again.

Clearly the parasites living in his gut had not diminished the tremendous strength the man had always possessed.

More of the frame bent and ten more panes broke into cascading shards and glittering glass dust. The frame now flexed like a living thing as its delicate geometry was spoiled and the weight of iron and glass struggled to find a new balance.

Bell had to drop his knife in order to hold on to the heaving frame. It felt like he was clinging to the back of an unbroke stallion. He sensed the structure was already too damaged to survive. There would be no new equilibrium.

Gly was there to prevent him from backing off the dome, so he did the only thing open to him. He got to his feet as the iron frame twisted and tossed like it was some monstrous creature in its death throes. His knees juddered and nearly buckled, but he stayed upright, and just before the catastrophic collapse, he danced along a slender beam to the symphony of tons of glass shattering. The final heave came just as he leapt for the deck and the once-elegant dome came apart entirely and vanished into the darkened room below.

Bell tumbled when he hit the deck and came up in a fighting stance. Gly rushed over and the two circled each other.

"You're finished now," Gly said with a smug sneer.

"You've got nowhere left to run," Bell countered.

"No need to run after you're dead."

"I'll be here till Liverpool." Bell hoped the longer he kept Gly talking, the better the odds a crewman discovered them in an unauthorized area. He wasn't too keen on his chances in a prolonged fight.

He tried to widen the circle as he moved. If the opportunity came, he'd be better off running and tracking Gly down later with more men. As if sensing Bell's intention, Gly moved sharply toward him in a diagonal that blocked the path between two of the big air scoops. Bell had been seconds away from racing down that alley.

Gly knew he'd been right and laughed. "You aren't getting off this roof alive."

"Then neither are you."

Gly had several inches on Bell and more reach, so he started firing punches from outside Bell's range. Bell danced back or deflected most of the shots, but a few got past. There wasn't a ton of power behind them, but four hits to the cheek started to hurt. Then came a fast step in. Bell tried to match by stepping back, but hit the ship's rail. Gly rammed his fist into Bell's stomach. Bell rolled left and took another punch on his shoulder that sent a wave of pain up and down the injured arm.

Bell then went on the offense, throwing sharp jabs with enough speed to ram them through. One cut Gly's lip against his teeth and soon blood dribbled from his mouth and dripped from his chin.

Back and forth they went, trading punches that grew less effective because both men were tiring. Bell knew what was coming next as Gly threw a roundhouse that missed by a mile. He moved to keep the rail at his back, and when the big Scotsman had had enough of boxing and rushed in to grab Bell in a crushing bear hug, Bell was ready. He took a step back, making certain Gly was committed, and then he grabbed his opponent's hand and twisted his torso with everything he had.

Gly's momentum and the strength of Bell's throw heaved Gly over the rail. Ten feet below was the boat deck, and Bell was already legging over the railing to jump after him, even as Gly continued to sail through the air. He hit the canvas cover laced over one of the long lifeboats. Like a circus net, the spread of the canvas acted as a spring.

Bell saw the horror in Gly's face as he bounced off the boat cover and was launched over the main rail like an India rubber ball. His hoarse scream started when he was forty feet from the water and cut out a short second later.

Bell was stunned by the turn of events, but kept focused. He finished climbing over the rail and lowered himself until his feet were dangling above the deck. He let himself drop and rushed to the rail. There was another passenger there who'd heard the scream and was looking over the side.

"Was that a man who went overboard?"

he asked, shocked.

"A stowaway. Do you see him?"

Bell scanned the waves, but couldn't see evidence that Gly ever resurfaced. The ship was in the process of adjusting her heading, and moments after he'd reached the rail, the bulk of the *Lusitania*'s hull hid the spot where Gly would have augered into the sea.

"No," the man finally replied. "Should we tell someone?" He noticed Bell's disheveled appearance and gazed at him suspiciously.

"I was just with the master-at-arms. I'll let him know and I'm sure he'll tell the captain."

"Oh, okay."

"You go off and enjoy your evening, sir. I'll take care of everything."

Bell felt a little hollowed by the turn of events. Gly was gone, for sure, but it hadn't seemed like a victory.

37

Bell was nearly certain Gly had died on impacting the hard cold sea because he couldn't have righted himself in midair the way a cat does and hit feet-first. And on the off chance the collision didn't kill him, the water was cold enough that twenty or so minutes was enough to cause hypothermia and death.

When he and the others eventually told the captain what had taken place, Bell wanted there to be little chance he would turn the ship around to look for a man who was now doubtlessly a corpse. He took his sweet time returning to the dining room. He first went to find his pistol, which a passenger had turned over to the bartender in the smoking lounge. He would need Master-at-Arms Smith's assistance to get it back.

Passengers were eating off a shortened menu due to the fight and fire in the kitchen, but they seemed to accept the situation since a few early arrivals had a story to tell about witnessing three stowaways being apprehended. Bell didn't see Peter Smith, but Inspector Pierpoint stood just inside the dining hall door, leaning against a wall. He straightened when he saw Bell enter the bustling room.

"Where the devil did you go off to?" he asked. "We could have used extra muscle."

"A fourth man snuck out of the pantry in all the confusion and tried to escape through this dining room."

"Fiends," Pierpoint said. "Did you get him?"

"He went overboard after a scuffle. What of the three you nabbed?"

"Down below. I was waiting to take you to see them." They left the dining room and made for the main stairs. "They refused to say one word, but we think they're German. We found a Hasselblad camera hidden in the pantry."

They met Head Purser McCubbin on the stairs. He was heading up while they were going down. "Ah, Mr. Bell. Pray tell, do you know anything about the destruction of the dome over the writing room?"

"I'm afraid that was me, my friend. I had to chase a fourth stowaway, who tried to make a run for it. Can you do me a favor and get me my gun from the bartender in the second-class smoking room? It was a rather far-ranging chase."

"Of course."

"Do you know where the prisoners were taken?" Pierpoint asked.

McCubbin nodded. "Lower deck steerage. Cabin next to the loo. I'll bring the pistol straight away."

"Thank you."

It took ten minutes to reach their destination. A pair of sailors stood outside one of the six-person communal rooms. "I'm Pierpoint. This is Bell."

"Aye, sir, we were told to expect you." He twisted the key that was already in the lock and opened the door for them.

Bell said, "When guarding someone, never leave the key in the keyhole. An enterprising prisoner can slide a piece of paper under the door and knock out the key with a pen or some other object from their side. With luck, the key stays on the paper and the guy inside pulls it back to him and, just like that, he's free."

"Does that really work?" Pierpoint asked with obvious doubt.

"Got me out of a locked closet at a distillery once."

Bell eyed the prisoners. The three spies

were sullen men, of average build and looks. Their hands were still bound by coils of kitchen twine that Peter Smith had obviously improvised when they were apprehended. There were two other men with him. Smith introduced one as Johan Pederson.

"I'm a translator," the mustached man said.

The other man was William Thomas Turner, the *Lusitania*'s captain. He was a large, sturdily built man with strong features and eyes as blue as Bell's. He had quiet authority and a solid commanding presence.

"I've heard things, Mr. Bell. Disturbing things about what you've done to my ship."

"I'm sorry, Captain, that my fight with the fourth stowaway unfolded as it did, and for the damage it caused to your ship. It couldn't be helped. I couldn't shoot at him with so many people around, and by the time we were alone I had already lost the pistol. I put the passengers' safety above my own and had to fight hand to hand at the end.

"If I may also say," Bell added, "I am currently employed by your government as a courier and believe they will cover the repair expenses."

"I'm glad you were aboard, Mr. Bell, and

I appreciate your regard for the passengers. I trust there will be no more disturbances." Turner glared at the three captives, then excused himself and left.

"Have they said anything?" Pierpoint asked.

"Not a word."

Bell asked Pederson if he would translate for him. "Of course."

He looked at each man and said, "In case you think you succeeded, I want you to know that I saw Foster Gly leave the pantry."

Even without first hearing the translation, the mention of that name made the three men exchange quick, nervous glances.

"He's dead," Bell said, "and your mission is a failure. I still have what you came to steal. Now talk and maybe the authorities will go easy on you. Otherwise, your lives are over."

Pederson felt no need to translate the profanity-laced tirades that were the responses. McCubbin arrived just then, a little winded and flushed. He handed Bell the Browning automatic. Bell thanked him.

He made a show of slipping it into his shoulder holster. "In that case, *meine Herren,* enjoy your cruise, and when I'm back in New York I'm going to make sure the

Bavarian Brotherhood is shuttered forever."

They understood some English because Bell walked away with a fresh round of curses hurled at him. He hustled back up to his cabin to change for the second seating of dinner. Joe was on his bed, dressed in his summer whites but with his jacket hung over the back of a chair. He was reading Conan Doyle.

"That took longer than I had imagined," he said, setting the book aside. "Did you hear about the skylight over one of the lounges? Thing came crashing down in a pile of iron and glass."

"That was me fighting Gly."

Marchetti flew out of bed with an incredulous cry. "What?"

Bell chuckled. "You heard me. He and three henchmen were hiding in a kitchen pantry. Ah, we need to find Pierpoint again. He should question whichever waiter was assigned to that space. It's possible he helped them sneak aboard undetected. Gly almost had me up on the navigation deck, but then I got the upper hand and he ended up over the side."

"That's incredible. You got your man."

"I didn't expect to find him here," Bell said, changing out of his soiled clothes. "Makes me wonder how he knew. There are certainly a few loose ends to tidy up once we get back, but that's a worry for later. For now, we get to enjoy being pampered and fed like kings for six glorious days."

They stopped at the purser's bureau on their way to the dining room so Bell could fill out telegrams written in company code to go out over the wireless in the Marconi shack behind the bridge. He reported that Gly was dead and asked that inquiries be made throughout Long Island's southern coast about a body being recovered at sea or washing up onshore. He added a couple of other orders and signed off asking about Archie Abbott. He'd spoken with Marion first thing that morning, but she hadn't yet been to Dr. Ridgeway's little private hospital and so had no news.

When Bell handed over the sheets, an assistant purser said, "Sir, just so you understand, the wireless is very busy on the first night at sea. These might not get out until late."

"That's fine. For the first time in weeks, nothing I do has any real urgency at all."

38

Gly's life was saved by the ship's helm. The *Lusitania* had just initiated a change in heading when he hit the water. Normally, the vessel's passage through the seas created a narrow zone of turbulence alongside her hull. But because the great ship had curled away in a more northerly direction, the area of turbulence spread out from her bulk like a billowing curtain of foam. Turbulent water has no surface tension, and it is this phenomenon that causes such severe injury upon impact. Some liken it to hitting concrete.

Gly landed far from perpendicular to the water, but he hit it in an area of roiling waves and agitated bubbles that allowed him to slide below the surface without breaking any bones. The impact had still been brutal, and he'd be black and blue along most of his left side for weeks, yet he had survived. He stroked for the surface and took a deep breath when he reached the waning sunlight. He managed to inhale water, but forced himself not to cough. He couldn't see the *Lusitania*'s railing, but that didn't mean Isaac Bell wasn't up there searching and, more important, listening for him.

The water was cold but not numbingly so. He had time before the temperature became an issue. Calmly, like he was simply preparing for a bath, Gly untied his shoes and let them float away. Next he unbuckled his trousers. Once he had them off, he lay back in the water with his neck arched. This position allowed him to float without needing his hands to maintain buoyancy.

It was awkward and disconcerting because waves kept washing over his face and he'd be forced to blow out through his nose to keep his sinuses from filling with water. He tied the pant legs together as tightly as possible and as near to the cuffs as he could. He relaxed out of his floating position and fitted the pants over his head like a yoke with the sealed cuffs at the nape of his neck.

He held the waist open with one hand and splashed water and air bubbles into the makeshift floatation device with the other. Once the pants had filled, he quickly plunged the opening into the water to trap the air in the legs that were around his neck.

Gly relaxed back into the trouser-float and found he had more than enough buoyancy to remain above the waves, reinflating the legs as needed.

He'd been in the water only a short time, but all he could see of the *Lusitania* now was the smear of coal smoke against the darkening sky. He marked her position and began gently kicking northward toward Long Island, some seven miles distant.

He was cold, certainly, but he'd just eaten while hiding in the pantry and so had plenty of energy to keep kicking and maintain his core temperature. He made sure to keep the pants wet, otherwise the air would escape through the weave.

After an hour, he was stiffening up from both the cold and the massive amount of bruising he'd suffered. He also struggled with holding the pants' waist closed because his hands were going numb. He'd held out hope that a fishing boat returning to port would pass close enough to hear him shout, but it hadn't happened yet, and with it soon to be dark it didn't look likely that it ever would. He knew he wouldn't survive the night.

Gly had been a scrapper all his life, fighting his way to adulthood on Glasgow's mean streets by using his size advantage and his utter disregard for any sort of civil rules. Someone wanted to fight him bare-knuckled, Gly would use a club. A guy came at him with a knife, he'd pull a gun. He never backed down, no matter the odds.

He eventually turned his aggression and disdain for others into a career as an enforcer, first for various crime syndicates in Britain and eventually the Continent when things got too hot. Later he found that legitimate corporations were often more ruthless than any street gang and paid far more than a two-bit Corsican pimp or an Italian mafioso.

He was working for a French mining firm, attempting to hijack a load of valuable ore some Americans had stripped out of a Russian island deep in the Arctic Circle, when his life derailed. And it was all thanks to Isaac Bell. Bell had been hired to help the miners escape Russia. His plans had gone awry, Gly didn't know how. What ensued was a running battle across the length of Britain, with the miners one step ahead of Gly and his men. In the end, Bell had outsmarted him. He'd been arrested in England but extradited to France with the understanding he'd go to prison for life in the savage Guiana jungle.

Gly never imagined he'd get the opportunity for revenge, but when he saw the Van Dorn detective crossing the lawn of the lighthouse inspector's house in Hoboken, he began to believe that maybe sometimes fate favors the wicked.

But then his own hasty plans of being snuck onto the *Lusitania* and recovering the vacuum tube from Bell had been a disaster. The delay leaving the dock stranded him and the three members of the Bavarian Brotherhood in the pantry. They were supposed to have been moved to third class and hidden among the countless steerage passengers. The delay meant their inside man couldn't get free from his supervisor. He'd told them to hold tight until after dinner service was complete and the kitchens were shut down for a few hours before the breakfast shift came on.

But then, of course, Bell came along. They'd worked out in advance how to act should they get caught, and it had almost worked. The two Brits had been fooled, but Bell had seen him slip into the second-class dining room.

It shouldn't have mattered. Gly had three inches on Bell. He should have won that fight. Three years ago it wouldn't have been close. But the worms in his gut prevented him from gaining back the muscle and bulk that he'd once boasted. He was so used to being eighty pounds heavier that he couldn't find a fight rhythm, and so Bell had tossed him off the navigation deck. In the few seconds before he hit the lifeboat cover, he had plans to rush back up and finish it once and for all.

And then he bounced off the damn canvas cover and hit the water a few seconds later. Had it happened to someone else, it would have been comical. But it was he who now suffered the humiliation. Humiliation that was going to kill him.

No, a voice roared in his head.

He started kicking even harder and found a way to hold the pants closed one-handed so he could flex his other hand and return the circulation. He was cold but not yet hungry. He had reserves of strength, but just as important, he had a will to survive that would not quit. He'd survived Glasgow slums and the most depraved penal colony on earth. He'd been given a chance for vengeance, only to fail.

Gly refused to accept that and so he fought on, ignoring the cold, ignoring the pain, focused only on surviving so that he could have his revenge.

The trawler found him twenty minutes later. With his head sandwiched between the two inflated legs of his pants, he didn't hear the low burble of the small boat's motor. Had it been any darker the men wouldn't have seen him, but just enough light remained for the captain to spot something in the water he didn't recognize, so he deviated from his run to port to investigate, and saw it was a person.

He chopped the throttle and waved to his single deckhand to be ready. The captain hit his horn a few short blasts. Gly finally turned and began waving and laughing. The boat slowed to a stop just a few feet from where he bobbed.

The deckhand had a boat hook that he held out to Gly. "Can you grab it?"

Gly reached out as clumsily as a toddler, his body racked by bouts of uncontrolled shivering. His fingers brushed the hook, but he couldn't get them to close around the metal tip. The man thrust it out again, leaning as far over the old boat's rail as possible, but it was no use. Gly was too far gone.

The motor revved aggressively and the boat accelerated. Gly was certain they'd given up on him and felt it was time to let his head slip out of his makeshift float and allow himself to sink into oblivion. Instead, the boat cut a tight circle across the waves and the captain laid them in close enough to Gly that the mate reached out and grabbed the back of Gly's shirt. It took the captain stepping out of the little pilothouse to lend a hand to drag the tall Scotsman onto the boat.

They stripped the pants from around his neck and the mate used a filet knife to slice off his sodden shirt. They moved him into the wheelhouse and set him on the floor next to a heating vent that fed off the engine, a filthy but thick blanket wrapped tight around his shoulders. Gly continued to shiver and could not speak, but managed to convey his thanks with his eyes.

"Don't know what you were doing out here, but you're lucky we come along," said the weather-beaten old captain. "We'll have you to shore in twenty minutes. Clever trick with your pants. Never seen that before."

He turned the boat shoreward once again and set the most economical speed, which for the old tuna boat was a lazy chug. The lights of a coastal town clung to the far shore, looking as distant as the stars but ever so slowly growing closer. Gly was in a catatonic-like state, so tired he wanted nothing more than to sleep, but still shaking so violently that he couldn't succumb to his exhaustion.

He was dimly aware that they'd arrived and that the two men were securing the boat to the dock. They helped him stand, and with one fisherman under each shoulder they got him off the boat. At the end of the jetty was a stand-alone little office with its lights on. They took him there and settled him on a chair opposite the harbormaster's desk.

"What's all this, Seamus?"

"Found him a couple miles out," the captain said. "No idea who he is or how he came to be so far out."

The harbormaster, a bear of a man with a dark bushy beard and a meerschaum pipe, bent low to look into Gly's eyes. "Can you talk?"

Gly tried to speak but got nothing out, as his body shook uncontrollably.

"We've got to unload our cargo," the captain said. "Keep an eye on him for a bit and then I'll take him up to the house."

An hour later Gly found himself in a ramshackle house on the edge of the village. The captain apparently lived alone in the two-room, tin-roofed house. It was tidy enough, but cluttered with maritime memorabilia, including an open shark jaw over the door that was as big as a basketball. Gly was on the couch, while the captain — Seamus, he recalled vaguely — reconstituted and heated a couple cans of Campbell's Beefsteak Tomato Soup on a single gas burner and added in some dried fish.

By now Gly only shook every minute or so.

The soup was only warm, not hot, and he could only use a spoon between bouts of shivering, but it was one of the best meals of his life. While he ate, the old captain brought out a pair of pants and a work shirt that had been mended a dozen times. He added a pair of socks and what looked like his Sunday-best shoes, but they were unpolished and actually dusty.

Onto the coffee table the captain set the wad of cash that had miraculously stayed in Gly's pants pocket throughout his ordeal. It was nearly a thousand dollars, bribe money to get aboard the *Lusitania* and keep him and the others hidden.

The old man tapped the roll of wet bills with a finger and stepped back. "I think whatever you were doing out there ain't none of my business. You want to tell me, that's fine, just don't feel you're obliged."

"Thank you," Gly said, speaking with a generic American accent. "I, ah, I got involved with some people I shouldn't have."

"That's what I figured. You're welcome to spend the night. I'm up and out about an hour before dawn, so I likely won't see you. Help yourself to another can of soup and be on your way."

"Thank you again."

"It's usually the sea that does the taking. Sailors, I mean. It's nice to get someone back from her for a change."

39

It was around noon the following day that Foss Gly turned off the road and onto the gravel drive that looped in front of the farmhouse belonging to Werner Dietrich, his and Max Hessmann's contact here in America and the last safe house open to him. It had taken two buses and a hitch-hiked ride plus an hour of walking, but he was here at last.

The old farmer came to the door a long minute after Gly started knocking. He grunted noncommittally and turned aside so Gly could enter. Dietrich had been eating lunch. Gly took the man's chair and helped himself to what remained. "I'm sorry, I'm starving."

"I'll make you more. You look like you need it. What happened?"

"What do you think?" he called out to the kitchen, where Dietrich busied himself with a fry pan and another breaded chop.

"The others?"

"Captured by the crew with the help of Isaac Bell."

"Who's that?"

"He's a Van Dorn detective, a man I am going to take great pleasure in killing. But that's for later. We have a more pressing problem. He still has the vacuum tube."

"That is not good."

"There has to be a way of preventing the British from getting it. That technology could allow them to disrupt all Atlantic U-boat operations. We need to contact Sektion IIIb. Max hid the emergency codebook in your barn with our equipment. Perhaps they have agents in Liverpool who can meet the ship."

"*Ja,* perhaps." Dietrich slid another schnitzel onto Gly's plate. "It is too dangerous to send a message now."

"I know. We'll do it tonight, if the wind doesn't pick up."

After sleeping through the rest of the day, Gly and Werner Dietrich got to work just as the sun was setting. The house and barn were too close to the road for what they planned and that meant they had to haul their gear out into a field. They loaded everything onto a small utility trailer that Dietrich hitched to a single horse. About a half mile behind the house was a small open space with a few trees among the crops where sat an abandoned Frick steam engine that had once run a sawmill when the land was originally cleared. The longitudinal crack in the main boiler tank was why the valuable piece of equipment was left to rust. Another quarter mile beyond the farmland gave way to a forest.

The wire was by far the heaviest single piece of equipment, too heavy in fact to unload from the rear bed of the trailer. They left it carefully coiled. Gly threaded one end of the wire through the spokes of the Frick's tall iron wheel several times and tied it off. The large envelope was made of the same doped material Count Zeppelin used on his giant airships. They laid it out neatly in the young corn plants. There was a loop on the other end of the long wire that attached to a hook that dangled from the envelope. Gly then tied a piece of rope to the steam engine and to the hook assembly as a temporary tether.

Then he set up the radio on the trailer bed along with the dry cell batteries to power it. Before his nap he'd given the set a thorough check, especially the cutting-edge vacuum tube. Dietrich ran a hose from the helium cylinder they left on the trailer to the envelope. They'd had to machine an adapter to make the connection because the gas cylinder was American and the inlet on the envelope was of a German design. Like all the rest of the equipment, it had already been tested.

They were set to go, except it was still too light out. They waited in companionable silence. Dietrich enjoyed his pipe, while Gly smoked his way through a half dozen American cigarettes. When it was dark enough, but before the moon rose, Gly opened the tap on the helium cylinder and began to inflate the large round balloon.

"What did you tell the company when you bought the gas?" Gly asked.

"That I was an inventor experimenting with model airships."

"Reasonable enough, I suppose."

"If we ever need to use this emergency radio again, I can easily go back without raising suspicion."

The balloon soon began to bulge and expand. The calculations had all been done in Germany, factoring the weight of the wire with the correct volume of helium to lift it into the skies. Soon the envelope had inflated to the size of a one-car garage and strained at the rope tether Gly used to restrain it.

The horse had been given blinders and a feedbag, but it acted nervous about the strange hissing sound it heard and didn't understand.

Dietrich uncoupled the hose and tossed the end onto the trailer. He took a moment to pat the animal's flank and whisper in her ear in German. Without ceremony, Gly cut the rope tether with a machete from Dietrich's barn. The balloon flew into the sky like a rocket, carrying the upper end of a thousand-foot radio antenna. It vanished into the dark sky in the blink of an eye, and the only way to know it was still climbing was the metallic whir as the wire coil rapidly unspooled.

It didn't take long before the aerial's meteoric rise came to a sudden stop when the wire snapped short against the Frick's metal wheel. Gly tested the tautness. The calculations had been perfect. The antenna was at its full height, but they'd be able to pull it back to earth using the horse. Max and Werner had inflated the balloon once before, but this was Gly's first time.

While the radio warmed up, he clamped a pair of leads from the back of the set to the aerial. The wire moved only marginally. There was no wind to speak of on the ground and only occasional eddies at a thousand feet. They couldn't have picked a better night.

Max Hessmann had always intended to use lighthouses when he'd been given this mission, but he'd insisted on a backup. He understood the risk that anyone could hear a broadcast from land, but felt it worth it in an emergency. Tonight would prove his forethought correct.

Gly was no telegrapher. It took him several minutes to tap out the sequence of letters from Max's codebook, transmitting the string of dots and dashes into the ether. To anyone happening to be listening on the proper frequency, they'd hear gibberish, just a long string of letters. However, back in Germany they'd be learning terrible news. The spymasters in Sektion IIIb already knew of the thefts from the radio ship, but the coded message informed them that the British tube was already crossing the Atlantic aboard the *Lusitania.*

He wasn't going to presume to tell them how to respond to this news, but felt he did his duty by sending the message. There would be no reply, he knew, so he powered down the radio and unhooked it from the antenna.

It took both men to pull the balloon down enough to loop the wire under a hook welded to the back of the trailer. Dietrich took off his horse's blinders, hopped up into the seat, and gave the reins a light flick. As they pulled away from the steam engine, the wire's anchor moved with the buggy and shortened every foot for each foot the horse walked. Gly sat in the back of the trailer and waited as the balloon was drawn inexorably to earth.

The darkened sphere appeared in the sky overhead when they were nine hundred and fifty feet from the Frick.

"I see it," Gly called.

Dietrich slowed the horse to a snail's pace, glancing over his shoulder to gauge the progress. He stopped when Gly was able to stand and reach the balloon's release valve. He opened it and helium hissed out in a roar that startled the horse and almost made Gly topple in the trailer bed.

"Easy, girl," Dietrich said soothingly.

Gly slowed the release of gas so as to not frighten the animal further. The envelope slowly deflated. As it collapsed, he hopped off the trailer to smooth it out as best he could atop the corn plants. After ten minutes, he was able to roll up the balloon like a carpet and stow it on the trailer. He unhooked the aerial and left the wire lying on the ground.

Dietrich turned them around, mindful not to damage more of the corn crop than necessary, and backtracked to the Frick engine. The final step was to untie the wire from the wheel and coil it back hand over hand, making certain none of the loops crossed or tangled. Once this was done, they got the wire back into the bed and returned everything to the barn. Gly was exhausted, having nowhere near recovered from his time at sea, but he wouldn't rest until the gear was returned to its hiding spot.

He and the old man finally staggered back to the house, too tired even for a nightcap of schnapps.

While the two men slept, the great machine of the Imperial German intelligence service swung into motion, ponderous at first, as all bureaucracies are, but soon humming along with Teutonic efficiency.

There were a number of spies operating in England who worked independently for the most part, for operational security reasons. It was determined that there wasn't enough time to coordinate any kind of operation using them with the *Lusitania* already on her way. It was also determined that the British would send a heavily armed contingent of men to meet the ship once it docked in Liverpool. The chance of intercepting the courier was slim at best.

The only realistic option was to sink the ship in hopes the courier didn't survive.

Twelve hours after receiving the transmission from America, High Command sent out five additional U-boats with orders to reach the Irish Sea at the best possible speed. It was unlikely that they would make their assigned patrol boxes in time to intercept the ocean liner. There were stepped-up British patrols in the English Channel. The radio ship *Ancona,* in Emden Harbor, sent out a vaguely worded report about targeting extra-large vessels, but there was no guarantee it reached any of the submarines currently on patrol, as they could not radio back a response.

Someone came up with an elegant plan that was guaranteed to succeed. The Kriegsmarine Zeppelin L7 was currently housed in hall number one, an enormous, enclosed hangar nicknamed Tobias, at the newly constructed airship base outside the town of Tønder. The zeppelins all carried wireless telegraphy sets and could directly communicate with the submarines if they were on the surface.

The airship was prepped in record time and took off for the Irish Sea, where several subs were already on station. The launch of the giant zeppelin was timed so it arrived in the patrol area under the cover of darkness and a full day before the express liner arrived on her way to Liverpool.

The weather was fine for the flight and the behemoth arrived on schedule. She could only linger for a few hours, as she needed to clear out before dawn. The radioman did manage to communicate with one of the submarines, the U-20 under command of Walther Schwieger. There was some confusion at first because the airship service used a different encoding system than the *Unterseeboots.* At last, though, the operator aboard the U-20 recognized the codes from his training days when he wasn't sure which service was for him and the message was relayed that the *Lusitania* must be sunk at any cost.

The airship loitered over the Irish Sea for a few additional hours but found no other surfaced U-boats and departed for the German coast long before sunup.

British code breakers in a five-story building near the Thames and operating out of what was simply called Room 40 had early on cracked the codes the German High Command used to communicate with their submarine packs. They heard the vague call about large ships but dismissed it. They knew approximately where the subs picketing the Isles were patrolling by the occasions when their commanders communicated with each other.

What they didn't know was how to break the codes used by the nascent German naval airship fleet. They intercepted the transmissions between the U-20 and L7, but had no luck whatsoever in transcribing them.

The *Lusitania* was sailing into a trap.

40

Isaac Bell and Joe Marchetti were eating a late lunch in the Verandah Café near the *Lusitania*'s stern when a passenger at a window table stood so quickly he knocked over his chair. Frantically he pointed out at the water until he found his voice.

"Torpedo. I think I see a torpedo."

The day was a warm one, so the back wall of the intimate little eating space had been opened to the boat deck promenade. Bell and Marchetti were in motion at almost the exact same time. They ran outside and over to the starboard rail. The seas were exceptionally calm. The trail of the torpedo's passage was a white slash on the otherwise monochromatic green water.

The weapon was twenty feet long and twenty inches wide and packed with over three hundred pounds of explosives. It used the release of compressed air to power pistons, which then spun a pair of counter-rotating propellers. The trail of bubbles the sharp-eyed passenger saw was the air exhaust escaping and rising to the surface. The weapon itself was ten feet underwater and well ahead of its bubbling wake.

Designed to defeat a battleship's foot-thick belt armor, the G/6 torpedo would slice deeply into the unprotected liner on impact.

Bell was an excellent shot and understood the artistry of leading a target. The ship was moving at about eighteen knots, blithely sailing into the path of the speeding torpedo. The weapon's speed was hard to judge, but he guessed it was traveling at better than thirty knots. Both men leaned far over the rail, and more passengers realized the one thing that they had all feared during the crossing, either secretly or aloud, was actually coming to pass. They were under attack by a German U-boat in sight of the Irish coast.

"It's going to hit," Bell said when the torpedo was still some distance off.

"Are you sure?"

"Midships, maybe a little closer to the bow."

The trail of exhaust bubbles was still fairly distant when the torpedo slammed into the liner's flank just aft of the bridge and detonated.

A geyser of water, wood, and steel rose nearly to the height of the funnel and the whole ship shuddered. When the column collapsed it drenched passengers as they lay sprawled on the decks from the concussive force. There were a few screams heard, but for the most part the passengers watched the destruction in silent awe.

A billboard-sized hole appeared where the torpedo struck, and surrounding it were many more hundreds of square feet of bent plates and popped rivets that gave the sea even more access to the interior. With her speed still up at eighteen knots, a hundred tons of water per second were being rammed through the aperture.

Almost immediately the ship started listing to starboard, while at the same time going down by the bow. The hull moaned like a muted whale song as it was slowly being twisted by the enormous forces at work.

Seconds after the first detonation, another great blast erupted deep inside the ship as cold water hit a hot boiler and caused it to rupture in a ghastly cloud of supercritical steam. Anyone who survived the initial explosion in the cavernous engine room would have been scalded to death.

Bell expected the *Lusitania*'s engines to be reversed to slow them down, but he felt no changes. The huge steam engines continued to pound out at a steady rhythm and force more water through the gaps in her outer plating.

"Can you believe the Germans would torpedo a ship like this?" Joe asked. "She's carrying women and children."

"And she's also carrying their stolen vacuum tube," Bell said.

Joe's jaw dropped. "Do you think we were targeted, you know, specifically?"

"I can't rule it out. There could have been contingencies if Gly failed in his mission. Perhaps if he missed a radio check, the Germans had to assume he didn't have the tube and so they painted a big bull's-eye on the *Lucy* and sent their subs out to sink her."

"Savages."

"This is a hell of a gamble. If the ship actually sinks, anti-German sentiment is going to rise to a fever pitch back home."

"What do you think? Are we going to sink?"

Bell considered the question for a moment. "On one hand I don't like that we're not slowing down, but on the other I can't imagine a single torpedo strike is a mortal blow to a ship this big. We'll need rescuing for sure, but I'm not sure she'll sink. That said, I prefer prudence over panic, so let's get the life jackets from our cabin and find Purser McCubbin."

The ship carried the latest Boddy life jackets for first- and second-class passengers. They resembled a sleeveless coat, but were padded with flotation material. The third class and crew had the traditional canvas vests with blocks of cork sewn into panels. Both men shrugged out of their suit-coats and donned their warmest sweaters before belting the vests around their torsos. Bell also retrieved a wad of cash he'd hidden under a drawer.

He gave half to Joe. "Just in case."

Less than two minutes after the impact, they could feel the list growing more pronounced.

They had to brace themselves against the wall as they headed for the main stairs aft. There were a lot of people about, scared, confused. Some had donned their life vests, while others looked mockingly at those wearing flotation devices, as if to say they were acting ridiculous. Because of the heavy list, one of the elevator cars had jammed up against its ornate cage, its cables slack.

Heading down the stairs was a dizzying effort because of the shift in angles. Bell had to step in the crease where the tread met the riser in order to descend. To make matters worse, he and Joe were moving against the multitudes trying desperately to reach the open deck. More than one person cursed them out in the vilest manner with little regard to the women caught in the crowd.

They finally fought their way to B Deck. The lobby was full of passengers and harried crew members trying to be as reassuring as possible. People continued acting rationally, but the situation could spiral into mass panic and a stampede in seconds. Over the constant strains of metal being bent floated the sound of children sobbing and some women weeping.

With Joe Marchetti in his wake, Bell weaved his way through the crowd to the purser's bureau. The room was packed with mostly male passengers demanding valuables from the ship's safe. The mood was ugly. There were only two assistant pursers behind the counter to verify claims.

Bell had to get even more aggressive, using a shoulder or elbow to get up to the counter. "Where's Mr. McCubbin?"

"Don't know, sir," a young purser said, handing a small case to a well-dressed gentleman.

Bell muttered an oath and slid back again, snagging Joe, who'd waited by the door. "Purser's not here. He could be anywhere, and we need to get into his safe."

"Should we check his cabin?"

"We aren't that lucky he'd be there. He's a public figure, best known on the boat, really. Likely he'll be topside to help keep people calm."

They went out onto the long promenade deck on the port side, the higher side of the ship, because it was easier to walk with a hand braced against the wall. The passengers standing at the rail had to hold on with both hands or they'd careen across the deck and into a bulkhead.

In just the few minutes they'd been inside, the ship had noticeably slowed. Bell didn't know if that was the result of an order from the bridge or that the engine rooms were so flooded the boilers couldn't produce steam. He also noted the *Lusitania* was settling even lower in the water.

He started to rethink their chances of rescue.

The two men made their way up to the boat deck. It was crowded like this was a typical sailing day, but there was no joy. Families huddled together, with fathers trying to assure their wives and children and for the most part failing. There were other passengers, traveling alone, who stood silent and bleak-faced. The children's cries were especially poignant.

When the ship had sailed into the German quarantine zone, Captain Turner had ordered all the lifeboats be raised up and over the rails as a precaution. Now handfuls of sailors were trying to lower them down to the rail in anticipation of the order to abandon ship.

They struggled mightily because the way the ship was listing to starboard left the heavy boats lying against the rail or even dangling inside it. They fought with oars to dislodge the sixty-eight-person wooden boats to no avail.

The specter of the *Titanic* disaster was fresh in everyone's minds. She didn't carry enough lifeboats for everyone and while the *Lusitania* carried more than enough for passage and crew alike, half of them might be unusable. Bell and Marchetti exchanged a knowing and grave look.

Bell called out, "Has anyone seen the chief purser? Mr. McCubbin? Has anyone seen him?"

No one even looked in his direction.

"Let's try the other side."

They had to lean far back as they descended the deck to the portside rail. People clutched at whatever they could to maintain their footing. Bell saw a friend, Alfred Vanderbilt, Willie K.'s cousin. Like all the family, he was wealthy beyond measure, well-educated, and cultured, but he also had a bit of a wild side and scandal seemed to follow him wherever he went. They'd spent a great deal of time together during the trip.

He seemed as unruffled by their situation as could be. "Good day for a swim, eh?"

"I'd have preferred a heated swimming pool. Any chance you've seen McCubbin?"

"I saw him aft about ten minutes ago." Vanderbilt then let his lopsided smile fade. "What do you think?"

"They can't launch the starboard-side boats."

"Grim."

"That's the word for it."

There came a loud clatter of wood and rope from the next boat down the line, where deckhands were trying to ready it for launch. The lifeboat swung violently away from the ship on its davits, yanking one sailor over the railing and leaving him clinging helplessly to the swaying boat's gunwale. The three sailors still aboard the liner had all been tossed back by the launch. Several women screamed.

The dangling sailor tried to pull himself up, but only managed to make his grip on the lifeboat more tenuous. He was going to fall in seconds. Bell pushed his way through the crowd and mounted the railing using the davit spar to steady himself. The gap was only eight feet, but he was aiming for a moving target sixty feet above the water with a man's life at stake.

For a fraction of a second Bell looked left and nearly lost his nerve at the sight of the *Lusitania*'s bow completely submerged. She'd slowed almost to a stop, but that hadn't lessened the influx of water into her belly. Portholes in the forward steerage compartments were only fifteen feet above the waterline when the ship was level. They were now underwater, and each sucked in tons of water every minute.

He timed his leap and threw himself into the void, arcing gracefully through the air and landing with flexed knees in the boat on one of the benches. He would have twisted an ankle had he landed on the curving floorboards. Momentum forced him to take one lurching step and then he turned, dropped to his belly, and reached out for the stranded crewman.

Bell's landing had sent the boat rocking once again, as hard as when it first swung away from the ship. The seaman couldn't hold on and felt his fingers lose their grip on the white-painted wood.

Bell clutched the man's wrist just as he began to fall. The strain was enormous, but the sailor had the presence of mind to grab for the gunwale again. Bell used his other hand to grasp at the back of the man's coat and pull. The sailor fought to raise himself up into the lifeboat, eventually using his elbows and finally knees.

A round of applause erupted among those who saw the rescue. Bell acknowledged it for just a second before he looked toward the *Lusitania*'s bow. It seemed to him as though the sea was absorbing the ship, drawing it downward foot by foot. He knew there was no coming back. Half of the bow forward of the bridge had disappeared. The *Lusitania* and an unknown number of her passengers and crew were doomed.

Bell used his pocketknife to cut off the painter line attached to the boat's bow and tied it onto one of the brass oarlocks. He kept the other end in his hand and jumped back for the rail. Joe and another passenger were there to help him over and back onto the deck. Bell pulled on the line and the lifeboat swung up against the ship's rail. Other men were there to hold it in place so

Bell could tie off this end of the rope, thus eliminating the daunting gap.

"Load it up," he told a deckhand. "Women and children first and launch as fast as you can."

"The order hasn't been —"

Just behind them came a roar of frightened shouting and fearful gasps. Bell looked to see what had happened. He saw all the lights had gone out. The electric dynamo that supplied the ship with power had failed. It wasn't so bad on the upper decks, where there was light streaming in through countless windows. Belowdecks would become a stygian realm of total darkness. Lord only knew how many people were still down there or how they'd find their way out.

Bell checked his watch. Barely ten minutes since the torpedo had hit the ship. At this pace she'd be gone in minutes rather than hours.

Overhead, a smokestack belched black smoke, coating those below with hot ash and soot. The guy wires holding it erect thrummed with tension as the ship's list cantilevered it out over the boat deck.

People had gone strangely quiet. The truth of their predicament was hitting home. Third-class passengers were arriving on the boat deck along with men from the engineering spaces, black with coal dust and grease. Bell saw a stoker crawl out of a ventilation shaft.

Bell said goodbye to Vanderbilt and he and Joe headed aft in search of McCubbin. The idea came to both men at the same time, and without word or thought they undid their life jackets and handed them to a pair of women as they passed. Bell also tossed overboard anything he saw that would float, mostly wooden deck chairs, but also the lids to the crates for the inflatable boats that were being lowered. Five hundred feet behind them the bridge slipped under the waves.

41

"It's going to be okay," Bell heard McCubbin's calming voice calling out as he and Joe reached the end of the deck where they had started when the torpedo struck. "The Irish coast is only a few miles away and our Marconi operators have been sending out our distress since the very beginning of this ordeal. There's a whole armada of boats heading our way. You'll all have a grand tale to tell when you get home."

Bell pushed through the last of the crowd. McCubbin had been standing on a chair from the Verandah Café to address the crowd of people around him. Even if what he said were all lies, they were the lies the passengers wanted to hear.

"James."

"Mr. Bell, where is your life jacket?"

"Gave it away," Bell said, as if the answer should have been obvious. "I need the key to your safe."

"At a time like this?"

A chorus of shrieks erupted from the water below. Bell rushed to the rail. Halfway to the sea, one of the lifeboats being lowered had suddenly dumped out its occupants. They'd plummeted into the water with no warning, with several landing on top of their fellow passengers. Many didn't appear to have life vests. The forty or so people began splashing feebly at the water, wailing and crying out for help. One person, a slender woman or maybe a teenage girl, remained motionless, facedown and quite obviously dead.

There were dozens, perhaps as many as a hundred people, in the Irish Sea already. They'd either jumped from the lower promenade deck or simply waded into the water as it crept up along the boat deck. A number of lifeboats had launched successfully and a few stayed close to the liner to rescue some of those stranded in the water, but others maintained their distance for fear of being swamped by the desperate.

"Dear God." A man at Bell's shoulder breathed and crossed himself.

Bell turned back to McCubbin. "James, it's possible this whole disaster is because of what we put in your safe. The Germans will do anything to stop us from delivering it, including this human tragedy."

The Englishman unbuttoned his jacket and shirt and felt around for the key. He snapped its lanyard and handed it over. "Pray you're not too late."

"Good luck, old friend."

"To us all, Mr. Bell."

Bell and Marchetti dashed forward, steadying themselves on whatever they could. It was so disorienting watching the sea consume the deck and realizing the water wasn't rising at all, but that the great ship, what they all considered as solid as terra firma, was sinking. They reached an outside staircase and had to use their arms and legs to crawl down to B Deck. The bottom few steps were awash.

Stepping into the water, Bell felt an electric jolt. It was cold. Not numbing cold, but certainly frigid enough.

Hundreds of people milled around on the shrinking patch of dry land that was the promenade. They all accepted that going into the sea was inevitable, but wanted to put it off for as long as possible. This close to the surface, the cries of people already adrift were louder and far more pitiable.

The two men went aft, away from the water, and entered the ship near the main stairs. People were still climbing up from below, wet from head to toe, miserable and shivering. A crewman with a flashlight seemed to be shepherding them like the proverbial Pied Piper.

"Promenade deck," he cried when he saw daylight streaming in through the windows. "Just like I promised you."

"Can I borrow that?" Bell asked, pointing to the man's multi-cell flashlight.

"Sir, it's almost completely flooded down below. Forget whatever it is you think you need and get outside."

"I have no choice."

The crewman's eyes widened, but he felt the conviction in Bell's tone. He handed it over, saying, "You're mad, mate."

Bell and Marchetti scooted down the stairs on their backsides like children. The ship had to be listing at more than twenty-five degrees and down by the bow at an equal angle. They had just minutes before the final plunge.

The water deepened and by the time they got to the C Deck landing, it was up to their chests, drawing heat from their bodies with every moment's exposure. Fortunately James McCubbin's cabin was just across the lobby and aft, where it was shallower. Bell played the light around. Floating in the water was all sorts of detritus, paper mostly, also a couple of bowls bobbing like bathtub toys, linen napkins that had drifted from the dining room, and a scum of white dust from all the intricate plasterwork that had cracked off the walls as the ship twisted in her death throes.

They both heard the screaming coming from around the backside of the staircase. It was distant and nearly drowned out by the rush of water filling the ship, but contained such unbridled terror that it cut through the interference and hit raw nerves.

They didn't have time for even a moment's distraction, but they forged through the rising water like rampaging animals. Around the stairs on the port side was the nursery, an area where haggard mothers could leave their youngest with dedicated teams of nannies while they enjoyed the ship's adult amenities. It was not a space either man was familiar with, and with the limited light from their torch, details were hard to work out. A wooden rocking horse and tiny desks and chairs swirled in the eddies of the rising water.

"We're here," Bell shouted.

"Help us."

"Through there," Joe said, pointing at the open door across the room.

They fought against what felt like a deadly

riptide, forcing their way forward, elbows high and torsos swinging to keep up their momentum. They passed out of the children's room. To their left were a pair of closets or possibly washrooms and ahead was a plain wooden door.

Only about the top eighteen inches had yet to succumb to the sea. Bell pounded on it with a fist. "Are you in here?"

"Yes."

"Oh, thank God."

"Help."

Three female voices sounded as one.

Bell reached under the water to grab the handle. "I'm going to open the door. When I do, water is going to flood that room very quickly and very violently. Hold on to something attached to the ship. Ready?"

"The door opens out because there's some pipes in here."

Bell tested the door anyway and while the knob turned easily enough he couldn't pull the door open against the pressure of there being more water on the outside than in the only partially flooded room. Doubtlessly water was filling the space from the crack under the door, however the chamber might not flood for many minutes, or hours perhaps, long after the *Lusitania* had slipped under the waves.

"There's a fire axe near the exit out of the main lobby," Joe said.

"Take the light and go. On the jump."

While Marchetti slogged back the way they'd come, and the water level had risen at least another inch, Bell shouted instructions to the trapped women. "Get yourselves away from the door."

There was little concern about over-penetration, but he was always cautious when it came to civilians and firearms.

Bell pulled his Browning and ducked underwater. He placed the muzzle against the door barely a quarter inch from the gap at the bottom and fired. The noise was atrocious because sound traveled faster in water and water doesn't compress. By feel he set the muzzle just above the hole and fired again. And again. Walking the line of holes up the door incrementally. He rose up to refill his lungs and replace the empty magazine. He dove a second time, repeating the procedure. Midway through the second magazine he could tell that the bullet no longer traveled through water on the far side of the door. The room contained only a couple of feet of water. He rose again.

"Are you all right?"

"Yes."

Bell released a relieved breath. He'd

feared a bullet ricocheting off the room's metal walls striking one of the women. "I have to keep shooting, but I'll angle the bullets down. Just stay where you are."

A bullet could conceivably ricochet off standing water, but less likely when it was churned and roiling. He needed only to reach down to find his next target, saving his ears the aural onslaught. He burned through his third and final magazine just as Joe sloshed back holding the light and a wood-handled axe.

Bell took the axe while Joe held the light steady. "Hold on tight in there."

He swung the axe, aiming for the middle of the door at a spot just above the waterline so he could throw as much force into it as possible. His healing wrist sent a sharp stab of pain up his arm. The blade bit deep and he had to saw it back and forth to pull it free. He hit it again and the door split along its grain, a crack that reached as far down as the uppermost bullet hole. Like the perforations on a piece of stationery, the holes allowed the tremendous pressure of the water to rip the door in two.

It collapsed in an explosive gush that pulled the two men off their feet and tumbled them into the room and then almost back out again when the surge hit the far wall and rebounded. They came up sputtering. The three women, porcelain-faced girls really, were dressed as stewardesses and clung to pipes. They'd been thoroughly drenched, but appeared unharmed.

"Come on," Bell encouraged them. "There isn't much time."

They each wore life vests, but didn't really know how to swim in them. After a few seconds wasted splashing around, Bell grabbed two of the girls by their collars and towed them out through the nursery and deposited them halfway up the main steps. Joe was right behind him with the third young woman.

"Off you go. Climb as high as you can and then get as far away from the ship as possible."

Bell and Marchetti turned away from the Englishwomen, who were lauding their bravery, and returned to their original mission. Bell took back the light and focused its beam on the corner where two pursers' cabins were located.

Something didn't look right. The wall opposite McCubbin's cabin had collapsed or more likely been blasted outward by a detonation in the engine room. The decorative panel that hid the flue for stack number three was blocking their way.

The panel was metal, jagged where it had been sheared off the wall and lodged tight across the little alcove. Bell gave the light to Joe and pulled on the metal with everything he had. It didn't budge. He dove under the surface, moving by feel, his hands in constant motion. At the floor he found an opening that seemed big enough. He tried squeezing through, but no matter how he worked his shoulders he couldn't make it. With his lungs nearly convulsing, he stopped fighting and popped back up to the surface. Joe could no longer stand and was forced to tread water in the rising tide and steady himself with a hand on the ceiling.

"There's a way through at the bottom," Bell gasped. "I can't fit. I'm too big."

"Never send a big guy to do a little guy's job," Joe said with bravado.

"Good man." Bell thrust the key into his hand. "The light should last long enough. You remember the layout of the room and where the safe is?"

"Sure do."

"It'll be disorienting, bedding and clothes floating around."

"I'll be fine. I went to Annapolis. Do you think I haven't had disaster training?"

Bell nodded. "Right. Off you go."

Marchetti sank out of sight. Bell could see

the light under the water as he swam for the bottom. He came up again after only a couple of seconds.

"What happened?"

Joe's face had gone deathly pale. "It's, ah, no good. I'm also too big."

"Joe, listen to me. You need to try harder than that."

"I did."

"No. You panicked. I get it. It's okay. But you need to hear me. There are thousands, literally thousands, of sailors' lives in your hands right now. If you don't get the vacuum tube, the Germans are going on a hunting spree across the length and breadth of the Atlantic, and those men, your brothers, are going to die."

"I . . ."

"Don't think. Just act. Now go."

"Yes, Mr. Bell."

He took a huge gulp of air and vanished once again. Bell watched the light disappear when it went through the opening and was blocked by Joe's body as he wormed his way past the obstruction. And then came a dim flash as he reached the other side, his torch visible from the surface.

A half minute passed and the light didn't reappear. It was okay. Plenty of time. Then, at the one-minute mark, Bell felt a growing sense of unease. Holding your breath that long wasn't impossible, but the cabin was tiny. It shouldn't take this long to get in and out. Had there been an air pocket? Why would it matter? The safe had a single key, not some intricate combination.

"Come on, Joe," Bell pleaded quietly as the deck shifted beneath him. The ship was settling faster now and the groans of twisting metal echoed near and far.

Finally he saw a murky aura down in the water. Joe was swimming back. It took only a few seconds, though, for Bell to realize the light grew no brighter. Joe wasn't coming closer. He didn't have an explanation, but his unease turned into something far darker.

A rising panic crackled through his system like an electrical short and he dove for the bottom. Joe's torso was visible, but he was stuck. The light was bright enough for Bell to see what had happened. The gnarled maze of twisted metal around the opening had collapsed as Joe was making his escape. Bell could see his leg was pinned just above the ankle, the water around it clouded red with blood.

Joe moved lethargically as Bell swam closer. His dark hair danced and waved on the currents, while his eyes, normally limpid and flashing, were clouded over in a blank stare. In one hand Joe held the dying flashlight. In the palm of his other wavering hand, torn and gouged by countless deep cuts, rested the machined cylinder containing the German's revolutionary vacuum tube.

He made a desperate motion toward Bell, extending his arm with the cylinder. As Bell took the device, Joe waved a weak farewell, his full cheeks exhaling a last breath.

Joe had become trapped on the sinking ship just eighteen inches from freedom.

42

Bell left Marchetti. But only for the few seconds it took him to scramble across the hall and return with the fire axe. Bell felt his own panic at seeing the life fade from Joe as he dove down beside him. The fissure that held Joe's leg was small, but enough room sufficed for Bell to slide the handle in alongside Marchetti's ankle. Bell planted his feet and pulled up on the axe, flexing every fiber in his body to exert the maximum force possible. He felt a slight give in the metal and instantly dropped the axe. Grabbing Joe by the shirt, he yanked his friend forward. Joe's bloody ankle cleared the gap, followed by his crushed foot, which dangled limp as a noodle.

Bell pulled him to the surface and was encouraged when he heard a rasping cough escape Joe's lips. Little space remained between the ceiling and the swirling floodwaters. Bell jammed the heavy cylinder into a trouser pocket. Keeping Joe's face above the surface, Bell struggled to swim against the sweep of water rushing through the ship. He finally reached the stair alcove and the crazily angled treads. He was exhausted from the ordeal and by the cold, but paused only long enough to strip off Joe's necktie and cinch it as a tourniquet around the injured man's leg. He lifted Joe onto his shoulders like a yoke and began climbing as quickly as he could. One full flight up and suddenly Joe came to life. The pounding of Bell's shoulder into his diaphragm had restarted his breathing and a gush of seawater erupted from Joe's mouth and nose. He convulsed a second time and even more fluid erupted from inside his body.

Bell would have liked to stop and attend to him, but it seemed that every stair he climbed vanished beneath the waves right at his heel.

He had no life jacket and knew the protective cylinder was too heavy to keep without extra flotation. When he got to the promenade deck, he was practically at the waterline. Before him more than a thousand souls braved the open sea. Some clung to floating debris, some relied on their life vests, and some, far too many of them, lay facedown and still. Seeing this panorama of death was one of the most disturbing images he would ever experience.

He set Joe on the deck. He was moaning feebly and couldn't open his eyes. But he was alive.

Bell unscrewed the brass cylinder's lid and slid out the vacuum tube still tucked inside a black felt bag. He doubted the delicate radio component would survive even a minute in his pants pocket, leaving him with only one option.

He worked up as much saliva as his saltwater-desiccated mouth would produce and swallowed the tube, rounded end first. It stuck in his throat for a moment, but he remained calm, working his muscles until it cleared and hit his stomach. He picked up Joe. The lad was so slim that he carried him as easily as he had Marion on their wedding night. He made his way past passengers and crew still too afraid to leave the ship. He peeled off Joe's shoes and his own. He then legged over the rail and eased himself into the water. Towing Joe once again, he swam away from the sinking ship in strong, even strokes for a minute before turning back.

From this perspective it looked like the ship had been sliced bow to stern in an angled line and the bottom two-thirds had been thrown away. She was sinking fast, accelerating to her death so that, one by one, her towering funnels vanished, while her three propellers gleamed in the sun. She was so thoroughly flooded that little air came rushing from the various vents and ports.

Nearby, Bell heard the haunted refrains of a thousand people weeping as they watched the liner in her final moments. Her stern rose high out of the water. She hung for a moment and then slid deeper and deeper until the sea washed over her fantail and the RMS *Lusitania* was no more.

After a few minutes of swimming, Bell came across a corpse still clad in a life jacket. It was an elderly woman in a dark dress. Certainly first class. In death the wrinkles of her face had smoothed out. Bell guessed she was a victim of the cold, or maybe the strain had been too much for her heart. As gently as he could, he removed her buoyant Boddy vest and then gave her body a slight shove. It was difficult to don the vest while keeping Joe afloat. He worked his arms into the device and tied off the belts at the front. He allowed the vest to take his weight to give his tired muscles a break. Hugging Joe to his chest, he couldn't relax for too long or he'd cramp up and the cold would settle deep in his chest. He noted the seas around him were far quieter than they'd been even a short time ago. A wave of death was sweeping through the water, taking the elderly and the very youngest of passengers first.

Bell started swimming sidestroke again. At the first opportunity, he got a life jacket around Joe. If anything happened to Bell while he was swimming, Joe would be able to float on his own. He didn't make for the distant shore. He calculated his best chance for rescue was to stay as near to other people or bodies as possible. He would have preferred proximity to the few lifeboats, but the men at the oars didn't want anyone else aboard, and they kept rowing away.

During his next rest, a bug-eyed man swam past him without saying a word. He just glanced in Bell's direction and kept going as though he had a destination in mind. He was the last living person Bell would encounter over the next three hours. He didn't want to count the number of dead, but did anyway. Seventy-three.

From around a distant headland on the Irish coast came a haze of smoke, the exhaust of a motley fleet of trawlers, Navy torpedo boats, pleasure craft, and various fishing vessels. Bell had been confident of rescue, as they had gone down so near to the coast, but seeing them come put a big smile on his face and he whooped aloud. He heard other distant survivors cheering as well.

Thirty minutes after that, Bell and Marchetti were pulled onto the deck of a trawler. Five other survivors were already aboard, huddled under mismatched blankets that must have been donated by townsfolk.

A crewman handed him a blanket and a metal mug with a gulp of warm tea at the bottom. "I learned quick I can't fill 'em, 'cause you'd spill most of it."

Bell took the mug in a quavering hand and, rather than drink it, let the warmth soak into his numb fingers. Joe remained unconscious. Bell wrapped an extra blanket around him, tearing off a long strip first. He took the cloth and wound it tightly around Joe's foot and ankle as a makeshift bandage until he could receive medical assistance.

It was dusk by the time the trawler's captain decided he couldn't take any more survivors unless he stacked them like cordwood on his deck like he had the bodies they'd recovered. They turned for Queensland. They arrived long after dark, but as Bell and the others staggered down the gangplank they were greeted by two long lines of people — soldiers, sailors, and townsfolk — who had turned out to give them an ovation under the glow of the town's gas lamps. A stretcher was quickly summoned for Joe and he was taken to the town's overrun hospital.

Bell spent the night on the floor of a hotel lobby, his belly full of stew and Irish whiskey. A general goods store had remained open, so he had dry clothes and new shoes. He'd given all but twenty dollars to the owner with instructions to cover any survivor who needed something but had no means to pay.

He'd also bought a small jar of castor oil for when the time was right.

He woke early the next morning and went straight to the hospital to check on Joe. Bell found him lying on a paper-thin mattress on the floor due to the overcrowding. His ankle was in a thick cast and his breathing heavy. He remained unconscious for most of the morning, his eyes prying open for just a minute. He focused on Bell's face as he sat beside him and he formed a weak smile.

"We got it," he rasped before passing out.

"We did," Bell replied, patting Joe on the shoulder.

He felt guilt at the severity of Joe's injuries, but knew he still had a job to do. Leaving the hospital, Bell found the town was awash in naval personnel, reporters, and representatives from a dozen charity organizations. Bell was asked by several people if he needed to go to the makeshift morgues that had been set up to identify any loved ones. He told them it wasn't necessary. Boats kept scouring the ocean and returning more and more corpses. Cunard personnel numbered and photographed them all to assist in identification. It was a lovely spring day on the Irish coast, but the grimmest anyone could remember.

Bell finally approached a Royal Navy officer who'd just come out of the city hall.

"Excuse me, Commander, may I have a word?" Bell extended his hand. "My name is Isaac Bell, and I was acting as a courier on behalf of your government. I was supposed to be met in Liverpool when we arrived, but now I'm not sure who to reach out to. I was told it will be days before I can send a telegram to your ambassador in Washington for instructions."

"Commander Brian O'Malley, Mr. Bell, and believe it or not, a few of us were sent here from Dublin with orders to find you among the living or the dead. I was just going over the register of survivors they're still compiling."

"I haven't checked in with anyone," Bell explained. "The Germans slipped agents onto the *Lusitania,* so I thought it best to keep my profile low until I could talk to someone in authority."

"Good thinking," O'Malley said. "I wasn't told what you were to carry, but do you still have it?"

"Safe as could be." Bell patted his stomach. The Irish sailor cocked a questioning eye. "As Holmes would say, 'Alimentary, my dear Watson.' "

"Huh?"

"I swallowed it." Bell showed him the castor oil.

"Ahh." Then the full implication hit. "Ohh."

Bell shrugged. "What do you chaps say, 'For King and Country'?"

"Let's go find the others I came here with. We have a car and can be at the Dublin ferry before you know it. Is there anything you need to do here, anyone you need to say goodbye to?"

"No. I have a friend at the hospital, but he is unconscious. They've dressed his wounds but fear pneumonia. He'll be here convalescing for some time, I'm afraid."

"I'm sorry, Mr. Bell."

"So am I, Commander. So am I. And we're the lucky ones."

43

One month later

They were still pulling bodies from the Irish Sea or finding them washed up on the coast. The disaster remained front-page news as the nation speculated about what the President would do, how he would retaliate for the one hundred and twenty-three Americans who'd perished when the *Lusitania* sank. Some in Congress were howling for blood, but so far Wilson had only sent a stern letter to the Kaiser.

The leadership in the War Department knew that if a declaration came, they were not prepared for battle, so in the weeks since the disaster, the top brass had worked around the clock to begin putting the nation on a war footing. Stores and munitions were purchased and plans drawn up. The country had no troop ships. Various shipping lines were contacted about the possibility of renting or leasing their fleets. It had been chaos.

Today had been the man's first day off since the telegrams from Queenstown arrived in America with news of the U-boat attack. He'd taken the train to New York and was now being driven east on Long Island. He hadn't been back since Christmas. He wished this was just a family visit, but he had work to do.

The driver parked in front of the old farmhouse and the two men approached the front door. His arrival had been expected and his grandfather came out before he reached the porch. "Look at you," he cried, "my favorite grandson. So important. That suit must have cost you a pretty penny."

"Hello, Opa," he said, and let the old man hug him.

"Come in, come in. I made your grandmother's spaetzle."

"This is Hans," the grandson said, introducing the driver. "He's a member of the Brotherhood."

They entered the house, and the old man closed the door.

Bell watched from down the road using a pair of binoculars resting on the car's windowsill. Behind him were the three other agency vehicles they'd used to tail their subject from Penn Station. Next to him sat

Helen Mills. The fact that Joe Marchetti's continued hospitalization in England had been caused by the men in the farmhouse made the hatred radiating from her right now such that Bell could almost see it shimmering off her, like heat from a sunbaked stretch of asphalt.

"Ready?" Bell asked.

"Yes," she said, her eyes on the distant house as if she could see through its walls. "Hell, yes."

They exited the car and the others followed suit. Bell looked at the passenger of the car directly behind them. "This is as far as you go."

"You made that abundantly clear in the office this morning," Archie Abbott said. "Lillian makes it abundantly clear every day, and Doc Rosenstein also makes the point abundantly clear whenever I see him. Four more weeks before I can get back out in the field. Got it."

Bell smiled. "Still good to have you almost back."

He had set up this operation while still in England, burning the transatlantic cables with instructions on what turned out to be the longest stakeout in the agency's history. Van Dorn was at his wit's end over the manpower expenditure, but Bell was adamant, especially when he received word the German vacuum tube they'd sent to Washington didn't work.

Their target was shadowed at his office and outside his apartment for twenty-eight straight days. An effort that provided no useful intelligence. It wasn't until he was finally granted a day off and beelined for New York, as Bell thought he would, that the Van Dorn team struck gold. They had no idea of his destination once he arrived in the city, hence so many cars to tail him, but all understood its significance.

The spy was likely making contact with the rest of his cell.

"Think he's here?"

Bell knew who Archie meant. "When it happened, I was sure he bought it taking a tumble off the *Lucy*'s lifeboat. After myself and a few hundred others survived all that time in the water, I put the odds at eighty–twenty he's dead."

"Why so skewed?"

"He didn't have a life jacket. For the most part, we all did."

The agents he'd chosen for the raid understood the tactics required for the assault. Bell spent a few minutes reviewing everything to ensure there would be no mistakes. They had a lot of firepower but wouldn't know what the other side brought to the fight until they were in the thick of it.

They circled wide around the property, keeping low so as not to be seen. It was a windy enough day that their crawling through the three-foot corn that grew almost to the back of the house went undetected. Two agents covered the rear door and two windows, one watched each side of the house, and Bell and Helen were going in the front, with James Dashwood, the best shot in the office after Bell himself, keeping flexible so he could rush where needed.

The clapboard farmhouse had so few windows he and Helen made it to a corner without being seen. She carried a .38 revolver. Bell had his Browning 9 millimeter in a holster at his hip and carried a Winchester 1897 shotgun with the barrels sawn off just past the five-round magazine tube. The round already in the chamber was what they called a breaching charge. It had the power to shred the guts of most door locks and handle assemblies, but wouldn't overpenetrate into the space beyond.

They slithered onto the porch under a big bay window and got to their feet in front of the door. Bell had never seen such determination in Helen before. Hell hath no fury . . .

He gave her a sharp nod, and fired from the hip, racking the pump to chamber another round even as the remains of the door swung back after being blown wide open. The noise had been thunderous. The two launched themselves through the door, Helen covering right, Bell to the left. From the back came another blast as the rear door was practically blown off its hinges. The plan called for only one man to enter the rear of the house. His partner remained outside covering the windows.

Four men sat around a table eating their lunch, each caught completely by surprise. The driver who'd picked up the spy at Penn Station had a hunk of black bread in his mouth, the old man had been so startled his dentures had fallen onto his plate. The master spy himself was as white as the good china plates his grandfather had honored him with.

And then there was Foster "Foss" Gly, sitting unnaturally rigid. He'd been as shocked as the others, but his ratlike instinct was priming his body for the natural flight-or-fight response. His heart rate was up, flooding his system with adrenaline. His eyes were dilating to bring in extra light, his nostrils flared to breathe easier and faster. Even his stomach had already stopped digesting his meal so every bit of energy was available for the next few seconds.

All of that had evolved to give a human a chance when encountering some wild animal in our distant past. It had worked more often than not, since the species hadn't gone extinct, but there was no real natural response to staring down the choked barrel of a pump-action shotgun.

"Clear. All clear," came the shout from the back.

"Go check the barn. You know what to look for."

Gly and Bell glared at each other, alpha males, apex predators, natural enemies, each shocked to see the other, but somehow not surprised.

"Everyone keep your hands flat on the table, palms up." In that position a person couldn't push themselves up from the table with much force.

Gly kept his palms flat.

Bell moved a foot closer so there was no doubt the Scotsman would take the full load of the shotgun's pellets. "Keep tempting me."

He rotated his hands.

Kurt Miller, Roosevelt's little toady, finally found his voice when he recognized the blond man on the other side of the twelve gauge. "Bell, what is the meaning of this? You followed me here."

"I've had you tailed every day for a month so I wouldn't miss this opportunity. And I have to say that you lead one boring life."

The outrage only grew. "Secretary Roosevelt is going to hear of this."

"Of that I have no doubt. I'll be happy to tell him how you fooled us all. I never would have suspected you but for two tiny mistakes and one major blunder. I saw you at the Bavarian Brotherhood's little cigar-smuggling party, not your face but your shoulders and their distinctive and rather unbecoming slope. I didn't recall that detail until you came by my office to pick up the vacuum tube and I realized it was you with your back to me that night.

"The second mistake was taking the bait when I told you we were leaving at ten. Doubtful an out-of-towner like you would know that's when the *Lusitania* sails. But you knew because you already had men aboard to photograph munitions in her hold. You phoned Gly after our meeting and he had himself added to the list of stowaways."

"This is ridiculous," the bureaucrat blustered.

"The blunder," Bell continued, "was having a couple of your Brotherhood thugs try to mug me on the train. The only people who knew of our morning meeting were me, my boss, your boss, and you. Neither Van Dorn nor Roosevelt are the Kaiser's man in America. And I didn't set up my own mugging, so that leaves only one. Oops."

"There could have been others in my office. Or yours."

"Stop," Bell said. "Just stop. You're caught. The vacuum tube was in your custody for a while. When we gave it to you, Joe Marchetti was sure it was in perfect condition."

"You can't prove I —"

Bell spoke right over him. "I'm sure I can interview the two guards who accompanied you back to Washington and they'll tell me that you had the case uncuffed on some pretext. I'd say you told them you had orders to inspect the tube at the halfway point of your journey."

Miller would have been an easy mark at the poker table. His expression was one of naked disbelief at how accurate Bell's guess had been.

"Those sailors were picked for their brawn over their brains, so I can see them falling for it."

James Dashwood called that he was coming in when he was on the front porch, always the smart thing to do around so many guns. "Sorry to say, there's nothing suspicious in the barn."

"Keep looking." Bell turned his attention back to the four men at the table. The realization was sinking in. Miller and his driver looked green. "Like I said. You're caught. Gly is caught, your driver's caught. By the way, fella, you really picked the wrong day to kiss up to the Bavarian Brotherhood leadership."

Now that he was no longer pretending to be Devlin Connell, Gly had started shaving his head again. He finally spoke. "I guess in the scheme of things this is an improvement for me. No more French hellhole. American prison should be like a vacation after that."

Bell chuckled, a low menacing sound steeped in intentional cruelty. "Here's the best part. When I realized you were involved in this espionage ring, I made contact with the French authorities on the odd chance I managed to capture you."

The smug look on Gly's face began to fade.

"They will be more than happy to take you back and I'm sure our government will agree to your return to Guiana."

Gly's blank face then sharpened, his eyes narrowing. Bell watched his hands. He hadn't flipped them yet, but the temptation was building.

"They also said that the remaining years of your sentence, which I believe is the rest of your natural life, will be spent in solitary confinement."

He was going to do it, Bell was certain. He surreptitiously slipped his finger into the Winchester's trigger guard. It was poor practice, but with a man as dangerous as Gly, he wasn't taking chances.

"You're going back to hell."

Helen moved toward the group of men, holstering her .38 and readying a pair of handcuffs. "On your feet, you monster."

Bell recognized her mistake a fraction of a second too late. "Helen, wai—"

Gly had stood as soon as she gave the order and she moved in to cuff him while Bell still had his shotgun in hand. Gly turned to present his back to her, his big hands crossed. She reached out to sling one cuff around his right wrist. Gly whipped around, swinging the heavy open cuff so that it slammed into Helen's temple. She started to collapse, but Gly grabbed her as a shield. He reached for her pistol with his left hand, drawing it from her holster and firing in Bell's direction, forcing Bell to the floor.

He then let go of Helen and made a headfirst dive through the window.

Bell couldn't fire the shotgun with Helen so close.

There were two rapid shots from outside when Gly fired at one of the Van Dorn men.

Bell jumped to his feet, his shotgun at the ready in case either of the other German agents tried to escape. It had all happened so fast that none of the men had moved. Helen staggered to her feet with a trickle of blood seeping from the wound at her temple. She appeared steady.

"You okay?"

"I think so."

"Coming through," James Dashwood called from the front door again. He had his pistol held low.

"Help Helen," Bell ordered. He tossed the shotgun to Dashwood and leapt through the window.

One of his men was lying on the lawn with his hand clamped to his thigh, the white handkerchief pressed to the bullet wound stained with his blood.

"Bad?"

"I'll live."

"Which way?" The agent pointed and Bell took off running.

At most he was twenty-five seconds behind

Gly. He wondered which of them was more motivated at this moment in time and guessed it was pretty even. The corn was thigh-high. Bell could see where fresh stalks had been pushed aside by Gly's bid to escape. He ran as hard as he could, his pistol gripped in his right fist, his eyes alert for the first sign of the murderous Scotsman.

He saw a small copse of trees and a rusty piece of abandoned farm equipment up ahead. He also saw a large silvery balloon tethered to the machine floating just a few feet off the ground. They'd speculated about something like this. The fifteen-foot-diameter balloon was used to loft a radio antenna. He figured it was only for emergencies. Miller probably had some intelligence to pass on to the German High Command.

In the distance was the tree line and a shadowy forest beyond. Any fugitive would be running for that with everything he had.

Bell raced on, but rather than close in on the old steam engine directly, he arced out to his right a bit and came at it at an angle. There was an open-topped wagon behind the machine and Foster Gly crouched near its open rear gate, expecting Bell to pass close enough for an easy shot. Anyone else would have run for it. Not Gly. He had to be the aggressor, something Bell had counted on.

Bell was coming up on his blind side and readied his gun as he came into range. Whatever feral sixth sense had kept the Scotsman alive for so long kicked in at that moment. He felt something, or perhaps heard Bell's breathing on the wind. Either way, he turned and saw that he was being hunted.

He and Bell fired at the same time. Both missed. Gly had cover. Bell was exposed, so he laid down suppressing fire in order to reach the edge of the steam engine with its large flywheel that once ran a belt for the saw. Gly fired off another shot.

Bell dropped the empty magazine from his Browning and reached for a fresh one, only to discover it had fallen out of his holster, likely after his jump through the window when he hit the lawn and tumbled like an acrobat. He still had one round in the chamber.

He came around the corner. The trailer was five feet away, the balloon floating serenely above it. The tether was regular rope, but a thick wire was also attached to the balloon. Their aerial. Gly was behind one of the trailer's tall spoked wheels. Bell timed his rush so that just as Gly raised his hand to fire, he triggered off his last round, forcing Gly to duck. Bell raced on with an empty pistol in his hand. Gly raised his weapon and fired. He missed again. The .38 was sized for a lady and he could barely get a finger around the trigger.

He let Bell come another few paces and then pulled the trigger again, knowing this time he couldn't miss. The hammer fell on the primer of an already spent bullet. Helen's pistol was only a five-shot to cut down on its weight. A fact Bell well knew.

Gly threw his empty pistol at Bell as he barreled at him. It stung Bell's hand as he batted it away and he threw himself at Gly in a cross block that slammed him to the ground. Bell rolled off Gly and got to his feet, ready to kick Gly in the head, but the tall thug was just as quick. They circled each other, hands flexing. Gly knew he didn't have time for a protracted fight. Bell had additional agents and they would soon be coming at him like a pack of hunting dogs.

He feinted a left roundhouse and then threw a lightning right jab into Bell's throat. Bell felt his airway close up and was left gagging and gasping. Gly got in two more blows, a left cross that nearly cork-screwed Bell into the dirt and a digger under the solar plexus.

One corner of Bell's mind remained rational and was telling him he was losing the fight and if things didn't change he was going to die in a Long Island cornfield. He backed himself against the trailer and stooped to pull the knife from the sheath attached to his boot. Gly rushed in before he could use the weapon and crushed Bell's arms to his sides in a bear hug. Gly no longer had the massive muscles that had once made his body nearly grotesque, but he still had the strength to crush the life out of a man. The knife dropped from Bell's fingers. Gly kicked it away.

Bell could barely draw oxygen down his damaged throat and felt his vision going to black. He reared his head back and snapped it forward as hard as he could. The cartilage of Gly's nose was crushed by the blow and he let go.

Gly staggered back, then regained his senses and charged into Bell like a raging bull. Bell was knocked to the ground and Gly landed atop him with all his crushing weight. They wrestled and rolled about, but Gly maintained an upper position, pinning one of Bell's arms to the ground. Beneath him, Bell felt the heavy wire of the antenna and its terminus with a J-hook attached to the balloon. He clasped his free hand around the base of the hook and slid it off the cable eye. He then used it as a weapon, pummeling Gly on his back and in the kidneys.

Gly reared back in pain and anger, rising to his feet and pulling Bell off the ground with him. Bell lost his grip on the hook, but pulled it through a belt loop on the back of Gly's pants before letting go. Gly was oblivious as he raised Bell up and tossed him like a rag doll toward the steam engine.

Bell landed face-first in the dirt, tumbling against the machine. He shook the dust out of his eyes to see his knife just an arm's length away. As he reached for the weapon, Gly stalked over and stomped a boot on the back of Bell's thigh, nearly snapping his femur. Bell's fingers clasped the knife an instant later, but his leg pain and weakness were too much for him to turn the blade on Gly. Instead, he raised the sharpened edge to the balloon's tether tied on the engine.

Gly raised his foot for a coupe de grace blow, when the rope sliced clean.

A second too late, he realized what was happening. He reached behind to yank the hook from his belt and had just gotten his hand on it when the rope drew taut.

The balloon and its human passenger shot into the sky so fast it was all just a blur, though Bell did see that Foss Gly's eyes had gone as wide as saucers. Without the weight of the metal aerial, the balloon shot past a thousand feet in seconds and kept climbing. It was designed to lift far more than Gly's weight and so there was theoretically no upper limit to how high it could climb.

For the first minute of the flight, Gly tried to free himself. A swift death from a fall was preferable to what he was about to endure, but no amount of struggling could loosen the hook from under his belt. And there was so much pressure on his waist that he couldn't unbuckle it and slip free either.

The cold hit just a few minutes into his flight. He'd already drifted over the Atlantic. The water looked distant and black. He shivered as the temperature plummeted and his breath froze around his nose and mouth. And still he climbed. His fingers turned blue, then white, and curled involuntarily. He couldn't feel anything below his hips. The air grew thin. It was hard enough to breathe with the belt digging into his abdomen and putting pressure on his diaphragm, and as the altitude increased each painful breath drew less and less oxygen.

Gly grew dizzy. His vision faded to gray. His shivering stopped as his brain realized it could no longer preserve his limbs and hoarded all the energy for itself.

And still the balloon climbed.

He died around thirty-five thousand feet, and then somewhere above forty thousand the balloon's doped rubber skin froze solid. As it had climbed and the air pressure decreased, the balloon had been steadily expanding, though not enough to pop it. The material was far too pliable, but at a certain altitude and temperature, the envelope froze up. Once in this state it could no longer expand and it shattered like the thinnest glass bulb imaginable. One second it was there, the next it seemed to have vaporized.

Gly's ascent ended. His descent took a little over two minutes and concluded with an insignificant splash in an uncaring ocean.

Back at the farmhouse, James and Helen had everything under control. Archie was just pulling up as Bell stepped out of the cornfield.

"I believe you were told to stay well away from the action," Bell admonished him mildly.

"What can I say. I waited for as long as I could, but then, well, you know me."

"I do. Gly survived his fall from the *Lusitania.*"

Archie glanced over at the porch, where their three prisoners sat with their hands cuffed behind their backs. "He isn't any of those three lovely gentlemen and I know you didn't let him go, plus there's the beginning of another shiner around your eye, so what exactly didn't he survive today?"

"Gravity."

"Huh?"

"Remember your idea about them using helium balloons to lift their antenna?"

"Yeah."

"Last I saw, Gly was at about ten thousand feet with no sign of stopping. If the cold doesn't kill him, the lack of oxygen will."

Archie shuddered. "That is officially on my list of top ten ways not to die."

"If memory serves, there are at least a hundred items on said list."

"Proof that I don't want to die other than as an old man asleep in my bed. What's next?"

"We deliver those three to Roosevelt, you go home and recover in the loving arms of a wife you probably don't deserve, while I take mine, who I know I don't deserve, to San Francisco for a month or until she's pregnant, whichever comes first. And then we figure out what we do if our nation goes to war."

Archie looked at Bell's disheveled clothes and bruised face. "You look like you could use a drink at the club first. I'm buying."

"You're on," Bell said. He gazed up at the sky and the high clouds overhead, where Gly had recently vanished. "Make mine a Scotch."

44

Bell hung up the phone in his office and called Helen Mills in from the bull pen.

"I need to meet a prospective client at the Cunard docks in twenty minutes," he said. "Suspected theft at the shipping line involving a woman. Can you accompany me?"

"Sure, boss," Helen replied, forcing a wan smile.

Bell had witnessed the joy vanish from her face weeks ago at the uncertainty over Marchetti's health. It had been over ten days since she had last heard from him in England and she was beginning to fear the worst. Bell had seen the strain and tried to keep her mind occupied with one assignment after another. It didn't seem to be working.

They took a taxi to save time, but the crosstown traffic barely allowed them to reach the docks in time. A large passenger ship, the *Carpathia,* famous for rescuing the survivors of the *Titanic,* had just arrived in port. The dock was crowded as a stream of passengers exited the gangway to meet waiting friends and family. Bell led Helen through the crowd to the base of the gangway, where he had a word with one of the ship's officers.

"We're supposed to meet your client here?" Helen asked.

"Yes," Bell said. "There he is now."

A crewman in summer whites started down the long ramp, pushing a wood and rattan wheelchair. Helen glanced up and turned flush at recognizing the figure in the chair.

It was Joe.

She began to rush up the ramp, then hesitated and stepped back to Bell.

"I thought you said this was a case of theft?" she said, tears streaming down her cheeks.

"It was. I have it on good authority that you stole that man's heart." He gave her a warm smile. "Case closed."

She squeezed his hand, then turned and ran up the ramp.

"Need a lift, sailor?" she called out as she approached Marchetti. Joe's head was down, so he hadn't seen her.

He looked up and smiled from ear to ear.

He'd lost more weight and was still awfully pale, but his eyes burst alive at the sight of Helen. He grinned that boyish grin of his. "I don't know about that. My mother warned me about brazen New York women."

"Trust me, Mr. Marchetti, you haven't seen brazen yet."

Some color blushed his cheeks. "Yes, ma'am."

AUTHOR'S NOTE

The *Lusitania* sank in roughly eighteen minutes. This is the time an average person will spend reading the scenes between when the fabled ship was first torpedoed until she slipped under the waves. Hat tip to James Cameron, who did the same thing in his movie *Titanic.*

ABOUT THE AUTHORS

Clive Cussler was the author of more than eighty books in five bestselling series, including Dirk Pitt®, NUMA® Files, *Oregon®* Files, Isaac Bell®, and Sam and Remi Fargo®. His life nearly paralleled that of his hero Dirk Pitt. Whether searching for lost aircraft or leading expeditions to find famous shipwrecks, he and his NUMA crew of volunteers discovered and surveyed more than seventy-five lost ships of historic significance, including the long-lost Civil War submarine *Hunley,* which was raised in 2000 with much publicity. Like Pitt, Cussler collected classic automobiles. His collection featured more than one hundred examples of custom coachwork. Cussler passed away in February 2020.

Jack Du Brul is the author of the Philip Mercer series, most recently *The Lightning Stones,* and is the coauthor with Cussler of the *Oregon* Files novels *Dark Watch, Skeleton Coast, Plague Ship, Corsair, The Silent Sea,* and *The Jungle,* and the Isaac Bell novels *The Saboteurs* and *The Titanic Secret.* He lives in Virginia.

The employees of Thorndike Press hope you have enjoyed this Large Print book. All our Thorndike, Wheeler, and Kennebec Large Print titles are designed for easy reading, and all our books are made to last. Other Thorndike Press Large Print books are available at your library, through selected bookstores, or directly from us.

For information about titles, please call:
(800) 223-1244

or visit our website at:
gale.com/thorndike

To share your comments, please write:
Publisher
Thorndike Press
10 Water St., Suite 310
Waterville, ME 04901